"Lyn Cote pens another heartwarming story in *Lost In His Love*. Finely drawn characters and lively plotting kept me longing for more! Cote fans will rejoice in book two of the Blessed Assurance series."

Lori Copeland, author of *Faith, June and Hope*

"Lyn Cote delivers with great characters, a touching story, and brings 1906 San Francisco to life on the written page. From the first chapter, her heroine's plight gripped my heart, and I struggled alongside her until the very end."

Jeri Odell, author of *Bouquet of Love*

"Lyn Cote has done it again! *Love in His Love* is a richly textured story with winsome characters and an ending that leaves us asking for more from this talented writer."

Lois Richer, author of *Mother's Day Miracle*

"How many times have we found ourselves, like Cecy, resentful and angry over our lot in life? Hidden in Cecy's story are the keys to set us free. Read, enjoy, and learn."

Gayle Roper, author of *The Document*

Lost
IN HIS LOVE

BLESSED ASSURANCE SERIES • VOLUME 2

Lost
IN HIS LOVE

A NOVEL

LYN COTE

BROADMAN
& HOLMAN
PUBLISHERS

Nashville, Tennessee

0-8054-1968-3

Published by Broadman & Holman Publishers, Nashville, Tennessee
Editorial Team: Leonard G. Goss, John Landers
Page Composition: Leslie Joslin

Library of Congress Cataloging Number: 99-045167
Dewey Decimal Classification: 813
Subject Heading: FICTION

1 2 3 4 5 04 03 02 01 00

To Elaine and Sue, my first readers
With thanks to Muriel, my faithful proofreader

Angels descending bring from above
Echoes of mercy, whispers of love.

Watching and waiting, looking above,
Filled with His goodness, lost in His love.
—FANNY CROSBY, "BLESSED ASSURANCE"

"FOR YOU, O GOD, TESTED US; YOU REFINED US
LIKE SILVER."

PSALM 66:10, NIV

"THE LORD IS CLOSE TO THE BROKENHEARTED
AND SAVES THOSE WHO ARE CRUSHED IN SPIRIT.
A RIGHTEOUS MAN MAY HAVE MANY TROUBLES,
BUT THE LORD DELIVERS HIM FROM THEM ALL."

PSALM 34:18–19, NIV

Historical Note

The San Francisco earthquake began at 5:12 A.M. on Wednesday, April 18, 1906. Eyewitnesses described it as a violent shaking with jolts and a circular motion. People were thrown from their beds. Roads split open. Electric cables snapped. Gas and water mains broke. Buildings fell. All in less than a minute.

Then the fires started. When they ended on Saturday, April 21, 500 city blocks downtown had been ravaged. Approximately 28,000 buildings were destroyed. Over half of the 400,000 city population were left homeless. Originally the cost of human lives was tallied at 478, but recent research by Gladys Hansen (formerly San Francisco city archivist) and Frank Quinn (formerly Registrar of Voters) has set the number closer to 3,000.

Facts here are from *Three Fearful Days* by Malcolm E. Barker.

PROLOGUE

"Let the little children come to me, and do not hinder them, for the kingdom of God belongs to such as these."
Mark 10:14, NIV

January 20, 1893

Papa's shouting shattered Cecy's sleep. Glass crashing. She sat up in her bed. In the blackness, she clutched her favorite blanket. She shook. Her teeth tapped. Would he come to her room and break things?

Mama's high voice cascaded over and around his vibrating tones. Anger. Fear. Anger. The loud voices fought back and forth. They might rush into her room. They might shout at her and break her china dolly's head. Cecy felt tears wet her cheeks. They might break her. *No! No!*

The door opened. Soft light glowed into the darkness. It was nanny.

"Nana!" Cecy cried out. She held up her hands.

"Hush, hush, sweetheart." Gently, Nana lifted her. "There, there. It's all right. I'm here. Don't cry."

"I'm scared," Cecy whimpered. Warm, soft arms closed around her. She heard Nana's soft words, but she couldn't stop trembling.

Nana carried her to the rocking chair, snuggling her close. The old chair began to move back and forth. *Creak. Creak.* She rested her head on soft Nana. Nana smelled sweet, like the powder Nana patted on Cecy after her baths.

From below, the voices shouted and cried, but Nana hugged her. Nana wouldn't let them break dolly or her.

Then Nana said the good words, the words that always let Cecy breathe easier. She closed her eyes to sleep. Nana whispered in her ear, "The Lord is my shepherd; I shall not want. He maketh me to lie down in green pastures: he leadeth me beside the still waters. He restoreth my soul…."

CHAPTER 1

"You prepare a table before me in the presence of my enemies."
Psalm 23:5a, NIV

January 20, 1906 LINC WAGSTAFF'S EIGHT-YEAR-OLD
daughter, Meg, gave his crisp, white silk tie one last tweak.
"There, Papa."

"Thank you, precious. That's perfect."

"Those tails look funny." She pointed at the back of his
black evening coat.

The tails felt funny to him too. Years had passed since he'd
attended a formal ball. A memory made him pause, a memory
of a Strauss waltz, the scent of rosewater, the feeling of Virginia
in his arms.... Linc dragged his mind back to the present.

To tease Meg, Linc flipped the long tails.

His daughter giggled, making her long, chestnut-brown
braids brush her shoulders.

"Linc, I found those gold cuff links at last." Gray-haired and plump, Susan bustled into the large upstairs bedroom; her black face a study of concentration. She carried a small dark box which she handed to Linc.

"Thank you. The final touch." He slipped one gold link into the buttonholes in each starched, white cuff. Standing tall, he turned to face his assembled audience—his Meg, dark Susan, and her grandson, Del. They ringed him in a semicircle. Pent-up dread and excitement made his heart thud in an ungainly rhythm. Tonight he would take a crucial step in a plan he'd mulled over for months. He took a deep breath. "So how do I look?"

"Like the fine gentleman you are." Susan nodded. "You do your mother proud."

"You look handsome!" Meg wrinkled the freckles on her nose and gave a little jump.

Ten-year-old Del looked unimpressed.

Linc ruffled the boy's tight black curls affectionately.

Del grimaced. "I sure don't want to wear that kind of clothes when I grow up."

"But he has to wear them because the ladies will be wearing really beautiful evening dresses." Meg spread out her arms like a lady wearing an evening cape. In her pink flannel nightgown, she paraded around the room in exaggerated sliding steps. "This is how ladies walk."

"You ain't a fine lady," Del scoffed.

"My mama was a lady." Meg paused, affecting an elegant pose. "I'll be a lady, too, when I grow up."

His daughter's mention of her mother caught Linc around the throat like a tight band. If his wife were on his arm, how different tonight would be. But now Virginia danced with the angels.

"Del, don't say 'ain't'," Susan scolded mildly. "Meg, you have a long time before you need to move like that. Now kiss your Papa good night. It's past time for prayers and bed."

Both children grumbled, but bid Linc good night. Meg's soft kiss made him reach down for one more hug, then Susan shepherded them out of the room.

Linc walked to the window. Alone in the shadows cast by moonlight, he looked out over the hill below his house. Virginia had been gone well over a year now. What would his wife have thought of San Francisco? "I'm a little nervous about tonight." Even though Virginia could no longer answer him, he never felt foolish speaking to her naturally as though she were in the room just behind the dressing screen changing for bed. "I wonder if I've bitten off more than I can chew with this enterprise."

Melancholy silence was the only response.

"But I have felt led here." Indeed, San Francisco had popped into his mind with such frequency after Virginia's passing that he'd been forced to acknowledge God's prompting.

Below the window, gaslights gleamed fuzzy and golden in the January evening fog. The City by the Bay shrouded by night. If he were an artist, he'd paint the mysterious scene below. But he was a journalist. He had much to accomplish tonight if his plans were to succeed. One last time before he set off, he bowed his head for a quiet moment of prayer. Afterward, he calmly picked up his silk-lined evening cape and black top hat.

A short drive in his automobile and he'd begin his new life. He hadn't wanted a new life, but it was the one that God had led him to.

❋ ❋ ❋ ❋ ❋

Fifteen minutes later he got out of his car in disgust. His new Chinese houseman, Kang, stood at the front of the vehicle, his hands folded. "Car not good like horse."

"At this moment I'm inclined to agree with you." Linc stalked out of the old carriage house at the rear of his new home. The cloying chill of the night air wrapped around him like a damp shroud.

"What you do now, mister?" Kang hurried along a step behind Linc.

"It's too late to call for a gig—"

The *ding-ding* of a nearby cable car bell interrupted. Linc instantly picked up his pace. "I'll take the cable car!"

"But, mister—" Kang remonstrated.

"I can't wait any longer. I'm almost past fashionably late!" Linc sprinted to the street, hailing the cable car. It lurched to a stop. Linc leaped aboard. He paid his two-penny fare and moved toward the bench.

Invigorated by his sprint, he looked at his fellow passengers, some workmen and a few women. He realized his evening dress had taken them by surprise. Despite the swaying of the vehicle, he made a half-bow. "Good evening, ladies and gents."

At his sally, most grinned at him. Linc flipped up his tails and sat down before he could unceremoniously lose his balance.

The cable car made its way up the next hill, straining and rocking. Over the grinding noise of the car, one of the workmen called to him, "Horses lame?"

Linc shook his head. "My automobile wouldn't start."

This announcement was followed by hoots. "Autos! Get a horse!"

This only made Linc grin more.

The old woman who sat beside him said, "Automobiles are of the devil. God made horses."

Accustomed to this attitude, Linc nodded politely, but without agreement. This new twentieth century was a mere six years old. Change, the possibility of even more progress, was what drove him tonight. The future could be better if only good men would try to make it that way. He couldn't turn a blind eye to the abuses of God's children or to God's prompting. Starting with the larger-than-expected inheritance to the quick sale of his Chicago home, surely God had blessed every step of his journey to this evening.

CHAPTER 1

Gaslights wrapped in wisps of fog passed by as the car went up and down hills. Finally he recognized Nob Hill. "This is where I get off!" Doffing his silk top hat in farewell, he descended from the cable car amid friendly wishes.

He walked down misty, winter-darkened California Street toward his destination, the Ward mansion. Mrs. Zebulon Ward always hosted the first ball after all the presentation parties held in the weeks following New Year's Eve. Fortunately for Linc, Mrs. Zebulon Ward knew Linc's step-aunt Eugenia Granger Smith of Boston.

Ahead, golden electric light radiated from inside the imposing, three-story, stone residence. Gleaming black carriages and motor cars lined up near the entrance. Arriving on foot would not add to Linc's consequence in the eyes of society. In the shadows of the high wrought-iron fence, he waited until the liveried footmen were busy helping two ladies from an opulent carriage. Quietly, he slipped from the shadows and followed the pair to the open double front doors.

He waited for the ladies to enter. When they had been relieved of their dark velvet cloaks, Linc stepped inside the huge foyer. The excited buzz of voices and bursts of laughter filled his ears. A footman relieved him of his cape and hat. He handed his invitation to another footman who carried it to the butler. The butler bowed, then read Linc's full name aloud to his hostess who headed the receiving line. "Mr. Lincoln Granger Smith Wagstaff."

Linc bowed over Mrs. Ward's kid-gloved hand.

"Lincoln, so good to see you. I just received a letter from your dear Aunt Eugenia yesterday. I was happy to write back and say I would be seeing you tonight." Wearing a diamond-studded stomacher around her waist and a dog collar of glittering diamonds, Mrs. Ward went on to make the debutante next to her aware of Linc's distinguished Boston Back Bay connections. She finished with, "Smiths have been bankers in Boston as long as there have been banks in Boston!" Mrs. Ward's high voice managed to pierce the hubbub of the huge ballroom which lay beyond.

Linc worked his way through the short line which consisted of Mrs. Ward's protégé, a shy motherless girl whom kind Mrs. Ward was bringing out this season, Mr. Ward, and his widowed sister. Linc smiled to himself—certain that the words: "banker" and "Boston" had escaped no one. Wouldn't it be amusing if someone approached him about a loan? After all, his stepfather's family's reputation and distinctions had very little to do with his own life. And he'd never before traded on anyone else's credit. Doing so made him feel like a quack selling snake oil. But his work included hobknobbing with the wealthy, the people he needed to influence to his cause. His research into who owned what and how much in California had led him directly to the people in this ballroom—especially one redhead.

Accepting a glass of ruby red punch from a waiter, he strolled through the gathering of San Francisco's top two hundred families. Though he wore the latest evening attire, the glittering rubies, sapphires, and emeralds and shimmering brocade dresses made him feel like a country rube. Bemused, he found a place off to the side where he could observe the assembly and still watch for his lady to arrive.

In front of him, a knot of young gentlemen collected. Linc idly listened to their conversations.

"Well, it's off once more," one gallant with brown hair and freckles intoned in mock seriousness. "The 1906 San Francisco marriage mart begins tonight."

"Why do you care, Archie? You'll never marry. Who would have you?" The fair-haired man beside Archie grinned.

Linc smiled to himself, glad courtship and marriage were not on his mind.

A rakish-looking man with straight, black hair stepped close to the fair gentleman and asked, "Finally looking for a wife, Bower?"

"None of your account, Hunt." Bower's words came out stiffly.

The obvious friction between the two men—one so fair and one so dark—piqued Linc's interest. He read the tension in the stiffness of their posture as well as the way they positioned themselves as though they were in a ring about to box.

"Still, I'm interested." Hunt asked airily, "Anyone you fancy in particular, Bower?"

Archie interrupted, "We all want to get another look at her. No mystery about that. They've kept the redhead under wraps for a year since her old man died—"

Redhead? So they wanted to see her too? Would that interfere with Linc's plans for her?

"Died and left her a fortune." Bower added pointedly, "That should interest you, Hunt. A wealthy bride."

"If one must marry, why not a wealthy bride?" Archie joked, attempting to calm the waters.

"Some of us need a wealthy bride more than others," Bower said acidly.

Looking stung, Hunt took a step forward. "What I do is none of your business."

"It is when you make my sister the object of your attentions for nearly a year. You trifled with my sister last year, Hunt. I've not forgotten that."

Linc stirred uneasily. What kind of game was Hunt at? Any man misleading an eligible girl was indeed suspect.

Hunt snorted. "I did nothing that I ought not. I didn't propose." Hunt paused to dust an invisible speck from his sleeve. "We just didn't suit."

The scornful edge to Hunt's words brought a faint flush to Bower's face.

"You two, stop it," Archie urged in an under voice. "Look!"

Linc obeyed automatically. Across the long room, a beautiful brunette in a fawn-colored gown was receiving Mrs. Ward's welcome. Near Linc, one of the young fashionable blades gave a barely discernible wolf whistle in approval.

"What's her name?" Bower inquired.

"Didn't you attend her coming-out?" Archie asked. "She's Fleur Fourchette—that Southern belle who's come to live with her aunt."

"Who?" Bower asked.

"Fleur Fourchette," Archie enunciated carefully. "She's from New Orleans, an old French family."

Linc silently admired the brunette's pretty face and shapely, petite form, but with only light interest. He wasn't looking for a brunette tonight.

The group of young men moved away from Linc, closer to the receiving line. A small orchestra, arranged at one end of the ballroom, quietly played a piece by Haydn. Humming the tune in a near-whisper, Linc watched the lovely Miss Fourchette smile prettily as Archie approached her. Archie motioned that he'd like to be included on the dance card that dangled from her wrist. Both Hunt and Bower appeared startled by Archie's pluck.

Linc judged Hunt and Bower to be in their late twenties, probably sons of men who made their money in the gold mines or building the railroads that now connected the east and west coasts. Restless young men, finished with education and trying to find a place in the scheme of things, overshadowed by successful fathers. Why then did Bower accuse Hunt of needing a wealthy wife? Why had Hunt trifled with Bower's sister? Though none of this had anything to do with his mission, Linc's newspaper reporter instincts stirred.

"Miss Cecilia Jackson." The words had not been spoken louder than any of the other names, but it was the name Linc had been waiting for. He heard it clearly.

His redhead had arrived.

�֟ �֟ �֟ ✖ ✖

CHAPTER 1

Approaching her hostess in the line, Cecy felt just as she had imagined she would—jittery, breathless, thrilled. Tonight her life, her real life, began. After a childhood spent in banishment and a year buried alive in mourning, she was free. She was a grown woman, an independent woman. The evening of her coming-out reception two weeks ago had been her trial by fire. She'd faced society for the first time and made a creditable impression. Tonight she would spread her wings and fly.

Her careful boarding school training was paying dividends now. As she passed a mirror in the foyer, she saw her serene reflection. No one would guess just how keyed up she felt. Looking out over the ballroom ahead, she imagined herself as the diva making her first stage entrance.

As Cecy shook hands with Mr. Ward, her gaze picked out that New Orleans' girl, Fleur. What a name. Fleur should have stayed in Louisiana where she belonged. None of the other debutantes vying with Cecy for the coveted title of "Belle of 1906" would give her as much competition. But as Aunty said, competition would make Cecy's victory all the sweeter.

When she and her Aunt Amelia reached the end of the receiving line, Aunty murmured her intention to find her place among the chaperones. "Cecilia, you are in high spirits, but remember your breeding. You are a cultured young woman, not a ninny hammer like most of the girls here tonight."

"Yes, Aunty." Cecy's gaze skimmed the dazzling room. Electric lights blazed from crystal chandeliers. Bunches of pink roses dangled from the branches of the chandeliers above, making the room as sweetly redolent as any rose garden in summer. Tall, rainbow-colored silk draperies hung between the columns that supported the mezzanine and ringed the grand ballroom on three sides. The orchestra played with restraint as though marking time until the dancing would begin. Tonight was as close to heaven as Cecy ever thought she'd come.

Without appearing to, she carefully scanned the gathering, assessing the gentlemen who would dance with her tonight.

Most were handsome, some even distinguished-looking. But they were all so obvious in their affected poses. Preening like peacocks on a terrace just like Aunty had so drolly predicted. Well, let them. They'd find out soon enough she hadn't come to be impressed. She had arrived to take her rightful place in San Francisco. She would no longer be denied what was hers by birth and wealth. She was a woman of means, of spirit, not just another ingenue.

"Miss Jackson." A gentleman with brown hair and a cheerful face bowed to her. "I'm Archie Pierce. We were introduced at your come-out. May I have a place on your dance card tonight?"

She hesitated, smiling prettily at him. She remembered his name. She'd memorized all their names and family connections. "Mr. Pierce. How could I say no to the first gentleman to ask? I'm so afraid of being left a wallflower tonight." As she said the words, she managed to smile demurely. "Shall I save you a waltz?"

"Miss Jackson, no chance of your being neglected tonight! I'd be honored to waltz with you."

As she wrote his name down, other men crowded around asking her for dances. Her dance card began to fill nicely. Her heart raced with the feeling of success. But even as she wrote names on her engraved dance card, she kept track of the other six debutantes around the room.

When she saw that she was one of the most sought-after debs, her fixed smile became genuine. She was where she belonged, in her rightful place. She would be careful to establish herself in her first season. Her dreams of being popular and respected would be fulfilled. Then she would have evenings like this for the rest of her life.

* * * * *

Linc remained in the background. Miss Jackson's beauty hadn't been exaggerated. Her hair was that highly prized warm auburn; her white skin creamy and unblemished except for a tiny enchanting mole at the corner of her mouth. How many young men this night would dream of kissing that beauty mark? Her eyes weren't the expected blue or green of most redheads. Her eyes were a rich brown, the shade of brown sugar. He'd been led to expect just another beautiful deb.

But the lady in the flesh disconcerted him. He went over the facts he'd gleaned about her. She was nineteen. She'd lost her father a year ago. Her mother was ill, so her Boston aunt lived with her as chaperone. She was the richest unmarried heiress in San Francisco, and that was what attracted his attention the most—her business interests.

He'd expected Miss Jackson to be a sweet pink rosebud that he would help to unfurl. Instead, she was a full red rose with thorns. The other debutantes fluttered around the gaily decorated room like colorful, but insubstantial butterflies. They tittered behind fans and tried not to be seen looking at the young men seeking their favor.

Cecilia Jackson, on the other hand, moved through the gathering like an aloof lioness. Linc watched the young bloods react. They couldn't take their eyes off her. Neither could Linc.

* * * * *

A trill of affected ladylike laughter caught Cecy's attention. Fleur was tarrying with a very handsome, raven-haired gentleman. She tapped his arm with her folded fan, then smiled up at him—the very picture of the coquette.

Outwardly calm, Cecy felt the pinch of envy. The dark, attractive gentleman was much too good to waste himself on a nobody from the South. Cecy recalled his name, Hunt, the son of a father in railroads. She'd make sure his name appeared on her dance card—more than once tonight.

A good-looking blonde gentleman stepped up to her. "May I have the honor of leading you in the promenade tonight?"

She knew his name, but said with a faintly confused tone. "You are?"

"Clarence Bower at your service, Miss Jackson."

He was being forward. A gentleman, still such a stranger, had no right to ask for a specific dance. "Oh, I'd much rather dance the schottische with you."

He flushed slightly. He had gambled and been gently reminded of his role. "If that is all you have left." He bowed. "Till the schottische."

As Cecy marked "Bower" beside Dance four, she noted the dark gentleman nod and leave Fleur's side and drift to another knot of men. Cecy indirectly made her way to his vicinity. She paused often to greet and nod to women who were the older sisters, aunts, or friends of the debutantes. These ladies, though not old enough to take seats among the chaperones, still need-ed to be cultivated socially. Aunt Amelia had instructed her that they were the hostesses and heads of committees that she would need to stand on good terms with now and in the future.

Cecy complimented them on their gowns and diamonds. Secretly she had the satisfaction of knowing her ropes of pearls had been crafted by Tiffany while her intricate ivory silk and satin gown had been designed by the House of Pacquin in Paris. How clever of her aunt to take her to the continent for her gowns. Cecy estimated only about half of the ladies present wore Parisian gowns. The others made do with designs from New York. Cecy's only regret was that, as a debutante, she must wear pastels and white. The richer hues were thought inappro-priate to an ingenue.

Then, just as she had plotted, she turned and faced Hunt. He greeted her formally.

"Mr. Hunt," Cecy purred. "We meet again."

His quick glance down into her eyes left no doubt he hadn't expected her to recall him. Little did he know how hard, during her long year of mourning, she'd studied San Francisco society from the newspaper columns and photographs. The facts she'd

CHAPTER 1

gleaned about Mr. Hunt were: he was approaching thirty and
except for a serious flirtation with Clarissa Bower last year, he'd
never yet shown any other lady serious attention. Hunt was just
the kind of man whose regard was absolutely necessary for her
future plans.

"You honor me, Miss, by your good memory."

"Have you forgotten me?" She pouted elegantly. She didn't
like his black mustache. It had an untamed look to it. That and
his hair, worn slightly longer than was fashionable, gave him the
look of a pirate.

"Never, Miss Jackson. Your beauty is not easy to forget."

She smiled slightly. "You are too kind, sir. Are you enjoying
the orchestra?"

"Not as much as I will when the dancing begins," he hinted.

"You like dancing?" She smiled with a touch of coyness.

"I'd like it more if it were with you. Have you saved a dance
for me?"

She glanced at her card. She had a few spaces open, the
quadrille and the first dance. Which dance should she bestow on
an admirer of Miss Fourchette? She looked up at him from
under her lashes. "Would the first dance, the promenade, be
agreeable, Mr. Hunt?"

"Honored, Miss." His face showed his pleasure.

Cecy let her mouth curve into a smile. How would Miss
Fleur like that?

The orchestra struck a chord for attention, then played the
opening bars of the Polonaise, the music for the promenade. Of
course, their hostess's shy protégé would lead the promenade.
Mr. Hunt tenderly lifted Cecy's hand and led her to the line of
paired couples. Cecy glanced at Fleur. The Southern belle had
netted a middle-aged man, gray at the temples. When all the
dancers were in place, the orchestra paused, then started once
more. Cecy sighed with satisfaction and gave Hunt an enticing
smile. Her first ball had officially begun.

✳ ✳ ✳ ✳ ✳

As the evening progressed, Linc watched a complex ball-room drama slowly build in intensity. Two overlapping conflicts became more and more pronounced. The most obvious was between blonde Bower and dark-haired Hunt. If Hunt showed interest in one of the debutantes, so did Bower.

Linc noted after they'd danced with Bower, young ladies often glanced at Hunt. Was Bower warning them away from Hunt? Sowing seeds of distrust? Had Bower decided to exact revenge on Hunt for slighting his sister the year before? *Am I imagining this just because I overheard them arguing earlier?* But Hunt did appear to smolder with anger toward Bower more with each new dance.

Overlaying the conflict between the two young men was the much more discreet and well-executed campaign of Cecilia Jackson versus Fleur Fourchette. The root of Miss Jackson's campaign against the Southern belle was easy to see. Miss Fourchette was much too good-looking for Miss Jackson to ignore.

To her credit, the Southern girl did not appear to even notice Miss Jackson casting lures at every gentleman who conversed or danced with Fleur. Why was Miss Jackson in such a rush? She had a whole season to solidify her reputation. Why did she seek complete conquest tonight? Begin as you intend to go? An interesting strategy, but it placed her on a collision course with Bower and Hunt. Did she have any idea of the dangerous competition she was fueling? Did she care?

The rollicking polka ended. The jaunty schottische began. Miss Jackson was swept away by young Bower. He appeared more pained than happy.

✳ ✳ ✳ ✳ ✳

As Cecy skipped and stepped around the floor to the bouncing tune with Bower, one face, out of the many, snagged her notice. He was a blonde stranger and not one of the young gentlemen who had sought her hand for dances. What caught her attention was how he looked at her. He looked as if he saw right through her. Who was he?

★ ★ ★ ★ ★

Linc watched Miss Jackson scan the crowd—for him? Had she really made eye contact with him? The electricity of her attention had connected them for a split second. She glanced at him again, then looked away.

"Hello, Wagstaff."

Linc looked to his side.

A journalist from the *Examiner* grinned at him. "Didn't think I'd see you here."

"Likewise." Linc shook the man's hand.

The newspaper man edged closer. "I'm the society editor tonight."

Out of the corner of his eye, Linc continued to monitor the redhead. She was bestowing Bower with winsome smiles and flirtatious looks. He whispered something into her ear. She blushed.

Linc made himself look away. "A promotion for you," Linc quipped wryly. "A nice easy beat to cover."

The reporter smirked. "The society column is the most bloodthirsty column in the paper and you know it."

Linc nodded, but eyed Miss Jackson with a sinking sensation. Over Bower's shoulder, she now cast glances toward Hunt.

Dancing with the pretty brunette, Hunt grinned back at Miss Jackson and nodded.

"Are you enjoying the unfolding drama?" the reporter asked.

This startled Linc. He didn't want unpleasant comments about Miss Jackson appearing in the society columns tomorrow. Their fortunes were linked by his central goal. Had any others noticed the dangerous currents on the dance floor? The way

Miss Jackson was fueling it, she, at least, must have noticed. He asked, making light of it, "You mean the daring Miss Jackson?"

"Thanks for my article's lead." The man pulled out a stub of a pencil and jotted down a note in a small, navy notebook.

The schottische ended. A number of gentlemen hastened to the lovely redhead to vie for the next dance, a quadrille. Hunt shouldered his way through them. Bower didn't give way, but stayed right beside the redhead. The two men squared off with her between them. Where was her aunt? She should intervene before....

"Well, Lincoln," Mrs. Ward spoke just beside him. "My protégé has made a good start tonight." Mrs. Ward nodded toward the girl who stood across the room.

Linc bowed automatically to his hostess, but couldn't take his eyes off Bower and Hunt. Hunt had taken the redhead's hand. Bower crowded close to Hunt speaking too low for Linc to hear. Linc said automatically, "I'm happy for her."

"You haven't been dancing," Mrs. Ward spoke distractedly. She frowned at the gathering around Miss Jackson.

"I'm just an observer tonight." Linc stirred inwardly, watching the drama. Miss Jackson looked triumphant as the two men drew even closer.

Mrs. Ward stared at her now, as did others.

Across the room, the heedless redhead made a show of deliberating between Bower and Hunt for the quadrille. The other supplicants took umbrage at this. The voices of a couple of the gentlemen rose. The scene reminded Linc of threatening clouds suddenly swirling into a thundercloud.

Mrs. Ward took a step forward. "Does she have any idea what trouble she's causing?"

"I wonder if she does," Linc mused aloud.

Bower and Hunt were now nose to nose—ignoring Miss Jackson. Another gentleman tried without success to remonstrate with them.

CHAPTER 1

Mrs. Ward drew in a quick breath. "They'll be shouting before long. Oh, this is dreadful. A scene in my ballroom!" Frantically, the hostess motioned the music for the quadrille to start.

Hunt tugged at Miss Jackson's hand. Bower took the other.

Miss Jackson flushed pink. Was she just now realizing what she'd sparked?

In a split-second decision, Linc strode right into the eye of the storm. He forced Bower and Hunt to give ground and release her. Linc seized Miss Jackson's hand. "Our quadrille begins," he said caressingly. "Let's not be tardy in joining our set."

Both Hunt and Bower objected. Linc didn't even glance at them.

Miss Jackson let Linc lead her into the set.

CHAPTER 2

"How shall we sing the LORD'S song in a strange land?"
Psalm 137:4, KJV

A FIRM HAND DREW HER AWAY from Hunt and Bower. Like a fuzzy cloud, shock shut her off from her surroundings. Cecy saw only to the end of her own hand. The beat of the music penetrated her mind. The firm hand led her. Her feet moved to the rhythm of the dance.

As waves lapping against the shore, perception returned to her by degrees. Radiance from the chandeliers above. The tap and shuffle of footsteps on the dance floor. The dance she moved in became more than merely four-four time. Sprightly melody flowed from the orchestra. She was dancing the quadrille with a stranger who'd rescued her from Bower and Hunt.

Sensing curious eyes focused on her, she blushed hotly. She tried to glimpse her aunt's face up in the mezzanine. But the intricate quadrille steps turned her away. Perhaps not seeing Aunty's stern face was a blessing.

As she had in her childhood, Cecy inhaled little breaths, pulling more air into her lungs, then more air, pushing against her corset stays. She'd taught herself this way of maintaining control in situations she'd been forced to endure. But performing the ritual now took her back too far, to unhappy times and places. She stopped herself from thinking of the sad past and concentrated on this night. What had gone wrong? Who was the man leading her expertly through the quadrille?

Keeping up with the movements of the dance, she glanced at the stranger who still held her hand. Why, he was the man whom she had glimpsed during the schottische. She studied him. He wasn't a youth like her other partners tonight. He must be in his thirties. His hair was dark blonde and his eyes clear blue. He was over six feet tall and wore his stylish evening dress well. But who was he? And why had he rescued her from the unpleasantness?

Then the stranger looked into her eyes—wrenchingly. She felt as though he took her heart out and read it with a glance.

Instantly, she looked away. He'd had that startling effect on her twice this evening. Her pulse pounded at her temples.

Expertly, he drew her into a quick spin. So near to her, only a whisper separated them. He smelled like warmed autumn spices. His hands guided her with ease. He possessed an indefinable air of assurance which she envied. Did he know how she trembled inside tonight-—though to everyone else's eye, she hoped she moved with confidence? Had he truly pierced her armor? Was that why she felt exposed to him?

He turned her so her back was against his chest. He led her in the promenade step; her one hand he held behind her back, the other he extended to the side in front of them. They dipped and swayed as one. His effect on her increased with each moment of nearness. He exuded force, power.... Her heart quavered within her breast. She felt as if she were losing herself to him.

His self-possessed manner was a beacon to her. She'd wanted to let her gaze linger on him. His warm breath feathered wisps of her hair at the nape of her neck. She shivered. No other partner tonight had evoked a reaction such as this from her. Why did all her senses riot at this man's touch?

The point in the dance came where the blonde stranger released her to cross the square and dance with another partner. She stepped mincingly to the opposite corner of the set of eight. Summoning her courage, she smiled coyly at the other man in their set who now faced her.

He nodded stiffly, no greeting in his eyes. The rebuff chilled Cecy like a splash of cold water after a warm bath. She reeled inside. Hunt and Bower were responsible for this! How could they have forced a contretemps in the midst of a ball? She'd done nothing wrong. The fault was theirs!

The disapproving gentleman danced with her briefly, then coldly released her to return once more to the blonde stranger.

He accepted her back, gripping both her hands. He stepped to her side and led her in a sequence of steps like "London Bridges." His presence swamped her composure. His powerful sway over her sensations, the general disapproval she felt—she wished the dance would end. She wanted to leave the ballroom, find a quiet corner and recoup her spirits. Covertly, she glanced at the faces of the ladies in their set. Not one would make eye contact with her!

Her spirit failed her. She made a misstep. Frantically, she looked to her partner. "I'm indisposed. Please lead me from the floor."

The stranger swept her into a waltz-like embrace. Restraining her, he increased his pressure at the small of her back and tightened his grip on her hand. "Courage," he whispered sternly.

His comment sparked her temper. Did he pity her? She stiffened her spine, fighting his influence. Who was he to tell her to have courage? She had strength. No man would dare call her weak. She gave him a furious glare.

He chuckled.

Oh, men were altogether contemptible! She averted her face. First, Bower and Hunt calling unwelcome attention to her by arguing like uncouth brats, putting her blossoming reputation at risk. They'd left her vulnerable to mocking like this.

She tightened inside, marshaling her will to survive, to succeed. She smiled brilliantly at the dancers in her set. The other ladies still didn't met her eye easily, but who were they to judge her? Envious cats. She let another artful smile steal over her face. She'd show them, all of them.

With a calculatedly enchanting expression, she looked at the stranger holding her.

He looked back unimpressed and amused.

Chagrined again, she held her smile in place. She'd teach him to laugh at her!

"Who are you?" she purred into his ear.

"A friend."

Was he going to play hide and seek with her? She tamped down her irritation. Honey gathered more bees than vinegar. "Friends have names," she returned coyly.

"I'm a friend of Mrs. Ward," he replied with maddening calm. "She knows my name."

His insult cut her speechless.

She tugged surreptitiously at his hold on her, but he held her fast.

He murmured, "Miss Jackson, please don't cause another scene within minutes of your first."

The injustice of what he intimated made her seethe. She hadn't caused the scene earlier. "If I want your advice, I'll ask for it," she hissed.

"You don't seem to know enough to realize *what* you need."

She gasped, then lifted her chin. "I won't forget your high-handedness."

"It's immaterial what you remember or forget. I know you probably won't accept my advice, but I'm going to give it to you anyway. You don't have to conquer San Francisco all in one night. Take your time. And don't be so obvious about competing with the New Orleans belle. She won't suffer from your actions. You will."

She gave him a startled look. This man was a mystery—overwhelming and taunting. "What do you mean?"

"Just exactly what I've said. I always say just what I mean—*if* I say anything at all." He spun her to the final four beats of the dance, then bowed. "Thank you for a lovely dance," he said loud enough for those around them to hear. Then he whispered, "But don't entertain San Francisco society with another scene tonight. Save something for the next ball." He grinned and walked away.

Oh, she wished she could curse! She swallowed with difficulty.

Her next partner approached her cautiously. She gave him a dazzling smile, but inside she rioted.

❋ ❋ ❋ ❋ ❋

January 21, 1906

Shrill laughter of children exploded in little bursts all around Linc. Meg, Del, and Linc stepped off the horse trolley. The amusement park on Haight Street had been chosen as their Saturday afternoon treat. The brightly painted signs offered carnival attractions, but Meg wanted to see the wild animals.

"There they are! I see a lion!" Meg shouted, tugging at her father's chilled hand. "Hurry, Daddy, I can't wait."

Meg towed him forward by one hand while Del held back on the other. Linc felt like the linchpin of a seesaw. Whatever was going on? "Del, don't you want to see the lions—"

"Tigers and monkeys!" Meg finished. "Come on, Del!"

"No, you go on. I'll wait here. That stuff's for kids." Del pulled away and went to stand by a street lamp.

Linc couldn't think fast enough to counteract Meg's enthusiastic plunge toward the amusement park on Haight Street. "Don't stray, Del! We'll be back soon!"

His impetuous, determined daughter dragged him into the thick of the crowd of parents and children. Fleetingly, he was reminded of another impetuous and willful female. He pushed away the image of Miss Cecilia Jackson sailing into the Ward mansion with all her colors flying. Or he tried to. Miss Jackson was as unruly in his thoughts as she had been in the ballroom.

"Look! It's a lion!" Meg finally halted in front of a cage. "OOOh, he's scary-looking, isn't he?"

The tawny beast chose that moment to give a mighty yawn.

"Scary indeed!" Linc teased. "He'll be asleep in a minute."

"Oh, Daddy." With gloved hands, Meg clung to the bars giving all her attention to the king of the jungle.

A lioness paraded out of the lion house. Again, Linc's thoughts strayed to the night before. The lioness had the same expression as the audacious redhead. Last night, as he had led Miss Jackson into the quadrille, she'd looked chastened, shocked at her own behavior. For those few moments, Linc had felt himself drawn to her. She'd seemed so innocent…, but that hadn't lasted even as long as their dance.

Linc glanced backward. Ten-year-old Del stood stolidly against the lamppost. Since the death of Del's parents, the boy and his grandmother, Susan, had lived with Linc's family. When Linc had decided to move to San Francisco, Susan had insisted on moving with them. No stranger was going to raise Meg, her best friend's only grandchild.

Chapter 2

What troubled Del now? The move from Chicago hadn't seemed to bother him in the first weeks. Lately, however, as soon as they left their home, Del became silent and moody. Had Linc's own sorrow been communicated to the boy?

Maybe Del would brighten as soon as his lessons with the new piano teacher started Monday. Del's musical ability had startled the teacher. Perhaps getting into a routine of school and music lessons again would lessen Del's homesickness. *Let it be so, Lord.* The old feeling of peace after prayer eluded Linc. What would ease his own homesickness for the life he'd shared with Virginia?

Not for the first time, Linc struggled under the weight of his own unhappiness, compounded by his responsibilities. His ever-present grief winnowed through him like the cold January wind. Suddenly he wanted to pull Meg to him, hug her. She was the only one who had the power to lift his spirits. Without betraying emotion, he waited until the urge to hold Meg passed.

Meg led him to the sleek tigers. Then he bought her peanuts in the shell and let her feed the chattering, cavorting monkeys. Linc nodded and smiled as naturally as he could. She was eight years old. She needed to have her childhood.

Finally, chilled to the bone by the winter dampness, they walked back to Del.

"You missed it all!" Meg said in disappointment.

Del looked at his feet. "I saw what I wanted from here."

"Let's go children." Silently perturbed, Linc drew them to the curb to wait for the next cable car home. "I'm sure Susan will have hot cocoa waiting for us."

✳ ✳ ✳ ✳ ✳

The four of them sat around the square kitchen table. The house was quiet. Kang was off doing the shopping. The new house still didn't feel like home. But this cheery room fostered a cozy feeling. Linc leaned back in his chair, drawing as much solace as he could from the warmth of the oven, the fragrance of beef roasting slowly, the sweet chocolate on his tongue.

Meg chattered on to Susan about the trip to the amusement park. Susan had helped raise him too. Linc patted Susan's hand, letting her know silently how glad he was she'd come with him to this new city. Susan smiled at him.

For a moment, he let his mind take him back to the old house in Chicago. He was a small boy, his mother, Jessie, and Susan talked back and forth as they busied themselves cooking a meal for the boarders. He recalled the cadence of their voices, not the words. The image made his heart ache.

Pushing away the past, he sipped his hot cocoa and studied Del. The lad's glum face tore at Linc's heart. Linc recalled the summer he'd been given his first dog, Butch. Maybe the children needed a pet in this lonely time.

Susan gave Linc an inquiring glance over Del's head. Linc shrugged.

Finally, Susan stood up. "Del, later you need to practice your piano. The tuner was here this afternoon. I bought you that new sheet music you wanted."

"You mean 'Maple Leaf Rag'?" For an instant, excitement flickered on the boy's features.

"Yes, but I expect to hear more Frederic Chopin than Scott Joplin. Do you understand me?"

"Yes, ma'am." Del became sober again.

"Now, Meg, you come with me. You have to spend time today on your embroidery."

"But I don't like embroidery."

"That doesn't matter. You're going to be a lady. Your mother started you on that sampler and I'm going to make sure you finish it." As Susan stepped behind her grandson, she nodded at Linc, clearly telling him to talk to Del and find out what he could.

Meg grumbled, but followed Susan out of the kitchen.

"Well...." Obeying Susan, Linc stood up. "Since the women are going to be doing women's work, we'd better go out and see if we can figure out why my auto wouldn't start last night."

"All right," Del agreed without enthusiasm.

They walked into the old carriage house, now the garage. Linc switched on the dangling garage lights and gazed around for a moment. Electric lights in a garage and his own automobile. He'd never get used to the wonders of this new century and the change in his living standard after the large inheritance from his stepfather. His stepfather's final request had been that Linc use most of the money to benefit children, not by endowing charities. His stepfather had told him to use his talents as a journalist to inspire others with wealth and influence to right the abuse of laboring children. Linc's voice with his stepfather's money behind it could change for the better the fortunes of children nationwide.

Del's unhappy face brought Linc back to the present. Mulling over how to help the child beside him, Linc lifted the hood and propped it open securely. The engine. This was when he really felt inept. He didn't have a mechanical mind. He understood the theory of the spontaneous combustion engine, but the theory didn't fix the car.

"Del, get that manual off the shelf and we'll go through the checklist again."

Del obediently fetched the large, black clothbound book. He began reading off the parts to be checked if the car wouldn't start: magneto, carburetor....

Linc paused, looking over at Del whose head was masked by the manual he held. "I want you to tell me what's bothering you."

The book slowly lowered, but still Del wouldn't look Linc in the eye.

"Come on. Whatever it is, we'll work it out."

"It's not something we can work out." Del looked up rebelliously. "We can't change our skin. I'm colored. You're white."

Linc wiped his greasy hands on a rag and recalled his own childhood and the names he'd sometimes been called. The closeness of his mother and Susan had made him a target too. "Has someone been bothering you at school?"

"It ain't just at school." Del balanced the manual on the bumper. "Everywhere we go—when we're together—you and me or me and Meg—people *look* at me." Del wouldn't meet Linc's gaze. "Don't you see them looking?"

Linc leaned against the car. "Sometimes," he admitted, "but when I was your age, people used to look at me the same way when I was with your grandmother in Chicago."

"They did?" Del glanced up.

"Yes, because there were so few Negroes in Chicago right after the Civil War. But they just figured that I was in Susan's care. They thought she was my 'mammy'."

Del rolled his eyes at this.

Linc shrugged. "They would have looked shocked if I'd told them the truth—that Susan wasn't my mother's hired girl. Susan and she ran our boarding house together as equals. They were best friends."

"But people didn't look at me funny in Chicago!"

"That's because they knew of the long-lasting relationship between our two families. Not that they knew of the friendship between us. For your family's protection, we've always had to let people believe that your family were our…."

"Servants?" Del scowled.

"Yes, unfortunately. After your grandmother married and left us, people just thought we were good to your family. Trying to make people understand the truth held real danger for you. Your grandparents found out freedom didn't mean equality."

He knew it would be futile to tell Del that, in spite of prejudice, he was a fortunate child. So many children, black and white, lived in squalor and abuse. Photographs that he'd seen taken by a young progressive, Edward Hines, still haunted him. Children with exhausted and hopeless faces atop shrunken, ill-nourished bodies. He couldn't get the images out of his mind.

Linc went on, looking grim, "If I could change things, Del, I would. But this century is still young, change is coming. I feel certain that the fortunes of your people will change year-by-year. Remember, your grandmother was born a slave, but your grandfather and father voted in elections. You will someday too."

"I don't like the way people look at me."

"God doesn't either, Del." Linc pulled the boy into his arms in a quick, rough hug. The dismal afternoon closed in on Linc. He could provide for Del, love Del, but he couldn't change the world for Del. Even at the beginning of a new century, he couldn't protect him from the consequences of being born dark.

❈ ❈ ❈ ❈ ❈

January 28, 1906

The congregation began singing lustily around Linc, "My Faith Looks Up to Thee." Feeling ill at ease in the imposing church he'd chosen to visit this Sunday, Linc held his red leather hymnal with one hand and rested the other on Meg's shoulder. On the way to the church, the morning fog and gray-felt sky had matched his wretched mood.

Without spirit, he sang along, "While life's dark maze I tread, And griefs around me spread."

The lyrics stung his eyes like soap, bringing tears. Unbidden, a plea echoed through him, *Virginia, I need you.*

As he struggled with his deep sorrow, the song went on heedlessly, "Be Thou my guide...Wipe sorrow's tears away."

Oh, God, I miss her so. The emptiness she left behind devours me day-by-day. When will I breathe easier? When will I stop waking in the night and reaching for her? Oh, God, the grief, the loss....

"O, bear me safe above…, Blest Savior, then in love, Fear and distrust remove."

Linc wrestled with his anguish, pushing it down, keeping it hidden. The mocking hymn ended. The congregation shuffled its feet, hymnals, and Bibles and sat down.

Shaken, Linc let himself down to the hard pew. Little Meg snuggled close to him. He tucked her tenderly into the curve of his arm. *Thank you, Lord, for Meg, my precious trust, Virginia's daughter.* If only Virginia hadn't gotten pregnant again! His recurring guilt tightened around his throat, making it difficult for him to swallow. Virginia had been so thrilled, another baby. The two of them had been buried together in the same coffin.

A rustling from behind swished up the gloomy aisle. Latecomers went forward to claim the few remaining seats in the front rows of the large, filled church. A flash of red hair underneath a fashionable hat snagged Linc's notice. Here? Did Miss Cecilia Jackson attend this church, out of all the churches in the city?

Yes, it was the debutante, with her austere aunt, arriving late and sitting several rows in front of him. Seeing her brought his confusion to the fore once again. Impressions and scenes from that evening spun through his mind like one of Mr. Edison's "moving pictures."

Glittering diamonds, gentlemen in evening dress, brocaded gowns shimmering in the light of electric chandeliers. At center stage, Miss Jackson, heedless and impetuous, had flirted audaciously, parading her finery, her wealth, her beauty around Mrs. Ward's ballroom. How could he expect such a slender reed as she to support the demanding work he felt called to?

The pastor's voice reading from Ephesians filtered into Linc's distracted mind. "Wherein in times past ye walked according to the course of this world… the spirit that now worketh in the children of disobedience…."

Child of disobedience! How exactly to describe Miss Cecilia Jackson! Last night her coquetry with Bower and Hunt had precipitated a nearly disastrous scene. For a few moments, as she stood obviously stunned, he'd felt drawn to her. He hadn't been able to stop himself from going to her aid. She'd seemed so innocent, so vulnerable. Any other modest young lady would have been crushed, brought to her knees by the near-scene. But within minutes, she'd seemingly forgotten the social faux pas and had actually tried to flirt with him. How did she have two sides—one audacious, one sensitive? She was an enigma—a troubling one.

The pastor's voice droned on, "Fulfilling the desires of the flesh,...were by nature the children of wrath...."

God, I must have misunderstood you! You can't have led me to her. She is a child of wrath. She's capable of causing discord, not harmony. How can she help children? I know she is the one who owns the factories I'm most interested in. You brought her name to my mind over and over as I studied the wealthy of this city. But you can't mean she is the one who is the key!

The reading went on, "But God, who is rich in mercy, for his great love...Even when we were dead in sins, hath quickened us together in Christ."

But she isn't what I expected. I don't feel equal to the task myself. How can a young woman, a girl who is so flawed, be in your plan? I've made a mistake. Where did I go wrong?

The Scripture reading drew to a close. "For by grace are ye saved through faith; and that not of yourselves; it is the gift of God: not of works, lest any man should boast."

These last verses, magnified by Linc's doubts, shouted at him. He bowed his head. God was sovereign. But doubt in his own ability riddled him. Already each morning dawned as a challenge. He struggled out of bed, made himself dress, greeted his daughter at the breakfast table. For Meg's sake, he had to continue to go about the business of living. *I'm not strong enough to carry this through, Lord.*

Moving to San Francisco had taken them safely away from the familiar reminders of his life with Virginia. Now a new challenge had been set before him. If Miss Jackson were to be of help to him, it would take effort and strategy. *I'm already struggling, Lord. Can I bear more testing?*

He opened his eyes and stared at the back of Miss Cecilia Jackson's stylishly coifed hair under a large fashionable felt hat. Her behavior the night of the ball had revealed much about her. Except for those brief moments at the beginning of the quadrille—she was vain. She was immature. She was heedless. Headed for destruction.

Well, we all are—without God's mercy. Linc drew a labored breath. The work he'd been given would affect many lives in serious ways, in ways that would ripple through coming generations. Uplifting children could change the next generation and the next. Much good could come from it. Miss Jackson was the key. She possessed the resources and could wield influence if she wanted to. It appeared he was stuck with her.

✹ ✹ ✹ ✹ ✹

Cecy knew how to appear to listen to a sermon. For years, she'd been marched to chapel every morning and twice on Sunday. But she never cared for the angry God who shouted from heaven and punished sinners. Whenever she'd imagined God, he'd always resembled her father, shouting and breaking things, terrifying her.

Cecy pushed these thoughts from her mind. At boarding school, she'd perfected the art of sitting perfectly still as though taking in every holy word, yet letting her mind roam far away.

When she had walked up the aisle today, she'd been startled. He was here, the blonde stranger. Aunty had said he'd extricated Cecy neatly from a scene and should be thanked. But Cecy hadn't told her how rude he'd been near the end of the quadrille.

Cecy would let Hunt and Bower know of her displeasure with them. Then she'd keep them dancing at the end of her string until her social triumph was secure. She'd also let this stranger know she wasn't to be insulted or criticized. Who did he think he was? Her father had left her millions and millions. Her circumstances had changed. She was free of the past and what was more, she was rich. Did this stranger think himself superior to her?

As the sermon began, Cecy's thoughts turned to more pleasant topics. Aunty was planning an afternoon tea to court more favor with the matrons of the city. Cecy was planning a party within a month to celebrate the opera season. She wanted to be associated with the arts, especially her beloved opera. The celebrated Enrico Caruso was scheduled to sing in San Francisco in April. By then, Cecy's social career would be well launched. By spring, she planned to be lauded "Belle of 1906"at the Easter Ball, then entertain—in her home—the Great Caruso himself!

CHAPTER 3

"The wise woman builds her house,
but with her own hands the foolish one tears hers down."
Proverbs 14:1, NIV

February 1, 1906   L INC STOOD IN MISS CECILIA Jackson's ornate ivory and gold drawing room near the facade of a Greek column. The sedate parade of Miss Amelia Higginbottom's first afternoon tea swirled before his eyes. Satins and silks in rich tones of purple, green, and brown, large decorated hats, lacy white handkerchiefs, the fragrance of lavender and heavier French perfumes—all created a heady montage of high fashion and higher privilege.

Invited to cover the event, he hadn't realized he would be the only male reporter present. Feeling conspicuous, Linc had drifted to his post, the column, where he could observe his redhead. The seven debutantes of 1906 had gravitated to two ivory-brocaded sofas that faced each other. A bevy of youth and spirit restrained by strict etiquette. In frilled, apricot silk, Miss

Jackson made herself the focal point by lounging on the sofa's broad rolled arm.

"Are you enjoying your visit in San Francisco, Miss Fourchette?" Miss Jackson sipped from her translucent china cup.

"Of course! San Francisco is so different from New Orleans." The attractive brunette's soft Southern drawl contrasted sharply with the touch of Boston in Miss Jackson's voice.

Linc was impressed by the turnout of San Francisco's finest. Miss Higginbottom had attracted the wives and daughters of the richest men in the city—the Big Four of the Central Pacific Railroad and the Bonanza Kings of the Comstock Lode. Miss Higginbottom, a newcomer, evidently had the right touch or maybe it was her broad Boston accent that impressed local society.

Mrs. Ward's protégé, a little brown sparrow named Ann, leaned forward. "I hear that your family is one of the oldest Creole families in New Orleans," she said with obvious awe. "What exactly does Creole mean?"

Linc wondered the same thing.

Miss Fourchette said self-deprecatingly. "Creole refers to the mixture of Spanish and French in New Orleans. My own family is descended from one of the original French colonial families."

"Really? But being raised in Boston, I know little of Southern society." With a trace of derision in her smile, Miss Jackson set her cup and saucer without a sound onto the inlaid, rosewood table between the two sofas. "How fortunate that your family survived the financial reversals of the Civil War."

Miss Fourchette smiled, but said nothing.

Smart girl, Linc commented silently.

The redhead had avoided him thus far. But he wasn't deceived. In the midst of conversation, she was observing him, sizing him up. She'd taken the effort to discover his identity. She'd invited him as the only guest reporter to write up this tea. Why?

✳ ✳ ✳ ✳ ✳

"Oh, the photographer's arrived!" Cecy exclaimed. *Thank heaven, this insipid conversation is boring me to death.*

"Photographer?" Ann looked around dismayed.

"Yes, I suggested to Aunty that I'd like a photograph of the other debs who came out with me." She'd thought long and hard to come up with a truly distinctive, modern favor for her guests. "Each of you will receive a framed print." And since most of the ladies attending were in some way related or associated with the debutantes, the gift should be deemed acceptable and especially thoughtful by everyone present. Miss Jackson motioned them all to follow her.

"How charmin'." Fleur smiled. "I'll treasure it."

Cecy smiled and nodded for the Southern girl to precede her.

Ann got up hesitantly. "I don't photograph well."

"Honey, you'll be just lovely." Fleur put her arm around the girl's shoulder and drew her along.

Hurry up, Cecy fretted inside. Finally the other girls trailed Fleur with Cecy bringing up the rear.

From the corner of her eye, she checked on where that exasperating man was. She'd put him in his place today. She'd show him just how charming, how popular she could be.

Aunty introduced Cecy and the other six debs to the photographer. Aunty gave her a warning look. Cecy nodded. She remembered Aunty's advice—she was to be very modest during the picture-taking.

Little Ann still hung back. Cecy wished she could take Ann aside and talk some sense into her. Cecy had spent most of her life afraid of her own shadow. Fortunately, after her father's death, Aunty had talked some sense into her. Why waste your time hiding in the shadows at the fringes of life?

The photographer smiled ingratiatingly. "Miss Jackson, will you stand beside the fern please?" She nodded graciously and took her place.

Cecy smiled, thinking of the freedom great wealth brought. In the Boston school to which she'd been banished by her father, she'd never been allowed to experience the privileged life she'd been born to. Only once had her parents shown any awareness of her as a person. She'd been given extra music lessons—more than any other student received. But she knew Aunty was the one who had requested them for her. Cecy still ached with traces of her past loneliness.

But soon she would forget her past. Her whole life lay before her and belonged to her exclusively. After a few months of mourning her father's death in San Francisco, Aunty had taken her to Europe, had shown her what life could be. She'd learned lavish hotel life, operas, parties, balls—champagne and flirtation.

In a few weeks, she'd give her first party for a visiting opera company. She could hardly wait. She would set the stage carefully, then the Great Caruso would come in April, just as her social triumph was complete.

Now she obeyed the photographer and tilted her head more toward him. She smiled for him—a real smile. For this good life.

* * * * *

Linc watched the photographer set up his cumbersome equipment in a corner of the drawing room. He arranged the six lovely girls on and around a love seat and a luxuriant Boston fern on a plant stand. The other ladies watched the proceedings with interest, calling genteelly to the young ladies to stand up straight, to tilt their heads in different positions and to smile. Linc thought the beleaguered photographer would explode with one of his powder flashes before the session ended.

Linc was aware of Miss Jackson's persistent, though covert attention to him. Whenever she thought no one was looking, her gaze drifted to him. Was there some surprise she had in store for him? His mind worked on two levels: one watching and taking mental notes about the occasion for the article he'd write up for *The Bulletin;* the other leaped ahead trying to decide what Miss Jackson would say when she did speak to him. What would he say in response?

The photographer arranged the seven lovelies in one final pose. The man shot his last negative, folded up his tripod and escaped. The debutantes drifted toward the two sofas again. Linc followed them discreetly.

Ann sat down, looking rosy with exhilaration. "I never had a photograph without my family before. How exciting!"

"Wasn't it?" Fleur agreed. "What a truly original touch, Miss Jackson. I only wish I'd thought of it during my New Orleans season last year."

Another young woman, very scrawny and plain, had followed them over after the photographing. She said in catty satisfaction, "This is your second season then, too!"

Linc tried to place her. He knew someone had pointed her out to him.

Miss Fourchette looked surprised. "Why yes, I feel almost greedy enjoying a second season. But my aunt, you know, has no daughter and she insisted I let her sponsor me here."

"Oh, I wouldn't want to have to do two seasons in two different cities," shy Ann squeaked.

Fleur smiled warmly and patted Ann's hand. "You've gotten off to a wonderful start. Mrs. Ward's ball was simply exquisite."

"And quite interesting at moments." The plain girl grinned knowingly; her eyes straying toward Miss Jackson.

If this girl kept these comments coming, she'd soon overshadow anything outrageous his redhead said.

Realization hit Linc. The plain girl was Clarissa Bower. No wonder she sounded cross. Why would Hunt ever pay court to such a lanky and unprepossessing girl?

Miss Jackson raised her chin; her eyes sparkling with unspoken wrath.

"Oh, you mean that silly little dust-up between those two gentlemen?" Fleur giggled. "High-couraged gentlemen can always be relied on to add a touch of drama to an evening."

Linc paused. Once again he was impressed with the lady from New Orleans. Did Miss Jackson realize the signal service Fleur was executing for her?

With a mischievous grin, Fleur went on, "Why at my first ball, two gentlemen threatened to duel over me."

"But that's against the law!" Ann objected in horrified tones.

Fleur gave her distinctive trill of laughter. "No duel took place. Though I suspect fisticuffs may have."

The debs tittered at this. The plain girl frowned.

"Well, some people find it gratifying to have men fighting over them, but I find it a dead bore," Miss Jackson spoke with airy unconcern.

Linc shook his head. Did she ever think before she opened her mouth? Fleur had effectively closed the subject without bringing Miss Jackson into it by name and dredging up the fiasco at the ball one more time.

"I hear that Victor Hunt has a new auto. Clarence got one, too," Clarissa said. "And they're going to have a race through the streets of San Francisco!"

Miss Jackson looked up, obviously intrigued. "An auto race. How exciting!"

"Driving an auto fast isn't safe." Little Ann sounded shocked. "They might be hurt!"

"I doubt that." Clarissa pointed her nose upward.

"I own an automobile myself," Miss Jackson declared. "And I intend to learn how to drive it too."

CHAPTER 3

She did? Linc was intrigued in spite of himself.

Every debutante stared at her.

Ann gasped. "Drive a car? By yourself?"

Miss Jackson chuckled. "Why not? It's even easier than driving a carriage. Autos don't rear up at the slightest thing. I'm looking forward to it."

Interrupting them, Miss Higginbottom clapped her hands asking for attention. Everyone, including Linc, turned to her. "Ladies, Miss Fourchette's aunt tells me that her niece is quite accomplished on the piano and has a lovely singing voice too. Please help me encourage her to entertain us with a song."

All the ladies dutifully clapped. Fleur rose with convincing modesty and complied. At the other end of the vast drawing room, she sat down at the baby grand piano and began to play and sing in a pretty voice, "I Dream of Jeannie with the Light Brown Hair."

Observing Miss Jackson discreetly move to the food-laden buffet table, Linc met her there. Nonchalantly, he busied himself choosing an appetizer from among the rich array of food: oysters on the half shell, salmon in aspic, fresh pineapple, petits fours, decorated cookies, sponge cake in rum sauce.

"Good afternoon, Mr. Wagstaff," Miss Jackson said in a quietly triumphant voice.

He casually bowed. "Miss Jackson." Then he turned back to the replete table. He sensed her chagrin.

"I found out who you are."

"I never doubted you would," he said blandly, then popped a feather-light cheese puff into his mouth.

"It was I who asked Aunty to invite you here," she preened.

"I thought so." He spread caviar on a cracker.

She bristled. "Don't you want to know why?"

"I know why." With an urbane smile, he accepted a cup of creamy tea from the Chinese waiter tending the table.

"You are the rudest man."

He looked at her. "Charming dress. Paris?"

"Yes," she faltered, looking thrown off stride, "by Pacquin."

"Do you really have an auto?"

"Yes, but—"

"Would you like me to find out when the race is?"

She gaped at him, her brown-sugar eyes unbelieving.

"I'd like to see the race myself, wouldn't you?"

"I couldn't go with you. You're just a newspaper reporter."

Ignoring her, he walked on down the buffet table. Miss Jackson followed him with a curt swish of her skirt. He glanced at her. "You haven't taken my advice. You're still competing much too obviously against Miss Fourchette. You're going to end up on everyone's wrong side."

"If you're not careful about offending me, I'll make certain you're not invited to any more society functions."

He shook his head at her sadly. "If you think that, then you don't really know who I am."

"Yes, I do." She sounded hoarsely desperate. "You're a journalist who's starting up a weekly newspaper on society."

This made him chuckle. "You're sources aren't very reliable." He walked away from her.

She discreetly pursued him until they were partially hidden by several potted plants behind a sofa. She hissed, "Don't walk away from me."

At the other end of the vast drawing room, Fleur accepted applause, then agreed to sing "Lorena." The mournful song settled over the room. Even Miss Jackson fell silent.

But two matrons sitting on the sofa in front of them leaned toward each other. From behind, Linc could see only their hats. The one in a brown felt hat said, "I don't care how good a front she puts up today. She caused that dreadful scene at Ward's—"

A lady in a mauve hat with a veil nodded. "I suppose you're right. My son's their age and he said Hunt and Bower have competed in school, in sporting events, everything."

"That's what I've heard. Didn't Hunt's father insist his son marry Clarissa?"

"I heard that too," the mauve hat nodded.

"If he doesn't marry her, the father will disown him."

"Never say so! Do you think he'd dare decide to marry a different fortune and confound his father?"

The brown hat bent as the lady under it took a sip of tea. "That could be. But anyway, to get back to that Jackson chit. She better watch out. Hunt is interested in her money, not her."

Linc watched Cecilia's face take on a stunned expression.

"And she doesn't have a mother to guide her—"

"And why is that? Where is her mother?" the brown hat asked archly.

The mauve hat bent forward. "You know she's still at that sanitarium south on the way to Monterey. Why, she's been ill for years now."

Linc felt a little sick at hearing such unsympathetic gossip. What was Mrs. Jackson in a sanitarium for?

The brown hat tilted backward. "Humph. That's one way to say it. As far as I'm concerned, there's bad blood on both sides of her family. Neither her father's wealth, nor her mother's social background can blind me to the truth. Bad blood always comes out. You'll see. I told Archie to have nothing further to do with that redhead."

Linc felt Miss Jackson stiffen beside him. Fearing she might actually respond, he took her by the elbow and led her away. A nearby anteroom at the side of the drawing room presented itself as a convenient retreat.

"How dare they?" Miss Jackson's low voice shook with temper.

"Every woman in that room shares the same opinion. I tried to warn you—"

"Aunty said," she went on in a tone of dawning disbelief, "the other night was merely a lack of tact by Bower and Hunt—a gaucherie. My family's wealth is greater than that of either Hunt or Bower. My mother's Boston—"

He implored her, "Your aunt is a stranger here. She overestimates the Boston connection. That might work against you. You need to take note—"

Her eyes flashed with anger. "Who do you think you are? I invited you here. I can make certain you're never invited to another social event. If you're going to succeed with your society paper, you need *my* good graces."

Giving her a bleak look, he shook his head. "You've been misinformed. My journal will be about social issues, Miss Jackson. I'm not interested in society news." He bowed and left her.

How did God expect him to use this young woman who was completely uninterested in anything beyond herself and seemed hell-bent on self-destruction? *There is none so blind as those who will not see.*

Applause for Miss Fourchette's last song greeted him as he reentered the drawing room. Miss Jackson came in right behind him. As she passed him, she gave him no recognition, but swept toward the piano.

Fleur stepped forward to meet her. "Are you going to sing for us?"

Miss Jackson nodded imperiously.

"Would you like me to accompany you?"

"No, thank you." Miss Jackson moved in front of the piano keyboard. "I will sing a capella."

After a nod, Fleur left her alone by the piano.

Linc sincerely hoped Miss Jackson's anger hadn't led her into something foolhardy. Was her voice equal to the challenge of singing without embellishment?

She touched one key, sounding one high note. Then she turned and faced San Francisco society. She opened her mouth. Her voice soared in glorious richness.

Linc recognized the aria from *Aida*, Verdi's opera of a tragic love triangle. When Aida discovers that the man she loves and her father will go into battle as enemies, she despairs— *"Numi pieta, del mio soffrir!"*

Linc stood, transfixed. The lady's rich soprano voice overwhelmed him, swept him beyond his surroundings. The despair she gave the melody transcended the words, "Pity me, heaven." Her own deep misery translated through her song notched deeply into his heart. He cried out inside, *Virginia!*

He couldn't take his eyes off her as she sang. In the late afternoon sun flowing down from the skylight, her hair flamed. Her creamy white throat vibrated with song. The aria swept on. No one whispered. No one looked away. Her voice took possession of them all. Linc tensed as the misery of the song comingled with his own deep sorrow. *Virginia! Cecilia!*

Her voice reached higher, higher until the final plea to heaven. She flung out her arms in a gesture of agony. She snapped off the last, wrenching note. She bowed her head. Silence.

The ladies surged to their feet as one. The virtuosity of the solo had been stunning. They applauded fervently. Linc joined them. He shouted, "Bravo! Bravo!" The applause continued. Miss Jackson bent in a humble curtsey.

For the first time, he was seeing the real Cecilia. She, too, had known grief, pain—agonizing loneliness. A beautiful, young woman with a heart full of emotion would have been a devastatingly irresistible combination. Linc longed to shout, *The woman you're hiding could shake San Francisco to its foundation! Take off your mask, Cecilia!*

❈ ❈ ❈ ❈ ❈

After struggling to write about the afternoon tea, Linc tucked the finished article inside his coat and walked purposefully up Market Street. He paused at the corner of Third Street. The *Call* and *Examiner* buildings stood on opposite corners there. San Francisco was famous for its newspapers.

As a newspaperman, he knew all the stories of this brash city. The *Examiner,* "The Monarch of the Dailies," was William Randolph Hearst's paper. Hearst's senator father had given his son the paper in 1887 as a Harvard graduation gift. Young Hearst had taken it from a four-page daily with five thousand subscribers to a ten-pager with over fifty thousand in only eighteen months!

Ten years before, The *Call* had been sold in an all-day auction with two bidders raising each other's bids by five hundred dollars at a time. The final price of $360,000 had been paid by John D. Spreckles, the son of the sugar magnate. Farther on, the *Chronicle* stood across Market at Kearney Street. Its building was a skyscraper. Its clock tower reminded Linc it was time for him to stop at the *Bulletin* office to turn in his copy on the afternoon tea.

As he walked the rest of the way to the *Bulletin,* he asked himself why he'd come to San Francisco, why he thought he could add anything to the newspaper world of this city. But the West needed a voice raised for social justice. Most of the work was being done in the East and South. The complacent fashionable circles here cried out for a shake-up. The wealthy in San Francisco needed to follow the example of his Boston aunt and many others to use their means as a tool of bettering the future of America.

But was he the one to do it? Learning the real Cecilia Jackson hid behind a veil had shaken his confidence. He'd believed Cecilia with her creamy complexion, brown eyes, and an enchanting mole at the corner of her mouth was merely a spoiled, rich deb. A girl who flaunted her wealth and had no regard concerning what that wealth might have cost others. He'd been so sure he'd had her all figured out. He'd been a fool.

He entered the *Bulletin* offices and dropped his copy at the city desk. Looking around at the cluttered desks and listening to the ticker tape run, he felt a sharp jab of homesickness. None of the desks here were his. He'd spent most of his adult life in

Chicago writing for one paper, then another. But his last few months there under a new, foul-mouthed editor had been the final stimulus to make him quit Chicago. Still, leaving the *Tribune* a month ago had been like tying off an artery.

Desperately alone, he walked back out into the chilly evening. Mist swirled outside. His spirits floundered. He started to head home.

"Wagstaff?"

Linc turned to see a tall, raw-boned man in the *Bulletin* doorway. "Yes?" He moved toward the middle-aged man sporting a mustache that resembled a walrus's.

"I'm Fremont Older, managing editor." He offered his hand.

Recognizing the name, Linc shook hands with him.

"Been wanting to meet you. Have a moment?"

"Certainly." Older, who'd started out as a "tramp" printer, was a big man in San Francisco journalism. But what did Older want of him?

Older led him back inside to his large office, and indicated the chair beside his desk. The two sat down facing each other. Older barked, "How'd you get the only invite to that Jackson tea?"

Linc looked up, amused. "Yes, it is a foggy evening."

"Eh?" Older glared at him.

"Sorry. Your directness startled me. I just endured an afternoon of genteel, ladylike conversation." Linc kept the sarcasm out of his voice. He'd heard some very unladylike conversation this afternoon—not only from the two hats, but from Cecilia Jackson too.

Older's face cleared and he chuckled. "Not much of an assignment for a newspaperman."

Linc nodded. For some reason, he didn't want to discuss Cecilia and why she'd invited him with anyone. She was still so young. That must be one of the reasons he'd been so fooled by her. He'd made the mistake of thinking she was past her first youth like he was. She was still an innocent in this world. He felt guilty for overlooking this, so he'd barely spoken to Susan about the tea. Writing the column had been a painful exercise in writing meaningless pleasantries. The hidden Cecilia Jackson was the real story.

"So what do you think of Miss Jackson and her stuffy Boston aunt?"

This was just the kind of question Linc dreaded. He hated being less than candid, but he didn't want to further rumors. "I'll admit it. I'm undecided," Linc replied cautiously. "I think I have her figured out, then she shows another side of herself." That was the truth—though barely.

"Hmmm. She fits her family then." Older steepled his fingers.

"What do you mean?" Linc looked up.

"Her father, August Jackson, wasn't anyone I would want to count as a friend." Older lowered his hands.

Linc digested this in silence.

Older went on, "He was the son of a German immigrant merchant who didn't come to pan for gold. He changed his name to Jackson and set up shop to extort money from the forty-niners. You know, one dollar for an egg. That kind of thing. When August came of age, he showed the same business sense and greed as his father. Instead of dissipating his father's wealth, he doubled it."

"I've heard Miss Jackson is the richest heiress in San Francisco."

"She is." Older stared into Linc's eyes.

Linc wondered what Older wanted to know. "What made you say you wouldn't want her father for a friend?"

Older leaned back in his chair. "The ability to make money was her father's only good trait. I'm not a religious man, but August Jackson violated at least nine of the Ten Commandments—more than once. I never heard him accused of murder, but he might even have been guilty of that. He had a nasty temper."

The words chilled Linc. He'd never known his own father who'd been a casualty of the Civil War, but his stepfather had been a true father to him. "Poor Miss Jackson."

Older shook his head. "I doubt she has much memory of him."

Linc gave Older a startled glance. "He died just last year."

"That's right. But his daughter grew up in Boston."

"I knew she went to school there, but I thought she was there for finishing school."

"No, she was sent away at seven."

"Seven?" Linc asked in shock.

"This is the story. August was so bad, no girl in San Francisco would marry him, no decent girl. So he went back East, put on a good show and married a Boston girl. Back in San Francisco, when the Boston girl finally realized what she'd married, she sent the daughter to boarding school in Boston near her unmarried sister, the same aunt that accompanied Cecilia from Boston."

"Why didn't the mother just take the child and go home?" Linc couldn't believe what he was hearing.

Older shook his head. "Father disowned her for marrying against his wishes. Most people think she might have been too stubborn to admit her mistake."

"Where is she now?" Linc thought of the gossip he'd overheard.

"At a sanitarium in the mountains. There are rumors, but no one knows for sure why she's there. It could be insanity or...." Older held his hands up showing his lack of knowledge. "So you see, Miss Jackson didn't have much luck with parents. And she's a stranger in her hometown. Everyone in society is waiting to see if she'll turn out anything like her father."

Linc frowned. Then Cecilia Jackson stood in more danger than she was aware of. She was playing a daring game trying to impress society. Was she aware that people might be watching for signs of her father's bad blood? Had she taken seriously the gossip they'd overheard from the two ladies in the hats? How could he warn her? Would she listen if he did?

"So how did you get the only invite today?"

Linc looked up. He couldn't tell the truth—that Cecilia had wanted to get the better of him, to make him dance on the end of her string. "I extricated her from a minor unpleasantness at the Ward ball. This was my thank-you from Miss Higginbottom." Maybe he could talk to the aunt, warn her.

"Makes sense." Older nodded glumly. "Are you likely to get more invitations?"

"Might." Grateful for the information Older had given him, Linc explained, "I've got Boston connections myself. My stepfather was—"

"I know. Boston bankers." Older grinned.

Linc smiled. Older had done his homework. But it looked like Linc hadn't done his. He'd been so interested in Cecilia's business interests and his own newspaper, he'd neglected the most important part, Cecilia herself.

"The *Bulletin* will be glad to buy any more society articles you can get."

Deep in guilt, Linc nodded noncommittally. "I really want to get my weekly up and going in a month."

"Weekly, eh? Heard you're a muckraker. You'll find a lot of muck to rake here, starting with Mayor Schmitz. Schmitz is just a political puppet for the Reuf gang. Corruption is so thick and rich in this town you could cut it with a butter knife."

"Politics isn't my focus."

"What is?" Older leaned forward.

"Children and their welfare. Have you heard of the National Child Labor Committee?"

"Can't say I have."

CHAPTER 3

Linc wasn't surprised by Older's blasé reaction. Right now newspapers saw nothing newsworthy about this topic, but that would change. "Well, you and the rest of this city will soon."

* * * * *

February 3, 1906

Leaning forward in her seat in the darkened opera house, Cecy lost herself in the melodious duet between Lt. Pinkerton and his Japanese bride, Cio Cio San or Butterfly. Cecy ached over the American's callous attitude to the beautiful young girl who loved him with all her heart. Cecy would never fall in love. Men couldn't be trusted. Seeing her mother earlier today had painfully pressed this point home. After the soprano's final notes, the theater lights came up. Act I was over. Cecy pressed her delicate handkerchief to her eyes.

Her aunt, dressed in sedate gray velvet, glanced around. "Gentlemen will leave their seats during intermission. I'm sure many will visit our box. Now Miss Fourchette is to our left. Be sure to give her a gracious nod. But I'll keep a discreet watch to see if she receives more visitors than you."

"Yes, Aunty." Cecy struggled to keep a smile on her face. While the opera was being performed, she could lose herself in it. Now she must be alert to the social tightrope she walked. On display once again. She'd show everyone she could attract gentlemen and keep them behaving as "gentlemen." And she must continue to draw more attention than Fleur. She wouldn't spend the rest of her life in the shadows, a pitiful spinster like her aunt.

Hunt, devastatingly handsome in black evening dress, stepped through the velvet curtains. "Miss Jackson."

Cecy extended her kid-gloved hand regally—though she really wished she could turn away. He bowed over it, then greeted her aunt. They exchanged pleasantries. Bower arrived with other gentlemen. Though both Hunt and Bower eyed one another, they never stepped over the line of decorum.

"Will you be attending our masked ball?" Bower asked close to Cecy's ear.

"A masquerade. How charming," she replied by rote. "I couldn't miss that."

The lights flickered. The men who'd spent the intermission in her box said their adieux and left for their own boxes. She felt relieved to be alone again with her thoughts about her mother.

Aunty's voice intruded on her thoughts. "Bower stopped at Miss Fourchette's box before coming here. I don't like that."

Barely hearing, Cecy gazed around the theater. Her eye caught a glimpse of that man, Wagstaff. Her face warmed. No matter how she'd tried to best him, she hadn't yet. There was something about him that drew her. What was it? He was handsome with his straight nose, square chin, and honey-colored hair. But his clear blue eyes pierced her, making her feel exposed, unmasked. And he never treated her like the other gentlemen—flattering her, waiting on her, begging for her favor. Mr. Wagstaff, on the other hand, never insulted her intelligence. Would he really take her to the auto race? Did she even want to speak to him again?

Her thoughts slipped back to her visit to her mother earlier that day. She recalled the feel of her mother's soft, weak hand in her own. Last year at her father's funeral, her mother had come in the care of a doctor and nurse. Cecy had only been able to speak a few words to her mother, but hadn't been able to tell if the lady understood her. But her mother's whispery voice today floated in her mind. What was wrong with Mother? What had left her a broken woman? When could she come home? Why did her aunt avoid any questions about her mother? The lights lowered. The curtain rose.

✳ ✳ ✳ ✳ ✳

Linc shifted in his seat. Puccini's *Madame Butterfly,* the tragic story of an innocent girl who gives her love to a cad, paralleled too closely the story of Cecilia's parents that Older had recounted to him. Did Cecilia know the truth about her parents? Or had her aunt concealed it from her? Should he try to warn her of the social peril that her father's deplorable reputation placed her in? Would she believe him if he did?

The opera finally ensnared him again. After three years apart, Madame Butterfly sang of longing for Pinkerton's return. She lifted her voice hoping his ship would again appear. The aria pierced Linc's calm, unleashing his own impossible craving for Virginia to return. A knot of agony clotted in his throat. He couldn't breathe. *Lord, I know she's with you, but I want her back! I can't let go.*

🐝 🐝 🐝 🐝 🐝

Restless, Cecy leaned forward in her seat. She couldn't rid herself of the images of her mother from their afternoon visit. Her mother's pale face. Her listless eyes. Cecy and her aunt had taken the hour carriage ride to the sanitarium in the mountains where her mother was convalescing. Cecy had been so anxious to see her mother, hoping she could finally speak to her. The year before, after speaking with Aunt Amelia her frail mother had collapsed and had returned immediately to the sanitarium. Aunty had said her mother was too sick to leave the sanitarium and that the doctors discouraged visits, so they'd gone away to Europe. Aunty had said that was what mother wanted. Cecy hadn't questioned her aunt's lead.

Today, Cecy had again hoped for a few moments of conversation, but that had proved overly optimistic. Aunty had spoken directly to her sister, but calmly. Mother had merely stared at them both—as though she didn't know them. Cecy had craved so much more. She'd been taut with anticipation and fear, too, that mother wouldn't want to see her. They'd been apart so long!

Finally, Cecy hadn't been able to hold back, "Mother, I'm Cecilia. Don't you remember me?"

"Cecilia?" Her mother had looked to her sister.

Aunty had nodded. "Florence, Cecilia and I are living in San Francisco now."

Trembling, Cecilia had taken up her mother's hand. "We want you to get better and come to live with us when you are able."

Her mother had stared at her, looking vacantly, but slightly scared. Finally she'd whispered, "I'm not well."

That was all she'd said, those few words and Aunty had refused to add anything.

A stage cannon fired. Pinkerton's ship had arrived in the harbor. In awful irony, Butterfly rejoiced singing of cherry blossoms. Tears ran down Cecy's face.

※ ※ ※ ※ ※

Act III was nearly over. Linc watched Cecy's profile clearly in the light from the stage. She sat in a box on the other side of the theater. Dressed in a soft shade of pink, she matched the silk cherry blossoms on the stage.

But her sadness showed itself clearly in the lines of her body: the dipping of her chin, the slump of her shoulders, the handkerchief dabbed at her eyes. Linc longed to comfort her, convince her that God's love could heal her—if only she'd let him. *How can I get through to her? The treacherous course she followed could bring more pain, more loneliness.*

On stage, learning of her husband's betrayal, Madame Butterfly sang in despair, "Goodbye, happy home, home of love."

Linc felt steel bands tighten around his heart. He looked up at Cecilia. He recalled her singing at the tea. Her voice rivaled the one he was hearing now. As Butterfly's voice soared higher in anguish, he recalled Cecy singing as desperate Aida. Now he knew this was true of Cecilia too. No wonder she'd looked so lost, sorrowful, so alone. She'd been abandoned, sent away by her parents. Now Linc glimpsed what God must see. Man looks on the outside, but God looks on the heart!

A sudden urge to comfort her, to draw her to him, to hold her in his arms and soothe her anguish with kisses and soft words rocked Linc to his foundation. He imagined the silky softness of her hair between his fingers.

Linc's chair began to sway. *Dear God, my chair is moving!* As though a wind blew through the theater, the stage curtains swished rhythmically. He sat petrified.

On stage, the fake front of the Japanese house crashed down.

The soprano screamed.

Some woman shrieked, "Earthquake!"

Linc leaped from his seat and raced toward the staircase to Cecilia's box.

CHAPTER 4

"Deliver me, O LORD,...preserve me from the violent man."
Psalm 140:1, KJV

BARELY KEEPING HIS BALANCE
on the undulating floor, Linc brushed through the curtains of
Cecilia's box. Cecilia was standing frozen, her eyes staring.

Her aunt pushed past Linc, "Get the girl!"

Linc swept Cecilia into his arms, his heart pounding.

At that moment, the theater stopped its rocking. Linc halted.
Nervous laughter rippled throughout the audience. The stage
curtains swished to a close. The soprano ceased screaming in
mid-shriek.

Linc looked down at the woman in his arms and murmured, "Cecilia." She smelled of spring flowers and her head
rested on his shoulder. In spite of the corset, her womanly softness brought a rush of remembrance that engulfed him. He

couldn't help himself. He tightened his hold, pressed his face into the velvety fold of her neck.

Her eyes cleared visibly. "Mr. Wagstaff?" she replied dazedly.

"Just a tremor." He carried her back to her chair. Aware of the impropriety of their intimacy, he tried to sit her down, but she clawed at his shoulders.

"Don't leave me alone!" Her voice sounded strained and thready.

The house lights went up. Linc didn't want people to see him embracing Cecilia—even in these circumstances. He knelt, sitting her on her chair, effectually hiding himself behind the sides of the box. "I won't leave you until you are recovered."

She clung to him.

"I promise." He captured her soft hands and tenderly drew them down. He spoke soothingly, "It was just a tremor. Nothing bad is going to happen. It's over."

"I've never felt anything like that," she stammered.

"We're both newcomers here. Boston and Chicago don't experience earth tremors." In the faint light, her pale beauty took on an ethereal quality.

She still trembled. "Someone screamed it was an earthquake."

"Everything's calm now." He drew his hands from hers—though breaking their connection pained him.

Her aunt hurried back into the box. "Cecilia!"

Linc rose and helped the distraught older woman take her seat.

Cecilia shook noticeably. "Aunty, are you all right?" Her voice broke on the last word.

Applause drowned out Miss Higginbottom's reply. The curtain rose. The lights dimmed. A few bars of the overture announced the resumption of the opera.

Still shaken, Linc bowed to both the ladies and walked to the rear of the box. He paused, unwilling to leave Cecilia though he must for appearances.

"Mr. Wagstaff, thank you."

At the sound of Cecilia's voice, he turned. "My pleasure." The velvet curtains fell into place behind him. He meant to walk back to his seat, but the lingering sensation of Cecilia in his arms made it impossible for him to return to sitting quietly.

He walked outside, going home to check on Meg, Susan, and Del. The haunting melody of the tragic heroine's aria followed him out into the clear, cool night.

✳ ✳ ✳ ✳ ✳

February 6, 1906

The scent of exotic spices, incense burning in a small outdoor temple and rancid garbage mingled in the air over Chinatown. The sun had proved sluggish today casting gloom over them, which Linc felt inside too. He eyed the crowded street, the strange Chinese symbols on buildings. A reflex of protectiveness in this foreign atmosphere tightened inside him. He squeezed Meg's hand and hurried to catch up with Del and Susan in front of them.

"This is different from Chicago," Meg whispered, staring upward at the balconies above.

"It's different than the rest of San Francisco." Del looked around.

Meg nodded, looking serious.

Chinese people, wearing a rainbow of bright cotton and shimmering silk hurried by them. Linc tried to keep his mind on the present scene, not the one from last night at the theater. He still hadn't decided what to do about Cecilia. Last night he'd watched her from afar, still trying to decide how to break through her sophisticated veneer. Then he held her in his arms and she'd awakened a part of him that he'd thought had died with Virginia.

"There may have been a few Chinese people in Chicago, but I never got to meet one." Susan huffed slightly going up the hill.

"Are we going to meet one today, Aunt Susan?" Meg skipped to keep up.

"Maybe."

"Why do the men wear those funny braids down their backs?" Del hunched his shoulders. "Braids are for girls."

Pushing aside the image of Cecilia, Linc wished he'd asked Kang more questions about Chinatown. "It has something to do with the conquest of China. If they cut them off, they wouldn't be welcome back in China."

"Why do they want to go back to China?" Meg asked. "China's farther away from here than Chicago, isn't it?"

A Chinese man, probably a rich Mandarin, in intricately embroidered, blue silk tunic and skirt walked past Linc. Another Chinese man in black cotton walked close behind with one hand in his pocket. Could he be a "boo how doy," a professional bodyguard? Kang had told Linc of tong wars and bodyguards who always had one hand in a pocket concealing a gun. Why had Susan wanted him to bring the children here?

"Last night I wanted to go back to Chicago," Susan said.

"Me, too!" Meg exclaimed. "I didn't like that tremor that shook us."

Linc recalled that extraordinary feeling of the earth moving, swaying. He'd never imagined a tremor could be so unnerving. Had he brought his beloved Meg to a place of danger?

"Yes, but it was kind of exciting, wasn't it?" Susan grinned wider. "I never thought I'd ever feel an earth tremor."

Linc shook his head. Susan, fearless Susan, who'd helped raise him and now in her seventies had insisted on moving to San Francisco with him.

Del looked at his grandmother as though she'd lost her mind.

Susan went on, "When I was a little girl, I never thought I'd ever see California, the ocean—"

CHAPTER 4

"That's not such a big deal," Del growled.

Susan halted. "I have had all I'm going to take of this bad attitude of yours, Delman Caleb DuBois," Susan said sternly as though unconscious of all the people on the narrow, crowded street who were listening.

"Look around you." When he didn't obey, she lifted his chin with her forefinger. "I said *look*."

Del's eyes shifted from one side to another, then Susan nudged him to scan the narrow, crowded street by rotating in a circle. People skirted around them, glancing at them curiously. One man stood in front of a Chinese café watching them intently.

"Now, Del, do you see how the Chinese people have tried to make a place for themselves here in this strange land?"

Linc felt a sudden kinship. He was trying to do the same. So was Cecilia, but so dangerously. Could he warn her?

Del nodded.

"Why do you think they came to California in the first place?"

Linc had come because of his own grief. He'd wanted to put half a continent between him and places that reminded him of Virginia. But God had led him to San Francisco. *God, you've opened every door for me along the way. But I don't understand why Cecilia Jackson is so central in my work. Shouldn't I find someone with fewer encumbrances? Help me see my way clearly.*

"I don't know."

"Guess," Susan commanded.

Del looked up, obviously puzzled.

Susan said slowly, "Think. Why would men travel across a whole ocean to be a 'coolie' to work on a railroad gang, pounding spikes or cooking for a hundred men at a time?"

Listening to Susan, Linc found himself wondering what had started Cecilia on her campaign for social success? Did she plan to marry Bower or Hunt? No, he had the feeling her flirting was merely on the surface. She didn't look as though she had any real affection for either gentleman. So why flirt and lead them on? It didn't make any sense. Did she even know the truth about her parents?

"It must have been bad in China," Del muttered.

"How bad?" Susan pressed him.

"Real bad."

Was Cecilia's past driving her hard? She badly needed guidance. Why wasn't her aunt warning her of the dangerous position she occupied? But Cecilia would never accept any advice—if he was right about her.

Linc noted the Chinese man still watching them.

Susan nodded, satisfied. "I know that some of this rebellious heart is your grandfather Caleb—God rest his soul—in you. But you have to learn life isn't fair."

Glancing at the boy, Linc wished he could shield Del and Cecilia, from the harsh realities they were facing. But he wasn't God. Linc had begun praying for Cecilia when he'd first felt she was part of the way to launch his weekly. Would he be able to persuade her to investigate the conditions of her own manufactories? He couldn't imagine the vain, willful young debutante having anything to do with such matters. Now his prayers would have to be more personal, for her protection, for wisdom to know how to prepare her.

Susan's voice called Linc back. "Del, you think your problems started when we came here. That's wrong. California isn't the problem. I faced hate in Mississippi, in Chicago, in Washington D. C. We moved here and here we're staying. Linc's got work to do here." Susan stared into her grandson's eyes.

Meg touched Del's sleeve shyly. "We got an automobile here, Del. You got a new piano. And we get to ride cable cars."

Del nodded.

The Chinese man stepped away from the entrance of his tiny café. He smiled suddenly. "Please, you come in. Tea and almond cookies on me."

Susan glanced at him in surprise.

CHAPTER 4

The man went on, "Bring the children in. I will tell them about China. Why my father came to California and what he did as 'coolie'."

Susan smiled. "Thank you. I'd like to hear that myself." She led the children and Linc into the gloomy-looking café.

Linc brought up the rear, wishing Cecilia had been here to benefit from Susan's common sense. But Cecilia was set on a willful path. One misstep and her life in San Francisco could be damaged forever. Linc needed her because God had led him to her. But what was God's plan for Cecilia? How could God use her as she was?

※ ※ ※ ※ ※

February 12, 1906

The fashionable people crowded Montgomery Street for the Saturday afternoon promenade. January had bestowed a clear, crisp day on San Francisco. The elite were on parade to see and be seen.

What was so wrong with Cecy's mother that Aunty wouldn't discuss it? All her questions had been ignored. Was it a fatal illness? An emptiness, a blackness squeezed inside Cecy painfully. She half-stumbled over uneven paving. She caught herself and walked on.

"Are you all right?" Aunty murmured beside her.

Cecy nodded. But horrible visions of her mother lying—frail and withered—on her death bed, brought tears to Cecy's eyes. She blinked them away. She cried out silently, *Mother, I want to know you!*

On the surface, she nodded and smiled to acquaintances. She felt like a mannequin. Phrases spoken by fashion modistes in Paris and London played through her mind. She was a stylish young woman in an ivory shirtwaist blouse and a matching brown woolen voile jacket and skirt. Her hat, a delightful, ivory felt, soft-brimmed and trimmed with red fox fur, had arrived just this morning from the milliner. Cecy had her chilled hands tucked into a matching muff of red fox.

Wearing beautiful new clothing, instead of an ugly school uniform, still pleased her. Each day brought fresh awareness of how burdensome trying to conquer society had become. But the only other choice, being ignored and slighted for the rest of her life, kept the false smile on her face. Aunty had become inured to her lot in life as a spinster. Cecy was thankful she had her aunt's guidance to avoid a similar fate. No one would ever pity Cecilia Jackson.

Horses hooves clip-clopped and carriage wheels clicked over the brick pavement. Darkly handsome Victor Hunt crossed the street and came directly to Cecy. "Miss Jackson. Miss Higginbottom." He bowed. "May I have the pleasure of escorting you?" He crooked both elbows, offering one to each lady.

Aunty Amelia smiled primly. "You don't want an old woman spoiling your conversation. Pray take Cecilia ahead. I'll follow."

Hunt grinned his thanks and immediately squired Cecy a few steps ahead of her aunt. "Your aunt is very understanding. I see you at every event, but we never have time for real conversation."

Cecy nodded, forcing a smile. She didn't like Hunt. A disreputable air clung to him and he often smelled of spirits. She had the feeling nothing would stand in the way of a goal he desired. Ever since the Ward ball, he had pursued her—or was it her fortune? Fool!

Hunt gave her a beguiling smile.

She wasn't beguiled. She smiled sweetly, but inside she hissed, *"I don't trust you."*

"I'd love to take you for a ride in my new REO auto. We'd finally have a moment alone then."

Just ahead of them, Fleur Fourchette alighted from a glossy black carriage with Clarence Bowers' assistance. For once, Cecy was glad to see the brunette with the Southern drawl. Cecy stepped forward. If Fleur were here with Bower, Cecy would make their twosome a foursome. Cecy didn't want either Hunt or Bower. But if Fleur became engaged to Bower, one of the most marriageable bachelors in San Francisco, Cecy would be cast in the shade. Also she couldn't let Hunt think she had any desire for a tête-à-tête with him. Which happened to be absolutely true.

Wearing a well-tailored, tweed lounge suit, Bower doffed his hat to Cecy. She gave him a welcoming smile. The two men exchanged stiff nods.

Out of the corner of her eye, she glimpsed Mr. Wagstaff across the busy street. He'd come to her aid at the opera—not Hunt, not Bowers. Mr. Wagstaff. Why? As she recalled the strength of his embrace, prickles ran down her arms. For those moments, she's felt secure, safe. Before Aunty's tea, she'd thought the newspaperman wanted to get close to her to further his writing career.

But she'd been wrong. His weekly journal was going to be about the plight of the lower classes, that kind of high-sounding pap that Aunty said was so insincere. But if he were only interested in using her to further his career, why had he come to carry her out of the theater? When she'd come to her senses, she'd been shocked at her own weakness over a mere tremor. Like some weak Nellie, she'd clung to him.

The man must want something.

As though she read Cecy's mind, Fleur said, "Miss Jackson, wasn't that tremor just shockin'? I couldn't sleep all night. I told Aunty I just don't know how y'all live here. There might be an earthquake at any time."

From across the street, Mr. Wagstaff had noticed her. He'd paused and glanced her way. An intriguing new thought about how this man might be useful to her began to insinuate itself into her mind. Was it possible?

Cecy smiled confidently at Fleur as though the earth tremor hadn't disturbed her at all. "Don't you have hurricanes in Louisiana, Miss Fourchette?"

"But the two can't be compared!" Fleur exclaimed, holding her rose-red felt hat against a gust of chill wind.

The two San Franciscan men smiled indulgently.

Aunty, who'd joined them, spoke up, "Mr. Bower, we are so looking forward to your masked ball tonight."

"I'm so happy you will attend," he said formally.

Cecy turned the new idea about Mr. Wagstaff over in her mind. Though she didn't let it show, she monitored Mr. Wagstaff's progress along the crowded street. She couldn't have ignored him if she tried.

"Normally I wouldn't allow Cecilia to attend a masquerade. Sometimes they become routs of the worst sort! But I know I can depend on your dear mother to make certain the young gentlemen keep the line."

"Of course, ma'am."

A short, uncomfortable silence fell over the group. Pondering Mr. Wagstaff's effect on her, Cecy pushed straying tendrils of hair off her brow. The wind had picked up. Her hat strained against her hat pins. Mr. Wagstaff threaded his way through the parading carriages across to the same side of the street as she. Could she persuade the newsman to help her once again?

Hunt drawled, "Well, Bower, have you finally decided what day you'd like our auto race to take place or are you going to admit defeat?" The lazy way Hunt said the words in contrast with the dark intent in his eyes startled Cecy. What was so pressing about winning an auto race?

"I hear you've been wagering—" Bower began.

Fleur interrupted, "Oh, you men. What does it matter who has the fastest car?"

Cecy spoke up with forced pertness, "Auto races are exciting. Aunty and I witnessed one in Monte Carlo." Cecy smiled widely. "Quite breathtaking."

Aunt Amelia nodded her agreement.

"Miss Jackson is more darin' than I." Fleur smiled. "She even owns an auto and plans to learn to drive it!"

"Really?" Bower exclaimed.

Hunt half-bowed to Cecy. "I'd be more than willing to take you out for a spin or two and teach you a few things."

Aunt Amelia frowned.

Cecy didn't like the innuendo in Hunt's words. She always wanted to draw away from him. He reminded her of the evil knight in a poem she'd read as a school girl.

Desiring to put Hunt in his place, Cecy waved to Mr. Wagstaff. He nodded, then strode toward her. She turned the idea over in her mind. Mr. Wagstaff was a reporter and reporters knew how to find out things. Now she needed information.

Frowning, Bower spoke with a touch of steel in his tone, "I've seen Mr. Hunt drive and he appeared to be more interested in speed than style."

Hunt's jaw hardened, but his words came out smoothly, "Miss Jackson can ask your sister how exciting a drive with me can be."

Aunt Amelia stiffened beside Cecy.

Bower took a step toward Hunt. Fleur touched his sleeve.

Mr. Wagstaff reached their group. "Miss Jackson, how may I be of service?"

His calm voice halted the tense exchange. Cecy was positive this man could find out about her mother's illness. But she'd have to think of a way to ask him without revealing her fears.

She grinned as a ruse flashed into her mind. She'd confound Hunt and create a way to talk privately with the journalist. "Mr. Wagstaff, I just wanted to remind you of your offer to teach me how to drive," she improvised.

She was pleased to see how chagrined both Hunt and Bower looked. That would teach them not to cause these unpleasant scenes. Really. Who cared about their silly amateur race?

The newspaperman bowed. "As soon as you wish, Miss Jackson."

Cecy beamed. The man was intelligent enough to go along with her ruse. He hadn't offered her lessons, merely to take her to the auto race. Hunt's stiff expression pleased her. She'd already tired of her flirtation with Hunt.

Her plan was perfect. A drive in an open car would preclude the need of her aunt's chaperonage and give her the privacy she needed to discuss the matter of her mother with him. But how would she be able to keep him from broadcasting what he found out about her mother? Well, she'd have to think of a way.

❋ ❋ ❋ ❋ ❋

February 12, 1906

At Bower's masked ball, Cecy curtseyed gingerly. Wearing a farthingale—a metal cage that fitted around her waist under her skirt and made it stick straight out from her waist—was disconcerting. Why hadn't Queen Elizabeth decreed more comfortable clothing? But the uncomfortable gown had done its job. Tonight, in the costume rented from Goldstein's, Cecy was certain no one had recognized her behind her mask, wig, and seventeenth-century costume.

Lincoln Wagstaff was in attendance; she was certain of that, too. At the tea party, he'd said her sources had been inadequate. He'd been right. Now she understood his Boston connection. And Mr. Wagstaff was her only hope to get to her mother. Aunty would never let her go anywhere unless she was chaperoned by Aunty or someone trustworthy like Mr. Wagstaff. Mr. Wagstaff was older and a widower, and their being together in an open car for an afternoon would occasion no comment. But she still hadn't thought of a way of hiding her true motive for visiting her mother.

A masked and hooded Medieval monk took her hand and led her into a merry polka.

What man was she dancing with? Dance cards had been dispensed with because no one was supposed to reveal their identities—until midnight when the masks would be taken off. Cecy had fallen under the spell of the daring atmosphere of the evening. She'd drunk two glasses of champagne, something she rarely did. She usually kept a clear head to navigate the swift social currents.

"Forsooth!" Cecy said in a husky version of her voice, trying to get the monk to speak and reveal his identity through his voice. "I did not know monks danced."

"My child, are you tempting me to break my vow of silence?" he demanded in a scratchy, false voice.

Cecy giggled. She knew she'd danced with this man before.

"If you promise me a kiss at midnight, I'll tell you now," he offered wickedly.

"The Queen of England never kisses monks," she teased haughtily. Who would be brash enough to ask for a kiss? Hunt? Perhaps? But the effect of wearing a costume might be making someone else feel just as she did—reckless.

As she gracefully stepped and hopped to the bouncy Polish music, she scanned the crowded Bower ballroom. She glimpsed a Musketeer with a blue-plumed hat over blonde hair. Why that might be Mr. Wagstaff! She must speak with him tonight. She didn't want to wait for their driving lesson a few days from now. She needed to find out the truth about her mother's illness. Whenever she imagined living the rest of her life without being able to know her mother, she panicked. Her mother may not have much time left!

The polka ended. She curtseyed her thank-you, then drifted toward the buffet table. By sending her away to Boston, her father had kept her apart from her mother for over ten years.

Now that her father was dead, why couldn't Mother come home? Didn't her mother want to come home? No, Cecy couldn't accept that. It must be her physical condition. And that must be why Aunty wouldn't tell her the truth.

"Your majesty."

Cecy turned to the Musketeer, who took her hand in a courtly fashion. She tried to decide if his blonde hair under the plumes were real or a wig. She couldn't.

"Would you favor this poor Musketeer with a waltz?"

Maybe she could figure out his identity as they danced. "I find you worthy, kind sir. Let us waltz."

He swept her into his arms. She tried to decide if this blonde Musketeer danced with her the same way Mr. Wagstaff had. She had no luck. Her partner, as tall as the newspaperman, danced excellently, but she had no sense of who he might really be. But then he didn't know who she was either.

At that moment, she heard Fleur's distinctive trill laugh. So Fleur was Marie Antoinette. She caught her partner's eye.

He winked.

Cecy giggled. Perhaps she could take the night off from competing with Fleur. For a few moments, she toyed with the idea of just enjoying the evening.

But at midnight, the masks came off. Everyone would know Cecilia Jackson had been Queen Elizabeth. So Queen Elizabeth must triumph over the French queen. Cecy must flirt and flatter.

A red-headed Little Bo Peep danced by with the monk. The monk winked at Cecy as he went by. Her partner stiffened. Why? Did her partner know the identity of the couple? She knew Bo Peep reminded her of someone. She was tall enough to be Bower's sister, but Cecy couldn't be sure. Did her partner dislike Bo Peep dancing with the monk or dislike the monk winking at her?

Feeling slightly fuzzy-headed because of the champagne, Cecy couldn't concentrate. Her mind returned to her main concern. She'd ceased asking Aunty about her mother's illness. All Aunty would say was that Mother had always been weak and was too sick to come home as yet. Sick with what, Cecy wanted to know. She had to find Mr. Wagstaff and her worry would be over.

The waltz ended. Cecy bent her head regally and swept away. A second blonde Musketeer who wore a red velvet doublet walked along the edge of the ballroom. Cecy followed him trying to analyze his walk, trying to decide whether he was Wagstaff.

"Your Highness."

A Harlequin, a jester wearing a hat with tassels, stopped her. She wanted to ignore him, but he'd just partnered Marie Antoinette. Cecy swallowed her irritation, smiled and let him lead her into the schottische. The Harlequin wouldn't speak. He answered her with nods and smiles. But she knew she'd smelled his spicy toilet water before. At the end, she turned to find the blonde Musketeer in red waiting for her.

Wordlessly he bowed, requesting a dance.

"I'm so thirsty," she stalled, trying to look for clues. She wished she hadn't drunk the champagne. Was it Mr. Wagstaff?

The red Musketeer led her to a darkened corner at the far end of the ballroom and seated her there. So this Musketeer wanted to speak privately? What would he say? He bowed flamboyantly, then left for the buffet table.

Cecy tried to relax in spite of the farthingale which prevented her from resting her back against the chair. The stiff ruffle around her neck made her hold her head very straight. How had English women put up with this?

She stiffly scanned the room trying to identify who was Mr. Wagstaff, who was Mr. Bower or Hunt. Unfortunately, she was able to recognize only several of the older people who couldn't hide their distinctive voices and way of walking.

The blonde Musketeer with blue plumes approached with two glasses of lemonade.

"What happened to the Musketeer in red?" Cecy took the glass from him. "Thank you, sir."

He bowed, then bent on one knee in front of her. "Your Highness, I've wanted a moment alone with you for a long time. Your loveliness and sparkling personality overwhelm me more each time we meet." He took her hand and kissed it.

Cecy was caught off guard. Men had paid her compliments, but nothing like this before. Why was he kneeling? Hunt had already proposed to her once and been refused. Was this Hunt thinking champagne and being masked would change her mind?

Aunty had been right. She'd warned her not to sit alone with any man like this at a masquerade. Ladies had to watch their reputations. Masked men were tempted to push the line as they never would dressed as themselves.

Cecy pulled her hand away. "Please, gentle sir, thou makest me to blush. Thou must not speak to your Queen thus." This Musketeer wasn't Wagstaff. His romantic speech proved that! Whenever they were alone, the reporter never failed to irritate her. Complimenting would make his tongue stick to the roof of his mouth. "La, I feel like dancing." She rose.

He clutched at her hand. "Please I've wanted to speak to you alone for weeks."

She deftly withdrew her hand. "The *galop* has started without me. I thank thee for the lemonade." She swept regally away.

Fleur, as Marie Antoinette, was dancing with a Mad Hatter, wearing an outrageous purple hat. The other Musketeer was dancing with the red-headed Bo Peep. Cecy hurried away. The *galop* was truly started. She must not be seen standing alone without a partner. Just as she reached the edge of the floor, the electric lights went out.

Shrieks, screams, and objections. The orchestra cut off in ragged peeps and the screech of violin strings. Cecy's own exclamation was cut off by a hand clamped over her mouth. The other hand grasped her around the waist. Her assailant roughly dragged her through the French doors and out into the garden. The cool night air made her gasp. She struggled against the dark form. But his strength overpowered her. The moonlight lit the garden with silver, but her assailant had her clutched with her back to him. She could see nothing of him!

"Help! Help!" Cecy screamed silently into the hand. She clawed the arm which held her like a vise. She tried to tangle her legs in her abductor's legs to trip him.

The hand at her mouth lifted.

She gasped, "Help!"

The hand struck her temple. Her senses swam. Suddenly released, she pitched forward, her head reeling with pain. "Oh…oh…" She slumped onto the wet ground.

Sounds of a struggle. An oath.

A man loomed over her.

CHAPTER 5

*"Faithful are the wounds of a friend,
but the kisses of an enemy are deceitful."*
Proverbs 27:6, KJV

MISS JACKSON, ARE YOU ALL right?"

She shrank from his hands.

"Don't be afraid. It's Linc. Linc Wagstaff."

She fainted.

Linc lifted Cecy from the cold ground. Had she been hurt? What had happened to the lights! Torn, he wanted to pursue the vanishing figure. The scoundrel had manhandled Cecilia! But Linc couldn't put her down, leave her unprotected.

One, two, then more pinpoints of light shone from inside the French doors. With Cecilia secure in his arms, Linc shoved his way back inside. He tried to be heard, but the deafening hubbub inside clamored unabated. Was everyone talking at once? *Dear God, help me before he gets away!*

But minutes passed in darkness while the servants brought in more dusty, tarnished, but serviceable candelabras and lit more and more candles. The kidnapper had gotten away! Linc cursed silently.

Cecilia stirred in his arms. He tightened his grip on her. She was so frail, so young. She stirred his heart. Someone had tried to harm her! *Lord, why did this happen?* Blood charged afresh through his veins, preparing him for a fight. He wanted to find the culprit, punish him, safeguard this lady. Leaning close to her, he said, "Cecilia, who hurt you?"

"He grabbed me!" Hysteria surged in her voice.

"Who?"

"I couldn't see him." She gasped, struggling with tears. "He covered my mouth." She whimpered.

As candlelight began to quell the darkness, the festive mood around them bubbled up again. Some man shouted, "Hoot man! Where's my bagpipe gone?"

Through the dimness, Linc finally located a sofa and set Cecilia onto it. She wouldn't let go of his shoulders. "Don't leave me!" Her voice rose, "He'll get me."

"Cecilia!" Her aunt drew up to them. "Let go of Mr. Wagstaff at once," she hissed, "before everyone sees you."

Linc straightened, withdrawing reluctantly from Cecilia's hold. But she clung to one of his hands. He gripped it in return. *Cecilia, I want to protect you. God guarded you tonight.*

Some man began singing off key, "You take the high road and I'll…"

He spoke to the aunt, "A man tried to abduct her. Stay with her, ma'am. The police must be summoned—"

"No!" The older woman flared up. "You're mistaken. You must be. No one would—"

Cecilia sobbed. "He dragged me outside, Aunty. I couldn't get away—"

The aunt leaned closer. "Hush, Cecilia, hush. Think of the scandal!"

Linc touched the older woman's arm. "I was following Miss Jackson to speak with her. The lights went out. Somehow I heard or felt what was happening. Some man tried to carry away your niece. Doesn't that concern—"

"Not another word!" She faced him, glaring, but lowering her voice, "Just a prank. High spirits at a masked ball! A young swain mistook Cecilia for his latest flirt. A dalliance in the garden. Mistaken identity—that's all this is."

Linc clamped his mouth shut. He longed to shake the woman. This was no prank. Cecilia was in danger. *Father, what should I do?* Wrestling his outrage under control, Linc bowed. "May I be of further assistance?"

The off-key singer suddenly broke off his song. Someone else shouted, "En garde."

"Don't leave me." Cecilia sat up. "Don't leave me."

Her piteous tone squeezed his heart sharply.

"You're indisposed, Cecilia. We're going home." Miss Higginbottom looked into his eyes. "Mr. Wagstaff, will you escort us to our carriage?"

"Yes, I will, and I'll follow you home too," he insisted.

Widespread, loud laughter drowned out his last words.

The Aunt smiled sourly. "Thank you, but you must speak to no one about this prank. I should have known better than to have allowed Cecilia to attend a masquerade."

Linc bowed once more. He wouldn't say anything now, but this wasn't over. Thank heaven, he'd been at hand.

※ ※ ※ ※ ※

February 25, 1906

"Miss Jackson." Linc led her down the steps to her carriage house. The date for the auto race and Cecilia's first driving lesson coincided today. Both of them wore long, buff-colored dusters—auto coats—over their clothing.

She also wore a large hat with a trailing veil. The cool breeze played with the veil, flaring and lifting the ends of it. Even in the unflattering driving garb, she was beautiful.

Linc hated having to tread lightly, keeping his true concerns hidden. The danger Cecilia had been exposed to the other night still made him seethe. Her foolish aunt had tied his hands. His hands itched to carry Cecilia away from the danger surrounding her.

"So this is your vehicle." He walked around the gleaming, dark green runabout. "Electric?"

"Yes, Aunty said I couldn't possibly crank the starter—"

"She was right. And there's always the danger of a backfiring engine and a broken arm." *Or being abducted.* He looked at her unable to hide his concern any longer. "Are you recovered from your shock?"

"What shock?"

He grimaced and hardened his tone, "The end of the masked ball." With the open car between them, he watched her. Anxiety tightened his midsection. Would she be honest with him?

"Oh, that." She wouldn't meet his eyes. "Aunty said it was just due to high spirits." Cecy indicated the car. "Now what do I do first?"

Take what happened at the masquerade seriously. "You don't have a chauffeur?"

"I told you." Her voice deepened, "I intend to drive myself."

You'll drive me to distraction soon! He had to get her attention, convince her she stood in danger. She didn't comprehend what an alluring vixen she was, that she was playing games with highly combustible young males. He nodded, tamping down his agitation, but he asked blandly, "You want to maintain the car yourself too?"

"Maintain it?"

"Of course. Autos take a lot of maintenance or they don't run. This morning did you check your brake rods, steering connections, springs, and tires?"

She stared at him.

"Then we'll start our lesson with those. They must be checked every time you plan to go out for a drive or you might as well stay home—*unless* you're in the mood for a hike."

"No need to use sarcasm." She nodded and moved close to him at the front of the vehicle.

Intensely aware of her light floral fragrance, he opened the hood and began pointing to the parts. He asked her to name them one by one. Perhaps truth would open her eyes. Observing her intently, he remarked, "It's funny, isn't it?"

"What?"

"Hunt was dressed as a monk at the ball. A little out of character, don't you think?" He caught a flash of fear in her eye.

"Really?" Her voice didn't betray her fear.

Linc had discovered from Bower that someone had cut the tangle of electric wires into his house. "Yes, would you like to know who was who at the masked ball?"

He tried to read her rich brown eyes.

But she lowered her thick, chestnut-brown lashes, then looked away. She said lightly, "Why not? You were the Harlequin. Who was dressed as the blue-plumed Musketeer?"

"Bower." Trying to figure out who the culprit was, Linc had talked to Mrs. Ward and discovered everyone's identities.

"Was his sister Bo Peep?" She glanced away.

"Yes." He needed to find out if she'd really accepted her aunt's explanation of the kidnapping he'd interrupted.

"I'm not surprised." She pointed to the engine. "What is that part again?"

"The steering connection." Could he steer her into the direction of safety? He had to make her realize the flirtation she encouraged was much more complex than she guessed.

She leaned over for a closer look. "When I was waltzing with Bower, the blue Musketeer, he didn't like Bo Peep dancing with the monk."

"I see." Linc had looked into Hunt's reputation and found him dressing as a monk to be sadly ironic. Hunt wasn't just another dashing society gentleman. The innocent who stood beside him wouldn't understand what made Hunt less than desirable.

What would Cecilia say if he told her Hunt still flirted with Clarissa when he thought no one was looking, that he probably had done more than hold hands with Clarissa Bower? But he couldn't tell her that! One didn't discuss such lurid topics with a decent young girl like Cecilia. How could he warn her? His frustration tightened his jaw.

"Can we drive now?" she asked abruptly.

He nodded, then opened the driver's door and helped her in. "Now, Miss Jackson," he cautioned, "don't touch that starter switch until I take my seat."

She gave him a nervous smile.

Taking his seat beside her, he slid his goggles into place. "Put on yours."

She positioned her oversized goggles, then tied her large, off-white veil over her face. She was a study of intense concentration and it tugged his heart. Cecilia, so young, so intense, so lost. *Father, how do I reach her, protect her?*

He rested his hand on the tiller which jutted out from the red leather dash between them. "Do you understand how this tiller works?"

"Not really."

"Just lightly move it in the opposite direction you want to go." He'd been feeling as though an unseen hand had been turning him from his stated purpose in moving to San Francisco. Nothing was going as he had planned. He'd tried to go toward establishing his weekly newspaper. But the Divine

Tillerman steered him repeatedly back toward this beautiful young redhead. The lady slipped into his thoughts all too often.

"The opposite direction?" she repeated.

"Yes, while you push it to the right, direct your attention to the wheel nearest you."

She obeyed his instructions. "Oh, I see."

He hadn't made even a beginning toward including her into his plan to make a difference in this city, this state. His frustration grew daily. Her campaign to be the most sought-after deb had interfered with his own plans for her. He wanted to start discussing social justice, show her photos of ragged four-year-olds working barefoot in Louisiana shrimp processing plants, eight-year-old miners with blackened, desolate faces. He hated being drawn more and more into her social life. But how could he ignore Cecilia—beautiful, willful Cecilia? She needed his maturity, his guidance. Flirting with danger seemed to be her favorite past time.

After her near-abduction, Linc had begun investigating Hunt and Bower in earnest. Bower was beginning a promising law career. On the other hand, Hunt had proved to have a dark side he concealed. A gambler, he spent time in the brothels of Chinatown. Many Barbary Coast bartenders called him a mean drunk.

"Can I start it now?"

He said a silent prayer for safety, for wisdom, then nodded.

She flipped the switch on the dash. The vehicle moved forward. "Oh!" She trod hard on the brake. Both of them lurched forward.

"A little startling, isn't it?" He wished she'd be as conservative in society as she was in her car.

"I'm sorry I jerked you about so." She blushed with obvious embarrassment.

He wished she was always so open to instruction. "I did the same the first time I stepped on my brakes. Now just ease up a little on the brake pedal."

She cautiously obeyed. The car rolled forward.

"Now push the tiller gently, very gently toward your left and we'll drive around in a circle a few times before we venture out on the road."

She followed his instructions and they made several wide circles in the large open area of the stable yard. The Chinese groom and coachman watched from the safety of the stable doorway. Linc's mind lingered on Hunt's motives. The story about Hunt's father insisting his son marry Clarissa was true. The older Hunt thought a well-connected and dowered marriage would settle his wild son down. Linc didn't agree.

"I think this time you might as well drive out onto the street. Remember to brake gently at the end of the drive to check traffic."

She did as he suggested. After she'd driven tensely several blocks, she smiled. "This is fun. I knew it would be."

"Yes, but always remember an auto isn't a toy. If you aren't aware at all times of the vehicles, horses, and people around you, you could hurt someone and yourself seriously."

For once she didn't argue, but nodded soberly. Maybe he could bring her to her senses about leading on Hunt and Bower any further.

Linc cleared his throat. "Are we still headed for that auto race this afternoon at Golden Gate Park?"

"Yes."

He let a few minutes of silence pass. Why would Hunt with large debts and expensive tastes and vices court disaster by turning away from Clarissa Bower? "Your aunt was wise about your driving an electric auto. Not only is it easier to start, but it also runs so quietly it won't startle horses nearby. That will make driving much safer for you."

She nodded, intent on the tiller.

He drew a deep breath. "I wish your aunt was as concerned about your safety at the masked ball. No one can convince me you weren't nearly abducted two nights ago."

CHAPTER 5

"But Aunty—"

Linc couldn't hold back. "Your aunt is more concerned with your social standing than the true danger you stand in."

* * * * *

Cecy made herself show no reaction. Aunty had told her to refuse to discuss the incident with Mr. Wagstaff if he brought it up. But Cecy couldn't follow that advice. She had to discuss it with someone. Aunty wouldn't talk about it with her and she couldn't free herself from remembering those awful moments of fearful helplessness. She glanced at him from the corner of her eye. "What danger do I stand in?"

"I've thought of two motives for someone kidnapping you—"

"Two?" she objected. "I could think of only one."

"Ransom?"

"Yes, what other reason could there be?" Her pulse beat a quick tempo—molto allegro.

He chose his words with care, "Have you thought someone might want to compromise your reputation, so you would have to marry him—"

"Compromise...marry? I don't understand." His words buzzed in her mind, not settling down to be understood. She stopped to let a pedestrian cross in front of them.

"You would disappear for a night, don't you see? In the morning, your reputation would have been in tatters."

Cecy tightened her hold on the tiller and herself. Primitive fear made it difficult for her to breathe. "You can't mean that! I don't understand. Everyone would know he took me against my will!"

Linc shook his head. "Miss Jackson, unfortunately the world would be harsher to you than the man. And *everyone* would prefer the man marry you quietly and cover his sin and scandal. Once a young woman's reputation is tarnished, she is shunned. It isn't right, but that's the way of the world."

Cecy clenched her jaw. Memories of her favorite music teacher, Miss Canty, washed through her mind, stinging like acid. Cecy recalled all the shocked, nasty whispers. The dance master had compromised the lady, but the school had let her go, not him. Cecy couldn't, wouldn't allow that to happen to her! Then reliving those terrifying moments in Bower's garden.... Her hand shook.

Mr. Wagstaff put his hand over hers. "I'm sorry to have to upset you like this, but I'm worried about you."

Many young men had touched her hand in the past month. Not one had touched her the way this man did—always to comfort her, to bolster her. His touch somehow released a soothing warmth inside her. His calm, sure strength flowed from his hand to hers, making the contrast between his confidence and her own uncertainty clear.

She wanted his strong arms around her. She'd cry out, "Help me! Help me go to my mother! I don't care anything about either of these men! I just want to be left alone!" But she couldn't. This man had helped her many times. But what did she really know about him? Only his family connections and his career. He was a stranger, after all, a question mark.

She willed herself to relax. "I'll be fine. No more masked balls for me and I'm going nowhere without my aunt. And you always seem to be in attendance, too. You will come to my opera party tonight?"

He nodded.

"I'm planning a surprise treat for my guests." She forced a lighter tone. "Now let's get to the race. Won't everyone stare to see me drive up?" She cast him a tremulous smile, laced with bravado.

Mr. Wagstaff withdrew his hand from hers. "Let's proceed."

Street signs passed by: Filmore, Pierce, Scott, Divisadero, Masonic.... As Cecy steered down the streets, she barely noticed people pointing, gawking, shouting at her. She bolstered her nerves. She would go on with her plans. It wouldn't be for very long, just till the Easter Ball. She would succeed. She had left weakness, timidity behind forever. No man, not Bower, not Hunt—would deter her from the coveted appellation, "The Belle of 1906."

And for finding out the truth about her mother, she'd decided learning to drive was the key. The sanitarium was within the range of her car. In a few days, she'd just invite Mr. Wagstaff out for a spin and they'd merely drive to the sanitarium. She'd speak to her mother privately, maybe her doctors. Everything would work out.

She drove through Golden Gate Park where mothers and nannies strolled with buggies and children. The breeze rippled through the high trees. A fashionable crowd had gathered along a small lake in the park. Cecy waved her free hand.

"Miss Jackson! Is that you?" Many young ladies and gentlemen greeted her. Their attention acted as a balm to her ragged spirits.

In his calm, no-nonsense way, Mr. Wagstaff instructed her how to park the auto. Then he helped her out. She drew back her veil, pulled off her goggles and driving gloves and tossed them onto the car seat.

"You did it!" Fleur Fourchette rushed up, clapping her hands in glee. "How amazin'? Were you scared?"

"No, indeed not. Mr. Wagstaff showed me exactly what to do. It was exhilarating!"

"I am quite impressed." The Southern belle smiled at them.

Cecy nodded, but looked away, searching the crowd. "Are the racers here yet?"

"I'm here!" Bower appeared at her elbow in a driving coat.

She wanted to draw back from him. This was Mr. Wagstaff's fault. Whoever had tried to kidnap her had been a stranger seeking ransom or a young man carried away by the rowdiness of the masked ball—just as Aunty said. Mr. Wagstaff's idea was too far-fetched.

"Mr. Bower." Cecy smiled, gazing at him from under lowered eyelashes. "I've been waiting for today—the race, then my opera company party. Two exciting events on one date."

Bower kissed her hand. "The daring Miss Jackson."

She savored this name which society columnists often used when referring to her. She would be known as a modern woman, a woman who'd been courted by many, but who had disdained all—a woman who didn't need marriage. A real smile overwhelmed her studied, artful expression.

"Miss Jackson." Hunt approached. He planted a light kiss on her cheek, then he greeted Fleur also.

Hunt had kissed Cecy so quickly, so unexpectedly, he stunned her. A man might steal a kiss from a willing maiden in a private moment. But in broad daylight, a man could kiss only his fiancée or bride. Hunt had tried to mark her as his publicly. She boiled with indignation. She had never encouraged or permitted such license! How dare he? Everyone around her looked surprised, shocked. Except for Clarissa. She looked pale, almost sick. Cecy wouldn't let Hunt disrespect her then discard her. "Sir, you have overstepped—"

Bower pushed in front of her. "Hunt, you've gone too far—"

Hunt took a step forward. "Who asked for your interference—"

"There are ladies present." Linc raised his voice.

His words shut both men's mouths. A few tense moments passed in silence.

The two adversaries faced one another. "Ready to start?" Hunt sneered the words.

Cecy took Bower's arm possessively. She'd show Hunt!

Bower placed his hand over hers. "I'm ready to best you, Hunt," he said intently.

The two angry men strode to their autos—Hunt's REO and Bower's Pierce Arrow. As previously arranged, Linc stood near the front of their vehicles, waiting for the assistants to crank the starters. Bower and Hunt donned their goggles and driving gloves. The Pierce Arrow surged to life. Then the REO engine caught. The assistants leaped out of the way. Linc raised the white flag.

"Wait!" Cecy shouted over the roaring engines . She'd teach Hunt to make free with her reputation. "My champion must wear my favor into battle!" She ran to Bower, untied her driving veil, then tied it around Bower's neck. Standing on the running board, she flashed Hunt a dagger-look letting him know he would be paid back in full for that careless, improper kiss.

Bower kissed her hand. "My lady!"

Cecy stepped down, her heart racing with her own audacity.

"Ready, set, go!" Linc slashed the flag down.

Hunt and Bower surged forward. Bower's Pierce Arrow took the lead. The cars were to race three laps over a loop of paved road around the lake some called Spreckles Lake. As the racers passed Linc the first time, he flashed the flag and shouted, "One!"

Cecy felt caught up in the excitement!

Hunt's REO was obviously outclassed by Bower's longer, more powerful car. Finishing another lap, the two drivers sped toward Linc again. "Two!"

On the last lap, Hunt sped up and edged close to Bower, crowding him. Bower didn't even glance at Hunt. He merely leaned forward obviously flooring the accelerator and moved another yard ahead of Hunt.

Cecy shouted, "Go, Mr. Bower! You can beat him!"

The two autos widened at the turn and raced on. Hunt still tried to edge ahead, but to no avail. Bower drove through the tape hastily strung up across the starting line. The young audience burst into applause and cheers.

Cecy rushed forward to congratulate Bower. He drew both her hands in his and kissed them. "Dear Miss Jackson."

Cecy cast a triumphant look at Hunt. He glared back at her. She froze. She'd heard of looks that could kill. Now she knew how one felt.

* * * * *

Tinkling laughter, dancers swirling around the polished floor, the fragrance of vanilla-scented candles—the spectacle drained Linc bit by bit. He couldn't shake his feeling of apprehension. Cecilia's long-awaited opera party was in full swing. As usual, Linc primarily stood back as an observer, even though he was invited as a guest, not a reporter. He felt like he was at the Cinograph Theater watching a movie, depicting the lavish French court before heads rolled in the Revolution.

Cecilia, dressed in the most extravagant ivory satin and velvet gown, played the part of a French countess, seductress. She floated through the gathering with a constellation of admirers, mainly Bower. In addition, the principals of the opera cast of *La Boheme,* still in costume, mixed among the pillars of San Francisco society.

Hunt made his entrance and went directly to the beautiful, Mimi, the soprano of the opera cast. Linc observed his flushed face. Could Hunt be inebriated already? Linc's somber mood deepened. Who knew what that kiss this afternoon might provoke.

* * * * *

Gliding through the slower Boston waltz, Cecy couldn't remember ever feeling so blissful. The visiting opera company boasted younger, more attractive singers than usual. Her daring decision to include them as guests, not merely entertainment, had added a definite éclat to the whole evening.

Hunt danced by, holding the soprano tightly in his arms. Cecilia would deal with him tonight. His presumptuous behavior this afternoon at the auto race rankled her. She'd put him in his place once and for all and stand no more nonsense from him. But more important than that, she had a surprise for everyone, her own personal triumph. Her link to the opera would be forged this evening. Tonight she put the past behind her forever. She'd never be alone, cast out, or ignored ever again.

✹ ✹ ✹ ✹ ✹

"Mr. Wagstaff?"

Linc glanced down into Fleur Fourchette's pretty face. "Good evening, Miss."

She smiled, but her eyes held worry. "I was hopin' I might speak to you."

Linc gazed at her. "About?"

"Miss Jackson...." She bit her lower lip.

The melody for a two-step started. To forestall speculation about them, Linc led the lady into the dance. The bouncy tempo contrasted with the young woman's serious demeanor. They stepped and bobbed to the American rhythm.

Finally she glanced up. "That kiss today worries me."

Linc nodded, encouraging her to go on.

"Miss Jackson is angry. So is Mr. Bower and his sister."

"I didn't like it either."

"No gentleman would." Miss Fourchette's voice vibrated with outrage. "You and I are both strangers here, so perhaps we are aware of things others more familiar overlook."

"What are you trying to tell me?"

"Miss Jackson should flirt less." The Southern belle looked away. "Mr. Hunt is not a boy to be trifled with. I don't think she comprehends...."

"The stakes are higher than she realizes?" he asked gently.

"I fear they are," the lady murmured.

The two-step ended. Linc bowed, thanking Miss Fourchette for the dance.

With renewed purpose, Linc spotted Cecilia and headed for her. Just then the small orchestra struck a chord for attention. Everyone quieted.

Cecilia's aunt stood beside the orchestra leader. "Thank you for your attention. As part of this evening's entertainment, our friends from the opera company will sing a brief selection from *La Bohème*. I'm sure those of you who haven't attended one of this company's superior performances will do so soon. Monsieur Rodolfo and Mademoiselle Mimi, if you please?"

The tenor and soprano who portrayed two of the four poor young "bohemians" in Paris drew in front of the orchestra. In Italian, they sang the duet of their first meeting. In her cheap apartment, poor Mimi asks her neighbor, Rodolfo, to light her candle with his.

Linc understood bits and pieces. Earlier when he'd attended the opera, the bittersweet lyrics had brought Virginia to mind. Rodolfo sang in a mellow tenor the poet's song, "…all my lovely dreams, my dreams of the past, were stolen away…."

With stunning purity of tone, Mimi responded, "talk of love, of spring dreams, and fancies…."

The words had no power over Linc now. He had to prevent the imminent disaster. Moving through the crowd, he approached Cecilia's aunt. Perhaps she didn't know of Hunt's insult to her niece today. He slipped close to her. Though he faced forward so no one would know he talked privately with her, he whispered, "Miss Higginbottom, are you aware that Hunt kissed your niece today at the auto race?"

"Kissed her?" Her tone could have frozen boiling water.

"Yes, Bower and he nearly came to blows over it."

"I had entrusted Cecilia to your care, sir."

Linc acknowledged this with a nod. He had done his best, but Hunt had crossed the line. Linc replied grimly, "I did take care of her, but I cannot control a man who isn't in control of himself. Are you aware of Mr. Hunt's poor reputation with women?"

"Cecilia didn't inform me of Mr. Hunt's latest affront. But I have persuaded her to depress that man's pursuit of her."

The woman's words hadn't reassured Linc. The duet ended and was greeted with applause. The aunt went forward to thank the singers.

He located Cecilia conversing with the singers. Threading his way toward her, he intended to make her listen to him.

He touched her shoulder. "May I have a word with you?"

She finally turned to face Linc, but frowned. "Just for a moment." She accepted the arm he offered her. Leading her away from the center of the room, he longed to shield her from the menacing undercurrents in her own ballroom. But now that he had her to himself, he scrambled to think of the right words to say. Yearning to hold her, he shook himself inwardly. He had to stop her from doing herself harm. "This afternoon I believe you saw a side of Victor Hunt you've been blind to before."

She gave him an exasperated look. "Is that what you wanted to talk about?"

He nodded. "You are a gently-reared young lady, so I cannot be plain about this. But Hunt has a very bad reputation— especially with women."

She shrugged. "I'm not interested in Hunt. That outrageous kiss was too much. I don't need or want that man's attentions as he will soon learn—"

Bower approached them. "Dear lady, this is our dance."

With profound resignation, Linc bowed. Cecy walked away on Bower's arm. Soon they danced the new ragtime one-step. Miss Fourchette danced by and sent a worried glance at Linc. He nodded, then went back to his role of observer. He longed to go home, leave these people to their own tensions and sins. Were he and Miss Fourchette the only ones here who were thinking clearly? But God had sent him to San Francisco and Cecilia. Linc couldn't leave his post. Cecilia must be protected.

※ ※ ※ ※ ※

The clock struck two o'clock. Cecy glowed with anticipation. Her moment, her triumph had come.

Bower led her to the orchestra. He bowed, kissed her hand, and left her. Bower was always the gentleman. She would reward him with a chaste kiss this evening and let Hunt know that she had rejected him.

Rodolfo joined her. The orchestra began to play the pensive music from the final scene of *La Boheme,* the scene where, as they recall their first meeting, Mimi dies in Rodolfo's arms.

Aware of the surprise in the faces before her, Cecy bowed to the gathering. Then she sang to Rodolfo, "I've so many things to tell you, or one thing—huge as the sea, deep and infinite as the sea...I love you....you're all my life."

🐝 🐝 🐝 🐝 🐝

Cecy's exquisite voice and passion tugged at Linc's emotions once more. She made him forget the tensions in the ballroom. Her voice had the power to lift him out of himself to see life in all its fullness. God had given Cecilia the gift of song, the gift to touch hearts, make them feel pity and draw them to a sensation of glory, of human love. If she only knew of God's love!

Cecilia's voice soared with pathos, tragic love, then death. Many women dabbed at their eyes. The orchestra fell silent. Cecilia, as Mimi, sank into Rodolfo's arms. He cried out in agony, "Mimi! Mimi!"

In the echoing silence, Hunt lunged forward. "You sing like an angel!" He went down on one knee. "Dear lady! Be mine!"

Cecy straightened up hurriedly. "You forget yourself, sir!"

Hunt stood. He pushed the tenor who was trying to shield Cecilia away. "I love you! Be mine!"

Bower, Archie, and Linc, among others, rushed forward. Behind them, Clarissa shrieked, "No! No! He loves me!"

Archie turned back, took hold of Clarissa and strove to draw her away.

Bower grabbed Hunt by the shoulders. "You're a disgrace. How dare you address a lady when it's obvious you're stinking drunk?"

CHAPTER 5

Linc tried to thrust himself between Hunt and Bower. Rodolfo dragged Cecilia aside. Hunt swung at Bower. The two men struggled. They crashed into the assembled orchestra. The players scattered clutching their instruments.

Ladies screamed.

Linc pursued Hunt and Bower. He had to end this embarrassing scene before someone got hurt. He circled the two men warily. But he could find no opening to push between them. *Father, help me stop them. This could destroy Cecilia!*

The two men were evenly matched. Bower answered each of Hunt's blows. But Hunt's drunken state started slowing him.

Linc edged around them waiting for a chance to help Bower subdue Hunt.

Bower delivered what should have been a stunning blow. But Hunt dodged it. Reaching behind him, Hunt suddenly flashed a knife in Bower's face.

CHAPTER 6

"Rescue me from the mouth of the lions...."
Psalm 22:21a

Shouts. Bright lights. Horrified gasps. The glitter of honed steel stunned Linc. Bower caught Hunt's wrist. Linc jumped back—fearful of causing more harm than good by interfering. The knife reduced fisticuffs between gentlemen to a bar-room brawl.

The two men struggled; the knife their focus. Their grunts and tortured expressions cast a common horror through the stunned audience. Linc felt it freeze him inside too. No one spoke. Not a whisper.

Linc broke free of the nightmare. He edged forward waiting for the moment he could help Bower.

Hunt tripped Bower. Bower stumbled forward.

The knife flashed up, slicing Bower's cheek.

More screams. Outcries.

Cecilia sailed past Linc—straight at Hunt. She threw herself on him—shrieking, "No! No!" Her attack shocked Hunt. He sprang back, dropping the knife.

Linc rushed to Bower. He pulled out his handkerchief and pressed it to Bower's face. "A doctor!" he shouted, but his voice was drowned by Cecilia's.

"You worthless men!" she screamed. "You've ruined everything!"

Hunt, looking dazed, objected, "But—"

"Do you think I'd marry you? Either of you!" Her voice vibrated with vitriol. "Never! I will never marry! You disgust me! I hate you! I hate you all!"

Linc had to stop her from doing more harm to herself. He turned and neatly slapped Cecilia's cheek. A shocked gasp echoed through the gathering. "She's hysterical. We need a doctor." Cecilia collapsed against him, white-faced and sobbing.

He caught her. "A doctor," Linc implored. "Summon a doctor!"

The crowd was still frozen in alarm. Then Bower's mother thrust herself through the ring around the players. She rushed to her son's side. "Clarence! My son!"

As though awakening, Hunt jerked, turned and pushed his way through the throng. This released the audience from its stupor. Voices burst forth in condemnation, panic.

Still burdened by Cecilia, Linc shouted, "Stop him! Stop Hunt!"

But it was too late. The rogue had escaped.

Cecilia struggled vainly in Linc's arms. "Let me go. Oh, let me go. They've ruined everything."

✸ ✸ ✸ ✸ ✸

March 5, 1906

Cecy looked down into her coffee cup. Instead of creamy coffee, she saw blood, red blood. She closed her eyes, but the stark image of scarlet blood, dripping, oozing down Bower's starched, white shirtfront lingered. She covered her face with trembling hands.

But closing her eyes only turned her vision inward. Her memory dredged up another haunting episode—the Saturday promenade on crowded Montgomery Street, just days ago.

Cecy, walking beside her aunt, strolled bravely down the avenue. They were to face society after the "dreadful scene" as Aunty called it and turn popular opinion to their side.

"Aunty, I feel sick. Maybe we should have waited until more time has passed before appearing in public."

"Nonsense. No one can blame you for what happened the other night."

The knife fight had made the front page of every Friday newspaper. Headlines like: "SWAINS FIGHT DUEL OVER LADY LOVE," "DASTARDLY FIGHT AMID THE HIGH LIFE" still made Cecy cringe. "But the papers—"

"Journalists! They always indulge in lurid detail and gossip. No genteel person will pay any attention to such disgusting sensationalism."

Mrs. Ward and her protégé, Ann, approached them.

"Mrs. Ward." Aunty smiled sweetly. "Good day."

The lady barely glanced in their direction.

"Cecilia—" Ann began.

Mrs. Ward quickened her pace, pulling Ann along with her. Ice shards pierced Cecy's heart, nearly making her cry out.

"Well," Aunty huffed. "I never liked that woman. In Boston she wouldn't figure in society at all. Her father was a buffalo hunter for the railroads for heaven's sake!"

As in a trance, Cecy continued walking beside her aunt. Each step took on a more hideous quality. People, strolling or riding by in carriages or on horseback, ignored both of them— pointedly. The sound of the horses hooves became magnified like a roaring in her head. Cecy began to shrivel, fade, become invisible.

Fleur Fourchette, sitting beside her aunt in her carriage did look at Cecy—but with such pity! Humiliation clogged in her throat like bitter coffee grounds. After that, each averted glance, each snub sizzled into her mind like a hot iron.

At the end of the block, Aunt Amelia motioned for their coachman to pick them up. In the bright mocking sunshine of early spring, they had driven home in agonizing silence. Upon arriving home, Aunty had taken to her bed and hadn't permitted Cecy into her room since.

Now, the smell of buttered toast and eggs brought Cecy back to the present and made her nauseated. She shoved back her chair. "I'm not hungry." She lurched past the butler and fled to the conservatory at the rear of the first floor. In the past three days since the opera ball, Cecy found refuge amid the plants of the conservatory. From the glass dome above, the pale light of morning hung like a pall over the room. She sank into a chair beside a drooping fig tree.

Waves of panic rippled through her. The silence of the huge mansion pressed in on her. The servants spoke in whispers and crept around the house as though someone were dying. Maybe they were right. She'd faced much in her life, but how could she face this—ruin, social death? Even her ability to feel anger at Hunt had waned. In spite of the agony it caused her, she'd read each day's papers because of her concern for Bower. Was he recovering? He had been as innocent as she, but he had suffered too.

She stood up abruptly and hurried to the library where a more private phone was. Picking up the ornate receiver, she waited for the operator's voice. "Please connect me with 236."

The connection was made. A formal voice said, "The Bower residence."

"Hello…." She almost gave her name, but decided against this. "How is Mr. Bower, Clarence Bower?"

"Mr. Bower's condition is stable. Who may I say is calling?"

"Just a friend. Thank you." Slowly, she put the receiver down. She hadn't expected an injury to his face to be serious, but there was always the danger of infection and sepsis. But at least, the man who'd come to her assistance was mending.

But what am I to do? For a second the thought of appealing to God flickered in Cecy's mind. She snuffed it. Even if God were here, he didn't care anything about Cecy. He'd proved that years ago.

She paced the Aubusson carpet in front of a wall of leather-bound books. With each step, the injustice of the rejection she was suffering swelled inside her. Resentment, scalding anger drenched her. "I did nothing wrong!"

"Miss?" Her butler stood in the doorway.

"Yes?"

"Your aunt would like to see you in the foyer."

"Foyer?" Why was Aunty there? Cecy brushed past him and sped down the hallway and grand staircase.

The appalling sight that met her checked her instantly. Cecy couldn't think. Valises? What was happening? "Aunty!"

Her aunt faced her. She wore a black traveling suit. Valises, hatboxes, and a trunk surrounded her. Why had she packed everything? "Aunty, what's wrong? Has someone died?"

"Cecilia, I have decided it's time, past time for me to visit your grandfather in Boston."

Visit? Boston? Cecy reeled as though she'd been slapped. None of Cecy's luggage had been brought down. "Boston?"

"Yes, I leave in an hour by train—"

"Leave?"

"Yes, I must wish you farewell for a time." Aunty pursed her lips in a chilling grin.

Clutching the railing, Cecy cried out, "You can't go! You can't leave me!"

Aunty spread her mouth in a flat, frigid smile. "You've established yourself here now, so I feel I can leave—"

"Established? No! It's a lie!" She ran down the steps. "You—"

"*Cecilia,*" Aunty checked her sternly. "You must learn not to let your emotions run away with you."

Cecy stopped on the bottom step. "You can't go. Everything's awful! I need you!"

"I think not. You're exaggerating." The older woman fiddled with one of her jet hat pins.

Cecy felt as though the hat pins were being jabbed into her skull. "If you're leaving, then I'll go back to Boston with you—"

"No! That's not possible!" Aunty scowled. "You force me to be unkind." Her aunt's voice chilled further with each word. "You'll be socially unacceptable in Boston as well as here. This isn't fifty years ago. There are telephones, the telegraph. Everyone in Boston knows of this by now!"

"Europe then," Cecy pleaded, desperate.

Glaring at Cecy, her aunt shook her head. "I had high hopes for you. We could have had a good life together. But you have proved to be a complete disappointment to me." Aunty's voice rose shrilly. "After all my efforts, you managed to spoil everything."

"Don't say that. There must be some way we can repair—"

Ignoring her, Aunty adjusted one of the buttons at the wrist of her black glove. Her voice hardened. "There is no longer any connection between us. I warned you about the lot of a spinster in society. To be accepted, I must be absolutely scrupulous in my social connections."

"Aunty!"

"I'd hoped you would take after your mother's side of the family." She paused to fix a cruel stare on Cecy. "But you are your father all over."

Cecy choked on panic, pain, and shock.

"Goodbye, Cecilia." Her aunt turned her back and marched to the door. The butler and footmen carried her luggage outside. The door shut.

CHAPTER 6

Her knees trembling, Cecy sank to the carpeted step. Feeling faint, she held her head in her hands and moaned without words. A quivering possessed her. She couldn't stop shaking. Tears flowed. Time passed.

Finally, she dragged herself into her room and collapsed onto her bed. The curtains were drawn; the room lay in shadow—just like her life. She tried to think, but she couldn't. Thoughts, words, images spun out of control.

Why think? Think of what? Her life had ended. Aunty, the only family she'd ever known, had abandoned her. Tears oozed from her eyes. How could she still have tears? Didn't a person at last expend all the tears they had and dry up? Was the supply endless? Moaning hoarsely, she buried her head in her feather pillow.

'You're just like your father'…. Like her father? No! Never! Her aunt's heart-crushing words pounded her down into total despair.

I can't be like him. She felt suffocated, drowned in hopelessness.

She flung herself off the bed and struck her head against the wall. "No! No!" Slumping to the carpet, she felt as though bony hands were dragging her down into a swirling black abyss.

✻ ✻ ✻ ✻ ✻

"Miss Jackson?" a timid voice whispered hours later.

Cecy opened her eyes. The room was dark.

"Miss Jackson?"

It was her maid. "Go away," Cecy muttered. Her mouth was dry and tasted bad.

"Cecilia."

At the sound of a man's voice, she shrank back. "Go away! I can't see anyone!"

Firm, heavy footsteps shuddered from the floor through her as he crossed the room.

Mr. Wagstaff bent, gathered her up, lifting her in his arms.

"No," she whimpered. "Go away. Please."

He spoke to the maid. "Turn on a light."

"No!" Cecy countered.

"Now!" he ordered.

The girl obeyed his command.

"Please pack her a bag for an overnight stay."

"What are you doing?" Cecy gasped. "What do you mean an overnight stay? I'm not going anywhere."

He ignored her feeble struggling and carried her out the door. "I'm taking you home with me."

CHAPTER 7

"Let not those who hate me without reason
maliciously wink the eye."
Psalm 35:19b, NIV

THE NEXT FEW MINUTES CECY was barely conscious of what was happening. He'd wrapped a coat around her and carried her outside. Cool air revived her only partially. She couldn't focus on the sights and sounds around her. Her neck turned to rubber. She had a hard time holding her head up.

"Just lean on my shoulder." Linc drove what must have been his automobile. She felt the tension and jiggling that came with an auto ride.

She wanted to ask him questions, but she couldn't form words. She gave up and slumped against him. After days of loneliness, she nestled against his shoulder—so broad, comforting, solid.

After a time, he stopped and lifted her again.

"Where are we?" she whispered.

"Home."

Then a door opened. Bright light and warmth enveloped her. For some reason this made her weep again.

"Susan, here she is."

"You bring her right upstairs." A woman with a strong voice answered him. "I'm going to put her to bed with warm milk."

Cecy glanced around. An old black woman followed them up a staircase. "It's not proper. I shouldn't...."

"Don't fret about the proprieties," he said soothingly. Susan will stay with you all night and tomorrow we'll get a more suitable chaperone."

Too deep in despair to argue, Cecy felt Linc lay her down on a soft featherbed. What did a chaperone mean to her now? She was ruined anyway. He began unbuttoning her shoes. He shouldn't be undressing her, but she couldn't bring words to her lips.

"You can do her shoes, Linc," the old woman objected. "But that's all."

"Yes, Susan." Linc sounded amused.

The old woman continued, "You go down and get that warm milk from Kang. I'll have her in a nightgown by the time you get back."

"I don't like milk," Cecy muttered.

"Nobody asked you that," the old black woman said kindly, but firmly. "You'll drink your milk or else."

Cecy gave in with a sigh. Her spine lost its strength. She felt wobbly as she lay on the soft bed.

"When was the last time you ate a meal?" The old woman nudged her as she unbuttoned the many buttons at Cecy's back.

"I don't know. I can't remember."

The old woman's voice had irritated Cecy at first. Now it soothed her. And feeling her corset loosen, then pulled away forced a deep sigh from Cecy. Her eyes drifted shut.

"Don't go to sleep on me. I'm too old to lift deadweight. You roll over when I tell you to."

Cecy thought she nodded.

"Roll toward me."

Cecy followed directions and soon she was dressed in a very loose, soft flannel gown.

A tap on the door. "Come in," Susan ordered.

Cecy opened her eyes. Linc walked in with a steaming cup on a small silver tray. He put the tray down on a bedside table "Here's your milk."

"That's fine, Linc," Susan said. "Meg and Del are waiting for you to say prayers with them."

"All right."

"You go on. I'll get Miss Jackson all tucked in."

"Good night, Cecilia." Linc touched her cheek gently. "Everything will look brighter in the morning." He walked out closing the door behind him.

Cecy whispered in her mind, *He called me Cecilia*. Tears came again, but they were warm tears of gratitude.

The old woman propped her up against several pillows and said kindly, "Now here's your milk. You'll feel better if you drink it."

Cecy took the cup and sipped obediently. She wished she could think. But her head felt like it was stuffed with cotton wool.

The old woman sat in a chair beside the bed and rocked and hummed an old spiritual Cecy recognized, "Swing Low, Sweet Chariot." Cecy's mind idly took up the tune, singing it silently to herself. The sounds quieted Cecy, leaving her calmer.

Cecy closed her eyes and sipped the warm, sweet milk. For a brief moment, she felt safe. Then sad thoughts attacked. Tears of shame slid from her eyes down to the soft flannel gown.

"Now don't go letting sadness take over. Linc brought you here. You're safe now. He won't let anyone hurt you. You're not alone."

Cecy didn't have the strength to argue. Her tears flowed, unchecked—inexhaustible.

* * * * *

March 6, 1906

"OK. You're all buttoned up." The black woman said from behind Cecy. "I'll show you downstairs. Breakfast is waiting on us."

I can't face anyone! "I'm not hungry." Cecy frowned.

"Don't say that." A little girl with brown braids popped into the room. "Aunt Susan doesn't like us to say that. I smell bacon, don't you?" Without ceasing to chatter, the little girl took Cecy's hand and led her out the door. "I think we're having pancakes today, too. I like pancakes—"

"Who are you?" Cecy looked down into the cheerful, freckled face.

"I'm Meg Wagstaff. My papa is Linc Wagstaff. He's your friend. He brought you here because you're sad because your aunt had to go away. You're Miss Cecilia Jackson. I read about you in the articles Papa wrote—"

"You're Mr. Wagstaff's daughter?" Cecy hadn't ever given a thought to this man's personal life.

The child stopped, looking up in surprise. "I just told you that!"

They reached the top of the staircase. As Meg led her down the steps, Cecy felt a little unsteady and gripped the railing. The little girl didn't need to lead her to where breakfast waited. Cecy smelled bacon, melted butter. Her stomach growled.

Meg giggled. "You sound hungry."

"Don't talk like that to your elders. Miss Jackson was too upset to eat yesterday." The old black woman had followed them downstairs.

"Sorry, Aunt Susan," Meg recited and made the words a song.

CHAPTER 7

It sparked Cecy's memory, bringing to her ear the singsong response that she and the other boarding school girls had used: 'Yes, Miss. No, Miss.' But this happy child made her reply sound pert and teasing, not beaten down and hopeless as she and the others had been. Cecy smiled at Meg. "I do sound hungry."

The little girl wrinkled her nose and grinned.

Aunt Susan stepped ahead, slid open the pocket door and ushered both Meg and Cecy into a small dining room.

Meg let go of Cecy's hand and ran to her father. She threw her arms around him. "Good morning, Papa! I brought her down. See?"

Linc hugged his daughter, then rose from his place at the head of the table. A small black boy at the table stood also.

"Good morning, Cecilia," Linc said. "Del, will you please help Miss Jackson take her seat?"

Cecy waited, silenced by seeing Mr. Wagstaff in these new surroundings.

Wearing a serious expression, the boy came around the table and pulled out the chair to Mr. Wagstaff's right.

Linc made the introductions. "Cecilia, Del is Aunt Susan's grandson. Del, this is Miss Jackson."

Nodding, Cecy sat down and shyly smiled her thanks at Del. The boy nodded soberly, then returned to his place across from her. Meg took the seat beside her while Linc seated Aunt Susan at the foot of the table.

Cecy looked at the faces around the table. She'd assumed that Aunt Susan was Mr. Wagstaff's housekeeper. But house-keepers weren't seated at the table by their employers. What were the relationships of the mixed group around the table?

The door from the kitchen opened and a Chinese house-man walked in carrying a huge platter of scrambled eggs, bacon, golden pancakes, and fragrant maple syrup.

Cecy's appetite leaped to life.

The houseman set the tray on the sideboard. "Good morning. I see the lady has come down. Lady, you drink tea or coffee for breakfast?" He pinned her with a bright questioning look.

The mention of coffee brought back the memory of trying to drink a cup the morning before and the dreadful vision of blood. "Tea," she murmured.

Meg tugged Cecy's sleeve. "Are you going to be here when Del and me—"

"Del and I," Aunt Susan corrected as she stirred cream into her cup of coffee.

Meg grinned. "Are you going to be here when Del and I get home from school, Miss Jackson?"

Cecy couldn't reply. Where would she go now? What would she do? She was ruined. Aunty had left her!

Mr. Wagstaff cut her frantic thoughts short. "Miss Jackson will stay with us (during the day) a day or two while she makes plans for the future." Mrs. Hansen, across the street, has agreed to let her spend nights with her.

"Oh, good!" The little girl stared up into Cecy's eyes. "I want to show you my dollies and the new dollhouse I got for Christmas—"

"Meg," Aunt Susan reminded, "be quiet now. Your father is going to say grace. Then you better get busy eating breakfast, so you don't get to school late."

Mr. Wagstaff grinned.

"Yes, Aunt Susan." He bowed and asked a blessing for the day. "And, Lord, we thank you for your word, 'sorrow endureth for the night, but joy cometh in the morning.'"

As he prayed, Cecy tried to make sense out of the unexpected family she found herself in. But she couldn't.

"Amen," Linc intoned.

The houseman put a pot of tea on the table near her. Cecy waited to see if he would sit down with the family too.

"Anyone need anything else?" the houseman asked.

"No, thank you, Kang. Another excellent breakfast," Aunt Susan said.

The Chinese man smiled, bowed, and went back through the door to the kitchen.

"Do you like pancakes?" Meg asked Cecy again as she offered Cecy the blue-and-white china serving plate.

"Yes." Cecy laid her napkin in her lap and took the plate of pancakes from the child. Her hunger made her feel light-headed and slightly nauseated. Her head buzzed like a hive full of bees. She forced herself to put food on her plate and take a bite. She had to eat to have a clear head to think.

✹ ✹ ✹ ✹ ✹

The children left for school. From the end of the drive, Meg looked back and waved cheerfully, then she skipped around the corner out of sight.

Cecy stepped away from the door. Meg had taken the pleasantness of the spring morning away with her. Cecy folded her arms around herself as though chilled.

Linc pulled out his pocket watch. "You need to go up and fetch your driving coat, gloves, and hat. We'll be leaving right away."

Cold fear suffused her. "Where are you taking me?"

He touched her arm. "After I take you across the street to meet Mrs. Hansen, I'm taking you to my office."

"Why?" What awaited her there?

"Because we have work to do and there we can talk privately." He gave her a long look. "Now be a good girl. Go up and get your things. We have a lot to do before we head back here for lunch."

She obeyed him. She wanted to argue, but how could she? Her only plans had been to go to her room and weep alone. Upstairs, as she reluctantly put on her auto duster, hat, and gloves, she realized that fortunately she'd be unrecognizable under this automobiling garb.

Heartened, she joined Linc in the drive beside his Pierce Arrow. After a short visit with Mrs. Hansen, he helped her into the passenger seat, then went to the front to crank the starter. Within minutes, they chugged up, then down the hills of San Francisco toward busy Market Street. When they arrived, Mr. Wagstaff parked, then helped her out of his vehicle and into an imposing office building. A few men glanced at her, but without interest. Relieved, Cecy preceded Mr. Wagstaff into the elevator. After the brief elevator ride, he unlocked a door and ushered her into a nearly empty office.

"Where's the rest of your furniture?" she asked, looking around.

"We'll discuss that later." He pulled a spindly chair close to his desk which occupied the middle of an otherwise bare, large walnut-wainscoted room. Then he sat down in the only other chair and turned it to face her. "Now let's discuss where you go from here."

"What do you mean?" Her pulse sped up.

He took her hand. "There are just the two of us here. You've been cast as the culprit in a very nasty scandal. Yesterday your aunt left town—"

"How did you know that!"

"A friend saw her leaving and called me. We need to talk about what to do about this."

A sob tried to work its way up and out, but she fought it under control. "Why do you care?" She almost added, "No one else does."

He covered her hand briefly with his other, then released her. Leaning back, he considered her. "I had heard about your father's reputation."

"What?" Her eyes widened. What did that have to do with anything?

"I wanted to warn you that your father's reputation put you in a precarious position socially." Leaning closer to her, he rested his elbows on the arms of his chair.

CHAPTER 7

"I don't understand."

"Tell me what you know about your father." He watched her trying to judge her reaction.

She wiped her moist eyes with a lacy handkerchief and looked away. Of all the unpleasant topics he could have brought up this was the worst. "I don't want to talk about my father."

"You can trust me, Cecilia. Don't you know that by now?"

His voice didn't coax her. He merely spoke the truth. She sensed it.

"My father was not kind to my mother," she said in a scared, dead voice. *Or me.*

"That's what I understand. Most of San Francisco did not think highly of your father because of how he treated your mother and everyone else. They were waiting to see if you would take after your mother. Or your father."

Aunty's final words echoed in her mind, *'You are your father all over.'* Cecy burst into tears.

Without a pause, he took her hands pulling her up. "Cecilia, I'm not trying to hurt you. I'm trying to help you. We've got to figure out what you're going to do."

"Why didn't you warn me?" she sobbed.

"I tried to. You wouldn't listen." He folded her into his arms.

She knew she should push away from him. Letting a man hold her was wrong. She didn't want any man to hold her. But in the past few days, too much had transpired.

And his embrace was so comforting and strong. And she was so alone. She pressed herself deeper into his embrace, seeking more contact with him. Why didn't he kiss her? Did he think her shameful, too? The sensation of his body close to her....

✾ ✾ ✾ ✾ ✾

The scent of her perfume, a profusion of spring flowers, filled his head. She was warm, close and so hurt. He bent his head, tempted to brush her lips with his. He whispered her name like a prayer.

She pressed her lips to his. For brief seconds, he savored the sensation of Cecilia's kiss. Then he slid his face away from hers.

His hold around her tightened, but only to prevent her from pressing nearer. He understood her need to be physically close. And he had crossed the line toward intimacy, but he wouldn't take advantage of her vulnerability. How could he be attracted to this woman when his heart still belonged to his sweet, lost Virginia? But Cecilia did attract him. *God, forgive me. God, lead me.*

He continued to hold Cecilia, but he tried to hold her as he would have held Meg. But he couldn't ignore the effect she had on him. Holding Meg was nothing like holding this vibrant, enticing woman. He couldn't push Cecilia away. First of all, he wanted to hold her, then he feared she'd feel rejected if he abruptly severed their closeness. Being near and not giving in to the desire to kiss her became torture. But he held her still within his arms, keeping the embrace chaste.

He yearned to tell her so much, but having a heart-to-heart talk didn't seem to be what Cecilia needed to pull herself together. Words meant nothing to her now. How could he tell her of God's love for her? Every day, he walked in a suffocating fog, knowing God waited—willing to heal and guide him. But his own grief obscured his connection to God. Cecilia wouldn't understand this. And he'd let her kiss him, promising something beyond friendship, something he couldn't give her.

She stopped crying. He knew he should put her away from him, but he still couldn't let her go. Though he felt guilt, her attraction worked through him like a steady flow of electric current. The desire to capture the sweetness of her lips tried him once more. He prayed for strength. This time he held fast. Gently he urged her back on the other chair, then cleared his throat. "I think we better get busy about what we came here to do."

She lost her dazed expression and eyed him warily, dabbing at her tear-stained face. "What was that?"

"I need you to look over the office. Then we will go shopping for office furniture."

"Shopping?" She stood up. "I couldn't!"

"Where we'll be shopping," he rose and took her hand. "I doubt you'll meet anyone you know." He drew her to the door, grateful she hadn't spoken of their kiss.

✹ ✹ ✹ ✹ ✹

Soon Cecy walked beside Linc through the furniture warehouse near the Embarcadero. Cecy had been reassured by its vast proportions. Evidently most of the shipments of furniture arrived here first. Only a few customers, salesmen, and workmen shuffled through the narrow aisles. Cecy and Linc stopped to look at an assortment of leather chairs.

Linc said casually, "Do you think I should go with the red leather or brown?"

"The red looks more imposing," she replied in a flat voice. She didn't care a fig about furniture. Turning away, she touched her lips. She'd kissed him. She'd longed to have him hold her again, make her feel safe, wanted. But what did she know about this man? "Is Meg really your daughter?"

"Does it surprise you that I have a daughter?" He sounded amused.

She still couldn't put the bubbly little girl with this man, who was always so serious. "I just never thought about it." Listlessly she stroked the back of a Queen Anne-style chair. "Where's your wife?"

"After our son was stillborn, Virginia died in childbirth about eighteen months ago." He looked away. "How many chairs do you think I should buy?"

Cecy didn't like the way he said his late wife's name with near-reverence. It made her jealous. While he'd held her in his arms, had he thought of his dead wife?

"Who is Susan?" She watched him closely.

"Susan was my mother's best friend."

"Your mother's best friend?" She stared at him, open-mouthed.

"That surprises you?" He raised an eyebrow, throwing her on the defensive.

"I never knew black and white people could be best friends. How did they...." She paused.

"Get to know one another?"

She nodded soberly.

"My mother was a Civil War widow who ran a boarding house to support us."

"You were poor?" She couldn't keep the surprise from her voice.

"Yes, in many ways, rich in others. My mother was a wonderful woman." He paused to smile. "She took Susan on as a partner to help her run the boarding house."

"Why didn't she just hire Susan?"

"Because Mother didn't know how much to pay her, so she offered Susan one-third of the weekly profit whatever it was." He sat on the arm of a wing-back chair.

"Then how did you become related to Boston bankers?" She stood in front of him.

"Through my stepfather."

She nodded knowingly. "Oh, your mother married well the second time."

He shook his head and grinned. "My mother would have said she married well both times. She adored my father."

"If you say so." She ran her fingers over the top of the chair he sat in. The leather, smooth and cool, pleased her fingertips. No doubt some love matches existed. Anything was possible. She glanced at him. She was near enough to kiss him without anyone observing them. Why had that idea come to her again?

Chapter 7

"So you see, Susan helped raise me. Del is Susan's grandson. His parents died of typhoid when he was only five. Susan and he came to live with Virginia and me at that time."

The story of Susan and Del didn't interest her much. But Meg's freckled, smiling face did. "I like Meg."

His face lit with a brilliant smile. "She's my treasure."

Cecy strangled a sob deep inside. An ache, an old one, clenched within her. Her father hadn't treasured her.

"Your father should have treasured you," he said quietly.

At hearing her own thought said aloud, she shied like a frightened filly. "I don't want to talk about him!" How could he have read her thoughts so clearly?

A salesman approached them. Cecy glanced away, regaining her composure.

In response to the man's question, Linc ordered the four red leather chairs Cecy had preferred. Then the salesman led Cecy and Linc to a section of smaller desks. He left them to look over the stock while he went to help another customer.

"Cecilia, help me choose a reception desk for my outer office first. I don't intend to hire a secretary yet, but I may in the future."

Cecy idly looked over the selection of wooden desks.

"Did your aunt tell you when she'd be coming back?" Linc asked close to her ear.

"I don't think she's coming back," she replied hesitantly. He'd forced this admission out of her.

"What?"

Cecy compelled herself to go on sliding open, then closing desk drawers and comparing wood grain with her hand.

He glowered in the dim light. "I didn't think highly of your aunt's handling of this whole situation. Though she must have known, she didn't warn you how dangerous flirting with a man like Hunt could be. Now you tell me she's abandoned her responsibility to you!"

117

The anger in his voice startled Cecy. Could he be right about her aunt? Had Aunty misled her?

He stared over her head. "You may spend a few days with me, but I think it's imperative you go back to your own house as soon as possible."

"I'm sorry to be an imposition," she answered stiffly. She wished she could say "I'll go home tonight." But to her mind, going home again equaled descending into her grave. She couldn't face that empty house and silent servants.

"You're not an imposition." He glanced down at her with a worried expression. "But Susan isn't an adequate chaperone—not in the eyes of society."

Society. The word stung her tongue.

"During daylight Susan and the children offer you enough protection in society's eyes from me. Then you'll go to Mrs. Hansen," he said lightly. "Don't worry. You will make a comeback." He touched her shoulder.

The injustice of what she'd suffered reared up inside her. "Of course, I will." But the words rang hollow in her ears.

"That's what I said." He drew her attention to the desks again. "What do you think of this desk? Like it?"

"It's fine." She scarcely looked at it.

"Better take a closer look. It might be yours."

"Mine? I don't need a desk." She stared at him.

"I was going to offer you a position on my weekly journal."

"Me? A journalist!" What nonsense was this?

"You don't need to make it sound like an exotic tropical disease." He grinned at her.

"Why would you think I'd want to be a reporter?" she demanded tartly. "They've made my life miserable spreading this scandal." She turned her back to him.

"Don't take the headlines personally. The reporters didn't make Hunt pull a knife at your ball."

She wouldn't look at him.

CHAPTER 7

"I've thought this over carefully. I think you might have what it takes to be a writer. And you need to take action to repair your reputation."

"I can't talk about that now." Though she spoke with bravado, inside she began shuddering again.

"Think about it. I've wanted to interest you in my work since we met. You could do a lot of good. Plus your writing for a social-issues magazine would give society something to think about, throw them a curve ball. They think they've consigned you to that dismal mausoleum of a house of yours for a life sentence."

These statements brought to mind the grim image of her mansion, all hooded windows and gray stone. Mr. Wagstaff had described it and her situation too accurately for comfort. But become a reporter? How shocking! She was a well-bred lady— no matter the scandal. A lady work as a journalist? The idea was ludicrous.

"When you do finally go home, we need to find someone to act as your chaperone."

"I can't make any plans now!" Thinking of a chaperone brought her mother to mind. If her mother were well, she could come home and serve as chaperone. But Cecy hadn't gone to the sanitarium to see her mother in many weeks. Her plans to go had been postponed. Her mother wasn't well, was she? Had Aunty misled her about that, too? She'd wanted to go to see her mother to find out the truth, but how could she face her mother after this?

He rested his hand gently on her shoulder. "We have a few days to act. But I warn you, just a few days. No more."

🐝 🐝 🐝 🐝 🐝

After ordering a desk and chair which would do for a future receptionist and one which Mr. Wagstaff thought she might sit at, Cecy and Linc drove home and walked past just-budding yellow daffodils into the front hall.

Cecy was just untying her veil when Susan stepped out of the parlor. "Hello, Linc. Miss Jackson, you have a visitor in the parlor."

Cecy turned to bolt.

Linc caught her by the arm, stopping her. He said calmly, "Who is it, Aunt Susan?"

"It's I."

The soft Southern drawl made Cecy strain against Linc's clasp on her shoulder.

He tightened his grip. Giving Cecy a stern look, he said "Miss Fourchette, we're happy you came."

Cecy wanted to run up the stairs and hide under her bed. She couldn't face her triumphant rival.

But her rigid boarding school training leaped to her rescue. She lifted her chin and pasted a brave smile on her quivering lips. "Miss Fourchette, how kind of you to call."

Susan beckoned them back into the parlor. "I'll get tea." She left them.

Drawing off her gloves, Cecy sat down on the nearest chair. She felt like a poker had been jammed up her spine. So Fleur had come to pity her and crow over winning their social competition.

"Are you well, Miss Jackson?" Fleur asked.

"The other night was a dreadful shock, of course." Cecy made herself smile sadly. "But I am recovering."

"I've been havin' dreadful nightmares. I close my eyes and see blood."

This shook Cecy. Maybe she wasn't the only one who had suffered. "How is Mr. Bower?" Sincerity crept into her voice.

"He's recoverin'. He's so sorry that you've been…."

"Blamed?" Cecy snapped.

"It is unfortunate," Fleur agreed without hesitating. "And unfair. When Mr. Bower recovers fully, he intends to do what he can in your behalf."

CHAPTER 7

"Is he still mending?" Cecy asked, still seeking more reassurance.

"Yes, they permitted me to see him today. When I told him your aunt had left—"

"How did you know that?" Cecy fired up. A hot flush burned upward from her neck.

"Miss Fourchette was the person who called me to alert me that your aunt had left." Linc crossed his legs and folded his hands.

"Your aunt drove by my window with all her valises and trunks piled at the back of the carriage," Fleur explained earnestly. "I'd been so worried, then to see her leavin' you. I didn't know what to do!"

"You shouldn't have worried." Cecy's throat tightened as though it were closing up. "For a short while I will be staying with a neighbor of Mr. Wagstaff's. And he has offered me a position on his weekly journal. He has reminded me that there are more important things in life than parties." Cecy swallowed with difficulty. "I fear I've spent too much time enjoying myself in San Francisco. It's time I settled down to more serious pursuits."

"Is that so?" Fleur asked with a bewildered expression. "I wasn't aware of your ambition. Your voice, so beautiful...I would think...."

"I do love to sing, but after all, opera isn't the kind of life I'd enjoy. Much too frivolous."

"I see." Fleur goggled at her.

Good. Cecy began to feel just a tiny bit more like herself with each word she spoke. She wouldn't go back to being a timid ninny. Mr. Wagstaff had been right. She couldn't just let them dispose of her, forget her. But she did need a proper chaperone.

Cecy drew back her shoulders, sitting even straighter. "And I'm merely staying with Mr. Wagstaff's neighbor until my own dear mother is able to join me at home."

"Your mother is feelin' better then?"
"Yes," Cecy lied boldly.

CHAPTER 8

"My heart has turned to wax; it has melted away within me."
Psalm 22:14b, NIV

I N THE STILLNESS AND CREEPING
shadows of early twilight, Cecy perched on the edge of the
feather bed in Linc's guest room. Susan had insisted Cecy take a
nap after lunch. Cecy had resisted the idea, but as soon as she
laid her head on the fluffy down pillow, she'd fallen asleep. Now
glancing at the softly ticking bedside clock, she couldn't believe
it was just a few minutes before five, nearly evening. The hours
since breakfast felt more like days. She'd gone to Linc's office,
shopped for office furniture, faced Fleur Fourchette and bluffed
her with Linc's offer of a job...

Linc? She'd never thought of him as anything but Mr.
Wagstaff, though a handsome gentleman, a man who could also
be counted on to alternately irritate and protect her. She pon-
dered this change.

Closing her eyes, she remembered his sweeping her into his arms the night before, his strong hands on her ankles as he'd unbuttoned her shoes, his arms around her this afternoon as he had comforted her. His warm lips against hers. At the thought of kissing him, her body radiated heat.

When she had vacationed on the Riviera last year, a French Count had stolen a kiss from her. Evidently Linc knew more about kissing. She hadn't been tempted to kiss the French Count back.

She touched her lips. Linc. Linc had held her in his arms and kissed her. A week ago that would have been unthinkable. A week ago she'd been Miss Cecilia Jackson, heiress and debutante. Who was she now?

Why did Linc always turn up just when she needed him? Why had he offered her a job? What did he want from her?

I don't want to need him. Or anyone else.

The image of her aunt, dressed all in black like a crone turning her back and marching out the door, flickered painfully in Cecy's memory. She couldn't trust Linc—no matter how kind he seemed. If she couldn't count on her aunt, the only one who had visited her every week all those years since she'd been sent away to Boston, whom could she trust?

No one.

Restless, she stood up and began pacing on the braided rag rug beside the bed. Her interview with Fleur Fourchette came back in detail. Facing her rival had blessedly brought her to her senses. Linc's idea of her writing for his muckraking newspaper had been laughable at first. Now it showed merit.

San Francisco society had consigned her to lifelong seclusion and shame. How dare they? Who did they think they were? Because one San Francisco man, Hunt, had no breeding whatsoever, *she* was blamed!

More agitated, she moved away from the bed and paced the length of the room. Could she write for a journal? Be another of the few women journalists in America, women like Annie Laurie or Ida Tarbell?

Cecy had met Baroness de Bazus here at several balls. Originally as Mrs. Frank Leslie, the baroness had taken over management of *Leslie's Illustrated Weekly* after her husband's death. The lady's status as one of the most influential and celebrated journalists and publishers in the United States explained why she got away with using Baroness de Bazus, a French title from her family. In Europe, such pretension would have been quashed. Here it was relished. Was there a possibility that Cecy, too, could reap that kind of reputation and influence?

After her father's funeral, Aunty had counseled that since Cecy never wished to marry—never wished to be under any man's thumb—that Cecy at all costs must be acclaimed a "belle." Society scorned a spinster and held her to a higher standard of propriety all the years of her lonely, barren life. But Aunty had explained that a woman who had been a social success, a belle who could have married well, but inexplicably chose not to, would not be treated like other spinsters. Often society conjured up a rumor of an impossible love to explain the belle's not marrying, which only added to the unmarried beauty's mystique. She could even indulge in eccentricity and be socially sought after.

With the flash of his knife, Hunt had killed the possibility of Cecy being proclaimed a "belle." She'd thought her life had ended that night. But being a career-woman might serve her ambition to be free of male interference.

Below the white-curtained window she looked out, she saw Linc in his large Pierce Arrow driving up with Susan, Del, and Meg. While pacing, she hadn't thought about it, but the house had been silent. Where had the family gone while Cecy napped? Wasn't it late for the children to come home from school?

She hurried to the side window to watch Linc pull up to the carriage house in back. As soon as the car stopped, the little boy, Del, jacketless, jumped out and ran toward the house.

Cecy heard the side door open and slam, then furious feet pounding the wooden floor downstairs. Within seconds, she heard agitated voices—Linc's, Susan's and Meg's. Cecy moved to her door to listen.

Meg was crying.

Who had hurt Del? Meg? Cecy opened her door just a crack.

"Sugar," Susan said from the first-floor hall. "I know you're upset, but you're going to make yourself sick. Come with me. I'll wash those tears off your face."

Meg tried to answer, but started hiccuping.

"I'll go to Del." From below, Linc's voice sounded disturbed. That surprised Cecy. Even when she'd been nearly kidnapped, he'd sounded unruffled like the calm at the center of a storm.

Not wishing to be caught eavesdropping, Cecy pulled her door almost shut though still listening to Susan huff and Meg clatter up the steps.

"I don't like that school." Meg hiccuped.

Susan wheezed as she climbed, each of her steps slow. "I don't either."

"I'm not going there any more!" Meg declared.

"Your father and I need to talk that over—"

"I won't!" Meg cried hysterically. "I won't!"

Cecy sucked in her breath, fearing she'd hear a sharp slap. She trembled for the child. At school, seeing others slapped for impudence, she'd never once spoken out of turn.

"Sugar, we'll talk about that when you're calmer. You can trust your papa. He won't let anyone hurt you."

"They hurt Del! But I hit 'em and hit 'em—"

"You're just getting yourself into a state." Susan's voice sounded firm, but gentle. "There will always be mean people in this world. You did right to fight them. But you have to calm down or you're going to be sick. Please."

"I feel sick." Meg sobbed.

"Come into the lavatory. I'll wash your face and hands, then we'll put a cold cloth on the back of your neck. That will help."

"All…right," Meg choked on her words, then sobbed between hiccups.

Cecy longed to comfort the little girl, longed to thank Susan for being so kind. But she was a stranger in this house. For just a second, a soothing voice—somehow similar to Susan's—flickered in her memory. Had it been her mother's?

Cecy turned back to the exchange she'd just overheard in her mind. Who had hurt Del? And why? She listened to the sounds of Susan soothe Meg, then take the child into her own room.

Quickly, Cecy smoothed her hair and dress, then slipped out the door. Her curiosity over Del and what had gone wrong at their school propelled her silently down the steps. She heard Linc's voice immediately. He was in a room toward the back of the first floor. She tread cautiously down the hall and drew close to the door, which stood open just a fraction.

"I hate them." Del repeated, "I hate them."

"They said they hate you," Linc replied in a steady voice. "Why didn't you tell me things were getting out of hand at school?"

"I don't care about that. I hate them."

"You mean you're just like them?"

"I'm not anything like them!" Del shouted.

"If you hate them, then you are just like them—"

"You don't know how I feel!" The boy began weeping.

A pause. Cecy's heart went out to the child. She'd felt just the same way after the opera party. Hunt had dealt her a death blow. She hated him. Why shouldn't Del hate his tormentors?

Linc said, "Perhaps not. But I do care how you feel. I love you."

Silence, then the sound of the boy crying.

Cecy backed up and tiptoed into the parlor. Linc's words, 'I do care how you feel. I love you,' echoed in her mind. She sat down, pondering Susan and Linc and their love for two very fortunate children. A presence, a memory, nibbled at her conscious mind, but remained elusive. Someone had loved her once.

✷ ✷ ✷ ✷ ✷

March 10, 1906

The rosy spring dawn radiated over the green hills of San Francisco. Cecy perched on the front seat of Linc's Pierce Arrow as she traveled out of the city to her mother's sanitarium. He'd asked Cecy if she wanted to drive her car, but though she didn't admit it, she was too jittery to drive.

Cecy's stomach objected to the wide, turning motion Linc made around a curve as they started down into a valley. She'd been feeling slightly ill for the last half-hour.

"Cecilia, what did the doctor tell you over the phone?"

His frank question relieved her. She was glad he'd dropped the pleasant conversation they'd both labored to keep going since they set out an hour ago. "He said that Mother could see me if she felt up to it." Her voice betrayed her by quavering on the last phrase.

He nodded. "If she is able to come home, Susan said she'll come and stay with you until you hire a nurse as a companion to your mother."

Cecy cleared her thick throat. "That's very thoughtful."

"Susan is angry your aunt didn't stand by you. She says family stands by family—no matter what."

Cecy gave a mirthless laugh. "No doubt Susan would believe that." She'd thought her aunt had been the only one in her family who wouldn't disappoint her. Tears threatened, but she steeled herself against them.

Linc glanced sideways at her. "I'm sure your mother will wish to help. But she has been ill a long time and might not be able to."

"I know. I know." *I have to try! I don't have a choice!*
Something which felt a little like hysteria ignited in the pit of
her stomach. What if her mother couldn't come, wouldn't
come? Cecy couldn't imagine having to hire a stranger as a
chaperone. How humiliating. *I won't do it. I'll defy convention first
and live alone!*

Linc's even voice called her out of the vortex of emotion.
"You were sent away to school when you were very young,
weren't you?"

"Yes."

"Did your mother ever visit you in Boston?"

An arrow of remembered pain pierced her. "No, my father
wouldn't let her at first. He said I should adjust to school before
she visited me." *Adjust to being abandoned.*

"And then?"

"And then she was too sick to come." Desperate in her
loneliness, Cecy had written many times over the years, inviting
her mother to school events, begging to come home for the
summer. In all those years, no one but Aunty had ever come.
Her father had paid for her school, clothing, music, and summer
camp fees, but she'd only received civil replies via his lawyer to
her letters. He'd had his lawyer write her. Why had her father
hated her so? She closed her eyes trying to block out the suffering she'd endured.

"The sanitarium's just around this bend."

"Yes, I recognize where we are now." She opened her eyes
forcing the past back like a lion tamer lashing a whip at a beast,
driving it back into its cage.

Soon they drove through the gate. The gatekeeper swung
the black wrought-iron gate closed behind them. Its clang res-
onated through Cecy's every fiber.

Linc glanced over his shoulder looking uneasy. "I take it this
is one of those exclusive hospitals for the very wealthy?"

"Yes, the security is very good here… Aunty said." For a
fleeting second, she yearned to lean her head on Linc's broad

shoulder. Maybe he'd take her into his arms and she could forget all about seeing her mother. Why did she even think her mother would want to see her?

A staff doctor welcomed them at the impressive carved, double oak door entrance. He led them down an empty corridor to his office, their careful footsteps echoing. They sat down by his desk and he faced them.

Cecy drew herself up, clutching at the shreds of her tattered courage. "Is my mother well enough to see me?"

"Yes, I think she is." The doctor, an earnest-looking young man, steepled his fingers and gazed at her over them. "I explained to her earlier this morning that you and Mr. Wagstaff would be coming for a visit. You mentioned that you hoped she might be able to come home with you for a visit?"

She nodded.

He eyed her warily. "May I be frank, Miss Jackson?"

"Please." The word scraped her throat like a nail file.

"The last time you visited, your mother seemed so much more agitated. But this time when I said only you and a gentleman were coming, she seemed much calmer. Miss Jackson, has anyone told you about your mother's condition?"

"No." Why had she quietly accepted the polite phrases with which Aunty had covered up her mother's illness? Why hadn't she insisted Aunty tell her the truth?

He stared at Cecy with a worried question in his eyes.

"Please tell me doctor. My aunt was not open with me about my mother's condition, but I'm very concerned about her."

He leaned his chin on the back of his hand. "Your mother's illness is a combination of things, but primarily, she is, or was an inebriate."

Cecy gasped. Her mother? No!

"You had no inkling?"

Cecy shook her head.

"Let me explain. I'm relatively new here, so I went through her file thoroughly. What was written there made me curious about her, so I made a point to evaluate her myself."

Nodding woodenly, Cecy couldn't take her eyes off him.

"I think your mother experienced *delirium tremens* years ago and was admitted here because of that."

"What is *delirium tremens?*" she asked haltingly.

The doctor exchanged glances with Linc. "When a person imbibes alcohol too liberally over a long period of time, the alcohol takes its toll on the mind—"

"My mother is unbalanced!" Cecy nearly rose.

"No, no. *Delirium tremens* does not last if steps are taken. As soon as the alcohol consumption decreases, the mind usually recovers its natural tone."

"Then my mother is rational." Cecy clutched the wooden arms of her chair.

"Yes."

Thank God. Cecy felt weak.

Linc leaned forward. "Does she have physical problems, too?"

The doctor nodded. "She is very frail and suffered damage to her liver which is common in inebriates."

"Is that why she has stayed here for over seven years?" Linc persisted.

"Please tell us," Cecy pleaded.

The doctor paused. "I believe your mother preferred staying here to going home. I believe your parents' marriage was a deeply troubled one."

Cecy's jaw tightened. *To say the least.* "But she could go home now if she wants to?" Hope flickered.

The doctor pinned her with an unswerving gaze. "Yes, but I insist she lead a very quiet life. No going to parties, etc. She is accustomed to an orderly, tranquil life. I warn you too much change might trigger her returning to alcohol which could begin the damaging cycle all over again."

"Quiet would be no problem." Cecy's eyes remained downcast. There'd be no chance for more parties now.

"Very well." The doctor stood. "I'll take you to your mother then."

He ushered them out into the green, carpeted hall and the wide corridor. The atmosphere was hushed, but not repressive. Cecy marshaled her resolve to see this through. No matter how this might end, she had to find out if she and her mother could become family to each other, or at least acquaintances.

The doctor left them in a spacious sun room at the end of the hall. Cecy sat down on a cushioned black wicker chair. Linc settled unobtrusively onto one a few feet away. She wished he'd sit nearer. She craved his solid presence.

Within minutes, a nurse dressed in a white uniform with a white cap strolled in sedately with a thin, frail woman by her side.

Cecy stood. "Mother."

Her mother halted and stared at Cecy. "Amelia isn't with you?" Her voice was barely a whisper. The nurse walked away quietly.

Cecy's heart raced. *Would her mother be angry with her over Aunt Amelia leaving?* "Aunty has gone back to Boston."

"Why? Why has she gone? When will she come back?" Her mother's gaze pierced her.

Cecy didn't flinch from telling the truth. No more secrets, no more lies. "She said your father needed her. She won't be back."

Her mother took a tentative step forward. "How do you know that?"

Cecy forced herself to tell the plain facts. "She said she washed her hands of me."

"She won't be back then?"

"No."

"What a relief." Her mother shut her eyes, then opened them. She smiled faintly. "Now I can go home."

CHAPTER 8

✹ ✹ ✹ ✹ ✹

Cecy and Linc sat alone in his cozy parlor. Cecy cupped a mug of warm tea with both hands. A golden fire in the hearth added a cheerful glow to the quiet room. The soft shades of blue and the crackle of the fire gave her a mellow feeling. Her new confidence flowered like the pink buds on the almond trees she'd seen today as they drove through the city. All wasn't well, but her midnight had passed.

She glanced surreptitiously at Linc as he read the evening paper. She'd never really known any man as a person, never had a friendship with a man. Was friendship with a man possible? He'd held her. They'd kissed. What did that mean to him, to her? Had they crossed the line to romance with that kiss?

Before she'd been so busy flirting with Bower and Hunt, she'd merely accepted Linc as another man pursuing her. But even at the beginning, he wasn't like any other man. He was different, special. Would it be possible to love a man, to love Linc?

For just a second, she fantasized that she and Linc were husband and wife with children upstairs. The image brought her peace, then disquiet. *I can't think such thoughts!*

In two days, she would order out her large carriage. She'd ride out in it to the sanitarium to pick up her mother and luggage and bring her home to Nob Hill.

Linc closed his paper, then sipped his coffee. "We'll go tomorrow and hire a short-term nurse to help your mother make the transition. Also to stay with her while you're working at the journal with me."

Cecy nodded. So much had happened today at the sanitarium. Her mother was coming home at last. For the first time since Cecy was seven years old, they would live together in their own home. Joy and fear leap-frogged inside her. But doubt still plagued her.

What had gone so dreadfully wrong between her parents that her mother had preferred a sanitarium to her own home? Why had her mother seemed so relieved when she learned that Aunt Amelia had gone back to Boston for good? Now that Cecy thought about it, when Aunty and Cecy had visited that first time, her mother had shown fear. Aunty had frightened her mother, but at the time, Cecy hadn't connected her mother's fear with Aunty's presence. Now she felt too much a stranger to ask her mother why.

Old whispers, secrets were rustling all around Cecy. She'd thought she'd understood what had gone on in the past between her parents, her mother and Aunt Amelia, but now she sensed much of the past lay beneath the surface of her life like a dangerous coral reef beneath uncharted waters.

She pushed all these unsettling feelings and thoughts aside and looked to Linc. "I don't mean to pry, but did something happen the other afternoon to the children at school?"

He frowned. "The children are having some problems adjusting to their new school. Children can be so cruel."

Cecy understood that with her whole heart. Her own school days had been filled with taunts and slights. Children unerringly seemed to pick the weakest among the group to torture. *I'm not weak anymore. I'm strong. I am.* "I'm sorry to hear that. They didn't go to school today?"

"No, Susan and I have decided to finish this school year teaching them at home."

"I see." She didn't like the hollow sound of his voice and sad look in his eyes. He didn't deserve this worry. He'd come to her aid so many times, she wished she could help him, but what could she do?

"I expect you will be busy for a few days getting your mother settled, but then I want you to begin accompanying me on a few interviews."

CHAPTER 8

"Are you positive you think I could be a journalist?" She set her cup onto the doily-covered table between them, then folded her hands.

"You're an intelligent woman. You'll try it and see if it catches your interest."

She nodded with conviction. She recognized his effort to bolster her confidence. She was grateful for it. And yet she resented it.

Susan slid open the pocket door. "Miss Jackson, Meg would like you to come and say prayers with her tonight."

"What?" Cecy's eyes widened.

Susan came into the room. "She usually says prayers with her father, but tonight she'd like you to tuck her in."

Cecy looked to Linc for guidance.

He merely nodded. "Would you mind, Cecilia?"

"No, but…"

"She's waiting," Susan prompted, folding her hands over her ample girth.

Cecy rose slowly, left the parlor, and walked up the stairs. She hesitated at the open door to Meg's room.

Standing beside a doll-sized cradle, Meg hugged her porcelain-headed doll close. "It's time to sleep, Matilda. Now don't you worry. You won't have any nightmares tonight." The little girl tucked her doll into its cradle with a small hand-stitched crazy quilt.

"Doesn't Matilda say prayers?" Cecy asked feeling ill-at-ease.

Meg looked up with a serious face. "Dolls don't have souls. When I'm a real mother, I'll say prayers with my babies like my mama did."

Cecy drew closer. "I'm sure you will. Did you want me—"

"Yes, come on. I wanted to say prayers with you tonight." Meg tugged Cecy over to her high bed.

"But why?"

"Because I like you. You talk nice and you're pretty."

Cecy swelled with pleasure. A genuine smile lifted the corners of her mouth. "I like you, too, Meg."

Meg knelt and pulled Cecy down beside her. The hardwood floor brought the reality of the moment to Cecy.

With sharp poignancy, Cecy dreaded hearing the chant, 'Now I lay me down to sleep. I pray the Lord my soul to keep. If I should die before I wake, I pray the Lord my soul to take.' She'd been forced to recite that aloud until she was fourteen. *I can't say that!* "You say the prayer, Meg, and I'll just say amen."

"Dear Father in heaven," Meg began. "I love you. I'm trying to like it here in San Francisco, but it's not easy. Please make people here like Del and me."

Cecy floundered. This cozy conversation was prayers to Meg?

The little girl continued. "Bless Papa, Susan, Del and Miss Jackson, my new friend, and her mama. Hug my mama in heaven and tell her I still miss her." Then she began to recite, "The Lord is my Shepherd I shall not want...."

The Twenty-third Psalm. Cecy had heard it thousands of times, but hearing it in this child's voice released a memory from deep in Cecy's misty past.

Before Boston, before she'd been sent away, someone had held her close and prayed this over her many times. Someone had loved her. But the voice Cecy heard in her memory wasn't her mother's. Whose was it?

CHAPTER 9

*"How long must I wrestle with my thoughts and
every day have sorrow in my heart?"*
Psalm 13:2a, NIV

March 12, 1906

A S THE AFTERNOON SUN WANED,
the butler held the door open for Cecy. She waited for her
mother to precede her, but the lady froze, staring up at the
stone front of their house.

"Mother?" Cecy murmured. "Is something wrong?"

Her mother shook her head and slowly crossed over the
solid brass threshold.

The butler closed the door behind them. "Miss Jackson, I
took the liberty of ordering tea for the two of you in the conservatory." He relieved them of their coats and hats and handed
them to the footman.

"Thank you." Cecy took her mother's arm. The older
woman looked around as though she'd never seen the house

before. The ride home had been an agony of uncomfortable silences and forced pleasantries.

This is my mother, the person I should feel the closest to in all the world.

They were strangers.

Silently they walked into the conservatory. Cecy applauded her butler's choice of setting for her first tea with Mother. Of all the rooms, this one filled with luxuriant plants, many of them flowering in white, salmon pink, red, and lavender, overcame the hollow emptiness of the mansion. The fragrances of frangipani scented the warm room and mist hugged the high glass dome above them.

As Cecy urged her mother to a comfortable chair, she wished she could ask about the hazy memory which had come to her when Meg recited the Twenty-third Psalm in her prayers. Instead, she asked politely, "How are you feeling?"

"I'm tired." Her mother sat, but still held herself very straight, not letting her spine touch the chair back. Just like Cecy had been taught by Aunt Amelia, her mother's older sister.

The butler entered bearing a tray with tea, petite sandwiches and butter cookies. He served them efficiently. Cecy smiled her thanks and he withdrew.

She sipped her sweet tea slowly, trying to come up with a topic. Her mother gazed at the fall of small lavender orchids across from her. A minute or more ticked by. "Did I tell you that I am thinking of writing for a new journal?" Though calm on the surface, Cecy felt questions bubbling up from deep inside her. *Why did you marry Father?*

"A journal?"

"Yes, Linc...Mr. Wagstaff...the man who came with me to the sanitarium is beginning a new journal and has asked me to try my hand at writing for it."

"I see. Do you like to write?" Her mother's gaze met hers.

This question hadn't occurred to her. "I suppose I'll find that out when I try it."

Her mother nodded. "Is Mr. Wagstaff a friend of yours?"

"Yes, he is new to San Francisco, too." *Mother, why did you let Father send me away?* The old ache, the old loneliness sluiced through her like ice water. Her first glimpse of the Boston school came up before her mind's eye, forbidding, terrifying.

"Where was his home?"

Cecy blinked. "What? Oh, Chicago."

"Really? Have you been to Chicago?"

"I suppose I passed through there by train on my way to and from Boston." *Will you react to my mentioning Boston?* She watched her mother.

Her mother looked away. "The plants here are very beautiful."

"I come here when I'm troubled." *Mother, when I was seven, did you care or even want me with you? Will you ask me what's troubling me now?*

Pause.

Her mother lifted her translucent cup.

Cecy stared as the light in the room shone through the lip of the cup. If only her past, her mother's, could be that transparent.

"The butler's a stranger to me. How long has he worked here?"

Disappointment clutched Cecy's dry throat. She forced herself to sip her tea again. "I don't really know. He was here when Aunt Amelia and I arrived near the end of last year." *When and why did you turn to drinking spirits? Did Father drive you to it? Or were you already an inebriate when you wed?*

"Cecilia, who's your business advisor?"

The question startled Cecy. It was the first interest her mother had shown in something other than commonplaces. "Mr. Edmonds."

"Edmonds. Have you spoken to him recently?"

Cecy tried, but failed to read anything from her mother's bland tone and emotionless face. "No, I've been preoccupied with…other matters."

"You should see him soon."

"Do you think so?" *Why, Mother?*

"Yes, writing is fine and good, but a woman should never assume a man is watching out for her, especially where money is concerned."

Cecy hid her face behind her teacup. What had prompted this advice? She'd met Edmonds briefly twice, but hadn't seen him for several weeks.

"Are you seeing anyone?" Her mother didn't meet Cecy's eyes.

"No." *Why would I want to see someone?*

"The doctor said that you aren't leading an active social life right now."

Cecy gave the pat answer she'd already used with others. "I decided I wanted to pursue a more serious life. Becoming a journalist will be more satisfying than being a debutante, don't you think?" *Why didn't you want to come home while your sister was here?*

"That sounds reasonable. I never thought of you pursuing a career."

Neither did I. Linc said Aunt Amelia gave me bad advice. Could you have warned me? Why didn't you try?

The butler ushered Susan and Meg into the conservatory.

"Meg?" Cecy rose. Her mood lifted just sighting Meg's face, brimful of suppressed excitement. "I didn't know you were coming, too."

"I brought a present for your mama." The little girl skipped over to the lady.

"Who are you?" Cecy's mother asked.

Cecy touched one of Meg's red-ribboned braids. "Meg is Linc Wagstaff's daughter." Cecy motioned toward Susan. "This is Susan, Mr. Wagstaff's family friend. She'll spend the night with us. The nurse I've hired will start tomorrow."

"Want to see your present?" Meg leaned closer.

Cecy's mother framed Meg's rosy face with her frail, white hands. "What a sweet face you have."

A muffled meow emanated from Meg's red spring coat. The little girl opened it and drew out a tiny, gray-striped kitten.

"Oh, my," Cecy's mother breathed.

Cecy cast a worried glance at Susan.

Susan lowered herself into the chair beside Cecy's. She smiled reassuringly.

"Want to hold it?" Meg asked.

The lady nodded.

"Papa said it's a girl kitty." Meg gently lay the tiny ball of silky fur into the lady's hands. "You pet it like this." Meg demonstrated by stroking the kitten's head with one finger. "We have to be careful. She's very little."

"Yes, she is." Cecy's mother stroked the kitten too. The furry baby mewed and rubbed against her hand begging for more attention. "Cecilia, may I keep the kitten?"

The childlike question hurt Cecy. "Mother, this is your home. You can have whatever you wish."

Cecy's mother smiled. "Meg, where did you get the kitty?"

"Our neighbor's cat had kittens. Last night she brought them over for me and Del to pick."

"So you got a kitty too?"

"Yes, I got a girl kitty and Del got a boy kitty."

Cecy sat back down. The kitten had obviously done her mother good. Her pale, drawn face showed more color and had become animated as though her mother had just awakened.

"Who's Del?"

"He's my grandson," Susan spoke up with a smile.

"Del and me... I mean, we don't go to school anymore. And I'm glad. I wouldn't want to leave my kitty home alone."

Cecy's mother nodded.

"What are you going to name her?" Meg stared up at Mrs. Jackson's face.

"I don't know. What do you think?" The lady gazed seriously at Meg.

Wearing a sailor blouse, Meg swished herself side to side, making her navy pleated skirt swirl. "I was thinking she needs a pretty name, something for a real little kitty."

Cecy couldn't help herself. She grinned at Meg.

"Well," Cecy's mother said, "when I saw you walk in, I thought, what a pretty little miss. Why don't we call her Missy?"

"I like that!" Meg clapped her hands.

Missy cringed and meowed piteously.

"Don't be afraid, Missy," Cecy's mother crooned. "I'll take care of you."

Cecy felt her over-sensitive emotions roll and swirl inside. Why did she feel like crying?

Meg leaned over, petting and also cooing to the kitten.

Susan cleared her throat. "Ma'am, if you'll permit me, I think you are in need of a nap."

The lady sighed. "Thank you. I am tired. So much excitement today."

Susan stood and walked to the lady. "I'll go upstairs with you to your room."

Cecy eased forward to the edge of her chair. The staid butler appeared.

"Mother, your room is all ready for you." Cecy stood, unsure whether she should accompany Susan or not.

"Thank you, dear. Coming home…." Her mother suddenly appeared near tears.

Tears nearly overcame Cecy again. Why did she feel like this, so helpless, so disconnected? "If you need anything, mother, just let us know. Susan is going to spend tonight in the room next to yours. Tomorrow the nurse I hired will stay with you when I have to be out."

Her mother rose, treasuring her kitty in the crook of her arm. On her way out of the room, her mother paused. "You know being here with you and seeing this sweet little girl, it brought Millie Anderson to mind."

"Millie Anderson?"

"Don't you remember her, Cecilia? But you were so young, I suppose you don't remember Millie. She was your nanny. Such a dear woman. It would be lovely if you could find her. I'd love to see her again."

Cecy stood, stunned. An image, a voice from the past flooded her. "Did she recite the Twenty-third Psalm to me?"

"Oh, yes, every night at bedtime."

Her mother's simple words rocked Cecy to her core. Images, a voice, an elusive fragrance from the past flooded her.

Following the butler, Susan led Cecy's mother from the conservatory.

Meg wandered over to Cecy and sat down beside her. "Don't cry. I like your mama. And she got to come home."

Her eyes shut holding back tears, Cecy felt the little girl hug her. Tears streamed down her face. *Nana, I remember you. You loved me.*

🐞 🐞 🐞 🐞 🐞

March 15, 1906

Cecilia's hands were clenched in her lap. Her lovely face was drawn and over-serious. Linc would have to think of some way to cheer her up.

He would have liked to put her at ease, but he didn't want to bring up how obvious her nervousness was. Was she nervous about accompanying him to an interview? Or something else?

Susan had let him know how tentative relations were between Cecilia and her mother. When Cecilia had faced Fleur, she'd bounced back temporarily. But dealing with an ill, depressed mother had cast a shade over her again. How could he lift her spirits?

He parked the car at redbrick Fire House Number One where Fire Department Chief, Dennis Sullivan's office was located. He helped Cecy out of the car and escorted her inside. She gripped his arm. He'd brought her along to inspire her with a desire to write, to interview. Originally he hadn't meant to have Cecilia write for his journal. He'd merely wanted to influence her to take action to rectify the abuse of child labor. She had the right business interests, money, power, connections or so she'd had these before Hunt. He hoped his new plan for her worked. The stakes were high. At least, the human stakes were high.

A gangly-looking young man wearing fire department insignia on his stiffly starched, navy blue uniform ushered them into the fire chief's office.

After the introductions, Linc and Cecy sat down side by side facing Sullivan over his desk. Linc took out a notebook and pencil. Cecy followed suit.

"Which paper did you say you were writing for?" Sullivan asked.

"The article's for my weekly journal, *Cause Celebre.*"

"Haven't read that one."

Linc grinned. "This interview will appear in the premiere issue later this month. *Cause Celebre* will tackle issues other papers avoid."

Sullivan snorted. "So that's why you're here. I've tried to interest the *Examiner, Call, and Bulletin* in my worries, and they all say a story like mine is bad for circulation. Nobody wants to think about a possible earthquake."

✳ ✳ ✳ ✳ ✳

"Do you think there will be another earthquake?" Cecy glanced at the slender man with graying temples, her interest caught.

"Heavens, yes." Sullivan grinned sheepishly.

CHAPTER 9

"So tell us what needs to be done—if and when another earthquake strikes." Linc poised his pencil over his paper.

Cecy wrote "Earthquake Measures" on her page.

"It's impossible to predict when an earthquake will hit," Sullivan began. "But let's be realistic. San Francisco has seen them before and will see them again. That hasn't changed, but our population density has increased and everyone has gas piped into their houses! Even if they've hooked up to electricity, most people cook with gas now, not wood. Cracked or broken gas pipes are an open invitation to fire."

Cecy hadn't expected interviewing the fire chief to be vital, interesting. Fleetingly she recalled the first unbelievable and terrifying moments of the tremor that night at the opera. "I hadn't thought about that," Cecy murmured as she wrote in her notebook.

"You and a lot of other people—our esteemed Mayor Schmitz included. In 1860, the city fathers showed more foresight than the jokers we have today. Back in the sixties, they constructed large underground cisterns throughout the city to fight fires. But these are old now. They need to be repaired and reactivated. The biggest problem in fighting any large-scale fire is getting water. If gas pipes break, water pipes can break, too. If water pipes break—"

"You can't get the water to fight the fires." Linc scribbled on his pad.

Cecy glanced at Linc. His tone had been unexpectedly grim.

"Give that man a cigar." Sullivan nodded.

"So why aren't the cisterns being reactivated?" Cecy asked. She waited to jot down the man's answer. She'd not gotten down all he said about cisterns.

Sullivan grunted. "Money, of course. The Reuf gang that got Schmitz elected is too busy siphoning off municipal funds to be concerned about a little thing like the safety of the citizens."

"Graft?" Linc demanded.

Sullivan leaned forward urgently. His concern clear in the tautness of his posture and in his grave expression. "If they won't give us water, we need to purchase high explosives to fuel firebreaks. But they nixed that, too."

"Firebreaks?" Cecy glanced up from her notebook.

He looked at her assessingly. "Yes, a trained fire department can devise and explode a series of firebreaks, lines of dense high rubble which serve as a barrier to the spreading flames."

The vision of sweeping, unchecked flames abruptly halted Cecy's pen. *Could this actually happen?*

"Pretty tricky business," Linc muttered; his face looked pained.

"You can say that again." Sullivan's face flushed with irritation and his voice grew gruffer, quicker. "If it isn't done right, the explosives just provide more fuel for the fire. Spreads the fire. But when I ask for money to bring in professionals to train my men, all I get are excuses. No money. They're fools, every last one of them. Fools."

❋ ❋ ❋ ❋ ❋

Linc pulled away from the curb. "Well, that's your first interview. What did you think?"

"I think the people of San Francisco should be told what their fire chief needs for their protection." She spoke with a passion which startled her. The images of an earthquake and flames had fired her imagination. "I can't believe the municipal government won't give him the money he needs!"

Linc grinned. "See I told you, you have what it takes to be a journalist."

She paused, looking at him. "I may care about the issue, but that doesn't mean I can write about it." She doubted her sketchy notes would be sufficient.

"Writing is something you can learn. Caring about inequities and abuses of power and wanting them to change for the better can't be taught. That must come from the heart." He smiled at her.

His approval warmed her through like summer sunshine. But why did she want, need his approval? She couldn't afford to depend on anyone again. Everyone she'd ever trusted had let her down. Everyone, except perhaps, Millie Anderson.

Her mother said her former nanny had insisted on traveling with her to Boston, but father had dismissed her and hired a new nurse to take Cecy across country to Boston. Her father's need to isolate her from anyone who loved her didn't make sense. What could Cecy have done to offend him so and at such a tender age?

Hesitantly, Cecy glanced at Linc. "My mother would like to locate someone."

"Who?"

"Her name is Millie Anderson. She worked for mother when I was a child. How does one locate a person?"

Linc swerved to miss a startled horse. The hack driver shook his fist at them. "We'll ask at the employment agency. Often they will keep track of people throughout their many job changes. If that doesn't work, we can always advertise in the classifieds."

"Thank you. My mother seemed to want to see her again." *Just as I would.* Perhaps Millie could answer questions from the past. Cecy felt like she was chasing wraiths, shadows.

Linc drove up to Cecy's house. "Our next appointment is in a couple of days. We're going to tour a cannery and investigate working conditions. I told the manager we just wanted to do a story about how a cannery works. But really it will be a story that pinpoints some dreadful conditions I merely glimpsed when I made the arrangements."

"I see." Cecy barely heard him. She dreaded going back to face her mother. Not being able to ask her mother all the questions she needed answers to was becoming harder and harder on Cecy. This made finding Millie even more pressing.

Linc parked and came over to help her out of the auto. Feeling warm, she unbuttoned her coat while the butler let them in the front door. A footman received their driving coats, hats, and gloves.

The butler smiled slightly. "Miss, your mother and the nurse are in the conservatory with Susan, the child, and kittens."

Cecy and Linc walked to the conservatory. Susan, Meg, and Cecy's mother were teasing Missy and Meg's kitten with a ball of blue angora yarn. Linc and Cecy greeted the others.

Linc looked around. "Where's Del?"

Susan looked serious. "When we were ready to catch the cable car, I couldn't find that boy."

After being introduced to the nurse, then asking Cecy's permission, Linc walked over to the phone in the conservatory. He called home. "Kang, is Del there?"

Linc frowned and hung up. "He's still not home. We should probably leave a bit earlier than we thought."

"Oh, Papa!" Meg moaned her objection.

This caught Cecy's attention. Why was Linc concerned about Del? Had there been more trouble?

Cecy nearly asked, but the butler appeared. He announced a call for Miss Jackson. Cecy stepped to the phone and picked up the receiver. "Hello."

"It *is* you, isn't it, Cecilia Jackson?"

"Yes, who's this?"

"This is Clarissa Hunt calling."

The new combination of names jumbled in Cecy's mind. "Clarissa Hunt? You mean, Clarissa Bower?"

"No," the other woman snapped. "I mean *Mrs. Victor Hunt*. Victor and I just returned from our elopement."

"You eloped with Hunt?" A weakness snaked through Cecy. She clutched the telephone table.

"Yes, I did. So now you know he loved me, not you," the woman gloated. "He was just pursuing you to give his father a hard time because he didn't like being told whom to marry. It offended his pride."

Clarissa believed that drivel? "He stabbed your brother because it offended his pride?"

"That was just an accident! Victor would never mean to hurt my brother! You pushed between them. You're the one responsible for the injury to my brother."

I didn't bring the knife! Every bad thing she'd learned about Hunt rushed through her mind like a runaway locomotive. This woman was in danger of suffering a life just like Cecy's own mother! "Clarissa—"

"I just wanted to tell you myself, go back East. You're not wanted—"

Cecy broke into the stream of spiteful words. "*Clarissa,* if you ever need help, call on me *please.*"

"What? Why would you say something that ridiculous to me? I've married the man I love and who loves me. I have all I'll ever need or want. Just stay away from my husband!"

Cecy's anger flared. "Isn't he too much in love with you to be tempted by me?"

Clarissa slammed down the receiver in Cecy's ear.

Cecy hung up slowly.

"Who was that?" Linc asked.

"A fool, a stupid little fool."

🌟 🌟 🌟 🌟 🌟

Cecilia's crushed expression brought him to her side. He took her arm and walked her a few paces away into the cover of the lush green plants and tall, potted trees. "Who was it?"

"Mrs. Victor Hunt." Her voice dripped with sarcasm. "Clarissa called to tell me she's blissfully happy, married to the man she loves and that I am the one who scarred her brother's cheek." She turned her face away from him.

He came closer to her. "Cecilia," he murmured thickly. She needed someone to protect her, smooth the way for her. Her vulnerability drew him. He wanted to calm her fears, pull her into his arms, run his fingers through feathery-soft tresses.... *No! I can't.*

Her hands clasped together, she turned back to him. "Linc, it's no good. Nothing will change what has happened—"

His hand pressed her soft lips together, stopping her words. Then his hand slid over her ever-so-smooth skin to cup the side of her cheek. "We won't think of the past. I'll lead you into the future."

"It's no use." Her lone tear slipped down over his hand.

Cecilia! I still love Virginia.

She leaned into his shirtfront. "I have no future."

"I'll show you you're wrong. This city is larger than you think." *Don't kiss her.* But his lips refused to obey him. Leaning down, he kissed her fragrant, auburn hair. *I can't do this. I love Virginia.*

She leaned her head back to kiss him in return.

He gently slid his lips from hers. *Oh, Cecilia, what am I going to do with you? Virginia, forgive me.*

CHAPTER 10

"Fools mock at making amends for sin..."
Proverbs 14:9, NIV

March 16, 1906   THE SKY THREATENED RAIN, BUT
Linc offered his arm to Cecilia as they set out down Market
Street for a Saturday afternoon promenade, a new and different
one from the one she was used to on fashionable Montgomery
Street. After Clarissa Hunt's nasty call, he'd wanted to cheer
Cecilia. Introducing her to the avant-garde, the literati of San
Francisco seemed a good way. Now he had qualms.

Since he was a journalist, he moved freely among San
Francisco's bohemians. He also associated with the bon vivants
of high society, and a third group, the members of the small
church he and Meg had joined recently. But he knew those
same church members would be shocked to see him here on
Market Street today.

He had learned from childhood how to mix with all classes, colors, and types of people. His parents with their wealth and zeal for social issues had led the way. Both of them had also shocked other Christians with their involvement with "undesirables."

"Who are these people you want me to meet?" she asked petulantly.

"You'll meet writers, actors...."

"Really?" Her budding interest was obvious by the lift in her voice. "Will any singers be here?"

"Could be." But would Cecilia be able to see these people as they were or only the persona they showed in public? "The artistic community parades down Market Street on Saturday—"

"While the hypocrites, who think Hunt is a fine young man, walk Montgomery Street?" she said in a brittle tone. Her chin lifted defiantly.

"Perhaps you're not ready—"

"Just because the so-called elite have cut me from their lists, I refuse to vanish from San Francisco. You're the one who has encouraged me to take a different path, aren't you?"

"To become a writer." *Not a rebel.* "This trip to Market Street is just to widen your experience. Bower hasn't recovered enough to help smooth matters over yet. I still expect you to take your place again in society. I don't want you to burn any bridges. Miss Fourchette said both she and Bower would help."

"How can they help me? Hunt is Bower's brother-in-law now. They'll all close ranks. I'm nothing to them." With a wave of her hand, she made a cutting gesture.

Linc tightened his grip on her. Her cynicism grated on him. "Don't always assume the worst about people."

"It's safer that way." With a toss of her head, she quickened her pace.

"Have I ever failed you?" he challenged her. She was too young to view people in such a dark light. What did she think of him?

"No, but I've only known you two months." She looked away haughtily.

Cut to the heart, he halted mid-stride searching her face. "If you feel that way about me, we can go home right now."

Her arch smile turned into a puzzled frown.

He held her motionless. "You may have known me only two months, but it has been a very rocky two months. Now, do you trust me or not?"

She grimaced. "I trust you more than anyone else in San Francisco."

How deeply had this troubled young woman worked her way into his heart? Too deeply. He took a painful breath. "If that's the best you can do, I'll have to settle for it. But believe me, Cecilia, I do care about you. I would never hurt you."

"I know. You're Meg's father." Her chin dipped low, almost shyly.

"What does that mean?" He started walking again.

She looked away. "Your daughter shows what kind of man you are. She loves you."

Before Linc could react, a handsome man with a shock of blond-gray hair walked up to Linc. "Wagstaff, who is this poor beauty you have hornswaggled into being seen with you?"

"Miss Jackson." Linc shook hands with him. "May I introduce you to Mr. Bierce?"

"This is the scandalous Miss Jackson? How delightful!" Bierce bowed over her hand. "Welcome to the rogue's promenade!"

Looking bemused, Cecilia curtseyed.

Bierce appropriated Cecilia's other arm. "How do you stand Wagstaff? He's so upright he makes my teeth ache."

Linc groaned. But he had been acquainted too long with men like Bierce, who found inspiration at the bottom of a bottle, to be surprised by this reaction. So he kept his voice light, "Just because I don't want to drink with you all night on the Barbary Coast—"

"Linc," Cecy emphasized her use of his first name in an obvious attempt to keep Bierce at a respectable distance, "has hired me to write for his—"

"His rag? We keep waiting to see it—"

"Two more weeks!" Why hadn't Linc recalled how Bierce charmed women? Linc tugged Cecilia away from the man. His stepfather had regularly taken Linc to rescue missions where they'd tried to help men climb out of the bottle. A drunk could be very charming at first. Linc didn't want Cecilia charmed.

Bierce nodded knowingly. "So it's that way. You're a two-some?"

"I'm just protecting her from a masher," Linc declared.

Bierce roared at that.

"Hey, Wagstaff!" another man hailed them. "How's that rag of yours going?"

Linc introduced Cecilia to McEwen, an editor of another avant-garde paper.

A lady—rouged and sporting an outrageous pink feather boa—swept up to them, obviously startling Cecilia. "Lincoln, introduce me to my rival!"

Linc bowed. "Miss Jackson, Miss Bonnie LaRoux, a lady of the stage."

"Oh, you're the scandalous redhead! Delighted, I'm sure." The actress touched gloved hands with Cecilia, then turned to Linc. "I've gotten a part in that new play opening at the Alhambra. I start tomorrow. Two weeks of rehearsal. Then you must come and see me."

"Wonderful. What play?" Linc inquired.

"Oh, it's the classic, *She Stoops to Conquer.* The producer wanted a touch of class, attract the upper crust—who wouldn't know a classic if it bit...."

* * * * *

Cecy felt her spirits lift as the five of them strolled together, greeting other strollers. No one lifted a nose at her or behaved as though she weren't there. Quite the opposite, they all appeared thrilled to meet her and laughed about her scandal. Many also made slighting comments about Victor Hunt. Being in the company of those who mocked scandal shocked her at first, but gave her a new freedom. Who would have dreamed Linc had friends like these? She needed to know him better.

McEwen cocked a bushy eyebrow at her. "You sing, don't you?"

Cecy nodded with a smile.

Miss LaRoux exclaimed, "What do you sing, my dear?"

"Opera," Cecy replied shyly.

"Divine! Caruso is coming in April! I can't wait to hear him!"

A prickly thorn of regret pierced her. She'd planned to fete Caruso during his visit. But not now.

The five of them ended up at Delmonico's for an early steak dinner. Both exhilarated and uncertain, Cecy glanced around the circle of people surrounding her. She wondered at the contrast of this gathering to the rigid social strictures she'd lived within all her life. She began to relax. Daringly, she ordered champagne for everyone—in spite of Linc's frown. He toasted her, but she noted his glass remained unsipped.

The champagne bubbles tickled her nose and she giggled. The electric lights and gilded rococo mirrors dazzled her eyes. The tart, witty conversation ebbed and flowed around her. The words weren't important. Being a part of a group again was.

After her third glass of champagne, the actress eyed Cecy. "So how wealthy are you, dear?"

Cecy nearly choked on her mouthful of steak. No one had ever asked her that question before. But the worst part of it was, she didn't know the answer! Her mother's advice came back to her. Yes, she would talk to her business advisor and find out her financial worth. Something this basic, she should know.

"Bad taste, LaRoux." Bierce shook his head. "The oppressed never ask the oppressor how much she has in the bank—especially at dinner and before the check's been paid. Bad form."

Cecy looked around warily. What were they talking about? Who was an oppressor? Had she offended them in some way?

"They are both just showing their lack of breeding," McEwen apologized. "Socialism is the topic of the day."

"Socialism?" Cecy looked to Linc for guidance.

Linc grimaced. "Karl Marx, a German—"

"According to Marx," Bierce supplied, "each man should put in what he is able and take out what he needs."

"Which sounds good, but isn't very realistic." Linc rested his elbows on the white damask tablecloth.

"Why, Lincoln?" the actress asked as Bierce lit the cigarette she held in a long ivory holder.

"Because," Linc replied with a sardonic twist, "the poor can be just as greedy as the rich. Being poor is no virtue."

"But isn't your rag intended to do exposés?" McEwen demanded.

Linc picked up his glass and stared through the pale amber champagne. "Yes, you see, the poor can read all about the rich in every evening newspaper. But the rich know nothing of the poor."

"Oh, let's talk about something amusing." Miss LaRoux waved her boa gaily. "The poor are a bore."

After the flamed dessert, Linc stood up. "I'll get the check this time, but Miss Jackson and I have to be leaving."

"The night's young," Bierce objected.

"Miss Jackson is expected home." Linc pulled back Cecilia's chair.

Flushed warm, Cecy looked up. "Must we?"

Linc offered her his hand. "Your mother is waiting up for you."

She rose then and felt a little wobbly. "I enjoyed meeting you all so much. You must come for dinner at my home sometime."

"Of course, dear," Miss LaRoux replied. "You just let us know. We'd love to hobnob on Nob Hill."

McEwen nodded. "We will wear our best bib and tucker for the occasion."

Bierce rose and kissed Cecilia's hand. "You'll find you have much more fun as the scandalous redhead. You'll see." He winked.

Linc drew her away. She waved goodbye. Outside, he flagged down a hack and helped her in. The evening mist floated on the night breeze, a promise of rain.

Sighing, Cecilia leaned her head back. "What exciting people."

"I'm glad you enjoyed yourself. I wanted you to see that there are many kinds of people in the city." Linc's arms steadied her on the bumpy ride home.

"I knew that. I just didn't know they'd be so much fun."

"They are fun—this early in the evening," he cautioned her.

"I don't know what you mean."

"I know you don't. There's a lot of life that you haven't seen. That's my point."

Cecy couldn't make sense of his answer, but she felt lighter than air, like the bubbles in the champagne she'd sipped throughout the meal.

✷ ✷ ✷ ✷ ✷

Soon the hack let them down at Cecilia's home. She was giggling to herself and Linc tried to keep her quiet knowing that gossips were probably at their windows listening. Before they even reached the top step, the butler opened the door. Linc almost picked Cecilia up as he hurried her into the house.

Just inside the door, she burst into laughter. "My shoe. I lost my shoe. I'm Cinderella!"

The butler scurried back outside and, within seconds, returned holding the shoe. Linc bent to slip it onto Cecilia's foot, then he rose and took her arm, bracing her.

"How did that shoe get off my foot?" Cecilia trilled. "Oh, I lost two shoe buttons. When did that happen?"

"Cecilia?" Her mother, dressed in a lavender flannel wrapper, stood at the top of the curved staircase.

Cecilia straightened and looked up. "Mother?"

"I was worried, dear. I couldn't go to sleep. You said you'd be back much earlier."

"I'm sorry, Mother." With Linc holding her shoulders, Cecilia clung to the post at the base of the balustrade. "We had dinner with friends."

"That's nice," her mother said doubtfully. Her sad expression touched Linc's heart.

The nurse came up quietly behind the lady and touched her arm.

"Well," her mother began, "as long as you're—"

Breaking from Linc's hold, Cecilia stepped forward and tripped somehow. She gave a trill of a giggle.

Linc caught her before she fell. But when he looked up, he glimpsed Cecilia's mother's white, stricken face.

✾ ✾ ✾ ✾ ✾

March 17, 1906

With Del in the middle, Linc sat in the front seat beside Cecilia who controlled the tiller of her electric runabout, motoring them to the *Bulletin* office. Inquiring at the employment agencies hadn't paid off, so Linc had told her she needed to place a classified ad to locate her old nurse, Millie Anderson.

As they drove past trees, budding white along the street, he fought himself from gazing at Cecilia's lovely profile. More and more, Cecilia glided in and out of his thoughts. Her rich brown-sugar eyes, that little mole beside her upper lip.... Now her auburn hair glowed against the azure sky.

He nearly cursed.

"Is this the turn?" She grinned at him with a saucy glint in her eye.

He nodded. "You're in a good mood."

"I am." She grinned again. "Mr. Bierce called me. He's such an amusing man."

"I've heard that." A needle of jealousy poked Linc.

She giggled. "Anyway we started talking about the operetta opening next week."

"What about it?"

"We're going to get up a theater party for it. Would you like to come along?"

"I'll consult my extensive social calendar," he replied dryly. He wanted to help Cecilia establish herself as a writer, if possible, help her reconcile with her mother, and put her in touch with God. All these didn't include theater parties or his kissing her.

"Bierce said the hero and heroine in *The Mikado* are Nanki Po and Yum-Yum." She giggled again.

"You haven't seen *The Mikado*"?

"No, but it sounds like such fun!"

Linc's mood lowered. During the past two weeks, Cecilia's depression had worried him. Now her giggling concerned him more. He thought she'd be interested and cheered by a glimpse of bohemian life, not fascinated by it. Had he led this young beauty, already so dear to him, into the path of temptation? *Dear God, no.*

He opened his mouth to voice a warning. He shut it.

All last night he'd poured his heart out, begging God to take away his attraction to this lovely young woman. But his grief over losing Virginia kept intruding—separating him from God. Linc knew that nothing in this world or the next could truly separate him from God—unless Linc himself held back from God. And he had held back from God ever since Virginia's funeral. The same, old empty feeling inundated him.

Cecilia interrupted his thoughts. "I can't wait to go out again and have fun."

"I understand." He did. A young, vibrant woman needed to be out having fun. On the other hand, he was a widower with a child, or more exactly, children to raise. Very aware of the sullen child sitting beside him, Linc knew Del needed him now more than Meg. Taking the children out of school hadn't helped at all. In his misery, Del had shut out Linc and Susan, even Meg. *God, what can I do to get through to him?*

Cecilia parked her car in front of the newspaper office. They got out and went in together.

Linc escorted her to the Classifieds Desk. "I'll leave you here. I want to talk to Fremont Older." Maybe a chat with the crusty editor would help him see things more clearly. Over the weeks working together on society articles for the Bulletin, an unlikely friendship had sprung up between Older and him. He now trusted Older with confidences and asked for advice from the editor who knew everything about San Francisco or so it seemed. With a hand on Del's shoulder, Linc guided the boy to Older's office. Linc leaned in at the door. "Got a minute?"

"Sure. Come on in." Older said a few more words into the phone, then hung up. "Haven't seen you for a while. How's the heiress?"

Linc sat down and gave a half-grin. "Please don't beat around the bush." He pulled Del close to his side. The boy glanced at Older, then stared at his feet.

"Hear she's been staying at your house. What's that all about?"

"She's back home now. Miss Jackson's mother is living with her."

Older looked shocked. "Her mother came home?"

Linc nodded. "Miss Jackson persuaded her."

"What happened to your Miss Jackson? Did the papers tell the truth?" Older leaned back thoughtfully.

"Everything happened to her. But the papers didn't get much right."

"Remember—I told you that Hunt was a nasty piece of work."

"I believe you. What I can't believe is that this city is choosing Hunt over an innocent young woman—"

"San Francisco takes care of its own. Did you hear Clarissa Bower and Hunt eloped?"

Linc nodded mournfully. He patted Del's shoulder affectionately. The boy stiffened in response.

Older barked a dry laugh. "How much do you want to bet there'll be an early baby soon?"

The same thought had occurred to him, but Linc shook his head and frowned, indicating he didn't want such conversation in front of Del.

"And who is this young fellow you have with you?" Older nodded toward Del.

"This is Del, my housekeeper's grandson." He felt the same twinge he always felt when he couldn't speak the plain facts about his true relationship to Susan and Del. But rarely did anyone understand even after detailed explanation. Susan never even tried to explain.

Older stared at Del. "Need a job, son? I could use another messenger boy. It's a good job, days only."

Del looked up with a startled expression.

"No thanks," Linc replied. "Del has school work to do."

"He can read a little, can't he? Count to a hundred? What else does he need?" Older asked briskly.

Linc hated this popular attitude. He bristled inside. "Del's father and grandfather were both professors at Howard University in D.C. I expect him to follow in their distinguished footsteps." Linc had hoped visiting a large newspaper office might catch Del's interest, not bring up again the whole matter of how the world looked down at him. He gripped Del's shoulder reassuringly.

"You don't say?" Older glanced curiously at Del. "Now when is that rag of yours going to get off the ground?"

"I'm working on the first issue now." Linc wished he knew what Del was thinking. Maybe it had been a mistake to bring him here. "I plan to get the first issue out in late March."

"Good. I've been curious to see this muckraking journal. Still focusing on children?"

"Yes, but I followed your suggestion and talked with the fire chief, Sullivan. After that tremor, I wanted to know what he'd do about the fires which would be sure to follow any major earthquake."

"You'll get used to the tremors." Older dismissed his concern. "And I warned you, the public won't thank you for stirring up that subject. They don't want to know—"

"Well, I want to know," Linc insisted. Remembered images of leaping flames—roaring, crackling—froze Linc inside.

Linc made himself relax. "At eight years old, I survived the Great Chicago Fire."

"Oh! There'll be a hot time in the old town tonight," Older recited the old lyrics.

Linc hated that song, so he merely nodded. "I've moved here with my family. I don't want my eight-year-old daughter going through something like I did." *God, keep her safe.*

Older eyed him.

Older considered this with a grim expression. "Glad you went ahead and did that interview. I've wanted to do it myself, but the suits upstairs said no—bad for circulation. But this might shake people up—especially our do-nothing, prettyboy Mayor...."

※ ※ ※ ※ ※

March 19, 1906

Early morning darkness still held its sway over California. Along the coast road, Linc drove by the glow of feeble headlights and a full moon. Cecilia napped beside him. He followed the uneven dirt road toward a huddle of waterfront buildings. Moonlight shone on the waves slapping the rocky shore.

The scene was anything but idyllic. Crude shanties, dilapidated storefronts—weathered and splintered from salt spray—hugged both sides of the road. The stench of fish and saltwater hung in the air.

He recognized the cannery he'd visited before and parked in front. A lone dog barked in the pre-dawn stillness. Linc folded up his collar against the damp chill before dawn. This was the day God had called him to San Francisco, the day he'd planned for, worked for. For this morning—he'd left Chicago, made himself accepted in San Francisco society to meet Miss Cecilia Jackson. Today he would finally put her to the test. He'd measure the true size of her heart and the mettle of her spirit. In spite of himself, he yawned. He couldn't hurry the dawn. *Dear Lord, bless my labor this day.* Making up for lost sleep, he closed his eyes and dozed.

✳ ✳ ✳ ✳ ✳

A keening, screeching whistle woke Cecy. She sat up in Linc's front seat. What was it? Bleak kerosene lights flickered in a string of buildings. The maddening whistle continued. The rank odor of rotten fish hit and, half awake, Cecy gagged. "Are we there?" she demanded, raising her voice.

Linc sat up beside her. "Across the Bay," he shouted back. "This is the cannery." He pointed to the building in front of them. He helped her out and they entered the drafty warehouse-like factory, open on one side to the sea. The whistle broke off.

But Linc spoke close to her ear. "Remember. I'm here to do research for an article, maybe a book. But it will be impossible for us to write anything down. Just keep your eyes and ears open and remember what you take in."

Stopping them, a tall, cadaverously thin man in a canvas slicker loomed over them. "You two ain't here to work the catch. Who are you?"

"I'm Linc Wagstaff and this is my assistant." He offered his hand. They shook. "I have permission from your boss, Mr. Boynton, to observe how a cannery works. Are you the foreman?"

"Yeah, but what-'cha want to know what we do here for?" The man spat tobacco out of the side of his mouth.

"Maybe I'll write an article in the paper or a book about it," Linc answered blandly.

The man rubbed his stubbled chin. "Ya don't say? You're sure you talked to Mr. Boynton?"

Linc nodded.

The man considered this a moment. "OK, just don't get in the way. We got a sardine catch to work."

"Don't worry. On an article like this, I usually work along with everyone so I can get a feel for the job."

Cecy couldn't make sense of what Linc was saying. People, no doubt from the shacks around the cannery, had begun streaming in. The fish stench made Cecy's stomach roil dangerously.

"Won't-cha get your good clothes dirty?" The man objected dryly.

Linc shrugged. "These are my work clothes."

"Swells, huh?" He tossed Linc a long dirty, oil-cloth apron. "Wear that. It'll help a little. Follow me."

Linc shrugged on the apron and hurried after the foreman.

Cecy struggled with her revulsion. Intending to escape to the safety of the Pierce Arrow outside, she opened her mouth to shout, 'I'm going to the car.' But a dreadful rumbling, groaning came from the seaside opening.

Frightened by the din, she hurried ahead to keep close to Linc. Visiting a cannery had sounded so inoffensive. Now inside the cannery, the reality hit her from all sides—the horrific noise, the filth-encrusted walls, the grinding of crushed shells and debris under her feet, the wretched stink of it all.

Catching up with Linc, she snagged his sleeve. She tried to be heard over the noise, but failed.

He shook his head, then followed a motion from the foreman toward the sardine boat unloading its catch. Linc hovered beside the foreman.

Cecy hung back, standing by a beam, watching the fishermen on the boat deck scramble to send the silvery run of wiggling sardines down a huge funnel into a kind of small boxcar. As each was loaded, men appeared and trundled the wheeled cars farther back into the cannery. The building had been empty only moments before. Now ragged men, women, and children teemed everywhere around her.

She turned her head to watch the contents of the cars being dumped onto long, metal tables. Instantly, swarthy unkempt men and gaunt women and children—who stood on rickety crates—pulled out short, fine knives and began slitting the small fish and flinging fish entrails to the floor.

At the sight, Cecy retched and retched, but thankfully her stomach was empty. Finally, she closed her eyes and leaned back against the beam, fighting for control. She would have fainted, but the thought of touching the filthy floor made her fight for consciousness.

Something tugged her skirt. What? Her eyes flew open. She glanced down.

A small, wailing child, still in baby skirts—grimy ones—clung to the fold of her dress. The child held up its arms. Cecy looked around desperately for a mother seeking a child. No mother looked up from the work of gutting sardines.

Confused, she frowned down at the toddler. What was a baby doing in this awful place? And the baby was barefoot! She snatched the child off the filthy floor. *That can't be healthy.*

She carried the baby over to the nearest table. She leaned close to one of the women. A slimy blot of fish insides landed on Cecy's cheek. She exclaimed, flicking it off.

Then another separate collection of horrific noises—rattling, rumbling, squeaking—descended from the floor above. Cecy couldn't make herself heard above the din. The women at the table all motioned her back toward the middle of the room.

Queasy, she put the child on her hip and picked her way through the crowded room—filled with tables and frantically laboring men, women and children. In the center of the room, a stove had been stoked and feeble warmth hung around it. Boxes had been set around the stove—away from the chill seaside drafts.

She glanced down into the boxes. Babies! Babies wrapped in tattered blankets slept in the boxes. A dilapidated carriage stood to one side. It held two babies. A lone wooden chair sat by the stove. Had they just dumped their babies here? With no one to care for them? How dreadful, sad. Bewildered, Cecy sank gratefully onto the rickety chair.

Within seconds, more sleepy, shoeless toddlers in soiled dresses crowded around her. Each grabbing a piece of her skirt, they clung to her, leaning against her, knuckling sleep-crusted eyes. Some crying; some somber.

Poor babies. Abandoned. Deserted. Her heart was wrung. She clumsily patted a dark-haired child whose tears ran down dirt-lined cheeks. "There, there," she murmured into the surrounding maelstrom. The child looked up at her solemnly and used her dress to wipe its eyes and nose.

A warm wetness oozed over her lap and down her legs. The toddler sitting on her had no diaper. *Oh, no.* She closed her eyes in resignation. Surrounded, she couldn't move without disturbing, distressing the little innocents further. She felt their loneliness, abandonment. Their eyes pleaded, 'Why doesn't my mother hold me? I need her.' She stroked another small, downy head. *Poor little ones.*

They couldn't understand why they'd been yanked from warm beds and brought into this horrifying, noisy, and filthy place. She still longed to escape this repulsive cannery, but she couldn't leave these little innocents here—like she had been deserted in Boston—left to cry all alone.

※ ※ ※ ※ ※

Linc found Cecilia still sitting by the cannery stove. Her hair had come loose. She had fish guts smeared down one cheek and dirty fingerprints on the other. Her white collar was grimy. She smelled of sardines or, at least, she must. He did. In her arms, she held a swaddled, newborn Oriental baby. She'd never looked more lovely to him.

"Cecilia."

She glanced sideways to him. "Linc," she said the word with what sounded like heartfelt relief.

"Are you ready to go now?"

She glanced around. "All the other babies have been taken home, but I still have this one."

A short Chinese couple stopped beside them. They both bowed. The woman bowed again as she lifted the baby from Cecy and said something in Chinese.

The husband translated, "Wife say thank you hold baby. Our first son. One week old."

"Congratulations." Linc shook the man's hand, then pulled a dollar from his pocket. "This is for the baby." The couple smiled and bowed and smiled again. Then they turned and straggled out with the last of the gutting crew.

Noise still rattled and groaned above them.

"We've been here forever." Cecilia stood up stiffly and stretched.

"Eleven hours. It's 4 P.M."

"I said forever. Take me home now!" Her hair slid completely down to her shoulder. She leaned on his arm.

"I'm exhausted too." He led her outside into the sunshine.

167

Cecilia paused beside his auto.

"What's wrong?" He held the door open for her.

"I'm too dirty to sit in your car." She looked down at herself. "I'm filthy." She started to cry in little gasps. "Why did you bring me to this awful place?"

He stared into her eyes. "Have you ever been filthy before?"

She gave him a startled and disgruntled look. "What has that go to do with anything?"

"Everything. Answer me. Have you ever been filthy?"

"No! I've never even been mussed before in my life. I wasn't allowed."

"Exactly. You've never been filthy. How could I make you understand what it means to be filthy if you'd never even been mussed before? They . . . " He motioned around him. "They live in it—filth. Did you imagine a cannery being anything like this? How did it make you feel?"

"No, I imagined men doing something with fish—"

He pressed her. "Not the children, not the babies—"

"No!" Gazing intently at her surroundings in the daylight, she turned around in a complete circle. Her voice came out harsh, accusing, "I'll tell you how it made me feel. I thought I had a reason to hate society, but I didn't know the half of it."

Free to voice his passion at last, Linc gripped her shoulders. "That's why I must write. God has called me to go into this wilderness, to shout for justice, to lift up the helpless. This is what I came to San Francisco to do. People must know this, understand this. It's bad enough for the men and even the women—but what about the children, the babies? Do you see?"

She nodded solemnly and gazed into his eyes. "I'd like to meet the man who owns this cannery. I'd like to tell him *just* what I think of him."

CHAPTER 11

"The righteous care about justice for the poor...."
Proverbs 29:7a, NIV

March 24, 1906   Cᴇᴄʏ ʜᴀᴅ ᴅʀᴇssᴇᴅ ᴡɪᴛʜ ᴄᴀʀᴇ in one of her new "journalist" outfits, a severe, brown, gabardine suit with an ivory cotton blouse. No ribbon, no lace, no ruffles. Prepared for business, she sat beside the imposing oak desk in her father's office, a room she had previously avoided, awaiting Mr. Edmonds, her business adviser.

She had called his office every day for three days. He'd finally returned her third call. She hadn't been able to get Miss LaRoux's question out of her mind. How rich was she? Edmond's reluctance to answer her calls worried her too. Why would he avoid her?

She also wanted to ask him to find out who owned sardine canneries, especially those across the Bay. Her visit there still haunted her. She intended to confront that heartless factory owner, definitely an oppressor. If he didn't change the conditions there, especially for the women and children, she would write what she had seen there in Linc's journal and name names. For the first time in her life, she found herself passionately concerned about something beside music. Linc had seen that sleeping passion inside her and had given her a way to let it out. Linc....

Her butler opened the massive door to the formidable office. "Miss Jackson, your business adviser."

Mr. Edmonds marched in, all business, in a starched white shirt and black suit. "Well, Miss Cecilia, what's this all about? I'm a busy man." He used the tone he would have used if she had been a small child.

She bit back an epithet to that effect. Instead, she smiled coolly.

He looked around.

Was he looking for a chair? But she hadn't asked him to sit. The footmen had removed the other chairs—at her request. She smiled benignly and kept him standing, reminding him he worked for her, not she for him.

"I need to know the extent of my wealth." She folded her hands.

"Why would you need to know that?" He bristled like his stiff, broom-like mustache. "Your father left you and your mother enough money to make you secure for the rest of your lives. That's all you need to know. Business is too heavy a subject for a woman. It will only confuse you."

"But it's my business." She waited, serenely composed like Queen Victoria in her photographs.

"Your father—"

"My father is dead. My mother is ill. The business is my responsibility now." She watched him struggle with himself.

"You're worth about twenty-three million." He tamped down his salt and pepper mustache, showing his aggravation with her.

That much! "Cash?"

He laughed dryly. "Of course not. You have about eight million liquid, that means in cash. The rest is invested in stocks, real estate, and businesses. Is that all you wanted to know?" He gave the impression that he was about to leave.

Cecy raised one hand. "For now. I want a detailed list of my holdings, stocks, etc., and where all my cash is kept, the banks, you know."

Above his stiff white collar, a red flush crawled up his neck. "A detailed list? Whatever for?"

"My mother has encouraged me to become more interested in our finances."

"Your mother knows nothing about business, nothing! Everything is taken care of!" he blustered. "You don't need to get your nose into my business—"

"I think I reminded you once that it is my business." She tilted her head in a haughty way, worthy of her Aunt Amelia.

"Your mother is the primary heir. If she is concerned—"

"I told you she is the one who has prompted this interview. Now why are you behaving as though you don't want to give me information about my own finances?" She gave him a narrow look.

"I have nothing to hide." The red flush completely suffused his bulbous face now. "In his will, your father entrusted everything to my management."

"And I don't intend to change that unless I'm forced to." She paused significantly. Edmonds should have guessed her father's recommendation certainly didn't count favorably with her. "Now when may I expect to receive a complete accounting from you?" She smiled with exaggerated sweetness.

"It will take some time for me to draw up a complete list for you," he said stiffly at last.

She considered him with a long silence. "Would a week be enough time?"

"I could have a cursory list by next Monday."

"That will be fine for a start. Oh, another matter, would you look into who owns sardine canneries north of Monterey?"

"Canneries?" He looked as though he were about to ask her why, then changed his mind. "If you wish."

She nodded regally. "Until Monday then."

Looking like a volcano about to erupt, he bowed and left with haste.

She smiled at his retreating form. *I did it. I am taking charge of my life.*

She stood up, feeling better than she had in days. The visit to the cannery had left her feeling deeply soiled. She'd come home and stripped off her clothing, told her maid to burn them; then she'd scrubbed herself clean with a brush.

Now she felt upright, powerful, energized in a new way. Thinking about finances had not been a part of her life before. In fact, she realized she'd been living in a foggy dream in many ways. Now she thought she saw rays of light piercing the darkness in her life. She hoped Millie Anderson would come forward soon and she could, at last, have the answers about the past.

She had to go to Linc, tell him. He'd understand.

Stepping out of her office, Cecy met her mother.

"Cecilia, what did Edmonds say?"

She patted her mother's arm, then stroked the silky kitten her mother carried everywhere over her arm. "Everything's fine. He will bring me a detailed listing of my assets by next Monday. He says we have over eight million in cash."

"Good. Good." Her mother stared at Cecy as though wishing to speak further.

Though distracted, Cecy waited, hoping for something more than polite concern from her mother.

The nurse, a few steps behind, cleared her throat and made a motion to direct her mother on.

"Nurse," Cecy said, "would you please wait at the top of the stairs?"

The woman nodded and moved away.

"Mother," Cecy lowered her voice, "is there any specific concern you have about our finances that I should know about?" She watched the lady closely.

For once, her mother didn't look away when asked a direct question. "Cecilia, money is power and…freedom. Men know that. That's why they keep it from us. Never forget that."

The words nearly brought tears to Cecy's eyes. It was the very first real exchange of ideas she'd heard her mother initiate. "I won't forget. I'm going to see Linc now."

Her mother's face brightened. "Please give Susan and little Meg my regards. Invite them to come for tea again soon."

"I will." Cecy felt heartened by her mother's cheerier expression. For the past few days, the lady had seemed depressed again.

Her mother looked into her eyes. "Have you had any answer to your advertisement about Millie Anderson?"

"Not yet. But Linc says I should keep it running. These things often take time."

Her mother stroked the gray-striped cat. "Very true." The kitten began purring. "You'll be home this evening, won't you?"

"No, I've made arrangements to attend *The Mikado* with friends, then we'll go out to dinner."

Instantly, a shadow of concern clouded her mother's face.

"Linc will be my escort. Don't worry." Cecy smiled.

"Of course." The lady turned to join the nurse. "Just remember a lady must guard her reputation jealously."

Cecy gasped silently with a phantom pain. "Don't worry about me, Mother." But she'd already lost her reputation, thanks to Hunt. Everyone had agreed to protect her mother by remaining silent about the scandal.

✳ ✳ ✳ ✳ ✳

"Miss Cecilia!" Meg opened the red front door and grinned broadly.

"Hello, Meg." Cecy stepped inside, warmed by the child's welcome. "How are you?"

"Fine." But Meg frowned and twisted one of her red-ribboned braids around her finger. "Del left without asking Aunt Susan or Papa's permission first."

Cecy paused and smoothed the girl's soft wisps of stray hair back from her face. "Is that so?"

"Can you play doll house with me?" Meg looked up expectantly.

"Good day, Miss Jackson." Susan had walked up behind Meg. "But I'm sorry Meg can't play now. Maybe later."

The little girl's expression crumbled with disappointment.

Cecy looked to Susan pleadingly. "Not even for a little while?"

Though smiling kindly, Susan shook her head. "No, I'm sorry, but Meg can't miss her study time."

"But Del's not here," Meg grumbled.

"That's Del's problem." Susan turned Meg by the shoulders toward the dining room. "Let's go get your spelling book out."

Susan walked away behind Meg.

Linc came jogging down the polished walnut staircase. "Cecilia! I'm sorry I have to go out now."

"I'll come with you." Cecy smiled her challenge. "My car's right outside."

With a click, Susan closed the pocket door behind Meg and herself.

Linc hesitated on the bottom step, resting a hand on the curved and rolled balustrade. "Cecilia, I have to go alone."

"Why?"

He shook his head firmly and approached her. "I need to drive through the Barbary Coast."

"Why there?"

Linc gave the deepest frown she'd ever seen on his face. He lifted his driving coat from the mirrored hall tree. "I got a call from Fremont Older. He said he thought he saw Del there."

"Del, at the Barbary Coast? It doesn't make sense."

"I don't understand myself." He opened the door to show her out. "I don't have time—"

"My auto is in your drive already. In fact, I've got you blocked in. I'm driving." She marched out to her shiny green car and let herself into the driver seat. The pink azaleas along the side of the house reflected her flush of victory. She smiled brightly at him. "Shall we go?"

"I can't let you drive to the Barbary Coast—even in the afternoon. Your reputation—"

"Is quite ruined already. I'm no longer the very proper Miss Jackson, remember? You're the one who drove me to a cannery. Now I'll drive you to the Barbary Coast." She positioned her driving goggles over her eyes. "If you don't let me, I'll just follow you there."

He put his hands on his hips, flaring his drab driving coat on both sides of him. Setting his driving hat on his head, he got in beside her. "Have it your way. I haven't time to argue with you. *Anything* could happen to Del down there."

Triumphantly, she let down her veil over her goggles, then switched on the starter. She backed the car into the street. They chugged down the hill, headed nearer the waterfront—straight for the notorious Barbary Coast.

A rush of forbidden excitement coursed through Cecy. Whispered phrases about Mickey Finns, Shanghaied sailors, opium dens, and ladies of easy virtue flitted through her mind. Tonight, when she met Bierce and the others, she'd have a tale to tell them. *She* had driven through the Barbary Coast!

The Barbary Coast was a dreadful disappointment. Just a lot of derelict buildings, scruffy-looking men with black hats pulled low over their eyes and slatternly women in bright garish dresses of magenta, crimson, purple, dreadfully cheap. Sneaky-looking mongrels slunk out of muddy alleyways. Seagulls squawked overhead. She turned to Linc. "I don't understand it. This isn't the sort of place I would think of Del wanting to be."

Linc looked grim, uneasy. "I agree. But Del...has been deeply confused, troubled since we moved to California."

I have been too. The forlorn thought echoed through her. "Oh?"

Linc looked at her as though testing her. "He can't understand why his color makes him count for less in the eyes of the world."

Cecy didn't flinch from his intense gaze. "You have to admit your household is different than most."

"I know, but my father was an ardent abolitionist. My mother a—"

"A woman who made Susan a partner in her boarding house, not a hired girl."

He raised an eyebrow at her. "You remembered that?"

She shrugged. "I don't understand it—"

"Don't you?"

"Susan is one of the sweetest women I've ever known. But—" She glimpsed Del. She stomped on the brake pedal. "Del!"

A large group of black boys in seeming consultation milled around at the head of a dark alleyway. Del stood at the center of the cluster.

Linc leaped out of the car. "Del! Del!"

The boys ran away headlong into the shadows.

His coat flaring behind him, Linc chased after them.

Cecy hit the accelerator and sped around the corner trying to head them off at the other end of the alley. She raced down the sorry-looking block. Ahead of her, the first boy in tattered denim overalls broke out of the alley. She pressed the pedal to the floor and surged forward to cut off the runaways. They yowled in shock. A couple couldn't stop and thudded against her car door.

Linc sprinted ahead and grabbed Del by the shoulder. Without a word, he yanked Del to the car, unceremoniously prodded him in next to Cecy, then got in himself. "Take us home, Cecilia."

"Hey! You can't grab him!" Some of the boys shouted, "Hey!" A few boys threw stones at the car.

Cecy spurted away. She couldn't make sense of what was happening. Why would Del, a boy so loved and protected, want to run away to be in the company of young toughs?

"I don't want to go home," Del blustered, almost in tears, pushing against Linc.

Linc stiffened and pressed Del back into the seat. "You're going home to your studies—"

"You can drag me home, but you can't make me study."

Cecy tried to soothe the boy. "Del, you're worrying your grandmother. Why are you doing this?"

The boy wrapped his arms around himself and stared at his feet.

"Answer us!" Linc demanded.

But the sulky boy refused to look up or speak. Cecy waited to see how Linc would handle Del. She waited in vain.

While she drove them home, Linc sat, as silent and gloomy as Del. She had barely stopped at their side door when Del vaulted over the seat and darted down the drive.

Linc jumped out of the car. "Del! Del!"

Cecy got out of the car, then halted. She watched Del disappear from sight. "Shall we go after him?"

Linc didn't move. "I don't know what to do." He raised his voice slightly and looked skyward. "God, I don't know what to do. He's so gifted musically. So much potential wasted.... What can I do? My love, even Susan's love, isn't enough. You will have to make the difference."

He stood there as though he actually expected to receive an answer. Discomfited, Cecy didn't know where to look, what to do.

"Cecilia."

She eyed him warily.

"You're still set on going to the operetta tonight?" He looked and sounded grim.

She nodded. She could understand his not being in the mood for gaiety. "I can go without you—"

"No. Sitting home worrying all night won't help. I've done all I can do. I'll pick you up about seven tonight."

"Fine." She got back into the car and drove away. Confused. Wondering.

❋ ❋ ❋ ❋ ❋

Gripped by powerlessness, Linc stood a long time in the empty drive, dead-sure Del was on his way back to the Barbary Coast. The same helplessness he'd felt when Virginia died filled him. Del was his responsibility. He'd failed him, just as he'd failed Virginia. He knew that wasn't true. He hadn't failed his wife. Why couldn't he rid himself of this irrational guilt? "God," he whispered, "I can't see my way. Help me."

❋ ❋ ❋ ❋ ❋

March 25, 1906

Cecy smiled and smiled. Her smile began to pinch at the corners of her mouth. In the darkened Tivoli Opera House, around her sat Linc, Miss LaRoux, Bierce and McEwen. The operetta, *The Mikado* had made everyone else laugh uproariously, but she had merely crimped up the corners of her mouth. Inside herself, she saw flashes of *Madame Butterfly* from the night at the Grand Opera House where she'd experienced that first earth tremor. Perhaps she didn't laugh because her life resembled the tragic opera more than Gilbert and Sullivan's light operetta about Nanki-Poo and Yum Yum.

The cast came out and bowed. The audience applauded enthusiastically. Cecy forced herself to clap and clap. Finally, the maroon velvet curtains swung closed; its gold tassels swaying. She nearly sighed aloud with relief. Now they'd leave the confining theater, escape her unaccountable low spirits. What was wrong with her?

The house lights came up. Linc glanced at her.

"I'm ravenous," Cecy said with counterfeit gaiety. "How about you?"

He took her arm. "You said you'd made a reservation at the Palace restaurant?"

She nodded. As the others got themselves together, he helped Cecy on with her amber velvet opera cape.

Outside, she wanted to ask him about Del, but Miss LaRoux, McEwen, and Bierce occupied the rear seat of the Pierce Arrow. The chic Palm Garden Restaurant at the grand Palace Hotel, just down from the San Francisco *Examiner* building was the crown jewel of downtown. They left the car to the valet in the famed Palace Great Court. Overhead, a glass dome and six-tiered stories opened onto the palmed court. She couldn't take her eyes from the magnificent sight.

Anticipating her role as hostess, she'd arranged a fantastic after-theater supper for her party—Consommé Royal, Salmon glace au four a la Chambord, Filet de Boeuf ala Provence, Pate de fois Gras, Cotelettes d'Agneau sauté au pointes d'Asperges, Sorbet, Salad al a Francaise, and for dessert, Napoleons. Bierce, Miss LaRoux, McEwen, Linc, and she had just sat down when the last of the party arrived.

The blonde ingenue rushed in, breathless from her performance at another theater. Miss LaRoux, who'd invited the lady to "even up" the numbers, performed the introductions. "Friends, this is Miss Effie Bond who's playing little Sarah Crewe in 'The Little Princess.' "

"Impossible," Bierce announced. "A lovely young lady like you can't possibly be playing a little girl."

Effie bowed her waved, golden head humbly. "It's all in the way I present myself, Mr. Bierce. We just had a great run with it at the Belasco in Los Angeles. Now bring on the wine. I'm parched."

Linc nodded to the head waiter. Pink Chablis, the first of seven wines for the various courses, flowed into their glasses.

Lifting her glass, Cecy drew in the chilled, pale pink wine. Soon, its chill turned to warmth which rippled through her. When she'd attempted to scale the heights of society, she'd needed a clear head. Now as the scandalous redhead, she could go to the theater without a chaperone. She could openly let this wine make every joke sound funnier, take away the worries about her mother, and troubling memories of the sad, helpless babies at the cannery. She took another tangy swallow.

By the light of the many electric chandeliers, she admired Linc's good looks. The glow glinted on his golden hair. On any other man, his blonde hair might not have been so manly, so handsome, but it fit Linc. He was different, special. His deep blue eyes looked out on the world, seeing the truth without flinching.

He had kissed her with tempting, insistent lips.

She ran her finger around the moist rim of her wine glass, then touched her lips.

He'd held her in his arms.

How warm and safe she'd felt then.

Everyone laughed. Having not heard the joke, she looked around, then forced a chuckle to fit in. Why did Linc keep frowning at her so? He needed a glass of champagne!

✻ ✻ ✻ ✻ ✻

Linc counted the glasses of champagne Cecilia drank. When the waiter came to fill it too soon, he waved the man away. After doing this twice, the waiter held back until Cecilia demanded her glass filled. Her laughter became giddy, tipsy.

Not wanting to cause a public argument, he hid his worry with effort. His deepest fear for her might have been realized. Each sip of wine Cecilia swallowed heightened his concern over her peril. Certain families were prone to certain sins. Her mother had ended up in a sanitarium with delirium tremens. *Dear God, how can I stop this from happening to Cecilia? Give me the words.*

The evening finally ended near 2 A.M. Gripping her elbow, Linc guided Cecilia out to his Pierce Arrow in the cool night breeze. Her exaggerated gestures and missteps told the tale he didn't want to know. She was more than tipsy tonight. When she giggled and muttered to herself, his mood lowered further.

He drove her through the empty, dark streets. Worry over Del had also gnawed him the whole evening. He'd turned Del's welfare over to God, but kept the worry, the guilt, to torment himself. He railed at his own lack of faith. He couldn't let go of his guilt over losing Virginia or failing both Cecilia and Del.

Where was Del? Had he come home after Linc left for the evening? He hadn't wanted to leave, but Cecilia needed his protection as much as Del. Susan had agreed. She, too, had turned Del's welfare over to God. Could she, could Linc do better than God, she had demanded. Linc had had no answer for her. How had everything gone from bad to worse? *God, where did I go wrong? Or should I just wait on you?*

But around him, the streetlamps glowed serenely, just as they had that first night he'd attended the Ward ball, just two months ago, a lifetime ago. What more could happen to them?

Eager to be home, he parked outside Cecilia's mansion and escorted her to the door.

"Why are there so many lights on?" Looking up, Cecilia bumped into Linc.

Though he wanted to carry her away and make her listen, he merely steadied her. "Perhaps your staff decided to wait up for you."

"I told them not to. Only the butler will be waiting to let me in. Oh, no. Mother... Mother might be ill." Had she slurred her words slightly? He helped her mount the steps. The butler opened the door. The warmth from inside made her feel even more flushed.

"What is it?" Cecilia asked. "Why all the lights?"

Linc piloted her over the threshold. He blinked adjusting to the bright lights in the large foyer.

"Cecy!" A warm, female voice rang out. "Cecy, my precious!"

Cecilia looked up, startled.

Linc watched a gray-haired woman, built on generous proportions, envelop Cecilia in her arms.

Cecilia gasped, "Nana! Oh, Nana!"

CHAPTER 12

"Without faith it is impossible to please God...."
Hebrews 11:6a, NIV

CECY'S HEART LEAPED, TUMBLED and cartwheeled. "Nana, oh, Nana!" She could scarcely speak. Tears flooded her eyes. Fearing to show such raw emotion, she buried her face against Nana's ample bosom. Oh, the scent of Nana's sweet talc—which she'd never forgotten! Cecy's thoughts fled. She could only feel.

"My sweet Cecy, my precious child, sweet girl, my own dear one...." Nana's soft words, spoken only a breath away from Cecy's ear, so only Cecy could hear...fell like a dew of blessing.

Cecy couldn't reply, only weep.

Finally, Linc's voice filtered through the warm cocoon created by Nana's embracing, presence. "Cecilia, your butler says he's made a fire in the library. I think you should move where your mother can be more comfortable."

Wiping her face with her hands, Cecy looked up. "I'm sorry. Of course." But she couldn't let go of Nana. So arm in arm, they led Linc and her mother to the room. Cecy sat beside Nana on a sofa across from Linc, who settled her mother into a wing-back chair; then he sat down beside Cecy.

Cecy's tears refused to cease. Linc leaned forward and handed her his man-sized, white handkerchief. She nodded gratefully.

"I knew you'd be happy." Her mother smiled one of the few smiles Cecy had seen during their weeks together.

The smile embraced Cecy like a long-desired hug. How wonderful her mother rejoiced with her!

Linc cleared his throat. "Miss Anderson, allow me to introduce myself. I'm Cecilia's friend and employer, Lincoln Wagstaff."

"I'm so sorry," Cecy said. "You must forgive—"

Linc raised his hand to stop her. "I understand completely. Reunions can overwhelm one."

Cecy clung to Nana's hand. "Where have you been? When did you read our ad?"

"After being away nearly a month, I just returned to my room at the boarding house this evening and my landlady gave me the paper. I read it and came here immediately. Couldn't believe you remembered me after all the years."

"I had forgotten, but..." How could Cecy explain how Meg's reciting the Twenty-third Psalm had brought back the memory? How could she have forgotten Nana?

Her mother sighed happily. "I told Cecilia I'd like to see you again, Millie."

"I'm glad." Nana squeezed Cecy's hand. "I've often thought about you, prayed about you, Cecy... I suppose I should call you Miss Cecilia now—"

"No, call me Cecy." Now Cecy knew where she'd gotten her secret name for herself. The name that was so dear to her that she'd never shared it with anyone else, but she'd never remembered why. Now she understood. Nana was the only person who ever called her Cecy. Why hadn't she remembered this woman who'd loved her so? Inside, questions bombarded Cecy.

But her mother's presence stopped her from asking them. They might hurt her mother and she couldn't do that. It was obvious her mother had already borne more pain than any human should have to bear.

How could she ask questions, such personal ones about her father, her mother now? Cecy needed a private moment with her old nurse. But would Nana answer the questions or decline to stir up the dreadful past?

Nana wiped her face of tears one more time. "It's late. I know I shouldn't have kept your mother up, but—"

"But I wouldn't let her leave until you came home." Cecy's mother beamed with another full smile.

"I'm glad." Cecy said. Evidently her mother also cherished happy memories of Nana, too.

Nana edged forward on her seat. "I should be leaving."

"No!" Cecy caught her by the arm. "I want you to stay." She thought quickly. "Mother has a nurse, but she needs a companion. Will you come live with us?"

"Oh, yes!" Cecy's mother clapped like a child. "We'd love to have you here with us. Please say you will!"

Nana's smile burst over her face.

Cecy experienced joy like a crest of music—like reaching the high note of a difficult aria.

"If you really want me."

"We do." Cecy took Nana's hand again. "Can you stay tonight?"

"I must." Millie chuckled. "I stayed up too late to go home without disturbing my poor landlady."

Somehow this made them all laugh.

Linc stood up. "Then I am the one who must leave."

Cecy rose and offered him her hand. "I'll walk you to the door myself." She waved away the butler as they stepped out the library door.

When they had separated themselves far enough from the others as not to be overheard, Cecy said softly, "Linc, I..." She faltered, then plunged on, "How could I have forgotten Nana all these years? Seeing her...such memories have come to me. How? Why?"

Though they kept walking, he took her hand. "I saw how this reunion affected you. Have other memories returned also?"

She warmed at his touch, his understanding. "Mostly feelings, images. How could I have forgotten someone so important?"

He frowned. "Perhaps being separated from her was too painful for you to bear."

"I don't understand. A person can't control her own memory like that!" Cecy tightened her grip on his hand, pulling it close to her breast.

Linc slipped his arm around her shoulder. "My stepfather would disagree with you. I recall a conversation we had once about his war experiences as an army surgeon for the Union. He said often soldiers in the hospitals would totally forget the instance and circumstances of their wounding. That they couldn't bear to remember was his explanation."

As she grappled with this idea, his closeness gave her confidence. "I don't know."

They reached the entry hall. Releasing her, he picked up the black top hat and white silk scarf he'd left on the green marble-topped table in the foyer. He bent and kissed her hand. He looked up.

She lost herself in his deep blue eyes. Heat suffused her. She yearned to step closer again, slip her arms around his neck and kiss him. Breathing in his scent of warm autumn spices, she could almost feel his lips coaxing hers. But she resisted. "Good night, Linc." Her voice trembled.

CHAPTER 12

"Good night, Cecilia." He walked out the door. Cecy closed it after him. She turned to go back to Nana and mother, wondering why, how this man—out of all the others—had the power to move her. Maybe it was just the wine and her unsettled emotions tonight. But she couldn't calm her pulse or purge the remembrance of the touch of his coaxing lips against hers.

☙ ☙ ☙ ☙ ☙

March 26, 1906

Driving down the streets of the Barbary Coast in the deepening dusk, Linc gripped the steering wheel of his Pierce Arrow. Gulls screeched overhead. Del hadn't come home the night before. At the breakfast table, as Susan tried to drink her tea, her hands had shaken. Kang had burned the toast. Meg had refused to eat, burst into tears, and run to her room. And Linc knew he was the one who had to find Del. *I've lost Virginia, Father. Please don't let me lose Del too. Should I have left Susan and Del in Chicago? But Susan had insisted.*

Before leaving this morning, he'd told Susan not to expect him home for supper. He would search for Del, but it would have to wait till the Barbary Coast awoke later in the day.

Somehow, Linc had put in an excruciating day's work at his newly-furnished office. The first issue of *Cause Celebre* needed only two more written articles before he sent it for printing at the *Bulletin's* presses. Now at the end of the workday, the haunts and dance halls of the red-light district were stirring, waking for another night of sin.

Lord, help me find him. My spirit is weighed down to death over him. You know better than I what could happen to him here. Not just to his body, but to his very soul. I feel so guilty. Help me, Lord.

As he drove slowly down each alley and each narrow, dirty street, oppression pressed down on him.

Cecy's new friends deemed rubbing shoulders with the habitués of the Coast as daring fun. But they let themselves be fooled by the frantic laughter, garish colors, and the loud ragtime.

These didn't fool Linc. He heard tubercular coughing, saw the dawning of syphilitic madness in dilated eyes, the sunken sadness of those bound to opium. Sin gave pleasure for a season, but it was an exceedingly short season on the Coast.

He drove around the streets a second time, looking for the band of boys Del had been with before. No luck. He saw only a few black boys tap-dancing for pennies on the corner. But no Del.

Creeping back up the hills, he parked his car under a street light, then caught the trolley that descended back down into the Barbary Coast. Only a fool would leave a car unattended on Battery Street after dark. Clutching his walking stick, he stepped off the trolley. Night had fallen. A hint of fog puffed around him. Rats screeched down dark alleyways. Ragtime burst from the doorway of the first saloon he came to. He didn't want to go in, but he had to. The thought that Del might be in there emptying spittoons and begging for pennies, pained Linc.

The odor of stale beer and sweat hit him as he pushed through the swinging doors. Just inside, he waited for his eyes to adjust to the almost blinding light.

"Hello, handsome." A bleached-blonde saloon girl wrapped her arm in his and brushed against him suggestively. "Lonely?"

As discreetly as possible, Linc disengaged himself, then he bowed to her, doffing his hat. "Good evening, Miss," he greeted her as he would have the church organist. "Perhaps you could help me. I'm looking for someone."

The woman looked startled, then asked "Well, what's her name?"

He shook his head. "I'm looking for a young black boy, the son of my housekeeper."

"A kid?"

"Yes, he's a boy of ten years and I'm afraid he's strayed down here."

"What makes you think he's down here?" She perched one hand on her purple-draped hip.

CHAPTER 12

"A friend saw him."

She shook her head. "Gee, bad stuff can happen to kids down here."

"That's what has me worried."

"Come on back and talk to the boss. Not much gets by him." She waved for Linc to follow her to a small office at the rear. She tapped on the door.

A rough voice called for her to come in. Linc opened the door, then bowed the woman in.

"Hey, Harry, this gent's looking for his housekeeper's kid."

Harry looked up. "So? What's that got to do with me and you? Get back out there...." He finished the sentence with a vulgar reference to her purpose in his establishment.

She flushed red and turned to leave.

Linc took her hand and bowed over it. "Thank you, Miss."

"Anytime." She swished out the door.

"I ain't got any kids working for me," the man said gruffly, not taking his eyes from the figures he studied.

"Perhaps you could tell me if you have seen this lad." Linc lay a photograph of Del on the man's blotter.

With an expletive, the man snatched it up, then tossed it back to Linc. "What's the big deal about a darkie?"

"He's my responsibility." Linc waited.

The man squinted at him. "What does he do? Shine shoes? Dance? Sing? Pick pockets?"

"Of those, I would say music. He plays the piano."

"Check at the Blue Moon on the corner. They got a darkie band and dancing."

Linc bowed and left.

Del wasn't at the Blue Moon or the Last Chance or the Golden Slipper. Linc found him at Oscar's, playing jaunty rag-time with a drummer and horn player in a three-piece band. In the dim light, Linc slipped along the wall until he was adjacent to the band and sat down at a table. The syncopated music gave the cheap saloon atmosphere a cheerfulness it lacked on its own. Ordering a beer he didn't plan to drink, Linc waited, motionless, until Del glanced his way.

The boy froze, except for his fingers, which somehow kept up the beat. The drummer and horn player looked at Linc with edgy curiosity. The song ended. The drummer stood up signaling a break. Linc drew closer. Del stood up and faced Linc defiantly. "I'm not going home."

Linc observed the two men hovering protectively around Del. It reassured him.

Del glared at Linc. "Why'd you come here? I'm not—"

The drummer cuffed Del lightly, silencing him. "Okay, Mister, who are you?"

The man's touch had been light, fatherly. Linc offered the man his hand. "I'm Linc Wagstaff. I'm Del's guardian."

"I'm Long Jack and that's Short Freddie," the tall horn player interrupted indignantly. "Your boy said he was an orphan."

"He is, but his grandmother lives in my home and cares for my daughter, Meg." Linc spoke directly to Del, "Your grandmother is so worried about you she can't eat."

Del hung his head.

The drummer, Freddie, shook the boy by the shoulder. "I don't like it when people lie to me, boy. You told me you ran away from an orphanage."

Del reared his shoulder angrily. "I don't want to go home. I hate it there."

The drummer grabbed Del's shoulder and shook him again. "You're a fractious kid. That's what I see."

"Huh?" Del looked up. "How do you know that?"

Linc held back comment. What did the man mean?

Freddie bent and shook his large-knuckled, dark finger in Del's face. "If this man was mean to you, you'd be scared, not mad."

Linc smiled at the man's simple wisdom.

The drummer solemnly considered Linc. "We got to get started in a minute. Can he stay till the night's through? We need him or we don't get paid."

Linc debated with himself. "I'm in no hurry. I'd enjoy listening." He sat back down. He paid the waiter for another beer and offered the two glasses to the musicians. They nodded their thanks. A few sips and the "strutting" melody enlivened the dark saloon again.

Linc sat listening the rest of the night, watching how the two men treated Del. What should he do? He could shag Del home, but would that work? Would Del just run away again, run farther and into worse company? He'd gotten a good feeling about Freddie and Long Jack. *Oh, Lord, what am I to do with Del?* Worry, caution, responsibility circled in his mind like a dog chasing its own tail. The last note ended the evening around 3 A.M. His eyelids drooping with fatigue, Linc stood and approached the band. He spoke to the drummer. "Where's the boy staying?"

"He bunks with me and him." The drummer jerked his thumb at the horn player.

"You're keeping a close eye on him?"

Freddie nodded solemnly. The horn player, Long Jack, offered, "We could tell he been brung up strict an' proper. He don't swear."

Linc hid a grin. A sudden idea, one which shocked him and would shock Del, came to him. *Thank you, Lord.* "I think it's best the three of you came to lunch tomorrow. Del knows the way. See you about noon."

"What?" Del exclaimed.

Linc waved farewell and walked out. He hoped Susan would understand. Maybe the knowledge of where Del was and with whom would be enough to ease her mind. And maybe a few days of working for a living for strangers would teach Del more than he could in their snug home. *God, open his eyes.* A verse of prophecy echoed through his mind, "I called my son out of Egypt."

"God bless you during your stay in Egypt, Del," Linc muttered.

* * * * *

March 27, 1906

Once again her business advisor stood before Cecy in her father's office. In a prim navy suit, Cecy perused the sixteen ledger sheets he had handed her. Though she knew very little about stocks, bonds, real estate and the businesses listed in Mr. Edmond's secretary's neat handwriting, she took her time reading the entries. She reached the final page which listed the banks where her liquid assets were deposited. The second-largest sum was deposited in a Boston bank, her grandfather's bank, the grandfather she'd never met.

"Why is this large amount deposited in Boston?" Cecy showed him the page.

"That's your grandfather's bank."

"I know. That's family, not business." She took pleasure pointing that out to him.

"Your father deposited funds there when he married your mother. The investment is large, but has proved wise."

For a moment, Cecy toyed with the idea of instructing Edmonds to withdraw her funds from the bank. To do so must surely cause her grandfather trouble. Was that why her father had done so? To be able to bully her mother's father? To assume so seemed logical.

Cecy tapped the sheets together on the desktop. No, she wouldn't withdraw the millions. Linc would say it was unworthy of her and he'd be right. Her grandfather and Aunt Amelia were strictly business, not family anymore.

She looked up at Edmonds. "Did you find out about the ownership of the canneries across the Bay?"

"Yes, didn't you see them on page three?"

CHAPTER 12

Canneries were listed with her assets? No! She felt her blood drain from her head, making her feel faint. "Page three?" She shuffled through the sheaf of paper until she came to the right page.

"Yes, there toward the bottom." He leaned over and pointed to the neat notation. "You own all canneries there."

※ ※ ※ ※ ※

"Did you know?" As birds chattered in the leafy maple nearby, Cecy confronted Linc at the front door of his home. Before he could reply, she pushed past him. She came up short when she came face-to-face with Del and two black men she'd never seen before, just outside the dining room door. "Oh, you have company! Del, you came home? We've been so worried!"

Linc came up behind her. "This is our friend, Miss Jackson. Cecilia, this is Long Jack who plays the trumpet and Short Freddie, who's a drummer. Del has been playing ragtime with them."

Cecy's mouth dropped open—not only from the content of what Linc said, but mostly from his calm tone. She stared over her shoulder at him.

With his forefinger under her chin, Linc closed her mouth.

Susan stepped forward. "We were just going into lunch. Will you join us, Miss Cecilia?"

Cecy hesitated.

"I think Cecilia wants to talk with me first. Susan, why don't you and our guests go in? We'll join you in a moment." He took Cecy by the elbow into the parlor and pulled the pocket door closed behind them. "What did you want to know if I knew?"

Cecy paced the length of the room and back. "I own every cannery across the Bay."

"What?"

"I own every sardine cannery across the Bay!" Cecy threw her hands up in disgust.

"*Every* one?"

She glared at him. "Linc, you knew I owned that cannery, didn't you?"

He nodded. "But I didn't know you owned *every* one."

She hit his chest with both her palms. "Why didn't you tell me?"

He caught her hands in his. "Why?" He had a silly grin on his face. "I knew you would find out on your own."

This stopped her. "How? Why?"

"The way you said, 'I'd like to tell him just what I think of him.' I knew you'd find out who the owner was."

She stared at him. "What am I going to do, Linc? Those poor people, those children—babies." She leaned toward him, his strength drawing her irresistibly.

He rested his hands lightly on her shoulders. "What do you want to do about them?"

Where his fingers touched her she tingled. She tried to ignore the effect he was having on her and focus on the issue. She fought back, holding onto the thread of her thoughts. "How can I write about them? I'm the guilty one!"

"We're all guilty. All have sinned and fallen short—"

"Don't quote the Bible to me! I'm not in the mood." She plumped down on the sofa. "What am I to do?" She looked to him. "I can't own such a place. I couldn't live with myself."

❋ ❋ ❋ ❋ ❋

Linc rejoiced. Oh, Lord, how wonderful are your ways. Who can know your mind? I never guessed she would so quickly turn from disgust to action.

Energized, he sat down beside her. "Change takes thought, time, and work. And for you, a lot of writing. You need to decide how to change the conditions at the canneries while still making a profit."

"A profit? I'm worth millions! I don't need to worry about making a profit!"

Linc shook his head. She was so beautiful to him now—her eyes afire—her face flushed under that ridiculous driving hat and trailing white veil. "You may not need it, but your workers need the jobs which your reaping a profit makes possible. Those people want to work. They don't want charity. They need higher wages and better working conditions, not a closed cannery and hand-outs."

She stared at him, wide-eyed. "I can do that?"

"You've got millions! The canneries belong to you. You can do anything you want that's legal!" He wanted to pick her up and carry her around the room. And dance. And laugh. "My family was friends with Jane Addams in Chicago. Have you heard of her famous Hull House?"

She shook her head.

Linc felt an urge to kiss her, to let her feel the joy she'd given him. "You will and plenty more."

"I want to write about the conditions at my canneries."

"Yes!"

Her voice rose. "I can't bear it when I think of those babies and little children."

"So what would you like to do with them?" he asked, holding his breath to hear what she would say.

"They should be in their mother's or a gentle nanny's care in a clean place."

"Yes!"

She appeared to catch his enthusiasm. She grinned. "And after I've done that I'll visit all my factories and mines and make more improvements."

"Yes." Unable to stop himself, he drew her up and held her as though preparing to waltz around the room with her. "I'm at your disposal." Glancing down into her lovely face, he paused. "That is, if you want me."

She stood straighter. "I do."

"Cecilia, you're wonderful!" Impulsively, he jerked her forward, making her driving veil fly backwards and soundly kissed her.

Now that he had her firmly in his arms, he found he could not let her go. His mind leaped ahead. He saw himself loosing her hair, letting it flow down her back like burnished spun copper. Then he would brush it aside and press soft kisses into the hollow behind her ear....

Closing his eyes, he prayed for strength to stop, to let his thoughts go no further into such temptation. He released her gently.

She gazed at him, looking dazed.

"We should go into lunch," he said formally. Careful not to touch her and tempt himself again, he helped her off with her driving coat and hat. What had he been thinking? He arranged her wrap on the hall tree in the foyer, then he led her to the dining room. Pushing down his turbulent emotions, he asked calmly, "Have you heard of Booker T. Washington's Tuskegee Institute?"

She shook her head, but continued to look up at him with a questioning expression.

But his even, measured words had nothing to do with his true feelings. An awful realization rammed him hard. He could barely breathe. *Dear God, I'm falling in love with this woman.*

✴ ✴ ✴ ✴ ✴

March 28, 1906

Linc couldn't stop frowning. The same group of actresses and newsmen they'd seen *The Mikado* with had met at the theater to see Effie Bond as the little girl in "Little Princess." Now in her crowded, cluttered dressing room, they toasted her and played with a small monkey, one of the cast. Linc thought how Meg would enjoy the little fellow.

"No, no, Jocko," Effie scolded the monkey. "You must not try to eat Cecilia's boa. It isn't cricket."

CHAPTER 12

Cecy gave the chattering furry little comedian back to his owner. "I didn't know a monkey could be such fun."

"Well, some aren't." Effie slipped the monkey into a large willow basket. "Some bite, but Jocko is lovely—a born ham. Now go to sleep, Jocko. We have to do a matinee tomorrow too. So, darlings, where are we off to for supper? I'm famished!" She stepped behind a tri-fold, glossy black Chinese inlaid screen.

Cecy couldn't believe it when Effie began discarding clothing over the top of the screen. She couldn't really be undressing with them all standing around, could she? How shocking!

"Bonnie," Effie called. "Come back and help me with these buttons."

Bierce offered his help jovially and was rebuffed.

A little shocked, Cecy felt herself, little bit by little bit, beginning to become lighter, less weighed down. Champagne always lifted her spirits. The past two days had been so serious, so dark—though in a way strangely satisfying.

But tonight she could look forward to another lovely night of laughter, oysters and champagne and plenty of it. "Everyone," she announced cheerfully, "I'm officially now a journalist! Today, I finished my first article for Linc's journal."

Everyone applauded. Bonnie LaRoux stepped from behind the screen. "I don't know why you want to work. If I were filthy rich like you, I'd eat bonbons all day and dance all night."

Bierce lifted his glass to Cecy. "Don't listen to her. I'm proud of you. What's the article about?"

"It's an exposé of a sardine cannery and the terrible conditions. Linc and I worked there a day last week."

"A sardine factory?" Effie exclaimed, still hidden. "Why would you go to such a disgusting place? I give up. You journalists are insane!"

Linc said nothing. The two actresses meant no harm and it was neither the time nor place for a stern lecture about social responsibility. Why couldn't he get in the mood for an evening of light entertainment? He didn't usually let himself get so down. Guilt over betraying his love for Virginia tangled around his heart.

Cecy held her glass up to McEwen. He refilled it for her.

Linc wanted to snatch the glass away from her, but he couldn't. He'd made much headway with Cecilia in the past two days. He'd helped her grapple with the conditions at the cannery and write about the changes she'd already thought up. But that didn't give him the right to dictate to her.

"I said, I'm famished!" Effie stepped out, dressed in a low-cut, deep blue gown studded with shimmering rhinestones. "Where are we off to?"

"Why not Cliff House?" Bierce's smile glinted wickedly.

"I made reservations at the Poodle Dog." Linc held Cecy's fur wrap and helped her into it. "We're due there in fifteen minutes." The Cliff House was a notorious restaurant that had a particularly unsavory reputation. Linc would bind and gag Cecy and carry her home before he let her go to such a place.

"Let's be off!" Cecy giggled and drained her champagne glass.

Feeling grim, Linc gave her his arm. Unable to help himself, he leaned close to her ear and whispered, "Go easy on the champagne or we'll go home early."

Cecy giggled again. "Go home if you wish. I'm off to 'see the elephant'."

Outside, the March breeze blew deceptively warm around Linc's ears. In front of the theater, Linc arranged everyone in his Pierce Arrow, but inside himself, he fumed. "Seeing the elephant" was the San Francisco term for touring its nightspots. And Miss Cecilia Jackson was going home after supper—if it was the last thing he ever did. The worst of it was that he'd introduced her to these people! Why hadn't he anticipated her fascination with the excesses of the avant-garde?

When he walked into the Poodle Dog with Cecilia on his arm, the restaurant rang with tipsy laughter. Linc had had about enough of that giddy sound, thank you! The head waiter barely seated them before Cecilia ordered more champagne.

Sipping it, she looked around innocently. "Oh, there's an upstairs. Linc, why didn't you get us a table up there? I'd have preferred sitting above everyone."

Effie and Bonnie both burst into laughter.

Linc remained grimly sober. Cecilia didn't need to know why she, a virtuous lady, would only be welcome on the main floor. And he wasn't going to explain it to her.

"Cecilia," Effie lowered her voice conspiratorially, "the second floor has only private rooms for private assignations."

Cecilia looked shocked. "Assignations?"

Linc silently ground his teeth.

"Yes, Miss Jackson." Bierce grinned. "Just like in Paris where the gentlemen drive along the Champs Elysee with their mistresses to their left and their wives to their right."

"At the same time?" Cecy gasped.

Everyone at the table exploded into uproarious laughter—except Linc. Over the past few days, he'd been so impressed with Cecilia's desire to change her canneries for the better and her serious labor to express her experience at the cannery. Why hadn't these meaningful experiences satisfied her need instead of champagne? Why hadn't she let him cancel this theater-supper evening?

And Bierce was beginning to irritate him seriously.

Hours dragged on and on. Linc couldn't think of anything more boring than watching other people get tipsy. He'd barely pecked at his meal. He struggled not to glance at his watch every five minutes. Starting tomorrow bright and early, he'd think of some way to get Cecilia so busy she wouldn't have time for any more of these "champagne" evenings.

Finally, the creme brulee had been consumed over a discussion of the great Caruso who would appear in San Francisco in less than a month. Cecy invited everyone to dinner after the opera. Linc's head ached.

Discussion of the notorious Lily Hitchcock Coit from San Francisco's early days began. Linc hoped Cecilia wouldn't get any ideas of aping the notorious hoyden.

"She shaved her head?" Cecy obviously couldn't believe any woman would actually do that. "Why?"

"To wear different wigs for differing occasions." McEwen lit his cigar.

"She wouldn't have if she'd had your lovely auburn hair," Bierce said with a wink.

Linc contemplated crumpling Bierce's handsome nose.

"The Gold Rush days must have been so exciting—not like today." Cecy sipped the last of her champagne.

Linc summarily signaled away the waiter who'd come to bring another bottle of champagne. He pulled out his watch. "It's time I got you home, Cecilia. It's nearly 3 A.M."

"The night's still young." Bonnie yawned.

"Not if you have a matinee and an evening performance like I do, dear," Effie countered as she rose. "Will you drop me at my hotel please, Lincoln?"

Linc could have kissed the blonde.

Bonnie stood also. "You're right. I have an early rehearsal. I need my beauty sleep."

Effie chuckled. "Don't we all, dear."

"So you won't be going to 'see the elephant' tonight, Cecilia?" Bierce asked in a taunting tone.

Over my dead body. Linc nearly spoke the words aloud.

"If you've seen one elephant, you've seen them all." Effie waved her hand airily. "Good night. Parting is such sweet sorrow, etc., etc. Anon, dear friends, anon!"

Gratefully, Linc squired the ladies to his car and drove them each home in the cool of early morning. Finally, as he helped Cecilia out and up to her door, he vowed this would be the last "champagne" evening—if he had to lock her up until she came to her senses.

CHAPTER 12

The butler admitted them. Nana waited at the top of the staircase, dressed in a plain, white flannel wrapper. "Cecy, home at last."

Linc heard the relief in the old nurse's voice.

"Oh, Nana, we had a lovely time." Cecy walked unsteadily up the stairs.

Nana came down and met her halfway. Taking Cecilia's arm, she gave Linc a worried look.

He merely pursed his lips, then bid them a gruff good night.

Outside, he breathed in the damp air. The earlier clouds had receded leaving a crisp, clear night. Linc gazed up at the flickering stars. The stars glinted knowingly, almost mocking him—'You're in love with Cecilia.'

I don't want to be in love with her, with anyone. Virginia was enough for me. I have Meg. I don't want another love.

※ ※ ※ ※ ※

Ring. Ring. Ring. Lying in his bed, Linc surfaced from the deep sleep he'd fallen into. He got up and hurried downstairs to the phone. "Yes?" he mumbled.

"Linc! Oh, Linc!" Cecilia cried out. "Come, quick. It's mother!"

CHAPTER 13

"But if anyone causes one of these little ones who believe in me to sin, it would be better for him to have a large millstone hung around his neck and to be drowned in the depths of the sea."
Matthew 18:6, NIV

March 29, 1906　　　　　Hıs FEET SLIPPING ON THE WET pavement, Linc ran up to Cecilia's mansion, its lighted windows gleaming ahead in the warm, rainy night. The butler waited at the open door for him. "Thank God, you're here, Sir. The doctor is upstairs."

Linc jerked off his dripping hat and driving coat, then handed them to the manservant. "What happened? Where is Cecilia?"

The butler's dour face looked funereal. "In Mrs. Jackson's room. Follow me."

Through the shadowy foyer and up the curved staircase, Linc jogged side-by-side with the butler. Outside the bedroom door, the butler paused to open it. "Mr. Wagstaff's arrived."

Linc stepped into a darkened room in disarray. Blankets, ripped from the bed, lay on the floor. Nearby, a bedside lamp, shattered, littered the rose carpet. He moved closer. Cecilia's mother lay perfectly still. Was she even breathing? The gray-haired doctor, a forbidding expression on his face, stood on this side of the rumpled bed, Millie at his side. Linc recognized him. He was the same doctor who'd tended Bower's wound, the night of the scandal.

"Oh, Linc." Cecilia's voice quivered near hysteria. In the low lamplight, Cecilia, deathly pale, stood opposite the doctor on the far side of the bed. Her auburn hair flowed around her unbound. The panic in her eyes moved him. The giddy young woman she'd been nearly three hours ago had vanished.

Millie spoke up loudly, "Mr. Wagstaff, thank you for coming. Mrs. Jackson took too much of her sleeping tonic by accident. I don't know how it happened. I must have poured out the amount twice without realizing it."

"No, no." Cecilia wrung her mother's limp hand. "That can't be what happened. Perhaps the mixture was made too strong this time."

Linc sorted through the explosion of scattered thoughts in his mind. He prayed that what he'd feared most had not happened. He longed to take Cecilia in his arms, to comfort with gentle caresses—*No.*

The frowning doctor made no comment to this, but finished taking the patient's pulse. "I can't believe that the mixture was responsible." His voice was distinctly suspicious. "But your mother will live, thanks to her quick nurse's action, but she should not be left alone."

"She won't be!" Cecilia declared tearfully, kissing her mother's hand.

The doctor made a strange disapproving noise that sounded like an elephant swallowing, then gathered up his bag, bowed stiffly, and left.

Cecilia started to speak, but Millie, with the shake of her head, silenced her, evidently not wanting the doctor to overhear anything. Still in the middle of the room, Linc waited in suspense. What had gone so wrong in the three short hours since he brought Cecilia home?

Her eyes looked haunted once more. Had the champagne bubbles all dissolved and left her empty, unequal to the disaster around her? Like a telegraph tapping a message but through an invisible wire, her pain transferred to him. How had her mother nearly died?

Cecilia needed him. He'd meant to protect her, to keep her from further harm. He failed her. Just as he'd failed Virginia. He strove against the lingering sorrow that had kept him from feeling the old closeness to God. He drew closer to the bed.

Within moments, the butler returned. "The doctor is gone."

Linc nodded. The butler withdrew closing the door behind him.

Cecilia flew into Linc's arms. "Hold me. Hold me!"

He caught her and the temptation was too much. He crushed her to him, willing his strength to her. While she wept against his neck, her sobs ripped at his heart. He kissed her hair fiercely as though he could blot out her suffering with his lips. His concern for her blended with her attraction.

Even as he soothed her, his awareness that only a fine silk wrapper separated them grew and alarmed him. *I can't desire her. I can't love her.*

But all her youthful, innocent charms taunted him. *Dear God, I'm just man, made from dust. Take this attraction from me.* He began to loosen his hold on her. He concentrated on her sadness, her terror, letting his sympathy for her increase till it overwhelmed desire.

He was aware of Millie's silent presence. He loosened his hold on her and centered his thoughts on the problem at hand.

Dear God, what happened here? Father, help me say the right words. She's already been through so much.

"Calm yourself. Darling, please." He stroked her back— even as he gently released her. Leading her to a love seat, he eased her down to it. She wouldn't release his hand, so he sat down beside her.

He looked to the nurse. "Millie, could you explain what has happened here? I'm very concerned."

Millie turned and collapsed on a bedside chair. She looked drained. "Cecy, your mother will sleep for many hours yet."

Cecilia hung her head.

Linc braced her with an arm around her shoulder though he yearned to enfold her in his arms again. "Millie, please."

The old nurse twisted her hands together nervously. "Since we let the other nurse go, I have been giving Mrs. Jackson her sleeping medication. Tonight, I couldn't sleep. I tried to ignore it, but I received a prompting over and over that I should check her one more time."

She lifted the small, amber bottle on the bedside table. "Thank God, I obeyed that prompting. Because when I came in, I found it empty. I filled this back up with water, so the doctor wouldn't see it was empty. If it leaked out that your mother had attempted...." The woman fell silent as if the dread of what had taken place here sealed her lips.

She sighed raggedly. "I tried to rouse your mother. I must have come in right after she'd taken it. I was able to wake her enough to force her to throw up, then she fell unconscious again. I rang for the butler to summon a doctor in case he might be able to do more. But when he said she'd be all right...." She turned her head away as though hiding tears.

"Mrs. Jackson tried to take her own life tonight?" he asked, still not believing.

"No!" Cecy sprang up. "No!"

Linc pulled her back down and pressed her close against his side.

CHAPTER 13

The nurse went on, "She must have drunk the full bottle of her sleeping draught tonight after you came home."

"But why?" Cecilia choked on her words.

Millie gazed at Cecilia sorrowfully. She stretched twisting her neck as though loosening tightened muscles, then she focused on Cecilia. "You need to know. The truth will make you free. The facts are hard, but you need to hear them. Because...," Millie paused to wipe her eyes with a handkerchief. "Because it was your behavior that caused your mother to despair tonight—"

Cecilia gasped, then pressed her fist to her mouth.

An awful suspicion occurred to Linc. Had her mother feared her daughter was following her own tragic example, just as he had? He gripped Cecilia's shoulder tightly, hoping he was wrong. "I think you'd better explain."

The nurse nodded. "Cecy, you don't remember much about your parents, do you?"

Cecilia shook her head. "I've wanted to ask you, but I didn't want to hurt my mother."

Linc's anxiety inched higher.

"I'm dreadfully at fault." Millie bowed her head. "I should have taken you aside and questioned you, counseled you. But...." She sighed deeply. "I hated to stir up the ugly past. But I must do so now to prevent more disaster, more misunderstandings." She looked directly into Cecilia's eyes. "Tonight, your mother tried to take her life because she was afraid you are following her sad path."

Linc, proved right, regretted it. Cecilia crumpled in his arms. Her sobs vibrated against him. *This is my fault too. I put you in temptation's way.* He tasted bitter regret like sour acid in his mouth.

The nurse pulled a crumpled piece of paper from her skirt pocket. "These are her own words: 'I'm so sorry, my dearest daughter. My life has been a failure. Forgive me, dear Cecilia. I have always loved you, but I wasn't strong enough to protect you. Now I see you are turning to spirits, just as I did. I can't face it. So I will fail you again. Forgive me. Dear God, forgive me.'"

Cecilia moaned and lolled weakly against Linc's shoulder. Fearing she might faint and fall, he pulled her onto his lap. If only he could magically make everything right, save her this heartbreak.

"Tell me, Nana. Please...." Suddenly Cecilia appeared to lose control of her breathing. She began inhaling too fast, struggling to exhale.

Millie rushed over and blew repeatedly into Cecilia's face while she chafed her hands. "Cecy, dearest. Please Lord Jesus, protect this dear child. It isn't her fault. It never was...."

Cecilia caught her breath.

Millie exchanged worried glances with Linc as though asking if she should go on or not.

He nodded firmly, encouraging her. "Tell her. Now." *Put an end to this!*

Millie perched on the end of the tapestry love seat. Her face drawn, gray in the low light. "I don't know how much you know, Cecy, and I only know the barest facts myself. Your mother confided only in me and I kept her trust all these years. It all started when your father went to Boston to find a wife."

Linc's mind went back to the *Bulletin* editor, Fremont Older, who'd told him a version of the story Linc feared he was about to hear repeated. How much more would this nurse know than Older had?

"Your father became fascinated...." Millie paused to blink away tears. "With your Aunt Amelia."

"What?" Cecilia bucked in his arms. "Aunt Amelia!"

Cecilia's tone echoed his own disbelief. Had the two sisters been romantic rivals?

Millie nodded sadly. "Your aunt was quite striking in her youth, according to your mother. But very headstrong. Even though strongly attracted to one another, your father and aunt fought—constantly. At least, that's what your mother told me. Then they had one huge argument.

"Out of spite to make your aunt jealous, I think, your father turned his affections from Amelia to your mother. Your mother was being pressured by her father to marry his wealthiest friend—a man nearly seventy years old. Your mother, only seventeen, accepted your father's proposal instead and eloped with him.

"I've always thought she married just to get away from the elderly suitor, her father, and envious older sister. Your mother was the prettier one, you see. Her sister and father never forgave her." Millie drew in a shivering breath. "Then you were born—a month early, only eight months after their wedding." Millie frowned deeply. "Your father used this against your mother."

"What?" Cecilia trembled against him.

Linc tucked her nearer. "He accused her of already being pregnant by someone else when they married?" Linc asked, well aware of the implications of this and how powerless a woman would be in this situation. Momentarily, he wished August Jackson still lived, so he could thrash him.

Millie nodded. "It wasn't true, of course, and he knew it. Anyone could see the resemblance of Cecy to her father."

"I wish I wasn't anything like him!" Cecy cried out. "I always knew he hated me!"

"Was that the reason Cecilia was sent away?" Linc asked as he fought the urge to hate Cecilia's father. *A man who'd turn against his own dear child! The fool!*

Millie continued, "By then, Mrs. Jackson had given in to despair and more and more numbed herself with alcohol. Your father was a violent man. They had dreadful shouting and crying arguments."

Cecilia nodded against Linc. "I remember," she whispered. "Oh, I remember."

"Was the short pregnancy his only reason for his ill treatment of his wife and daughter?" Linc asked, trying to understand the twisted logic.

"Was it, Nana?" the young woman's voice quavered.

Millie pursed her lips. "I think he regretted marrying your mother. After all was said and done, I think in his way he'd loved Amelia, but had been too willful and stubborn to suffer a woman who wouldn't knuckle under to him. He despised your mother for the very reason he married her—her compliance. Also he wanted a son, but your mother never conceived again. For which she was truly grateful."

Linc added, "But in his eyes, it made his wife completely useless to him?"

Millie nodded disconsolately. "He taunted her that she was weak, not like her strong sister. Then he used your mother's attack of delirium tremens as an excuse to rid himself of both his unwanted wife and his daughter. He telegraphed Amelia and she arranged for the Boston school, everything."

Cecy gasped. "My aunt!"

Millie's faced turned darker. "I have no doubt she took great pleasure in destroying your mother's reputation further in Boston by whispering to everyone of her sister's drunkenness. She took revenge on your mother for stealing her love by helping to take her daughter from her. Truly, your aunt would have been a match for your father. They were both evil."

Linc nodded grimly, recalling all the times he'd wondered about the aunt's motives himself.

Wiping away tears, Millie sighed. "Your mother was sent to the sanitarium and I was dismissed. I thought my heart would *break* when I had to leave you." Millie choked back a sob. "But I had no money, no legal way of stopping your father. I had only my prayers. And I've prayed for you every day since your father wrenched you from me. Oh, why didn't I tell you the truth right away?"

CHAPTER 13

✴ ✴ ✴ ✴ ✴

A tap at the door startled Cecy. She'd been completely immersed in the agonizing past. Linc went to the door and Nana drifted back to Cecy's mother's side to check her pulse again. Cecy wrapped her arms around herself, feeling the chill in the room now that Linc's warmth had been taken from her.

After speaking to the butler, Linc turned back to face her. "I've a phone call." He left and returned within minutes.

"What was it?" Cecy leaned toward Linc, her hair falling forward. She tossed it back over her shoulder. "Is something wrong at home—Del?"

"No, but I have to leave—"

"No, don't—" She panicked. Feeling herself begin to gasp for air again, she held her arms out to him in silent appeal.

He strode to her and grasped her upper arms, urging her to stand up. "I wouldn't go if it weren't absolutely necessary. I will come back as soon as I can. I promise."

His strength eased the anguish of the revelation from her damaged past. *Don't leave me!* She wanted to convince him to stay, but she recognized the determined set of his jaw. Why couldn't he stay and hold her until her mother woke? She might still die. *Dear God, no!*

She repressed a bone-deep shudder. "You'll come back?"

"As soon as I'm able." He hesitated, then bent to kiss her softly on the lips. *Oh, his touch!* He tried to pull away.

But she threw her arms around his neck and clung to him.

The night Hunt had wounded Bower, her life had unraveled. Now all the effort she'd put into starting a new life was slipping through her fingers like silk thread. Only Linc seemed able to guide her. She needed him. She hated needing anyone. *But I'm not equal to face this alone!* She forced herself to let go. "I'll be waiting for you."

He nodded giving her his unspoken promise and left.

Feeling as though all the life had been drawn out of her, Cecy crept slowly over to stand beside Nana who put her arm around Cecy's waist. Cecy stared down at the limp form on the bed. Had the doctor been right? Would she wake?

How her mother had suffered! *Why didn't we talk about what was truly important?* Why had she feared probing the truth? She'd recognized her mother wasn't happy. "If she'd only spoken to me...."

"She's led a solitary life for so long...." Nana shook her head sadly. "I wish you'd seen her when she was so young, so pretty."

Cecy took a deep, calming breath. It had been a long time since she'd practiced the technique of bringing air in slowly and pushing out anxiety. When she'd come into her inheritance here in San Francisco, she'd thought her powerless days were in the past. But money couldn't help her now. The worst outcome, though, had been averted tonight. Her mother had been saved by Nana. "She will have a good life from now on. I promise. No more secrets. My father. My aunt. My grandfather—they will never touch her life, my life again. Never." Saying the vow out loud gave her strength.

Something, some tight sadness in Cecy unfurled, then dissolved. She took another deep breath, pressing down the last trace of her panic. "I feel different, Nana. You were right. The truth has set me free."

❈ ❈ ❈ ❈ ❈

Outside, Linc dashed down the steps to his auto. How much could go wrong in one dusk to dawn? He cranked the car in record time and raced away for the *Bulletin* office. Gray clouds shifted, drifted over the risen moon in the eastern sky. The story of twisted evil he had just listened to made him ache even more than the damp of early morning. Evil. Many in this new century scoffed at its existence. Even in the twentieth century, evil lived on.

He parked on Market Street and charged into the *Bulletin* building. The first floor was unusually bright for the hour, nearly dawn. The door to Older's office was open. Linc halted at it.

Looking back at him were Fremont Older, the man who'd befriended him, and the other San Francisco managing editors—whom he'd come to know casually over the past months—one each from the *Examiner*, the *Call*, and the *Chronicle*. This gathering of editors was highly unusual and he knew why they'd all come. Cecilia's life was headline material and they didn't want to miss anything. Somehow he—with God's help—had to turn them from using Cecy's mother's attempted suicide as another feast for the vultures.

"I'm happy you all came." His heart pounding in his ears, Linc stepped into the office.

"What's all this about?" the *Examiner* editor, a slender young man with spectacles, asked tersely.

Linc nodded his thanks to Older. "You've all been contacted by Doctor Smith?"

"So?" the *Call* editor, a rumpled middle-aged man asked.

Linc hardened his jaw, irked at the flippant attitude. "What he has done is beyond the bounds of honor. The best I can say of him is that he is a gossipy old woman, masquerading as a doctor."

"So? We knew that." The rumpled Call editor leaned back in his chair. "Let me guess, you don't want us to run the latest chapter in your favorite redhead's scandal?"

"It's news. We print news." The young *Examiner* editor shrugged.

The gray-haired man from the *Chronicle* kept his silence like Older.

"You print news, but not all the news. Some news goes beyond what is moral to reveal and you know that. Besides, the real story here is better than what you've heard." Showing a confidence he was far from feeling, Linc leaned against Older's filing cabinets.

The *Call* editor edged forward in his chair. "So?"

Linc thought quickly. Cecilia's reputation—what was left of it—hung by a strand. The scandal of attempted suicide outweighed anything already alleged against her. Suicide was a shame that clung and couldn't be washed away. The worst of it was—Cecilia would be blamed. He imagined a headline: "Heiress Drives Mother to Suicide." *No, I can't let that happen to her!* Linc wished he could wipe his damp palms and blot away his anxiety. Instead, he prayed for a persuasive argument, for God to move the hearts of these men. "First I want to get something off my chest. I think you all owe Cecilia Jackson an apology. Every one of you here knew the truth about Victor Hunt and you still painted her as the villain." He glared at them.

None of the others except for Older would meet his eye. Older nodded encouraging him to go on.

"Now in spite of everything, Cecilia Jackson has become a changed woman."

To save Cecilia and her mother, he would have to sacrifice his own scoop, his big story about her experience at the cannery and the changes she had planned.

"Why? Is she really writing for your muckraking journal?" the young editor quizzed him, looking over his spectacles at him.

"Absolutely. My first issue comes out in a week. Her expose on sardine canneries across the Bay—"

"Sardine canneries? What kind of punch does a story like that have?" the *Call* editor sneered.

"Miss Jackson wrote an exposé of the horrible conditions and the abuses of the workers—men, women, and children in the canneries owned by...." He paused dramatically, then made himself grin though he was shaking inside. "Miss Cecilia Jackson."

"What?" the rumpled man, slouching, unfolded himself, nearly stood.

"Is that so?" the bespectacled young man looked amused.

The *Call* editor couldn't conceal his shock. "Why would she do something like that? It doesn't make any sense."

Linc bowed slightly and spread his arms in a what-could-I-do gesture. "It was her decision. She went with me and worked a sardine catch there."

"Did she?" the *Examiner* editor grinned.

The middle-aged editor goggled at him. "A young lady of quality worked in a sardine cannery?"

Linc nodded. "You can believe it. She lasted the whole eleven-hour shift. The experience changed her mind about much. Her article not only graphically describes babies left unattended in flimsy boxes around the stove, but also four-year-olds—who if they were ours would never be allowed near a sharp knife—gutting fish while their mothers work nearby. She also outlines the changes she has already set in motion."

Older spoke up for the first time, "What changes?"

Linc glanced at him. He would thank Older later for calling to warn him of the doctor's betrayal revealing the suicide attempt. "First of all, in voluntary compliance with the new Pure Food Act, she ordered all the canneries across the Bay to be scrubbed spotless."

"That's good. Since I have occasionally had sardines on toast, I don't want you to tell me just how dirty it was," Older observed laconically.

Linc grinned at him. "I won't be eating another sardine for at least six months, if then. But let's get back to the changes. Next, she hired a mechanical engineer to go over the machinery to check for unsafe conditions, and he's been commissioned to improve their design for safety and increased efficiency."

"Is that all?" The *Chronicle* editor finally spoke. "I'm sure all this is interesting, but I have better things to do."

Linc ignored this and continued to give away all the facts with which he had hoped to snag the interest of magazine-buying San Francisco readers. "She has already signed construction contracts for a large building across the Bay that will serve as a settlement house. It'll include a nursery, an infirmary with a nurse, a day school, a bath house, and a laundry for all cannery workers."

"Something like Jane Addams' Hull House?" the young man looked up thoughtfully.

"A cross between that and a company town—only a good company town. The workers will be required to report to work clean and in clean clothing to meet new sanitary standards. No children under the age of twelve will be hired. All children and infants will be left at the nursery and day school while their parents work." Linc studied the men, trying to gauge their reactions.

The Chronicle editor asked, "How does she plan to still make a profit with all these new expenses? Lower wages?"

Linc proudly shook his head. "The cleanliness changes would be necessary in themselves since the passage of the Pure Food Act, so money would have to be spent in any case. But she has *doubled* her workers' wages and will still be able to make a healthy profit." Linc smiled. "She believes the newly designed machinery will have a good effect on the workers and will increase their productivity and keep her cannery well in the black."

The rumpled editor stood up. "Those kind of people won't appreciate this—this outrageous charity. Most of them are just ignorant and inferior—Chinese, Italians, and Poles. If you're finished—"

Linc swallowed a sharp retort. He couldn't afford to offend these men no matter how much he disagreed with them.

The young man lifted his eyebrows asking the *Call* editor to cede the floor to him. "I'm quite impressed with what you've said, Wagstaff. But you've not convinced me yet. What is your final word?"

Linc crossed his arms over his chest. He sent up one final prayer. "Well, it's a combination of points. Number one, would you like your doctor calling the paper to tell about your ailments? He has violated the trust of his patient. Is that something you want to encourage? And which is more likely to make a better story—a near-suicide or the reclamation of my scandalous redhead? If you run the suicide story, it will overshadow and weaken the story of Miss Jackson's reclamation—which will give you many more opportunities for copy! Let me remind you—she has a lot of factories."

The *Chronicle* editor rose. "Are you sure this isn't just a setup to get publicity in all our papers for your *serious* journal?"

Linc shrugged. He'd in effect given the competition all the thunder of his first issue. He didn't grudge this sacrifice for Cecilia, but would it work? "I'm not working on a shoestring budget. I can afford advertising."

"Well, if I can put my two cents in, I don't like Hunt," Older drawled. "Wagstaff's heiress deserves a fair shake. She's writing for him, you know. Remember, that makes her one of us."

A pause, then the editors left Linc alone with Older.

Linc closed the door after them and turned to face Older. "I can't thank you enough for warning me, then inviting them here." He shook Older's hand. "Thank you."

"Don't mention it. Bring your redhead in sometime. I'd like to meet her."

"You will. She'll want to thank you herself. Do you think I convinced them?"

"Time will tell. Either the scandal will run today or it won't."

� ✿ ✿ ✿ ✿

After the meeting at Older's office, Linc hurried back to Cecilia. He stood at the door to her mother's bedroom. Cecilia drooped beside the bed, holding her mother's hand while the lady slept on. Should he warn Cecilia another scandal was brewing?

He strode over the thick carpet to stand behind her. Willing himself to ignore her attractions which shook him to the core, he gently cupped her shoulders with his hands. "You should get some sleep. Where's Millie?"

"I sent Nana to get some rest," she whispered. "See, Mother's kitten came out from underneath the bed. I guess she hid during all the commotion."

Linc felt proud. Cecilia was bravely fighting despair. He glanced at the small cat which was curled up in the curve of her mother's waist. He reached out and stroked the cat's satin-soft fur.

"When I saw the kitten snuggle up to Mother, it made me feel better—I'm hoping the kitten senses everything is OK." Her voice quavered, "But I'm still afraid to leave. I'm afraid my mother won't wake up." A tiny sob escaped on her last syllable.

To reassure her, Linc stepped around Cecilia, closer to the sleeping woman. He felt the lady's cool forehead, then took her faint, but regular pulse. He leaned close to her face and felt her shallow breaths against his cheek. "Your mother is merely sleeping peacefully. When the drug wears off, she will wake up with a slight headache. She should be very thirsty. But we'll have to tempt her palate. Her appetite will be dulled."

Looking a bit surprised, she glanced at him. "You sound like you know."

"Though he came from a banking family, my stepfather was a doctor, remember? Unfortunately, I've been to many bedsides like this in my life."

"You have?" Hope lit her eyes.

Like a taut wire around a screw, her hope tightened his gnawing concern for her. Another scandal due out in the evening papers? How would she take it? "Yes, and your mother is going to be fine. Now you're going to get up and go have a bath—"

"No—"

"Yes." He coaxed her to her feet. The elegant robe gleamed in the low morning light. The temptation of holding her against him tested him once more. *Not now.* He reluctantly released her hand. "When your mother awakes, she'll feel more reassured if she sees you looking fresh and sober."

She buried her face into her hands. "I just want to see her open her eyes again. But I can't bear to face her. It's all my fault."

He took her into his arms, but held himself in check. Everything about her soft form without corset stays against him, her disheveled beauty tormented him. She needed him, but he must respond with honor. She was vulnerable now. And no matter what his feelings, this was no time to hint at love, especially love he wouldn't act on. Too much separated them— age, wealth, faith. "All this started years before you were born. I blame myself for introducing you to bohemian life. I didn't realize it would—"

"It's not your fault. It's mine."

He forced her lovely chin up. Her brown eyes pooled with tears. Her lips parted in silent invitation. "Cecilia, you know I'm a widower."

She looked confused. "Why do you mention that now?"

"Because for over a year now, I've held onto my guilt over my wife's death."

"Why do you feel guilt?"

"Virginia died in childbirth. We both wanted the child. But not at the cost of Virginia's life. The baby came with complications and was stillborn. When Virginia died just hours later, I wanted to wrap myself around her lifeless body and go down into the grave with her."

"Linc," her exclamation came in a heated whisper. *"No."*

Just speaking about Virginia's death brought the scene slamming back into him. A room much like this. A still body in a rumpled bed. Grief snaked around his neck like a hangman's noose. He had to fight for breath. "I know it's unreasonable, but I blamed myself. I still blame myself over and over." He gripped her by the shoulders. "Let go of it—the guilt. Just promise that you'll never again repeat the same behavior that hurt your mother."

Her eyes widened. "Never! I'll never take another drink. I swear it."

He wrapped his arms more tightly around her. Her sweet fragrance, though fainter, and the touch of her soft form in the silky wrapper filled his senses. *Dear God, take away this temptation.* "We'll fight guilt together."

"I'll try."

Nodding against her feather-soft hair just below his chin, he allowed himself to experience the joy holding Cecilia brought. The pain of loss began receding. He kissed her forehead, a mere brush of lips, then made himself release her. "Now you go, freshen up, and eat something."

"I couldn't —"

"I insist you eat, at least tea and toast. Now go. I'll stay with her till you return. Then I'll have to go home and do the same." He pushed her to the door. "Put on your prettiest morning gown for her, so she'll know you are happy to see her awake."

She went—though reluctantly—with many backward glances. Finally, she closed the door behind herself.

Linc eased his tired body onto the stiff-backed chair. A night of shock, worry, and a bare two hours of sleep had left him feeling hollow and weakened. Perhaps that's what had left him so open to Cecilia's attraction. Was he adequate to deal with the crisis looming ahead in the evening papers? *Oh, Lord, I'm so weary. Confused.*

An old spiritual Susan had sung a million times played in his mind—"I'm gonna lay down my burden, down by the riverside, down by the riverside...."

CHAPTER 13

Del hadn't come home yet to stay. What was happening to him right now? *Lord, I'm not equal to all this. Maybe when I was twenty, but not today.*

A scripture came to mind: "My burden is easy. My yoke is light."

"If you say so, Lord." He thought over all the intense drama he'd experienced since meeting Cecilia. "I've had about all I can handle. This has to be the last, the final crisis."

He gazed at the frail, sleeping woman. "Madam, I don't know if this second scandal is going to break over your daughter. I did my best. But more importantly, I love your daughter. And I don't know what to do about it."

CHAPTER 14

"...the truth will set you free."
John 8:32b, NIV

Wearing a morning frock of pale pink cotton, Cecy felt tired but fresher than she had in days. She lingered by her mother's bedside, still waiting for her to awake. Without warning—just hours earlier—Cecy had teetered on the brink of losing her mother one more time—this time forever. Now as she watched her mother blessedly breathe in, breathe out, she clung to Nana and Linc's reassurances that her mother would awaken again.

All these months in San Francisco, she'd thought she'd been walking on solid ground. But early this morning, the earth beneath her life had shifted. The most basic assumption about her life had been false. Aunt Amelia, the only one in her family she'd thought she could count on, had secretly despised her. No wonder her mother wouldn't come home while her sister stayed here.

One fact, however, she'd had right. Her father had hated her. Merely because he'd chosen to. Why would a man callously reject his only child without a reason? Had he known anything of love? *What do I know of love? I love my mother. I love Nana. And little Meg.*

Linc's handsome face appeared on the stage of her mind.

Recalling his embrace and kisses from the early morning hours brought a blush to her face. She pressed her hot cheeks with her cool hands. She admitted to herself if it had been possible, she would have stayed within his arms. Whenever he was near, she was so aware of him—the strength he exuded without effort, his calm authority in the face of any disaster, his golden good looks and his clear blue eyes which could see deep inside her. Did she love Linc? He certainly had stood as her friend. *Oh, Linc, stay close.*

But I can't love you.

Not after her father's rejection of her, not after her music teacher had been tempted, ruined, and sent away, not after her aunt....

Was that the real root? Hadn't Aunty introduced the plan for Cecy becoming "Belle of 1906" to prevent the stigma of spinsterhood when she never married. Had Cecy really wanted that for herself? No, she'd only wanted to be free, to make her own decisions, to live life filled with music.

Now she saw her aunt's twisted revenge. Her aunt had used her. Only with Cecy by her side and with Cecy's millions could Aunty live the extravagant life she'd evidently wanted, the one she would have lived if she'd married Cecy's father. In this revenge, Aunty would have had all the advantages of her former beau's wealth. She'd also reap the vengeance of standing as Cecy's parent while Cecy's own mother had remained hidden away and alone at the sanitarium.

Then, though she doubted what she saw was true, her mothers eyes flickered, then fluttered open.

"Cecy?" The lady's voice sounded thready, unbelieving.

"Mother." Cecy sat on the bed and gathered her frail mother into her arms. "Oh, Mother, I thought I might never see you again."·

"I'm sorry." The lady began to cry weakly.

"No, *I'm* sorry." Cecy kissed her mother's drawn cheek, then stroked it gently. "I know everything and I'll never drink another drop of alcohol. Never. I promise. But *you* must promise never to try to leave me again. Please." She straightened up enough to gaze into her mother's soft gray eyes, filled with tears.

"I just couldn't face seeing you end up like me."

"The end hasn't come yet." Cecy smiled. "You and I are together at last. Aunt Amelia, Father and Grandfather are out of our lives forever. They will never hurt us or separate us again."

"You know the truth?" Her mother whispered with a shaking voice. "Everything?"

Cecy nodded triumphantly. "Yes, Nana told me and I love you more now than ever before and nothing will ever come between us again."

"My daughter." The lady lovingly touched Cecy's hair. "Dearest daughter, my own sweet girl. I prayed for us to be together without secrets, then despaired. Even so, God brought it to pass now."

Though Cecy nodded, she didn't know if God or Linc Wagstaff were responsible. Then a thought stunned her.

Victor Hunt did me a favor.

Hunt's actions had set her free from her aunt by making her flee from the scandal, spoiling her aunt's revenge, reuniting Cecy with her mother, and making Cecy willing to let Linc show her more of the world. *What would I have done without Linc?*

✷ ✷ ✷ ✷ ✷

"Cecilia, I'm going to come and pick you up." Linc's voice over the telephone wires sounded urgent.

"But I don't want to leave mother. She's only been awake for a few hours." The thought of being separated from her mother made her feel hollow, sickened.

"I know, but something has come up and I need you here."

"But—" *Please, Linc, no.*

"This is for your mother's sake. Please."

Her mother? What had come up so suddenly? "All right. I'll be ready."

"Good girl. I'll leave now."

Cecy hung up. She tried to think of what excuse to tell her mother for leaving. Hadn't all the secrets been exposed? Though the room was warm, goose flesh zipped up both her arms.

※ ※ ※ ※ ※

Cecilia, dressed in her driving outfit, hurried by her butler and stepped outside into the misty rain. Linc met her on the steps. She tried to read his face, but his driving goggles and the dim March dusk made it impossible.

"Thank you for coming." Linc led her down the steps and walked her to his auto. The warm mist penetrated her driving veil as though the fading twilight clasped her tightly and wept against her face.

After being helped into the passenger seat, she glanced at him. "You look worried. What's happened?"

"I'll tell you everything as soon as we're in my parlor."

Cecy's anxiety tightened around her middle—tighter than her corset stays.

※ ※ ※ ※ ※

Linc closed the pocket door to his parlor. *Click.*

The sound made her shudder. Apprehensive, Cecy went to the fireplace and held her icy hands in front of the comfortable fire.

CHAPTER 14

"I have some bad news."

A leaden weight slid downward inside her. She spun toward him. "No! No more bad news." She shuddered.

Linc hurried to her and took her hands. "I'm so sorry. I've done everything I could, but there's a chance...."

"What?" Clinging to his strong, warm hands, she wanted to seek protection within his embrace once again. Inwardly, she took a step backward. *I can't depend on Linc. I have to depend on myself.*

Linc inhaled deeply. "There may be the possibility that the papers might spawn another scandal tonight."

All the breath went out of her. "No. Not about my mother."

"I'm afraid so." His arm braced her as she fought creeping weakness. "The doctor called the city papers this morning and told them he thought it was a suicide attempt."

She sagged against him. "I can't face anymore."

"Don't despair. The matter was handled better than I'd hoped."

"How?" She hated her weakness. *I can't faint.* She fought to take in small breaths.

He led her to a hearth-side chair and settled her into it. He pulled the white crocheted afghan lying over the chair arm and tucked it around her. Then he sat down across from her. "Remember—early this morning when I received the call, I left you? Older, the *Bulletin* editor, called to warn me, then he called the other three city editors to his office to meet with me. They'd all received the same call, just as Older had feared. I tried to persuade them not to print the story. I told them about your changes at the canneries to show that you have become a new woman."

She leaned forward, her hands clutched in her lap. "What difference will that make to them?"

"It might be enough to put them in sympathy with you. And remind them that now you are one of them, a journalist."

She sat back. "I hadn't thought about that."

"Anyway the editors handled it much better than I thought they would." He lifted a stack of papers from the floor beside his chair. "All of the papers did mention your mother's sudden illness, but none called it an attempted suicide."

He opened the *Examiner* to the place he'd obviously marked. "Mrs. Florence Jackson, widow of the late San Francisco businessman August P. Jackson, was suddenly taken ill early this morning. Mrs. Jackson, though unwell, had returned from a sanitarium to be with her daughter, Miss Cecilia Jackson, after the recent scandal. It is unfortunate that some rumors have been spread about Mrs. Jackson's illness today which are groundless.

"Evidently, Miss Jackson's experience of forsaking the city's social life has imbued her with a new, more serious purpose in life. She herself has embarked on a new venture into journalism. Read tomorrow's *Examiner* to learn more of her new social progressivism across the Bay."

He gave her a look of concern. "The others are similar to this."

"But it didn't say anything about suicide, just rumors," she objected.

"I know, but what if the doctor continues spreading the rumor? He may decide to. Men don't like having their word called groundless rumors. For that reason alone, I had to warn you. I didn't want to upset your mother. That's why I brought you here."

She rubbed her forehead. *Why does God hate me? Can't anything ever go right?* "What should I do?" she murmured.

"Exactly what you're doing now. Except...." He paused. "Perhaps your mother should go back to the sanitarium—"

"No!" She lurched forward; the wool afghan slid to the floor.

He held up his hand. "Just for a brief visit. It's no one's business that she was treated for alcoholism. If your mother is under the care of physicians at the sanitarium again, her illness will be seen as a relapse related to her previous stay. That should weaken any gossip the doctor might have spread or will spread."

"I don't want to lose Mother again." Pressing her elbows into her knees, she buried her face in her hands. "And what will it do to her, to have to go back there?"

"It will be for only a few days. She'll go willingly if we explain it to her. She'll want to do it to help you. I wouldn't urge you to do this unless I thought it were absolutely necessary." He paused and searched her eyes. *Was he asking too much?*

She gazed at him. "Is it necessary?"

He nodded. "But Millie could go with her. We can visit her every day if you wish. By the time she comes back, our journal will be out. Your new career as a social progressive will have been launched." He smiled at her. "This will all be forgotten."

As always, his smile reassured her. "Do you think so?"

He nodded. "It will be only a short separation. When she returns, your life together will really begin."

He made everything sound so reasonable. *How could she doubt him?* Her emotions seemed all used up. She couldn't think. "If you think it's really for the best."

Her easy acquiescence surprised Linc. She'd never agreed to anything this easily before. Maybe she had been finally transformed enough to accept suggestions.

"Cecilia, I pray that will be so. I think this..." he motioned to the open paper in his lap, "is from God. I don't think that I could have persuaded the editors without His blessing."

She frowned. "I know you're a person of faith. But I'm not. I'm sorry if that hurts you. But it's the truth. I haven't seen much of God in my life or my mother's."

"Cecilia—"

She straightened in her chair and looked at him directly. "But I'm going to go ahead with my work on your journal and on changing matters at my factories. Whether God loves me or hates me, I can't stand by and not change such...oppression. I'm not an oppressor."

"No," he agreed. *You've been oppressed.* "But just as you did at the canneries, you must go slow and make well-thought-out improvements. As a woman, you'll be held to a higher standard—always. If you make mistakes, others will use them against you—saying you are incompetent to handle such weighty matters. What did your business adviser think of what you've done with your canneries?"

"I didn't ask him, but he didn't look pleased. Why should I care?"

So like the old Cecilia. "Because it's never wise to put people's backs up. If you take time to persuade, things will go smoother. You'll be well thought of. I want you to have the kind of freedom I have. I associate with the intelligentsia as well as the fashionable and humble."

"I still don't believe I will want to associate with society. My aunt is well-respected in Boston and now you and I know the truth about her!"

Linc shook his head. "My Aunt Eugenia is well-respected in Boston too. I'm going to send her the first issue of my journal. Just wait until she reads what you've done here. All of Boston will hear of it. My aunt has spent her life working to lift up the poor. My aunt may be a snob, but she has a good heart."

"Unlike my aunt."

The desire to draw Cecilia close, to allow himself to feel the joy of stroking her soft cheek and kissing her fragrant hair engulfed him. He resisted. *That's not possible. Cecy must be a confidant, a friend, nothing more. I'm acting like a fool even thinking these thoughts. I can't forget Virginia.*

The pocket door slid open. Susan walked in. "Linc, Del is here."

"Where?" *Thank God.* Linc stood up and slid the papers onto the side table.

"He's in the kitchen. Kang's making him a snack." Susan folded her hands over her waist.

Cecy tried to read Susan's mood, but couldn't.

CHAPTER 14

"I'll go see him." Linc strode out the doorway.

Cecy had a physical reaction, a feeling of loss, to his leaving her. As he had talked, she'd been distracted by thoughts that strayed to the memory of Linc's embrace and kisses this morning. She longed for him to hold her again.

Then Susan stepped forward and opened her arms toward Cecy. "Miss Jackson, you come here. I have a hug with your name on it. I've heard you had a terrible day."

Cecy stood up and walked into the large woman's arms. Briefly, she rested her head on Susan's cushion-soft breast. "Oh, Susan, I never want another day like this."

"I know what you mean." Susan rocked her slightly side to side. "Most days pass before we know it. But some days live on in our memories. Some good. Some bad." She looked into Cecy's eyes. "Meg wants to see you."

Susan released Cecy.

Cecy brightened. "I'd love to see her. I'll go right up with you."

"Good. But if you don't need me to come along with you, I think I'll just sit down in here and rest some."

"You're all right, aren't you, Aunt Susan?"

Susan shuffled slowly to the chair nearest the fireplace. "I'm an old woman and those stairs are getting to me. Why this San Francisco have to be such an up-and-down place? Everywhere I go, I got to walk either steps or hills. Chicago was nice and flat."

Cecy giggled, then felt the wonder of hearing herself. After all that happened today, she could still laugh.

Cecy ran out into the hall and up the flight of stairs to Meg's room. The door was open. Before she could speak, Meg scrambled to her.

"Miss Cecilia, how are you? Your mama's sick!"

Taking Meg's hand, she let the child lead her into the room. "My mother's going to be fine."

"I'm glad. You lost your papa. I wouldn't want you to lose your mama too."

Cecy smoothed Meg's dark hair off her sweet, rosy face. This child must favor her mother. This thought caused Cecy a moment of disquiet. *Linc's life with Virginia has nothing to do with me.* "I'm not going to lose her, but she's going to go away for a while for a rest."

"Good. She'll be better then. Aunt Susan needs to rest a lot now too."

"Oh?" Cecy heard the worry in the child's voice.

"Yes, she has to stop all the time on walks. And she cries, but she says it's just being tired makes her eyes water." Meg looked up into Cecy's eyes with a serious face. "Del doesn't live here anymore. I think that makes Susan cry." Meg looked ready to cry herself.

Recalling Nana's sweet ways, Cecy drew Meg over to the rocking chair by the bed. She coaxed Meg onto her lap. Holding a child in her arms was still a new experience, a very pleasant one, with Meg. "You mustn't worry, dear." *How nice to have someone to call "dear."* "Your father will find a way to persuade Del to come home." *If anyone can, Linc will.*

"It's because the kids at school called him names because he isn't white like me. People don't like you if you have dark skin. I hate that."

Cecy couldn't think what to reply. The child merely spoke the truth. She could imagine how cruel the children at school had been. Adults weren't much kinder. Her mind went back to Clarissa Hunt's phone call.

"Don't worry, Meg. Your father will fix everything."

"Aunt Susan says faith is the victory," Meg said seriously.

"Well, Susan would know more about that than I would." Then Cecy indulged herself by hugging Meg close, rocking her. She kissed the little girl's cheek. How blessed Linc was to have this sweet child as his daughter.

★ ★ ★ ★ ★

Linc watched Del neatly "putting away" a stack of pancakes and a rasher of bacon. Kang poured Del a second glass of milk.

Del looked sideways at Linc. "I'm sorry I ran away. That was bad."

Linc nodded, wondering what was coming next. Had letting the boy see how the other half lived worked? *God, is he ready?* Or had Del just come home, driven by an empty stomach?

"But I like it down on the coast. Nobody picks on me."

Kang stepped forward and waved a spatula in Del's face. "Nobody pick on you here."

Linc glanced with surprise at Kang. The houseman hadn't ever come forward with an opinion about the family before.

Del looked startled too.

"You do bad, treat father with disrespect," Kang accused, still gesturing with the spatula.

"Linc isn't my father," Del objected.

"He is your father. He give you home, food, send to school."

"I can take care of myself now," Del blustered.

Linc thought Del's milk "mustache" cost him some credibility, but Linc kept his peace. Maybe Kang could make Del listen to reason.

"You get mad at school. Kids call you name because you colored. You think you the only one? They call Kang—'stupid Chinee. Hey, dumb Chinaman'. Kang no run away. Kang work and help family. When father die, he say, Kang take care of mother and sisters. You good son."

Kang put his hands on his hips. "Even dog know better than you. Dog do good to one who feeds him."

Del stood up. "I don't have to listen to you."

Kang pointed at the table. "Sit. Eat. You still full of foolishness. Someday you be sorry you show disrespect to father. Someday."

☙ ☙ ☙ ☙ ☙

March 30, 1906

"Are you sure you want to help me proofread?" Linc stood by his desk in his office. Electric lights gleamed against the shadows of dusk.

"Yes, I'm sure. That's what I've been hired on to do, isn't it?" Cecilia removed her russet gloves and tucked them into the pocket of her matching cape. "Should we get started?"

"Very well." He hung her wrap on the coat tree by the inner door. With the beautiful redhead in it, his office felt very small, almost confining. When she'd walked in, he'd found it harder to breathe.

Moments before he'd been all alone—but not at peace. His thoughts had been a snarl of worry about Del, excitement mixed with dread over the launching of his new journal and intermixed had been short flashes of Cecilia—the image of her beauty the first night he'd met her at the Ward's ball, the glory of her soprano voice as she sang *La Boheme* right before Hunt's attack, the saucy grin she gave him every time she flipped the switch to start her auto....

"Should we get started?" she repeated with a quizzical look.

"Here." He scanned his cluttered desk and picked up the sheaf of papers. He pushed away his musings. He would ignore her attraction. *He would.* "I just got the galley back from the typesetter. It needs to be proofread for mistakes."

He handed her a yellow pencil taking care not to touch her elegant fingers. He imagined turning her hand over and kissing her palm. *No.* He cleared his throat and said in a businesslike tone, "Lightly circle any mistake you find, then mark down the number of the line and note the mistake on the sheet."

"Shouldn't I check my own articles?" She glanced up at him.

Fighting the urge to interlace his fingers on each side of her head into the hair above her small shell-like ears, he stood straighter. "No, you're less likely to see your own mistakes. Your mind fixes things automatically before you see them."

"Really? I hadn't thought of that. But it makes sense." She sat down.

He reached over to switch on the green-shaded desk lamp. His hand brushed the nubby fabric of her brown tweed suit. This only served to carry his mind back to the sensation of touching the silky robe she wore that morning standing beside her mother's bedside. *Stop it. Now.*

"I'll get busy then." She picked up the top page.

He nodded, then went back to his own desk. He couldn't focus. The air around him felt charged. Her presence expanded in the room. He closed his eyes, willing himself free of her. He made himself look down at the page in front of him focusing on Cecilia's description of her impressions of the first day at the sardine cannery: "I wish, dear reader, I could part the veil of ignorance that separates those with wealth from those without. That day, across the Bay, I walked through that veil and looked upon the poor who came to work the sardine catch."

His pride in her increased with each word.

"What a stench! What noise! The machinery assaulted my ears so they soon felt numb from the horrific din. Men, women, and the veriest children all streaming in to work at hearing the sound of a screeching whistle. I am not a mother, but any mother's heart would have been wrenched to see little babes lie, as discarded trash in flimsy boxes—"

"Linc?" Her voice stirred all the passion and love he'd fought since she entered.

He sat up straighter. "Yes?" Her burnished auburn beauty captivated him anew. The lamp's light and shadows highlighted her womanly curves which the sober tweed suit was designed to hide.

"May I ask? Del's...all right?"

Her question sobered him. "Del still hasn't found his place."

"What do you mean?"

"I mean, he doesn't feel he belongs with me and Meg. But I'm sure he's finding out he doesn't fit in playing ragtime on the Coast either."

"I think I see what you mean. Is that the problem?"

In spite of her presence, worry over Del hung over him like a pall. "Yes, he doesn't fit the stereotype of a black boy. He never will." Each word he spoke took his spirits lower. "His way won't be easy, but I'm powerless to change the world as it is. Since Reconstruction, lynchings are the scourge of the South. For Del, life will hold dangers I can't ward off. He has to learn to go on with his life—as much as he can—in the face of the prejudice around him. He must learn to lean on God. God's strength is the only thing I know that will give him the endurance he needs for a lifetime. He must adapt because I don't see bigotry vanishing anytime soon. It's cruel, but it's reality. If he can't go on in spite of it...." This fear silenced him.

"I never really thought about people different from me. Susan isn't anything like I thought when I first met her. I admit at first I thought she was your housekeeper." She blushed. "But she's a wonderful person and I'm so glad Meg has her."

Cecilia's concern for Meg's care touched him deeply. He knew it sprung from her own harsh neglect. *This woman has a tender heart.* When they first met, she'd camouflaged it—or had her aunt's interference been to blame? He couldn't help himself, he grinned. "Susan is a rock. How is your mother?"

"I spoke to her today on the phone. She's glad she returned to the sanitarium. She wanted to visit some friends there. She says she's feeling stronger, but would like to stay just a few days—"

A tap at the outer door interrupted her.

Linc rose and went to open it. When he returned, he had a man and a woman with him.

Cecy looked up. "Fleur! Mr. Bower!"

"Cecilia." Fleur hurried to her and took both Cecy's hands in hers. "How have you been?"

Cecy looked to Mr. Bower. "Very well, thank you. But, Sir, I have been so concerned for you."

"I'm much better. Please call me Clarence."

❋ ❋ ❋ ❋ ❋

Cecy couldn't take her eyes from Bower who stood a little behind Fleur. "Are you really all healed then, ...Clarence?"

"Yes, though my face...." He grinned. "Has taken on an interesting scar."

The emotions from that awful night rushed back through her. "I'm sor—"

"Now it wasn't your fault." Fleur released her hands and stepped aside, so Clarence could bow over Cecy's hand in greeting. "We know you are completely innocent."

Linc quickly arranged four chairs into a cozy circle.

"I've wanted to visit you before this," Clarence said with his hat balanced on his knee. "But I wasn't well and my parents insisted I take no action until my sister's elopement had been accepted by society."

Cecy was shocked by his frankness and couldn't reply.

"You've heard that Hunt married Clarissa?" Fleur asked gently.

"She called me." Cecy remembered Clarissa's nasty phone call.

"No!" Fleur looked saddened.

"But she needn't worry. I had no feelings for Hunt," Cecy went on, looking at Clarence. His frankness made her brave. "Do your parents approve of the elopement?"

"They have no choice. Clarissa would have been ruined if her marriage weren't accepted. I rue the day my sister became infatuated with Hunt. I don't think he'll ever be finished sowing his wild oats. But I can't convince my father of that."

Cecy agreed with him, but merely nodded.

Linc spoke, "What can we do for you?"

Glancing sideways toward Clarence and Linc, Cecy compared the men—both were tall, blonde with blue eyes. Clarence was still handsome in spite of the vivid red welt on one cheek. But Linc, by far, was the more attractive man. His face showed strength and wisdom. The desire to pass her fingertips over Linc's lips as a blind person reading Braille came over her. *What a strange thought.*

Tugging off her pale kid gloves, Fleur replied, "Well, first we just wanted to see you two." She glanced to Cecy. "We have been reading about what you've been doing at your canneries. It's wonderful—exciting."

Cecy couldn't hide her pleasure. "It really *has* been exhilarating. For the first time, I feel like I'm doing something important with my life."

"It's wonderful." Clarence edged forward on his chair. "And we want you to know that we're going to do everything we can to smooth your way back into society—"

Cecy's heart jerked in her breast. "I don't—"

"Please let us continue." Fleur leaned over and touched Cecy's hand.

Cecy glanced down at Fleur's hand. A large diamond ring caught her eye. "You're engaged!"

Fleur blushed. "Yes, Clarence did the honor of proposing to me a few days ago. It will be announced soon."

Linc cleared his throat. "Congratulations, both of you."

"Yes, I hope you will both be very happy." As Cecy said the accepted phrase, suddenly she knew she actually meant it. "I'm really happy for you. Really."

Clarence nodded. "I'm glad because we came to ask you to be Fleur's maid of honor."

CHAPTER 15

"Do not boast about tomorrow."
Proverbs 27:1a, NIV

"MAID OF HONOR?" Cecy rose in her chair, then sank back down, gripping its supple leather arms.

Clarence lifted his chin and spoke rapidly, "Yes, Fleur and I talked this over. We consider you a friend and we think it will encourage your acceptance back into society."

Cecy noted Fleur had lowered her worried, brown eyes while Clarence had spoken. "But your sister," Cecy looked to Clarence. "Shouldn't she be matron of honor?"

His handsome face tightened grimly. "She won't be able. She'll be near the end of her confinement by then."

"She's expecting?" Cecy felt ill. Victor Hunt, a father? *No.*

Bridging his hands in front of himself, Linc leaned forward, his voice calm. "I understand your generous motive to help right the wrong done to Cecilia, but you may do a lot more harm than good."

He was right. Cecy looked at Clarence and Fleur. Clarence shifted in his chair, awkward, tense. Fleur sat, folded into herself, subdued. Neither looked happy like an engaged couple should.

Linc continued, "Please, if I may make a suggestion, wait until your sister recovers from her confinement. Then, since Fleur has no sister of her own, Clarissa should be the matron of honor. Passing her over for Cecilia, someone your sister views as a rival, may and will, cause hard feelings that could linger for years, generations." Linc paused, then smiled encouragingly. "Cecilia, of course, would make a lovely bridesmaid—among several other of your friends. It's very important that you don't pit Cecilia against your sister and her husband."

Cecy watched for the couple's reaction. When they didn't respond, she said hesitantly, "I think Linc's right. To be honest, we all know what kind of man Victor Hunt is. I was as naïve as your sister.... Life with him will not be...easy." Cecy couldn't tell them of her mother's tragedy. But she didn't want to see Clarissa cut off from help as she and her mother had been. She wouldn't wish such suffering on anyone.

In the lengthening silence, a cable-car bell clanged outside on the street. From under her lashes, Fleur glanced at Clarence.

Clarence grimaced, then relaxed in his chair. "You were right, Fleur. You told me she wouldn't think it was a good idea."

"Mr. Bower, your sister will need your support." Cecy looked directly into his eyes. She wanted to say so much more, but discretion prevented her. "I hope you understand."

"I do. I've already warned Hunt I'll be visiting my sister often." He gave her a look filled with meaning. A few more moments of polite conversation, then the happy twosome rose to leave.

Cecy stood next to Linc at the office door as they watched the elevator doors close behind the departing couple. "You were right. I didn't believe you when you said they would assist me back into society."

"I was proud of you just now." He rested one hand on her shoulder. "Your first thought was for Clarissa."

"I pity her. I pray she doesn't suffer from her poor choice to marry Victor Hunt." The disdain in her voice made crystal clear her opinion of Hunt.

But it also spoke of her own pain. Tentatively, Linc stroked her velvet cheek. "You don't have a very high opinion of men and marriage, do you?"

She slanted her chin up. But inside, she reacted to his soft touch. Her breath caught in the back of her throat. "Would you if you were me?"

The coldness of her tone pierced Linc, an icy needle through his heart. Did she doubt him too? Couldn't she see he was different than Hunt, her father? He'd started letting go of his guilt over losing Virginia. Could Cecy ever let go of her distrust of men? He pressed his case, pushing her to react. "Don't you think you might fall in love someday?"

"Never."

Her instant dismissal deepened his longing, his despair. His voice dipped lower as emotion expanded inside him. "What if someone fell in love with you?"

Whirling from him, she spoke facing away from him and with a harsh imitation of worldly wisdom, "No one will ever love me—except for my money."

Underlying all the sarcasm, he heard clearly the deeper pain. Just as he had pushed God away and clung to his own grief, she didn't believe she was lovable. He stepped nearer. "That isn't so." The creamy skin of her nape glowed in the light. He could barely speak, his words came out hoarse and low. "I'm in love with you."

She didn't move. She didn't appear to breathe.

Leaning toward her back, he let his own breath caress her neck, just below her ear. "I've fallen in love with you. I don't need your wealth. My own inheritance is more than I will ever need." He drew her shoulders back to him. The wool of her suit sensitized his fingertips. He whispered into her ear, "I love you—you, headstrong, passionate, lovely...innocent woman. I vowed never to forget my wife, but I love you. You're too young for me. I believe in God and the work he's given me. You have no faith beyond yourself. Yet I...love...you."

He turned her by her shoulders—fraction by fraction. Then his lips brushed against hers.

Electricity.

He murmured against her soft lips, even as he kissed her, "I love you."

He pulled her closer; his arms bound her. His kiss deepened.

Cecy felt warm and lighter than air—as though she might drift away from the earth. She slipped her arms around his neck, then she lifted herself on tiptoe, so she could return his kiss. His enthralling kiss.

The times before when she kissed him had been different. This time she sensed he'd lost restraint. The raw edge of his passion awakened her, made her welcome and return his kisses. She felt him loosen her hair pins. Her hair slid free.

With one arm, he cradled her head. With the other, he drew her radiant tresses forward over her shoulder. "You always smell of spring flowers." Lacing his fingers through her silken hair, he turned his head and kissed her parted lips.

Linc, Linc. All the jagged, sharp edges of her shattered emotions cried out for his healing touch. His insistent, intoxicating lips wandered down her neck. His fingers teased through her hair. Each tender kiss, each feather-soft caress soothed, healed her.

A warm tide flowed through her and she floated on the sensation. She'd never known such pleasure. All the operas she'd ever sung had glorified love, passion. Was this what Madame

Butterfly experienced in the arms of her American officer? Was this love, temptation? Was this what brought joy, then tragedy?

She pulled back, her hands pushed forward fending him away. "No. Don't love me. I want no man's love."

"Even mine?" His intense gaze halted her, held her motionless.

"Even yours." She turned her back to him and gathered up her wanton hair, twisting it back into place. "I will never marry. I thought you knew that."

"And I never thought I could love again. I've changed."

"You've changed." His voice caressed her. "Don't you think this intention might change too?"

"No. Don't love me, Linc. I will never love you." Still, she wouldn't face him.

He stared at her back, stiff and resolute. Finally, he spoke. The words gritted in his dry throat. "Let's get back to work then." He went to his own desk. "Please forget my lapse of decorum. It won't happen again." Each polite word cost him pain.

Without a glance at him, she moved to her desk and sat down to work.

Linc stared at her. *I love you. I don't have a choice. This love must come from God. I never sought it. I love you Cecilia, for better or worse, for richer for poorer, until death do us part. Just as only death parted me from Virginia, my first love, not my last.*

❋ ❋ ❋ ❋ ❋

April 6, 1906

In the brightly lit and crowded restaurant, Cecy couldn't take her eyes off Linc. Tonight he drew her attention like a beacon on a dark horizon. Devastatingly handsome in evening dress, Linc sat across from her at their table for four. Fleur, in deep rose satin, sat to her left; Clarence to her right. The diners at the table next to theirs burst into laughter. Lucchetti's, done in red, white, and green, the first-ever Italian restaurant for

Cecilia and Fleur, had been Clarence's choice for their dinner date.

"I was right, wasn't I?" Clarence grinned. "This is just the spot for a friendly dinner."

"Clarence." Fleur gave him a coquettish smile. "You know, I've never eaten Italian food before."

"Then you're in for a treat." His eyes on Cecy, Linc swirled the water in his glass, making the ice clink. "I haven't had spaghetti since leaving Chicago. Kang makes Chinese noodles, but no spaghetti."

"But I ordered the ravioli," Fleur objected.

"Even better!" Clarence lifted his glass of red wine and saluted his fiancée.

Cecy knew they were trying to cheer her and the light-hearted company was balm to her nerves. She hadn't wanted to appear in public after the last round of gossip over her mother's illness and her own new profession, but she'd given in to their urging. Since that horrible night she'd almost lost her mother, she hadn't been out in a social setting.

After the story about her mother's illness ran in the papers, both Effie Bond and Bonnie LaRoux had called to give her sympathy and encouragement. She felt their concern was genuine, not society's insincere show. Maybe Linc had the best attitude. He was at ease in society, at a filthy sardine cannery, and among the avant-garde. Perhaps she, too, could have that kind of easy entree into every level of society. She felt Linc's gaze on her though she wouldn't meet it. His kisses just a few days ago still haunted her daydreams, her night dreams. His kisses....

"Cecilia." Fleur touched her hand and nodded discreetly to the side.

Cecy followed Fleur's gaze and glimpsed Mrs. Ward and her protégé, Ann, sitting down at a table to their left. Cecy's pulse sped up. That final time she'd promenaded with Aunty on Montgomery Street, Mrs. Ward had cut her. Cecy recoiled from the humiliating memory. Fortunately, tonight she'd worn a hat with a short veil of cream-colored lace. She tugged at it to better conceal her face on the left side.

As though unaware of Mrs. Ward, Fleur said in a low voice, "We talked to Clarence's parents last night about our wedding. We've decided to marry in New Orleans in December, then we'll return to San Francisco after the honeymoon."

"In Bermuda." Clarence winked broadly at Linc. "Far from both our families and an island, so she won't be able to get away from me."

Fleur giggled delightedly. "Clarence, please. Behave yourself."

The engaged couple's happy teasing slit open a thin wall that covered a deep emptiness inside Cecy. Did Fleur and Clarence know how rare their sincere love was? Fleur, a sweet innocent, capable of love. Clarence an honest man. Cecy couldn't doubt he would make Fleur a good husband.

Clarence adjusted his already correct cuffs. "I am behaving myself. Linc understands me, don't you?" He winked.

Cecy glanced forward, knowing she'd find Linc gazing at her. When she recalled his fingers lacing through her hair, the veil hid her blush.

Linc looked into her eyes alone. "A honeymoon is a special time to hide away, just the two of you. Its memories will carry you through many spats and rough patches." Linc experienced a stab of regret and longing. The woman he loved sat across the table from him—unreachable. She might as well be standing on the other side of the Pacific. *Life and love are so fragile in this fallen world. Let me love you, Cecilia.*

"Thank you, Linc." Fleur nodded. "But, both of you, we'd still love to have you come to our weddin'." Fleur glanced at each of them in turn. "Would you consider comin'?"

Linc knew he should give his regrets, but he hesitated waiting to see what Cecilia would say.

"December is months from now." Cecy took a sip of her tea. "I'll wait and see how my mother is and if I'll be able to get away. But thank you for asking."

Did she mean that, Linc wondered.

With a flourish, the white-aproned waiter brought a large wooden bowl of lettuce, tomatoes, and green onions and tossed their salad at their table.

Taking her first bite, Cecy savored the tangy dressing over the greens and crisp croutons. Her veil masking her own eyes, she studied Linc, so handsome and distinguished. He'd told her he loved her. She knew he wouldn't have declared his love for her if he hadn't meant it. And she had rejected his love. She'd probably caused him deep pain, pain he didn't deserve.

Now witnessing the love between Fleur and Clarence made her wonder. Had she given Linc the answer her aunt had drummed into her? Not the one that might actually lie within her own heart?

But merely thinking this made her stomach clench. *No! I can't.* Her mother's face flashed in her mind. Pushing worry away, she turned to Fleur. "Are you going to hear Caruso sing?"

"Oh, I would love to." Fleur nodded. "I'm sure you'll want to. With your lovely singing voice."

"Yes, it's only a few weeks away. I'm really looking forward to it." A motion to her left stopped her. *Oh, no.*

Linc observed that Cecy stopped eating. *What had upset her?* Her fork clattered to the floor. He glanced up to see Mrs. Ward and Ann approaching their table. Why did they have to come here tonight of all nights? His first instinct was to throw himself in front of his love. But he couldn't do that. Instead, he rose politely.

"Miss Jackson, we thought that was you." Mrs. Ward's piercing voice cut through the hubbub of the restaurant. Her huge lavender hat with a bird perched high in its netting towered over Cecy.

Clarence stood too. Linc clutched his napkin like a weapon.

"Good evening, Mrs. Ward, Ann," Fleur greeted them.

Cecilia appeared to be frozen in her chair. She glanced neither to the right or left.

Mrs. Ward gushed nervously, "Congratulations, Clarence, and best wishes, my dear Miss Fourchette. I see you're celebrating your engagement with Miss Jackson and Lincoln. Good evening." Mrs. Ward moved to Linc's side of the table and offered him her hand. "Lincoln, I just received a letter from your dear Aunt Eugenia. She's so excited about your journal! The *Cause Celebre!* What a clever title! She's showing everyone in Boston her first issue."

With a swirl of white ostrich feathers, the lady turned back towards the table. "But your article, Miss Jackson, both Lincoln's aunt and I agreed it was the best of Lincoln's first issue. So moving! Your description of those poor babies brought tears to my eyes. Didn't you agree, Ann?"

Little Ann nodded enthusiastically. "I think you're wonderful. You're helping people—"

"Yes, such a good work," Mrs. Ward finished for her. "Cecilia," the matron lowered her voice, "your aunt astonished us by leaving so abruptly. I was so glad that your mother was able to come home. So sorry she had a relapse. Is she feeling better again?"

Cecy nodded woodenly. "She should be home again soon."

"When she is feeling better, I'll call. Do let me know. I'm sure she'd love to join our embroidery circle."

Cecilia barely nodded once more.

Mrs. Ward leaned close to Linc's ear in a flutter of ostrich feathers. "Tell Cecilia her aunt didn't receive a warm welcome in Boston." The lady turned to her protégé. "Ann, I think we should go back to our table now. Archie will be joining us— Oh! There he is. There may be another engagement announced soon." She tittered, then waved, returning to her table in a flurry of feathers and well wishes.

Linc and Clarence took their seats.

Fleur whispered, "Such a sweet lady, but she *does* talk so."

Clarence smothered a belly laugh.

Fleur threw her napkin at him.

He laughed out loud.

"Hush, Clarence, hush," Fleur hissed indignantly. "I declare you're embarrassin' me."

Linc glanced across at Cecy. Was she upset by Mrs. Ward's visit? Had she heard what the lady had said of her aunt? He studied her. She was staring wistfully at Fleur.

✹ ✹ ✹ ✹ ✹

April 8, 1906

"Rats," Cecy hit the leather dashboard of her runabout with both her hands. Around them the city hurried about its business under the gray April sky. Rain appeared imminent. "I could spit nails."

Linc agreed, but grinned at her colorful phrase. "You know what's happening, don't you?"

"Someone warned them." She turned to him. "Who?"

"Who do you think?"

"Edmonds." She hit the dashboard again.

"You win." He should have warned her to not let her business advisor know the day she planned to begin her factory inspections. This was the second factory they'd visited. Both factories had resembled ghost towns. Edmonds obviously had decided Cecy couldn't expose anything, if nothing was in operation.

"What can we do?" She glanced sideways at him.

"You're the boss lady," he said wryly.

"That's right. I am." She stared straight ahead momentarily. Flipping the starter switch, she backed out into the traffic. Two horses reared, objecting to her auto. She tooted her horn, grinned at the drivers' raised fists and waved as she drove away. "I will go to the warehouse I remember seeing on another list."

Linc frowned. "If we can't find any of your factories in operation today, maybe we can interview some workers."

"Not on your life. I won't put up with this." She swept around a corner making two men jump back onto the curb. "If

Edmonds bucks me any further, I'll fire him. I'll fire everyone and start fresh."

He grinned. Many things about Cecilia had changed, but her determination to have her own way had not. *August P. Jackson, this is your daughter. Too bad you didn't value her as you should have. But perhaps God wants the strength you endowed her with for his glory.*

Within a few blocks, Cecy pulled up to one of many seedy warehouses along the South End district. The afternoon sun was warm. Linc looked forward to shedding his driving coat.

"Cecilia—"

"Linc, I really don't like that name."

"You mean Cecilia?" He tried to gauge her mood.

"Yes, will you call me Cecy?" She lowered her chin.

"You mean like Millie does?" *What did this change signify?*

"Yes, please. I've never liked my name. Cecy is who I've always thought of myself as." Her voice sounded gentle like it did when she talked to Meg. Was she softening to him?

He turned toward her. "Really? Why do you think that is, Cecy?"

"Cecy is...Cecy is separate from my father, from the Boston school, from my Aunt Amelia. Cecy is me...myself connected to Nana."

"You still plan to call her Nana, not Millie?"

She looked thoughtful. "Yes, she will always be Nana."

"She's like a mother to you."

"Yes, and she was really the only one to successfully oppose my father."

"How do you mean?"

"Well, she took care of me, so that I...prospered. She protected me, shielded me from him. That was her victory."

She prayed for you too. He nodded. "You've thought deeply about this."

"Everything I believed about my life before the night of Hunt's attack wasn't true at all. Lies. My aunt had fed me lies, so she'd have her revenge and the life she wanted. She was concerned with herself not me. But she failed."

Thanks to God.

"I'm going to have the life I want my way."

Not God's way? But he kept his peace. He sensed this wasn't the time to speak of the possibility of God having a plan for her life. Now that he'd finally let his guilt over Virginia go, he felt God drawing him closer each day. "What does that life include?" *Does it include me?*

"I'm not sure yet. Not completely. But right now I'm going to clean up my businesses and do what I can to learn to write well."

"Good. But you aren't leaving open the door for love?" He couldn't have stopped himself from asking this question if he'd tried.

"Love." She thrust open her car door and stepped outside with a decided swirl of her skirt. She faced forward, only giving him her profile.

Following suit, he exited the car. But he bent forward resting his wrists on the top of the shining green door. He studied her as she struggled inwardly, such an inner conflict. And she held it in so tightly.

Over her shoulder, she glanced at him, then untied her driving veil and threw it back onto the top of her hat. "You are my best friend, my first real friend in my whole life." She leaned her hip against the car. "The other night I was thinking about what my life would have been like if I had been born lucky like Meg." Her gaze connected with his again. "If I'd been loved and kept at home, not sent away, I think love could have been a part of my life."

"You think it's impossible for you to love?" He could barely speak. His mouth was so dry.

"Linc, do you know what I felt when you asked if I couldn't leave the door open for love?"

"What?"

"Panic. The urge to run and not to stop running until I reached safety."

He wanted to hold her. He didn't move a fraction. "Love isn't always cruel, Cecy. Just because your mother—"

She pinned him with an ironic expression. "This is me, Cecy Jackson, we're talking about. What do I know of love? In all my life only Nana and my mother loved me, but I lost them both when I was seven years old. Do you know what that feels like?"

How could such a lovely, young face look so desolate? He longed to comfort her, but forced himself to stay on his side of the car. "I've known loss. I lost my father and a son I never got to know."

"And Virginia."

He looked away and sucked in his breath. A faint echo of his guilt screeched like a circling seagull over the warehouse. "Virginia is with God. I am free to love again."

"But I don't think I'm capable of loving any man." She faced him fully. Her brown eyes alive with suffering. "All I know is that the thought of trusting someone that much makes me sick with fear."

"Perfect love casts out fear," he murmured.

"Nothing is perfect in this world." She grimaced. "Don't preach to me." She straightened up and turned away from him again. "If I never hear another sermon, it will be too soon."

She folded her arms. "You said I was a changed woman and I am. After all the disasters I've gone through in three short months, I'm finally able to see my life the way it is. I'm going to live a good life, doing work I care about. Nothing will stop me now. And that's the last time I want to have this discussion."

He straightened, ignoring his sudden loss of energy. How could he shake her out of this cynicism? "Very well. I see you have your mind made up. Shall we go in?"

"Wait." She held up her hand. "You go in the office and keep the manager busy while I look around in the back."

"Cecilia, no—"

"Don't argue." She motioned airily and lightened her tone. "It's my factory. It's my story."

He grimaced, but headed for the door with the word "Office" printed above it in white letters.

Cecy walked around the other side of the dusty warehouse looking for another entrance. This time she was determined to glimpse what was really going on here, not what Mr. Edmonds wanted her to think was going on. She turned the corner of the building and came upon what must be the loading area. A gray-haired man was snoozing on a chair propped against the wall at the top of a short flight of steps. She ran lightly up and passed by the sleeping man.

Inside the warehouse, only dim natural light shone through high, dirty windows. Cecy walked quietly across the littered cement floor looking up at the landings of two higher levels. Had Edmonds closed down the operation here or was this just a time between shipments?

A door above her slammed back against the wall. "I told you get outta here!" The voice was a roar and markedly slurred. Was someone drinking on the job?

Cecy hurried forward.

"But you owe me three days wages," a child's voice whined. "I can't go home without it. Ma said."

Running toward the voices, Cecy rushed up the steps at the end of the warehouse. Just as she reached the top, a burly man with a tight grip on a child's shirt rushed for the steps.

Cecy held up her hand. "Unhand that child—"

The scruffy child strained against the brute, then the boy swung back and bit the hand which held him.

"You little—" The man's oath was drowned out by the child's yelling.

The brute struck the side of the child's head. The boy screamed.

Cecy launched herself at the man. "Stop!"

CHAPTER 15

The man swung around to face her. His broad shoulder hit her hard, right at the breast bone, just above her corset. She gasped one torturous breath.

Her own momentum multiplied the blow's force. She flailed frantically. Backwards. She was falling backwards down the steps—screaming.

Crushing pain as her head hit a step.

Blinding agony. Her back scraped splintered wood.

Tumbling over and over…toward the cement!

"Help me! Linc! Linc!"

CHAPTER 16

"Wealth is worthless in the day of wrath...."
Proverbs 11:4, NIV

April 10, 1906

HOSPITAL NOISES—A SQUEAKING wheel on a cart, the clipped tones of the nurse's voice, a low moan, a sigh—the late-night routine of nurses and patients went on around Linc as he kept his vigil. Cecilia—his own dear Cecy—still lay unconscious in the hospital bed in the stark white room. He lifted her limp, but warm hand and savored this slight contact with her. He murmured, "Wake up, Cecy. Please wake up."

The white bandages around Cecy's head stood out in the feeble light from the hallway. Hidden by the shadows were the black and purple bruises that surrounded both her eyes and the side of her face and chin. The doctors had told him her body had suffered bruises all over and two cracked ribs. She should have awakened before this. The doctors surmised the repeated blows to her head must have been the most serious of her injuries from the fall. And they must be responsible for her continued unconsciousness.

Kissing her hand reverently, he gently placed it back on the white muslin hospital sheet. He glanced at the newspaper in his lap. Cecy, now proclaimed a heroine, had made the headlines again. Photographs of the warehouse and little boy Cecy had protected stared back at him. He tossed it onto the bedside table. His back aching from sitting too long, he rose and began pacing at the foot of her iron bed.

He suffered not only from worry about Cecy's continued unconsciousness, but also from his lack of connection to God. Always in the past, he'd felt his Father near, but after Virginia's death that had changed. *Dear God, please hear my prayer. I know I let my grief over Virginia intrude between you and me. I've finally accepted her death and I've just started feeling connected to you again. But I confess I can't understand why this has happened.*

You sent me here to shout for justice for the children. If this wasn't so, I could have remained in Chicago. Del would still be with us. Cecy wouldn't be lying here like this.

Have I read your Spirit's prompting wrong? I thought I was almost to my goal. This young woman has become a part of my life, my journal, the work you sent me to do. This young woman, the woman I love, had changed, turned around. She was on a mission of mercy, injured while protecting a child. You were there. You let her fall. Why?

Two days have passed and she hasn't opened her eyes. She grows weaker and weaker. Help me, Lord. I can't find my way.

A memory from his past, the image of Virginia clinging to life in the hellish hours after their son's stillbirth, thundered through him. He had to sit down. *I can't lose, Cecy, Lord. Please.* Holding his head and hands, tears leaked through his fingers. He swallowed sobs, vainly willing himself to stop.

Give me strength, Lord. My faith feels like an ocean mist—no longer a firm foundation. I know you're there. Let me feel your caring. Linc waited, his head bent in prayer. Slowly, slowly acceptance came. God knew the woman he loved lay here. God was here with him.

A nurse stepped in and by the low light took Cecy's pulse and temperature. Standing at the head of the bed, Linc watched. "Any change?" he whispered.

"No, sir." The nurse smoothed the blankets and pillow and left without a word.

Linc leaned down and kissed Cecy's drawn cheek. "You have to come back to us. You must wake up and drink and eat soon. Your mother collapsed after hearing what happened. She can't take many more days not knowing. Millie had to stay with her at the sanitarium. Please wake up."

Cecy, you needed me. I wasn't there.

"Why did I let you go in alone? I should have kept you by my side." The vivid memory of hearing her screams from the back of that warehouse turned his veins to ice. He'd nearly throttled the drunk who sent her down the rickety steps. It had taken two men to pull him off. Linc's own rage had shocked himself.

At last, fatigue conquered him. Leaning back in the stiff chair, he fell asleep.

❋ ❋ ❋ ❋ ❋

A moan.

Linc blinked in the subtle light of dawn.

A moan.

He sat up, shaking off sleep. "Cecy?" He cleared his clogged throat. "Cecy?"

"Linc?"

He watched her lick her dry lips. Seizing her hand, he leaned forward. "Cecy, wake up. Please." Hope flared through him.

She squeezed his hand slightly. "Oh, where am I?" She groaned. "Everything hurts." She groaned again. "My chest. Oh, I hurt."

Thank you, Lord. His voice shook. "You took a fall. Don't breathe too deeply. You've got two cracked ribs."

"Oh, I ache so...." She touched the bandages around her head. "How badly was I hurt?"

"You're bruised and battered." He fervently kissed her hand. "But you'll heal. Now you're awake and everything's going to be all right." His heart beating a triumphant chorus, he rose to summon the nurse.

"Why is it so dark? Turn on the light. I can't see you."

Her fretful words froze him where he stood. In the early morning light, he turned back to her and looked into her eyes. He saw no indication that she was seeing him. He began to speak. He stopped himself. Slowly he passed his hand in front of her eyes, knowing they should automatically track this movement.

They didn't.

The floor felt as though it were spinning beneath his feet. He clutched the cold iron railing on the bed.

"Turn on the lights, Linc," she repeated, agitated. "Oh, I hurt so. Turn on the lights. I'll feel better just seeing where I am."

He passed his trembling hand in front of her face once more. No response.

Turning, he stumbled to the door. He shouted, heedless of the other patients and the early hour, "Nurse! Nurse! Call the doctor. I need him—now!"

Then he stood gasping against the door jam, too shaky to move, to pray.

❧ ❧ ❧ ❧ ❧

The budding pink azaleas along the house mocked Linc as he walked slowly up the steps to his side door.

Kang opened it for him. "Mr. Linc, we got good news for you."

Linc forced himself to step inside. He dragged his hat from his head. He tried to focus on Kang. "What did you say?"

"Del come back last night. Sleep at home."

Linc halted, staring at the smiling houseman. "Del? Home?"

Kang nodded repeatedly. "Aunt Susan much happy. She sing all morning."

"Good." Linc, drained, leaned against the wall. Del had come home, but Linc didn't feel anything. His emotions had been flattened.

"You tired. Miss Jackson still sleep?"

Linc shook his head. "She's not asleep. She's sedated."

"Good. Good. Come in. You need coffee. I make fresh."

Linc let Kang lead him in to the kitchen table. Linc lowered himself to sit. He ached all over. He couldn't get Cecy's hysterical cries this morning, when she'd realized she was sightless, out of his mind.

Beaming, Susan walked into the kitchen. Her obvious joy made his anguish seem darker, weigh heavier. "Did Kang give you the good news?"

Linc lifted his eyes reluctantly, then nodded. He tried to feel relief. He didn't. *I feel dead.*

"Linc, what's wrong?" Susan put her hand on his forehead as she had done so many times when he was a child.

Kang stood by the stove holding the coffee pot in his hand. "Something go wrong at hospital?" He looked at Susan. "Mr. Linc says Miss Cecilia wake up."

"She can't see." Linc's voice ground low in his throat. "She's blind."

"No." Susan sat down. "Lord, have mercy."

"She became hysterical. They had to sedate her with laudanum. I came home to get some sleep, change clothes. I have to be there when she wakes again." Her earlier shrieks enveloped his mind.

He covered his face with trembling hands. "I can't see what's happening, Susan. I can't see my way. I prayed, felt comfort. But then this.... I was so sure the worst was over for Cecy, that everything was going to get better now. How much can one person bear? I fear for her sanity."

Susan touched his sleeve. "You're in love with her." She stated it as fact, not a question.

"I didn't want to love her."

"You and Virginia were like your mother and father. You had a deep love. But we don't always choose whom we love."

"My love for her isn't the focus now. My love only led her into harm's way. I don't know what to do. I still have to call Millie and tell her. This could set her mother back again. Her nerves are so fragile. This is all so cruel." His voice broke.

"What exactly did the doctor say?" Susan took his hand in hers sympathetically.

"They called in an eye specialist. He said the blindness must be from striking her head repeatedly as she fell. They know so little about the causes of blindness. Her eyesight could return slowly or—not at all."

"Miss Cecilia's blind?" Meg's shocked voice made Linc look up. Meg and Del came in together.

"Yes, Meg." He choked on the words. He opened his arms.

She rushed into his embrace. "I don't want her to be blind! She's so pretty and I like her."

Meg's tears wet his neck. He patted her back and watched a subdued Del snuggle close to Susan's side. "Home for good, Del?"

"Yes sir," Del said solemnly. "I won't ever run away again. I promise."

"Why?" Linc asked.

"I don't belong on the Coast. I guess I don't belong any-where, but Freddie said I should stick with my family. That's what's right."

"I think Kang mentioned that also." Though the boy's unhappiness was clear, Linc gave a shadow of a smile, trying to encourage him.

Kang nodded but did not show much satisfaction.

"I'm sorry Miss Cecilia is bad." Del frowned.

His spirit dragging in the dust, Linc squeezed the boy's shoulder and nodded. "I feel so guilty. I should have been with her. I should have been there to break her fall."

"Seems to me that's exactly what you been doin' ever since you met her." Susan looked at Linc steadily. "You've been there to catch her every time she fell. Maybe it was time for her to hit bottom."

But I've hit bottom with her. Oh, God, I can't bear it. Please let her see again.

🜨 🜨 🜨 🜨 🜨

Feeling as though he dragged bags of cement behind him, Linc walked into Cecy's room.

"Who's there?" she asked anxiously.

"It's me, Linc." He walked to her bedside. Her bruised and cut face stabbed his conscience. If only he could smooth all the marks away. And her skin would be clear and healthy again and her eyes would greet him.

"You left me." Her accusing voice heaped burning coals on his head.

"Not until you fell asleep." His hand inched over the coarse muslin sheet close to her arm, but stopped just before touching her.

"They drugged me."

"You were hysterical."

"Go away." Her tone was petulant. One tear slid down her right cheek.

"I won't leave you."

"I said go away." She turned her face away from him.

He sat down beside her. "Cecy, I don't know what to say to you."

She rolled away from him in obvious pain, showing him her back. "I hate you. I hate everyone. Go away."

"I won't leave you."

"I...don't...want...you." She swallowed sobs in between words.

"I'm staying. I love you and I won't leave you."

"Leave me." Her voice was absolutely cold.

He didn't respond. Perhaps silence would be best. He bowed his head to pray. But no words came. His sorrow, his shock was too deep for words. *Holy Spirit, pray for my Cecy.*

Silence settled over them. The hospital routine went on around him. In the corridor, nurses passed by in their starched, white uniforms and caps. Later, orderlies brought the evening meal on wheeled carts. A nurse marched in. An orderly carrying a tray of food followed her. "I'm here to feed Miss Jackson."

"Take it away," Cecy ordered, her voice muffled by the pillow.

"I have doctor's orders to feed you." The nurse moved purposefully to the bed.

"I'm not eating," Cecy declared.

Linc startled the orderly by taking the tray. "I'll see she eats."

"I'm not eating." Cecy used her old imperious tone.

He leaned close to the nurse. She didn't know she was about to tangle with a wildcat. "Will you let me try?"

The nurse grimaced, then looked at the watch pinned to her breast. "Five minutes." She marched out.

"Cecy, you must eat." He set the tray on the bedside table.

"Go away."

It was time to get her thinking about more than herself. He knew she had a tender heart. "Cecy, I spoke to your mother—"

"No! Oh, no." Cecy groaned.

Each despairing sound stung his conscience. "It wasn't easy...she had to be told." He waited for her to say something. When she didn't speak, he went on "I told her you were temporarily blind—"

CHAPTER 16

"You lied to her."

"I don't lie. The specialist said in some cases like yours, sight comes back all by itself."

"My eyesight won't come back."

"You are taking the worst view—"

"Nothing in my life has gone right. Nothing. My mother should never have married my father. I should never have been born."

"Never say that."

She went on heedlessly, "But that can't be changed, so I don't want to go on. I can't."

"You will. I did after I lost Virginia."

Her voice rose, "That isn't the same. You don't know—"

"I don't know how you feel." He paused. "But I feel like part of me has died today. I care about you."

"You shouldn't."

"Think of your mother, Cecy. You must eat. Your mother can't lose you. Don't you see that?" He coaxed, "She's lost everything else. You're her only child. Will you abandon her?" He waited.

"No." She rolled slowly back toward him.

Relief overwhelmed him. "I'll crank up your bed and help you eat. You've got to get your strength back."

By the time the nurse returned, Linc had Cecy sitting up with a large, white napkin protecting her gown.

"She plans to eat then?" The nurse questioned sharply.

Linc nodded.

The nurse waited sternly with arms crossed.

Linc picked up the heavy, white bowl and plain spoon. "Looks like chicken broth, Cecy. I'll feed you this time. I don't trust the strength in your arms. Here's the first spoonful." He carefully piloted the spoon to her mouth. Cecy opened and swallowed.

The nurse walked out of the room.

Linc watched helplessly as tears rolled down Cecy's cheeks. He spooned another swallow for her.

Cecy's tears continued to wash down her face. In between spoonfuls, she let her anger pour out freely, "I hope your God is enjoying this.... He's been trying to destroy me since I was born.... But I suppose he'll have to settle with just destroying my life and humiliating me completely.... I hate him."

Feeling deep guilt for exposing Cecy to danger, Linc concentrated solely on each spoonful, blocking out her words. She was railing at God just as Job's wife had. He couldn't blame her anger. Only a person of deep faith could accept this adversity without complaint. Cecy had no faith. And he had no comforting words for her. His own anguish defied words.

✻ ✻ ✻ ✻ ✻

April 12, 1906

"I know you mean it kindly, but I'm not up to visitors." When she'd heard Fleur's voice, Cecy'd pulled the blanket up to cover her face and rolled away. Having felt the bandages on her face and being painfully aware of the stitches that had been taken along her chin, she couldn't bear for anyone to see her like this.

"I don't think you feel up to much of anythin'."

Cecy heard the scrape of a chair on the floor. A gentle hand touched her shoulder. "Please go."

"Don't reject my concern for you. I can't leave you, Cecilia."

"Fleur, I can't face anyone. Please." Cecy choked back tears.

"You don't have to face me, honey. I don't know if it's the custom here. But at home when neighbors have trouble, we go and sit with them. And you have trouble."

Cecy lay still. "Sitting with me will do no good."

"I must do it. I cannot ignore what has befallen you. Linc told me there's hope your sight may return."

"I am blind. I will stay blind." Her bitterness overflowed inside. Each word burned like acid.

"Where there's life, there's hope."

"No, it was a mistake I was even born. God wants to torture me."

"I have hope. God is love, not hate." Fleur's hand gripped Cecy's shoulder.

"This is my fate."

"I believe in providence, not fate, but we don't need to discuss that now. I'm staying to feed you lunch. Ann is coming tomorrow."

"No." The idea of people coming in to look at her like a freak show—*no.*

"You have friends and we won't abandon you."

Cecy couldn't speak. Every minute—day and night—impenetrable blackness clung to her. Her hands moved. She couldn't see them. She felt as though she'd become a shadow, a ghost in an endless night. The bleakness had slipped deeply inside, branding "doomed" on her heart. *I don't want to live if I must depend on others. I want my life back. But there's no way out....*

✳ ✳ ✳ ✳ ✳

April 13, 1906

"Today you're going to feed yourself," Linc spoke as he cranked her bed to the sitting position. Sunshine flooded the room. Having planned a course of action to get Cecy ready to leave the hospital, he placed a napkin in her hand. Earlier, he'd consulted the doctor and received his encouragement to take action. "You know what to do with this."

She spread it over herself. Doubts cluttered her mind, but she had to try to take some control of her life again.

"What? No argument?"

"I want to feed myself." The thought of being totally dependent for the rest of her life was unthinkable.

"Good. You're going to." Linc took her hands and led them to each utensil on the tray. "Here's your fork, glass of milk, plate. Now I've thought this over. And you should probably do fine if you use one hand to guide and one hand to eat."

Cecy felt the smooth plate and cool utensils with her fingertips. Hesitantly, she picked up her fork and positioned the other hand tentatively against the plate. Very slowly she brought the forkful of potatoes to her mouth. "This food is tasteless."

"I think that's a hospital rule."

She made no notice of his attempted humor.

The meal went better than Linc had hoped. He handed the tray to an orderly who'd come in.

"Now it's time to get out of bed." Linc pulled a white hospital robe from behind the door. "I have a wrapper for you to wear."

"Linc, I haven't been on my feet since I fell."

"I talked to the doctor this morning. You're able to walk. The longer you stay in bed the weaker your legs will become."

"You're not a nurse." The thought of leaving the safe haven of her bed made her shake inside. She wanted to walk, yet was terrified. "I can't see my way."

"I know. But you cannot stay in bed for the rest of your life."

She wanted to argue, but she knew she didn't have a choice. She couldn't spend the rest of her life in bed. Sliding to the edge of the bed, she swung over her feet, but she held out both hands to fend Linc off. "Be careful. My ribs."

"I know. I won't put my arm around you."

Cecy grasped his arm. An image flashed through her mind, another day when she'd been too petrified to take a step—Aunt Amelia leaving her on the doorstep of the Boston school years ago. She froze, waves of fear washing over her.

"Just take one step."

She grasped Linc. Terrified, she took a step.

"Follow my lead."

"I hate this," she whispered.

＊ ＊ ＊ ＊ ＊

April 16, 1906

Leaving the hospital after ten days was a relief, but everything...seemed strange, unknown, frightening. Though the morning sun warmed her face, Cecy clung to Linc's arm as he led her through the endless midnight to her own door.

"Welcome home, Miss. I'm so glad to see you recovered enough to return. The staff has been very concerned." She heard her butler's voice.

The sincerity in his tone touched her. "Thank you."

Linc led her inside.

"Take me up to my room," she murmured to Linc. The safety of her room drew her like a magnet.

"We'll have tea first." Linc drew her along with him.

The butler's voice announced, "Tea is ordered for the conservatory, sir. The others are waiting there."

"Others?" Cecy halted. Fear washed through her like chilled blood.

"Just Meg, Del, and Susan." Linc tugged her arm. "I couldn't bring the children into the hospital to see you. Meg has been beside herself over you."

"I don't want her to see me like this." She wanted to see Meg, but she feared upsetting the little girl.

"Cecy, the child needs to see you. This tea isn't for you." Linc drew her on.

She wanted to whirl away from him, refuse to follow. But her own home presented itself as a terrifying maze of objects to fall over, to bump into, to break. She'd lived there six months, but how could she make her recollections fit this dreadful murkiness that never knew dawn. The sound of voices made her stiffen. *I don't want them to see me like this!*

"Miss Cecilia!" Meg's own dear voice rang out. The clatter of a child's footsteps warned Cecy to brace herself for Meg's hug around her waist.

Cecy let go of Linc and bent over returning the girl's fierce embrace. "Meg, dear Meg." Her hand skimmed over the child's French braids, came to rest on her round, soft cheeks. Cecy kissed her smooth forehead and automatically tucked the stray wisps back from Meg's face. Joy flickered briefly in her heart.

"Come on." Meg clutched Cecy's hand. "I brought my kitty to see you. Come on."

The little girl threatened to pull her off her feet. "Wait." Cecy reached out to Linc for support. He took her other arm and led her to the wicker chair and after feeling for it, she sat down. The kitten was put into her lap under her hands.

This simple act brought an avalanche of remembrance—the scene of Meg bringing her mother a kitten that day they had brought her mother home from the sanitarium. *I'm an invalid now too!*

A small hand on her cheek startled her. She jerked in her chair. The cat jumped down with a thump.

"I was just wiping away your tear," Meg said.

A handkerchief was put into Cecy's hand. "Thank you." *Dear, dear Meg.*

"Why are you crying?" Meg asked. "We came to cheer you up because you're blind for a while. Are you crying because of that?"

Cecy dabbed at her eyes. "I was thinking of my mother."

"Oh, I miss her too. She always has peppermints in her pocket for me."

Cecy's heart melted. Meg's sweet purity was irresistible.

Susan spoke up, "I told Linc he's wrong. I think you should go to be with your mother at the sanitarium."

"I'm going. He can't keep me here." The news of her accident and blindness had debilitated her mother to such a degree she was bedridden. Cecy wanted to be with her and bolster her, but she couldn't do that here. Besides, she couldn't face people. She'd been stripped of her human dignity. Didn't Linc understand she just wanted to hide away? At the sanitarium, she'd be safe from prying eyes.

"He doesn't understand that at times like this a woman needs her mother."

"Thank you, Susan." Cecy tucked the handkerchief into her pocket. She recalled Linc had said Del had come also. "Del, are you here?"

"Yes, Miss."

The boy still sounded unhappy. "You won't run away again, will you?"

"No, Miss, I won't."

"Good." She wished she could let him know how fortunate he was. He was well and loved. But who was she to tell him to be happy? He was probably as miserable as she was. Otherwise, he wouldn't have run away.

Tea was served. Cecy tried hard not to spill it or act uncomfortable. She carefully felt for the table and put her cup down. She stood.

"Sit down a moment please, Cecy," Linc said. "I want to read you an article about Caruso. Evidently, he didn't sing last night and the performance of The Queen of Sheba by the New York Opera Company was not well received." Linc read all the reviews of the opera from all the papers.

Cecy listened in eager, but pained, silence. She'd looked forward to hearing the Great Caruso sing for months. Now she'd sit alone while the rest of San Francisco society thrilled to the world-famous tenor.

Finally, Linc relented and led her from the conservatory. They mounted the staircase. His arm guided her. "I'm going to leave Susan with you tonight."

"I have other servants—"

"Susan won't take no for an answer. It was her idea. She said your mother's mind will be easy if your friends are with you."

"But I'm going to the sanitarium tomorrow—"

"I'm taking you the day after tomorrow. Tomorrow night we're going to hear Caruso sing."

"No! I don't want anyone to see me like this!" How could he want to put her on display like that?

"No one will notice you. Effie Bond has arranged with the stage manager at the Grand Opera House to have you enter by the stage door. I've purchased seats back under the first balcony where we won't be seen. We'll go early—"

"No!" She actually felt faint.

"No one will notice us. You'll be veiled and dressed plainly—"

"No!" She squeezed his arm tighter.

"You're not missing Caruso. You're blind, Cecy. Not dead."

"I might as well be!" She pulled away from him, then stopped—afraid she might fall without his help.

He grasped her upper arms urgently. "I lost Virginia. I'm not losing you."

"You don't understand!" *I am lost. I have lost my life.*

*   *   *   *   *

April 17, 1906

Grimly, Linc sat beside Cecy in their seats at the Grand Opera House. She sat low in her seat. A heavy black veil covered her face. No one had recognized them. The spot he'd chosen for their seats had been in the shadows even during intermission with house lights up. He'd tried to take her hand in the darkness. She'd refused his overture, putting up a barrier of silence and polite coldness.

Linc knew the opera's story of obsessive love well. Onstage, Caruso and a formidable soprano sang in the final act of "Carmen." In the Spanish mountains, the temptress, Carmen, played cards with her smuggler friends. She drew the card of death. Carmen laughed and sang "You can't avoid your fate!"

CHAPTER 16

Linc glanced at the silent woman beside him. He was as blind as she. He had thought he was seeing clearly, but no more. Why did things go from bad to worse? *I'm in love with you, Cecy. But I can't change your blindness.*

Onstage, Caruso as Don Jose watched in jealous agony as Carmen sang of her love for his rival, a bullfighter. "*Si tu m'aimes*—if you love me." Her bullfighter left to meet the bull in the ring. Caruso confronted Carmen. She rejected him and he plunged a knife into her back.

Linc felt the blade go through his own heart. Not all his pleading had changed Cecilia's intention of joining her mother at the sanitarium. At Cecy's request, Millie had visited Cecy only once at the hospital. Cecy had insisted Millie stay with her mother. Would Millie have better luck persuading Cecy her life wasn't over?

Onstage, Caruso threw himself over Carmen's body, then was dragged away by police. Linc felt as helpless. Tomorrow he would rise early and drive Cecy to her mother. Would he ever get her to return? Even if she returned, would she ever be the same? Beside him, Cecy sat as still as a statue. Was she even listening to the opera?

The final musical note echoed and faded. Applause vibrated throughout the opera house. Roses, red roses cascaded from the balcony and private boxes onto the stage—bow after bow. Nine curtain calls.

Throughout it all, he and Cecy sat still—a quiet island in a thunderous sea. At last, the Grand Opera House was empty and Linc escorted her out of the theater, to his home. They'd decided it would be better after the short night to leave early in the morning from Linc's house. Her silence was impenetrable. Their only communication being his murmured directions to guide her along the way.

He parked in front of his garage. He rested his hands on the steering wheel. "Cecy." He cleared his throat.

"Are we home?"

"Yes, but before we go in—"

"Everything has been said already. I'm going to the sanitarium."

"That's not the question. The question is will you return...to me, give me a chance to persuade you we have a future together?"

"Linc, I've told you I'll be no man's wife."

"But—"

"Don't!"

He made a desperate plea. "Cecy, you must learn to walk by faith, not by sight—"

"No more platitudes. I'm tired. Take me in." Her flat tone left him nothing to say. She opened the door and stood waiting for him to lead her in.

Defeated, once inside he handed her over to Susan who led her away to the guest room.

Linc loosened his tie and shrugged out of his evening coat. Tired, but restless, he walked softly into Meg's darkened room. The moonlight shone over his beautiful child, Virginia's daughter. Standing over her, he'd recalled donning the same evening wear for the first ball in San Francisco. Meg had teased him that night about wearing tails.

That night he'd been grieving for Virginia. He'd thought he'd seen the worst, suffered his greatest loss. Tonight he loved a girl so different from him, wrong for him, he'd barely admitted even to himself. Now she'd suffered everything but death and he was going to lose her too.

He sank to his knees beside Meg's bed. Burying his face in the blanket, his hands clutched it. He wept. His soul cried out. *Dear Father, I've lost my way. I don't understand. I'm begging you. Show me the way, your way.*

CHAPTER 17

"Even though I walk through the valley of the shadow of death,
I will fear no evil...."
Psalm 23:4, NIV

April 18, 1906   "LINC, WAKE-UP."

Cecy's low, coaxing voice called Linc up from deepest slumber. Groggy, he sat up in bed and ran his fingers through his hair. "What? Is something wrong?"

He could barely discern her outline in the gray of pre-dawn. She stood against the doorway of his room. "I can't sleep. I want to leave now."

He picked up his bedside clock and tilted it to pick up the glow from the window. "It's only a little after 4 A.M. How did you find my room by yourself?"

Her tone became starchy. "I remembered yours was next to the guest room. I felt my way along the wall. I can't sleep. I want to leave now."

"But—"

"Now," she insisted, "I want to leave *now*."

He swung his feet to the floor. After a short, restless night, he wanted to delay, but maybe it would be better to go now.

He had to be back for an afternoon meeting with Sullivan, the fire chief, and Brigadier General Funstan, stationed at the nearby Presidio Garrison. They were scheduled to discuss yet again the army and city combining efforts to use explosives for firebreaks. City graft had siphoned off the funds and the first attempt failed.

Somehow this need to prepare for a large-scale fire had been goading Linc the past few days. That probably didn't mean anything though. Just childhood memories of the horrifying Chicago Fire kicking in at an odd time. But he didn't want to miss the meeting.

"Linc?"

He yawned and blinked, "Go sit in your room. I'll dress and come for you." He ignored the lead weight of dread in his gut. He didn't believe she meant to return. Today he'd lose Cecy, just as completely as he'd lost Virginia.

Ten minutes later in the foyer, he helped Cecy on with her drab auto garb. Then they walked out Linc's side door into the heavy, dewy morning. Spring fragrances—white azaleas, lilies, and lilacs—floated in the air. Purple bougainvillea cascaded over his neighbor's fence. Drops of crystal clear dew dripped—one drop, one drop—from the lower petals. The beauty mocked him.

Linc seated her in his car, checked to see that he'd brought out all her valises, then looked at his house once more, casting a glance at his daughter's window. He imagined how she looked sleeping peacefully, her kitten curled up at her feet. Why couldn't they all just stay here together—as a family?

He shoved his hands into his long coat's pockets. "Are you certain, Cecy, that you want to run away?" He couldn't stop himself. "You know I love you. Won't you stay with Meg and me?"

She didn't move, but continued facing straight ahead. "I will not change my mind."

He stripped away the last of his pride, his voice raw. "My love means nothing to you then?"

"I don't doubt you think you love me. I can't love you in return. Just look what has happened to me since we met in January." She made a sound of disgust. "Let's go. My life is as good as over and we both know it."

Feeling a deep weariness that had nothing to do with the gloomy hour, Linc cranked the auto, and drove them away from the life they could have shared. He felt more dead than alive. Loving Virginia had been as natural and uncomplicated as breathing. Loving Cecy was a circle of thorns wrapped around his heart.

Up and down nearly deserted streets, out of the city, they mounted the spring-green hills and left San Francisco behind. Dawn, a pink radiance above the dewy eastern horizon, stirred Linc's appetite. "We'll stop in the next town and have breakfast. I think I recall a café there."

"I'll stay in the car."

"No—"

A rumble from deep in the earth interrupted him. Crows overhead screeched. In fascination, he watched the leafy maple trees farther down the road sway and jump, flapping their branches like a chicken's wings. The car began to rock and shake. Linc jounced as though driving over a "washboard" road. "Earthquake!"

The world whirled back and forth like someone swirling oil over a griddle. The deep groan moaned louder, closer. Linc felt the control of his car wrenched from him. The wheel in front of him spun recklessly this way and that. Ahead, an old broken, roadside fence rippled like a flag unfurled in the wind.

He shouted. Cecy was thrown against him. He grabbed for her. She was pitched over the side of the car. She screamed.

The auto bucked. Helpless as a rag doll, he was thrown from the car too. "Cecy!"

"Linc, help!"

He tried to grab hold of something stable. Nothing was stable. The insane vibrations continued. He heard himself shouting, "Stop. Stop. Oh, God, help."

The world stopped.

Too demoralized to move, he lay panting flat on the dirt by the side of the road. The young wild grass tickled his nose. Once again the earth felt solid beneath him. But was it? He didn't trust it.

Slowly he got up on his knees and looked around. He closed his eyes and looked again. A gaping crack, a two-foot-wide fissure, separated him from his car. The maple trees ahead had ended their dance and lay uprooted across the road.

Overhead, the sun rose against a red sky. His mind chanted senselessly, 'Red sky in the morning sailor take warning.' Finally, as though some force activated his ears, he heard Cecy calling.

"Linc! Are you all right? Where are you? Linc!"

He staggered to his feet, still unsteady, jumped over the fissure and scrambled around the car. She lay on the ground writhing in great distress. He knelt beside her and lifted her into his arms.

"Linc! Thank God!"

"Where are you hurt?" He scanned her, but found no blood, only a few scratches.

She collapsed against him. "You're all right? Nothing hurt you?" She threw her arms around his neck. "You're safe."

"It was an earthquake. Are you hurt?"

"I don't think so. But hold me!"

For a while that's all he could do. Foolish thoughts jumbled in his mind. He almost said, "I want a cup of coffee with cream and sugar please." He shook his head, trying to shake his thoughts back to normal. *God, God, God.* He couldn't pray farther than that.

His mind calmed. He could think again. "We have to get back to town. Meg and Del might need me."

Though Cecy still clung to him, she stopped crying. "What about my mother...Nana?" Her hold on him tightened around his stiff collar.

Gripping her hands together, he looked at the trees blocking the road toward the sanitarium. "Your mother and Millie are adults in a protected place. Meg and Del are children. And Susan is not in good health. They might need me."

"I want my mother."

Her tone moved him to pity. "Cecy, we're going to my family first and you're going with me. They're in more danger in a city than your mother is at the sanitarium." He lifted her bodily and without opening the door, dropped her into the passenger seat.

"How do you know that?" she pleaded.

He got in and turned around, back toward San Francisco. "I just know."

Cecy cried softly.

Meg needed him and Del and Susan. He pictured them lying bloody, unconscious, crushed beneath rubble. "Cecy, your mother will be fine—"

"She has to be! I can't protect her. I hate this blindness." Cecy's voice rose to a shriek, "I'm helpless!"

Linc stopped the car. He gripped her shoulders. "Everyone's helpless in an earthquake. No one can stop the earth from shaking."

Cecy keened, "You'll leave me! Everyone leaves me! I'll be all alone! I can't see! I'll be lost!" Her words became frantic, nearer to wordless cries.

Linc crushed her in a fierce embrace. He spoke emphatically, "I—won't—leave—you. I—won't."

"You will! Everyone leaves me! I can't see. Help, help me!"

With all his strength, he forced her to lie motionless against him. Still she raved. He shouted in her face, "Don't you know I love you? I will never leave you!" Then he kissed her, forcing her into silence.

He felt her relax against him. Slowly he released her. "Now we have to get going. We're about an hour out of the city. We'll go back and get Kang, Susan, Del and Meg, and we'll all go to the sanitarium. I hope we'll all be safe there."

"But the earthquake might have been worse where mother is." Cecy still struggled with tears.

"I'm not worried about the earthquake itself. There's nothing we can do about it now."

He put the car into gear. "I won't sugarcoat this. You went with me to interview Sullivan. There is a special danger in the city after an earthquake. We've got to get the children out of the city."

"Fire," Cecy murmured gravely.

"Fire." He pressed down hard on the accelerator. The word, short and easy to say, sent a chill from his past through Linc. His mind sang the ditty he hated, "There'll be a hot time in the old town tonight."

Again, scenes from the Great Chicago Fire, forever etched in his memory, sprang to life. He'd only been eight at the time and had run away that night, so he'd faced the terrifying conflagration alone. Stampeding people—shouting and shoving—chimney's exploding from intense heat, showers of golden-red, burning sparks stinging with fire.

I can't let Meg and Del face that alone. Oh God, dear Lord, protect my family. Bring me safely to them, help me protect them. The words became a chant—repeating, repeating in his mind.

The gravel macadam road he'd driven over previously had been smooth. Now he navigated over lumps and deep depressions. Cracks lay in his path. He managed to negotiate the narrow ones. A few made him detour out of his way along the fissure until he found a narrower gap that he could drive over. Such a force, strong enough to break apart the earth, boggled his mind.

Cecy sat hunched against him as though fearing attack. He understood her alarm. He'd been terrified and he had his sight. Her new blindness had already pushed her into insecurity. Would she recover from this new blow?

Finally, Linc turned a bend. As the city below came into view, he stopped the car.

"What's wrong?" Cecy shivered against him.

"Smoke." The word rasped his throat.

"Smoke?"

"Fire." The ominous word clanged in his mind like a frantic fire bell, a death knell. On the skyline over the harbor, plumes of dark gray smoke ascended in the roiling columns. *It's begun.*

Buttressing his resolve, Linc drove his way through the littered streets. High in the morning sky, bright April sunlight mocked him. All around him lay scattered proof of the savage earthquake. Tall maples and oaks had crashed across intersections. Windows had fallen, shattering across roadways. Roofs had slid off houses and blocked his way. Water gushing down curbs spoke of broken water mains. In places, downed live electric wires shimmied and twisted, hissing like vicious snakes. Stopping to move debris or detour around it, he pressed on, yard by yard. In a macabre way, the billows of smoke downtown became his compass as he navigated the broken city.

His hold on the steering wheel became a death grip. *I have to get Meg and Del.*

People wearing only robes and nightgowns strolled the sidewalks aimlessly, carrying things they'd grabbed as they ran from their homes—birdcages, framed pictures, coffeepots. He had to be careful because a few stepped in front of his car as if unaware of it.

Shock. They're in shock.

As he drew closer to home, he saw clearly the outline of the proud skyscrapers downtown. The tall buildings had become skeletons, their brick and stone shaken off like snake's skin. And the columns of black-gray smoke billowed wider and darker then, obscuring his view. *Del! Meg!*

Linc turned a corner and screeched to a halt. A squad of soldiers blocked the road where they were tossing bricks from a shattered house that littered the street. One soldier motioned to Linc. "You there in the car! Get out and help us clear this street."

"But—"

"No argument. Martial law has been declared. We have the right to impress citizens to clear rubble from the streets."

"But—"

The soldier swung his gleaming new rifle toward Linc. Instinctively Linc's hands went up. His heart pounded.

"Now!" The soldier barked.

He obeyed.

"Linc?" Cecy called.

"He has a gun. Stay down." He left her clinging to the steering wheel. The soldier's rifle gave him no choice.

Linc bent and began tossing rubble onto the curb with the other civilians and soldiers. When the path had been cleared, he hurried back to Cecy.

"Hey, you're not dismissed!" the soldier shouted.

"She's blind. I can't leave her." Linc slid behind the wheel. "We're trying to get home to the children."

"All right, but remember—the Army is in control of the city. No alcohol can be bought or sold. Looters will be shot on sight."

"I don't drink. I don't steal!" Linc drove away with haste. The sight of armed soldiers in the streets had shaken him. Martial law hadn't been declared during the Chicago Fire. "Things must be worse than I thought. I have to get home and get us out of the city," he muttered to himself. He sped down the street heading for home.

Cecy clung to his arm, making it throb painfully, but he said nothing.

CHAPTER 17

He turned another corner and came smack into another group of soldiers. Most looked too young to shave, much less be in uniform.

"Halt! Out of the car!" The soldier at the rear turned and ordered.

Linc stared at the man. "What?"

"Out of the car!"

"Why? What did I do?"

The soldier fired his rifle overhead.

"Don't shoot him!" Cecy screamed. Linc leaped out and dragged her from the vehicle. He held her close to his side.

She quieted against him. "Are you hurt?" she asked with tears in her voice.

Linc called to the soldier. "She's blind. We're just trying to get to the children." Linc stayed by the car, but scanned the sur-roundings for cover.

"Sorry. I've got orders to confiscate autos for the use of the city and military government."

Linc objected, "But you can't just take my car. It's private property. I told you I'm on my way—"

Two soldiers climbed into the car, rendering the dispute null and void. Linc's Pierce Arrow was driven away—while he stood gaping in shock.

"Come with us." The soldier waved his rifle at Linc, motioning him to join the line of soldiers and volunteers. "All able-bodied men are needed to clear streets."

Incredulous, Linc shoved Cecy behind him. He faced the soldier. "I told you she's blind. I cannot leave her defenseless in the midst of earthquake and fire. You can shoot me if you want to, but I'm not leaving her!"

The soldier stared at them. "Lady, lady," he barked. "Are you really blind?"

"Yes!" she shrieked. "Yes!"

The soldier turned and ordered his squad to march on. Looking back, he shouted, "Refugees are gathering at Golden Gate Park and Presidio. Get your wife and kids there—pronto!"

Delayed fear hit Linc's stomach making him queasy. Soldiers with rifles loose in the streets, impressing civilians, shooting rifles! Had the world come to an end?

"Come on—before someone shoots us for looting." He set off on foot with Cecy trying to keep up with him. He judged they had about a mile or so to go to reach his front door. He sensed Cecy's hesitation to move so quickly, sightless, but he couldn't help hurrying her anyway.

He was rattled. She must be terrified. But she bravely kept up with him. He murmured, "Not far now."

"Linc, the children will be fine. I know they will."

In gratitude, he kissed her temple, then hurried her on. Finally, he found his street.

What was left of it. He halted.

"What's wrong?" Cecy gasped, huddled close to him as though he were a warm hearth.

"My house is down."

"Down?"

"Yes, its roof has slid onto the drive and the house is leaning on its side. The front porch is hanging over the sidewalk." Linc said the simple words, but couldn't believe them. Almost three hours ago, his house had been whole, now it hung and listed, a battered wreck.

"Hurry. Hurry," Cecy urged. "They might still be in there and need help."

Her words made him move. Pulling her with him, he pelted down to the hulking remains of his house. He left her at the curb while he went around it, trying to locate a firm place to set his feet, to enter. But the bricks and boards were cracked, broken at angles.

"Susan!" he called. "Del, Meg, are you in there?" He shouted this over and over. No answer came. He hesitated to venture inside for fear of being injured and unable to care for Cecy. "How do I get inside, Lord?"

At last, he fell silent, baffled, unable to think. *They should be here.*

"They're gone," a feeble voice called from across the street. "I saw what happened. I was up because my back was bothering me." It was Mrs. Hansen, who lived across the street and who'd let Cecy stay with her briefly. The white-haired grandmother, still dressed in her frayed print nightgown, stood in front of her leaning redbrick house.

Linc raced to her. "Where did they go?"

Mrs. Hansen paced back and forth on the crumbled sidewalk. "Everybody went off to Golden Gate Park. Fools, all of them. Don't they know—"

Linc interrupted, "Did you see my daughter and the others?"

"Yes, they went with everyone else." She motioned vaguely toward town, then folded her arms in front of herself. "I saw your colored woman run out with a child in each hand. She ran into the street. Things were still falling—"

"But they were all right?" Linc wanted to shake the answers out of her. But she already looked as frail as a leaf about to fall.

She nodded. "You lost your Chinaman."

"What?"

"He'd run out the side. The colored woman ran out the front so she made it—"

"What happened to Kang?" He whirled about and tried to detect any sign of his houseman. *Not Kang! No!*

"Your Chinaman ran out the side door. The roof came down right on him. I yelled to the men, 'Wagstaff's Chinaman is under the roof!' They tried to move it, but couldn't. They called and called. He didn't answer."

Disoriented, stunned, he turned to go, then paused. "You want to go with us? To Golden—"

"I'm not going anywhere. I filled everything I could with water. I'm not leaving my home over some earthquake."

Though the woman chattered on, Linc hurried back to Cecy. "Did you hear?" He pulled her up by both hands and hugged her to himself. Just touching her soft form bolstered him.

She leaned against his chest. "Yes, she said they are safe. But Kang's dead." Her voice broke.

Linc put his arm around her. He tried to think of what to do if it were true that Kang indeed lay dead under the roof. But Linc's normal emotions had deserted him. *I suppose I'm in shock too.* He looked into Cecy's face. *What was she thinking, suffering?* But he couldn't ask. They had to survive. They would talk later after....

"What are we going to do?" Raising her head, Cecy felt along his arm until she found his jaw, then cupped it with her hands.

He leaned his forehead against hers. "We'll go to Golden Gate Park. That's where people are headed—"

A terrible groan rippled through the air. The street under their feet began to roll again. The houses swayed dangerously, creaking, moaning, howling in protest. Weaving himself, trying to anticipate the quake's moves in vain, Linc threw his arms around Cecy. The old woman screamed.

The rolling stopped. Bricks crashed to the pavement and rolled down the hill. Choking dust billowed upward.

Linc was afraid to move. Would it start again? Was it just an aftershock or the prelude to another full-blown quake?

"Help!" Mrs. Hansen called. "Oh!" Her hands on her breast, she fell down on the pavement.

Pulling Cecy with one hand, Linc dashed to her side. She was gasping and pressing down on her breast.

"What's wrong?"

She couldn't reply. She grabbed his shirt.

He let go of Cecy and held the woman. He felt her stiffen, then go limp. He felt for her pulse. There was none. "She must have had a heart attack."

"She's dead?"

"Yes."

"Oh, the poor woman. The shock must have been too much."

Slowly he lowered Mrs. Hansen to the pavement. He tried to find her pulse again without success. *Gone.* "Wait here."

"Where are you going?"

"I'm going into her house and bring something—"

"You might be hurt! What if there's another quake?"

"Stay here. It's the least I can do for her. In fact, all I can do for the poor woman!" He ran into her precariously listing house, spotted a gray blanket over a chair, swept it up and ran back to Cecy.

Kneeling beside the woman, he gently closed her eyes, folded her hands and draped the blanket over her. He rose, bringing Cecy up with him. He bowed his head. "God, I commend to your care Mrs. Hansen and our dear friend, Kang," he forced out each painful word. "Amen."

He took Cecy's arm and headed down the hill. With every glance at the towering "smokestacks" downtown, he felt his anxiety surge again, again.

"Are we still going to Golden Gate Park?" Cecy murmured anxiously. With her free hand, she pushed ineffectually at the flyaway hair around her face. Her off-white driving hat had fallen backward and hung by its ribbons around her neck, bouncing with each step she took.

He wished he could shield her completely from the devastation all around them. Danger lurked only a heartbeat away— armed soldiers, fire, and aftershocks. "Yes, I just hope they are there." He hugged her briefly to his side. "Don't worry. We'll get them." They set off briskly.

An explosion.

Cecy cried out.

In the distance downtown, a scarlet flash of fire and a new spout of smoke ascended below them. The sight hit Linc like a mallet. "Dear God, the dynamite has started."

✷ ✷ ✷ ✷ ✷

Wild golden, molten fire raged along Market Street. Hot wind, ash, and sparks whirled high on scorching updrafts. Hearing soldiers coming, Linc towed Cecy to a gap between two buildings, not yet aflame.

"Keep silent." He pressed a hand over her mouth. The soldiers marched closer. He pushed Cecy into a doorway and froze.

"Hey you!" A voice boomed in the street behind him.

Oh, Lord, don't let it be me he wants. But Linc didn't move a fraction of an inch though Cecy started against him.

"Come out of that building with your hands up. Or we'll shoot."

A man's heated denial. A volley of shots. Crackling flames muffled the sounds. Soldiers marched away.

After several moments, Linc eased out of the doorway though he still pressed Cecy into its shelter. A quick glance told him the soldiers had passed.

"Let's go." Then he halted as a stream of squealing rats, the size of alley cats, raced just inches from their feet. The Barbary Coast and Chinatown were famous for underground passages and their inhabitants, these rats. Now they were fleeing just like the humans. "The Army should be shooting them. There's sure to be plague," he muttered to himself.

"What?" Cecy asked, her teeth chattering audibly.

Her blindness must be doubling, tripling her fear. But he could only say, "Nothing." He was powerless to change anything today.

Leading her away by hand, he thanked God she couldn't see the bloody corpse of the poor looter lying in the street. In fact, her blindness had been an unexpected protection. She hadn't been forced to witness bodies lying lifeless in the streets or watch them tossed like debris into fires. Life was cheap today in San Francisco. *Dear God,* he shuddered inside; he couldn't stop shuddering.

How much more could happen? He feared to say the question out loud. This day in San Francisco anything could happen. He fought the foreboding that crouched at the back of his heart and mind.

The crackle of the fire, sounding like a high wind through a field of ripe corn, triggered dreadful images from his childhood brush with fiery death. Memories of the Chicago Fire haunted him every moment—bellows of pain, pounding footsteps on a burning bridge, people splashing into the river screaming for help that never came.

At times, when dynamite was detonated, the past and present fused in his mind. In Chicago, the firemen had known how to use dynamite to create firebreaks. Linc knew for a fact the firemen here didn't. Why was Sullivan allowing this? With one eye on the smoke, he trudged along leading Cecy to Golden Gate Park. Would Meg, along with Del and Susan, be there?

At eight years old, he'd faced hurricane-strength winds and fire. Meg was facing an earthquake and a fire! A yearning to hold little Meg in his arms had become a deep thirst, a well of longing. Inside he repeated, *Keep them safe. Keep us safe.*

He'd never felt so removed from divine care. Shouldn't he feel closer to God now—when he needed him so? His fear grew despite his prayers. *I believe, Lord. Help, thou, my unbelief.*

✺ ✺ ✺ ✺ ✺

"How much farther? I'm sorry, but I'm so tired." Cecy tugged at Linc's sleeve.

Another blast of dynamite assaulted his ears. Airborne cinders blew over them, stinging like mosquito bites.

Cecy fretted, "Why are they still blowing things up? I thought they didn't know how to use dynamite—or have any!"

"Obviously the Army had some and has put it into the hands of the untrained." With an eye on the multiplying towers of sooty smoke, he pulled her along. "They'll just spread the fire! Fools!"

Skirting Union Square, Linc and Cecy stopped. Refugees in all types of dress and undress loitered around an informal soup kitchen on the street. The orange sun, though obscured by the smoke, dust, and flame, had begun its descent in the western sky.

"Is that coffee I smell?" Cecy asked in a wondering tone. "I'm so thirsty."

"Yes." And just like that his own hunger and thirst came alive. He led Cecy to the line.

"Hello, lady and gent, how about a cup of coffee?" a little man in a dark suit asked.

"Please." Linc gladly accepted two tin cups filled with the dark aromatic liquid.

"I only got bread and coffee. I made the coffee. The Army sent bread." His face blackened by smoke, the man tore pieces from a long loaf of bread.

"Thank you. Thank you." Linc accepted two large hunks of bread. "We haven't eaten anything today."

"Don't mention it. This won't last much longer. Fire is getting close. Keep those cups. I just picked up what people left out here."

"Thank you." Cecy said over her shoulder as Linc led her to an open spot on the curb.

Linc settled Cecy at his side. The bread was hard. They had to dip it in the coffee to eat it. The strangers around them sat so silently eating and drinking. It was eerie. He wondered why. Then he thought, 'we're all sleepwalkers in a nightmare.'

Cecy let go of his arm and urged him to go for refills of coffee. When they finished, Linc helped her to her feet. "Not too much farther till we get to the Park."

Boom! Another explosion. Glaring, red flames shot skyward only blocks away. Fiery sparks and cinders, some the size of silver dollars, showered down dispersing the panicked crowd. Linc ran with Cecy holding his hand. Up ahead, he saw another squad of soldiers. To avoid them, he rushed down a side street. "I never thought I'd be running from U.S. troops."

A huffing man running beside them said breathlessly, "They're not all regular troops. Some are National Guard—just young college kids pressed into service for the emergency." Since Linc had to run slower because of Cecy's still hesitant gait, the man sped ahead of them. Seeking shelter while they caught their breath, Linc led Cecy behind a destroyed storefront. He gasped for breath.

"Linc." Cecy pulled his coat. "I hear something."

"What?"

She held her finger to her lips. A faint sound blew to them on the wind.

Linc whispered, "What is it?"

"Please. I think it's a child crying."

Linc strained, listening in spite of the steadily increasing roar of the approaching fire. He could barely hear it. But it was real. "Come on." He picked his way through the wreckage, keeping Cecy behind him.

The sound remained insistent but faint. It led them to a house whose roof was partially caved in. "The sound is from in there."

"Go see what it is. I'm worried," Cecy urged.

Linc hung back. Cecy, blind, had missed the ghastly sight of hands and legs protruding from under wreckage which he had seen all that day. He fought his own revulsion. With the consuming flames advancing, he didn't want to abandon some helpless soul trapped beyond human help. He couldn't face it.

The pitiful whimper beckoned again.

"Go!" She pushed him.

He gathered his courage. "Stay here." Carefully he began to pick his way through the shattered rubble—wood, plaster, broken glass—which had once been a humble dwelling.

Then he saw her—a young woman. She was pinned under a beam—crushed, lifeless. *Dear God*. He scanned the area.

The whimper came again.

He knelt and looked under a nearby heap of smashed boards. A cradle turned on its side had formed a protection. The whimper was an exhausted infant's cry. How little? Still in the cradle. The poor baby must have been alone and overlooked since the early morning quake. Pity wrung his spirit.

In the cramped quarters, he got down on his belly. Reaching cautiously so as not to disturb ravaged beams and make them shift, he snaked his arm along the floor. Shards of glass, pushing up under his sleeve, scored his arm. Gritting his teeth, he touched a corner of a blanket with his thumb and index finger. He dragged at it.

He saw the baby, not more than a few months old, on the blanket. Slowly, slowly he inched the blanket with its precious cargo until the child was within his grasp. Rising to his knees, he reached in through the gap and lifted the babe to himself.

"Thank God!" He breathed. The little heart still beat under his hand. Linc stood up. "I've got it!"

"Turn with your hands in the air." A harsh voice commanded. "Drop it or I'll shoot."

Linc swung around.

CHAPTER 18

"…and that Rock was Christ."
I Corinthians 10:4c, KJV

A RIFLE SHOT.

Blazing pain. Linc shouted, fell backward. His grip on the child held.

Cecy shrieked. "Stop! He went in to get a baby. Linc!"

"Baby? What are you saying, ma'am?" Rough hands shook her shoulders.

She screeched at him, "A baby!" She pounded him with her fists. "We heard a baby crying. Linc went in…." She couldn't put her fear and anguish into words. Screams frothed up from inside her. She pressed her hands over her mouth, holding them back.

"Dear God! No!" The stranger dropped her shoulders. She heard hasty footsteps. The man's voice rose in panic, "It is a baby! What have I done?" The man cursed himself. "Here let me help you up, sir."

"My shoulder," Linc gasped. "Take care. I think you shattered my collar bone. I couldn't drop the baby—"

"When you spun around so quick, I thought you were going to shoot! I never shot at a person before in my life!" The young soldier helped Linc stagger out of the wreckage, clutching the crying baby, blood streaming from Linc's shoulder. Then he bodily lifted Linc over the last tumbled wall to the street. "But they told me to shoot anyone who was looting. I'm so sorry!"

Linc fought faintness and gritted his teeth against the pain, the searing pain. "Cecy, are you all right?"

Her hands, outstretched, reached for him. "Don't die, Linc. Please don't die."

"Soldier, give her...this baby. She's blind. Make sure she gets...a firm hold...before you let go."

"I shot a blind woman's husband." The soldier cursed himself again.

Cecy felt the man fold her arms together like a nest and lay the baby gently into it. "Linc, what should I do?" Cecy begged as she clutched the wet, crying baby to her breast.

Unable to respond, Linc pressed his hand to the wound staunching the stream of bright red blood flowing from his shoulder. He slid down on the curb. "You'll . . . know . . . what . . . to . . . do. God . . ."

"Linc?" She heard him moan, but he didn't answer her.

Within minutes, she heard a racing motor, squealing to a stop. She felt the swoop of air it brought. Hands took her by the arm and hurried her into a car. The young soldier explained rapidly, "I'm taking both of you to the military hospital at the Presidio."

"Linc?" Cecy cried out to him.

"Don't worry, ma'am. He's passed out. I laid him in the backseat. Dear God, don't let him die on me!"

Chapter 18

❧ ❧ ❧ ❧ ❧

Abandoned in her blackness, Cecy sat on a hard hospital bench and cradled the whimpering infant close and hummed softly. Inside the hospital came quick, harsh voices, voices of strangers. Running, rushing footsteps—raced back and forth, but no one stopped to give her news. Linc had been rushed away from her. She waited alone in the darkness...waited... waited....What was happening to Linc?

Hysteria simmered inside her, but she held it back. Raving would help no one, least of all this poor baby and Linc. Periodically, a distant explosion recalled to her the rampant flames devouring the city, block by block. Would it drive them from the Presidio into the Pacific?

Linc, Linc.

The baby in her arms mewled more and more weakly. Would they let the child die? She heard a woman's footsteps, lighter with tapping heels, coming near. She reached out with one hand. "Please, I'm blind. Help me."

"What's the problem?" A woman's voice.

In spite of the peculiar hospital odors, Cecy recognized the scent of rosewater. A lady. "Please I need food for the baby, diapers."

The woman's voice became kinder. A soft hand touched her arm. "Aren't you able to nurse?"

"No, the child is an orphan. We found it beside its dead mother. The child is growing weaker. Please—"

"How awful. We don't have many supplies for babies. It's a military hospital."

Cecy pressed her hand forcefully over the woman's, detaining her. "Could you find a wet nurse? The soldier said refugees were coming here. Maybe someone—"

"I'll try." The woman squeezed Cecy's hand, then left her. Her purposeful steps clicked rapidly away.

LOST IN HIS LOVE

"Please bring help," Cecy whispered to herself. She rocked the baby, grateful to have someone to hold onto. She bit her lower lip holding back tears. *I can't give in. I can't—if I let go, I'll start screaming and I won't be able to stop.*

Where was Linc's God? Would he send help for this defenseless child Linc had risked his life to save, for Linc himself? Or were this baby and Linc doomed like she? Every life she touched suffered. Why? She clutched the baby and rocked it, murmuring soothing words. *I have to hold on. I must.*

"Ma'am?" A deep voice addressed her. "I'm your husband's doctor."

So deep in misery, she hadn't heard him approach. She looked up imploringly toward the voice. "You mean Linc?"

"Your husband lost a lot of blood, but we removed the bullet and set his collar bone. I think he will recover, but I can't promise anything."

Oh, Linc, dear one. She swallowed with difficulty. "He was shot—"

"I know, by mistake. I'm terribly sorry. But we're full to bursting already. So many wounded, burned, and broken, and more coming all the time. As soon as your husband comes to, we'll have to move both of you out to a tent. We just don't have the staff or room. Have faith." A strong hand squeezed her shoulder.

He left her in the darkness—alone. Outside, some man screamed—a man screamed. She'd never heard men scream until today. Her shaking intensified. If only she could escape, but how, where? *Linc!*

❋ ❋ ❋ ❋ ❋

"Missus?" The quiet, feminine Chinese voice asked, "Missus?"

"Are you talking to me?" Cecy sat up straighter and turned toward the voice.

"Yes, Missus, I wet nurse, please."

"Thank God." The child had fallen silent and it had distressed Cecy more than all the crying. Had help come in time? "Take the child. Hurry please." She offered the silent infant up into the blackness.

Small hands took the child from her. The woman sat down beside her. She smelled of burned cloth.

"Are the fires still raging?" Cecy's throat felt very dry. The trembling in her voice announced her fear, but she couldn't stop shaking.

"You need water. You come. I take."

"I can wait." Cecy clutched the woman's cotton sleeve. "Feed the baby."

"Okay, Missus."

Cecy heard the baby cry out, then begin suckling loudly. She felt weak with relief. She bent her head into her hands. The child wouldn't die. She heard lighter footsteps coming toward her, then smelled the familiar scent of rose water.

"Ma'am? I see the Chinese woman found you. Is the baby eating?"

Cecy rose, reaching out for the hands of the kind woman. "Thank you. Thank you. How is my...how is Linc?"

The woman held Cecy's hands in hers. "The doctor told me he is just about to be brought out on a stretcher. We have a tent ready for you nearby. An army nurse will check on him at least once tonight." She pulled her hands from Cecy. "I'm sorry but we're short of morphine. I'm afraid he'll have a rough night. But that can't be helped. President Roosevelt has ordered the Red Cross on its way. Supplies are coming in."

"The Missus need food, drink." The Chinese woman's voice sounded from beside Cecy.

The woman touched Cecy's shoulder. "You will have to see that she gets in line for food. I must go."

Cecy reached out into the empty air to delay the woman. "Wait please. What time is it?"

"After dark. Goodbye. God bless."

Cecy sat down, listening gratefully to the sounds of the exhausted baby suckling. "My name is Cecy."

"I Kai Lin."

Cecy reached out, found the woman's shoulder and squeezed it gratefully. "Thank you for coming."

"I happy to feed baby."

"Where's your baby?"

"Baby die in Quake."

Feeling as though she'd been punched in the stomach, Cecy couldn't stop the moan. "I'm so sorry," she whispered.

"Very sad day, very sad." The woman's voice quavered with grief.

A thud of heavy, measured footsteps came toward Cecy. "Ma'am, if you will follow us."

"You stand please, Missus. The stretcher here." The Chinese woman tugged at her arm.

"Linc?" Cecy held her hands out in front of her.

"This Mr. Linc?" Kai Lin asked.

A stranger answered, "Yes, we'll show you the way. Follow us."

At the sound of the man's voice, Cecy let Kai Lin lead her away. "Linc? Can you hear me?"

"Yes." In the dark void, Linc's voice sounded faint and weak.

Panic hovered over her like a vulture, threatening her calm. "Where is your hand?" She held out both her hands into the nothingness, feeling for him. "Please...I need to touch you."

"Can't," Linc muttered.

"Hold up, Joe," a man ordered. They all stopped. "Lady, we've got him wrapped tight, his bad arm in a sling under his blanket. Both arms pinned down, so being moved wouldn't pain him more than necessary. Lower your hand about a half-foot. That's the stretcher. Do you feel it?"

"Thank you. Yes." The mere contact with the canvas and wood of Linc's stretcher reassured her. She followed along outside only a short way. The outdoor air was welcome. She felt free from the hospital and its terrors.

The stretcher halted. "Ladies, here's your tent. Wait outside while we go in and settle him on the cot. Then you can go in."

The stretcher was pulled from Cecy's hand. Cool night air closed around her. Now everyone was also in darkness just like she. With her remaining senses, she tried to take in her surroundings. The smell of burning was everywhere. Many voices—some high, some deep—murmured, rose and fell in the background. "Are there a lot of people here?" Cecy asked Kai Lin who pressed close beside her as though afraid they'd be parted.

"Yes, Missus, many people, many tents."

Cecy heard the men moving about in the tent, then they were back beside her. "OK. He's in there. He's out again, but breathing. There are two blankets for you. Be sure to get in line for food—quick. The lines will be shutting down soon. They're about out of everything." The men moved away saying good-bye, wishing them well.

"Thank you—very much," Cecy called after them.

"Missus? You bend please. I take you in tent." The Chinese woman led her inside the low tent.

Cecy held out her hands feeling around for Linc.

"Here, Missus. He's here." The woman took her hand and put it on Linc's cot.

"Thank you." She knelt by the cot, sliding her hands over Linc's form covered by the fuzzy wool blanket. She turned her head slightly. "How is the baby?"

"Baby fine. I go get us food now?"

"Yes, there is no chair?"

"No chair. Just one cot, two blankets. Nothing else."

"Could you give me one of the blankets to sit on, then please go and get food?" Cecy let Kai Lin help her sit down with a blanket around her. The Chinese woman put the baby into Cecy's arms. She left with promises to return soon.

With the baby in one arm, Cecy felt on top of the coarse blanket again until she found Linc's hand underneath. Carefully she covered his hand with hers, the blanket between them.

How had they survived the day? The fear she'd lived with for ten days since she had awakened blind had been crushing, oppressive. But today, her terror had grown to monstrous proportions. Now she leaned her head on the hardwood frame and canvas of the cot. "Linc, can you hear me?" No answer. Only voices outside. A dog barked. A baby cried out. A little girl yelled, "Mama, I want my Mama!"

The baby in her arms whimpered. Cecy let go of Linc's hand. The baby's cheek was wet with tears. "There, there, you'll be all right." But then she recalled that perhaps the baby was an orphan now. She knew how estrangement, abandonment, loneliness felt. Alone in the world. "Don't worry, little one. If we can't find your family, I'll never let you be lonely. I will take care of you always." She kissed the tiny palm, counting the chubby little fingers. "Your mama loved you. I will too."

But how could I take care of a child? I'm blind. She couldn't even take care of herself. Linc moaned in his sleep. What had that woman meant when she said there wasn't enough morphine? *Linc, please sleep. Don't wake to pain.* What if the nurse didn't come? What if he needed something and she didn't know what to do? What if he died tonight? Tears coursed down her face. But she rocked the baby and wept silently.

"You hurt, Missus?" The Chinese woman swished the canvas flap as she entered. "You afraid?"

"Yes, I'm frightened...dreadfully frightened. I haven't been blind for long..., at least, my eyes haven't been blind for long." Cecy remembered Linc's declaration of love for her this morning. How could she have doubted him, turned him away? "I'm afraid I'll lose the man I love. I didn't know I loved him until now."

"You not love husband? Father make marriage?" The woman took the baby from Cecy's arms.

Cecy realized the Chinese woman thought she was speaking of an arranged marriage. "Nobody here asked me if I were married to him. Everyone just thought we were married, so I didn't say anything. I didn't want to be separated from him." She patted Linc's blanket lovingly. "He's asked me to be his wife."

"Who belongs baby?"

"Linc found the baby in a wrecked house. The mother must have been killed in the quake. That's when Linc was shot. They...thought he was looting."

The Chinese woman put a piece of bread in one of Cecy's hands and a cup of coffee in the other. "They only have bread and coffee till morning." Though Cecy didn't have any appetite, she drank the coffee and forced down the bread. She heard the baby nurse again. Cecy and Kai Lin sat very close, each wrapped in her blanket. Kai Lin held the sleeping child. Cecy kept a hand on Linc. He lay very still. That worried her. He moaned and that worried her. *I don't know what to do.*

The hours crawled by tense and unchanging. Inside herself, Cecy's thoughts became clearer. *I do love you, Linc. I didn't see it until I nearly lost you.* She touched his forehead—burning, feverish. *I could still lose you.* Where was Meg? Del? Susan? *I'm afraid we may lose them. I don't want to live if you die.* The day had stripped her raw. Its memories—the earth's bucking and rolling, rifle shots, screams, moans, the crash, and pungent odor of dynamite and black powder—attacked her like hands slapping her, dragging at her. She clutched the blanket around her and fought for equilibrium.

A deep inhuman groan shuddered beneath her. A tremor! She screamed. The aftershock continued, rocked, startled the camp around them. Men shouting, little children screaming. Desperately, she and Kai Lin clung to each other, Linc, and the baby.

The darkness magnified Cecy's alarm. *Please, stop!* Finally the earth settled again. But the clamor outside their tent went on. Though silent herself, she felt each noise shiver through her, tightening her nerves, dredging up panic anew. Too many souls pushed beyond their limits.

From outside, over all the chaos, came the sound of one forceful baritone voice singing, "Rock of ages, cleft for me, let me hide myself in thee." He sang the opening phrase again and again until the outcry all around them calmed, stilled. Then he sang on, "Let the water and the blood, From thy riven side which flowed…." Voices, then more and more joined chorus, "Could my tears forever flow,…All for sin could not atone….." Cecy pressed her hands to her breast holding back loneliness, paralyzing fear. *I'm alone. Linc may die!*

The song around them swelled louder and deepened with emotions—heartfelt. "Lord, thou must save, and thou alone…." *Mother, Nana, Meg did they need help? How could I help them?*

"Nothing in my hand I bring, simply to thy cross I cling… Rock of ages, cleft for me…let me hide myself in thee."

Cecy felt Kai Lin move against her side. "I'm so afraid, Kai Lin." Cecy's teeth chattered.

Kai Lin spoke next to her ear, "You a Christian?"

The question startled Cecy. She glanced to where she felt Linc lay. "Linc is a Christian…," her voice faltered.

"Earthquake and fire take everything from Kai Lin, not just baby, family, husband, everyone."

Cecy leaned her face closer until it rested against the woman's soft cheek. "Oh, Kai Lin. I'm sorry."

"Lord give, Lord take away. Nothing we can do. But pray." The simple words did not hide the woman's raw pain.

Their heads touching, Cecy felt their falling tears mingle. "I've not prayed for a long time. Not since I was little girl." *When I prayed to stay with Mama, Nana.*

"I pray. God, help us."

Outside, the hymn ended. The camp stilled at last.

A lone woman's voice began to recite the words, the good words which bound Cecy to Nana, to Meg. "The Lord is my shepherd. I shall not want." Again more voices joined in. "He maketh me to lie down in green pastures. He leadeth me beside the still waters. He restoreth my soul." Soon, the words of the psalm swelled until the prayer surrounded their tent.

Hearing Kai Lin saying the psalm in her own tongue, silently Cecy mouthed the blessed words that Nana had taught her, "Yea, though I walk through the valley of the shadow of death, I shall fear no evil...."

Today, death had prowled all around her. Even blind, she had sensed it as though she crept fearfully through a dark forest alive with wild beasts. Were the children still alive? Were her mother and Nana safe? Or had death snatched them from her, just when they were about to be reunited?

The psalm outside ended with a heartfelt "amen." She heard other women weeping. How many women tonight would keep vigil over loved ones or beg to have them returned? Grief surrounded her completely, permeated her deeply. Inside, she could only say, "Dear God. Dear God."

She was praying. The shock of this realization rolled through her, dazzling her like a blazing illumination she experienced even without sight.

I don't have a choice. No choice, but to pray. I'm blind. Linc may die. The children are lost. I should be angry. But it's all gone, gone! I see now. I see Linc's love for me. She heard again Linc's voice, 'Go ahead and shoot me, but I'm not leaving her!' *He'd sworn he loved her, would never leave her. In the midst of earthquake, fire, and death, he'd protected and defended her.*

"How could I have doubted him?" she whispered. 'Greater love hath no man than to lay down his life for a friend'—the old Bible memory verse murmured inside her. Linc had defended her, had been shot protecting the tiny infant she held.

God, you brought Linc to me. You blessed me!

My father hated me, but surely Linc's love is greater, more powerful than my father's hatred! If I let the past rule me, my father wins. No! Never!

Lord, you brought me home to San Francisco, to my mother, to Nana, at last. You gave me Linc who loves me more than his own life. I cannot believe that you will part us now. But even if Linc dies, I'll know he truly loved me. You really love me.

Forgive me for hating you, blaming You. Free me, Lord, from my father's hatred. I choose Linc. I choose your love.

The words uncapped a deep spring of fresh, healing joy that surged through her. Then as though gentle hands clasped her under her arms, she felt lifted, lifted higher. She longed to sing, to voice her release, but the grand melody inside defied words, expression. All the beautiful music she'd ever heard or sung intertwined, vibrated through her, a mighty chorus of joy, a stirring prelude to new life.

Her hands searched the darkness and found Linc's face. She placed a hand on each of his cheeks. "I love you, Linc." Her blanket slid off her shoulders, she felt Kai Lin helping her, tugging Cecy's blanket back up around her shoulders. She whispered her thanks. Tracing her hands lovingly over Linc's form through the blanket, she kissed Linc's hand. *I love you, dearest of all.*

Though she huddled on bare, cold earth in an army blanket with the night chill around her, a warmth grew—not from outside, but from the inside. Love was warming her. Joyous melody cascaded in her mind. *Oh, God, you are beautiful, wonderful. Your love glows.*

She whispered, "My father didn't win. Father, I put my trust in you."

✹ ✹ ✹ ✹ ✹

April 19, 1906

"Cecy?" Linc's scratchy voice woke Cecy.

"Linc?" Her heart pounding, she moved to her knees and reached for his hand.

"Where?" he gasped.

She nearly wept with relief. "We're at the Presidio Garrison. You were shot." With one hand, she felt her way gently up to his forehead. But his fever hadn't broken. It was dry and hot.

"Baby? Children . . . found?"

"The baby's fine, but . . . the children . . . no, not yet." Speaking of the children clogged her throat with emotion. She focused on Linc to gain control. She reached toward Kai Lin who still slept beside Cecy and touched her hair. "Is it morning yet, Kai Lin? Please go get us some coffee."

"I go quick."

Cecy heard the rustling of the woman leaving the tent.

"Who?" Linc's voice sounded like a rusty hinge.

She lay her hand on the side of his face. "Kai Lin. She came to nurse the baby. How do you feel?"

"Hurt. Hot." His voice came out in forced gasps. "Children?"

"I described them to the soldier who shot you two days ago. He promised to look for them. We will find them." Cecy blocked out any thought that harm had come to their dear children. They were lost but Susan was with them.

Cecy pulled a crumpled handkerchief from her pocket and wiped his forehead. When the nurse came again, she'd beg for more medicine. Even aspirin would help. Surely they had to have aspirin.

"Fires?" he asked.

"Yes, fires still burning," Kai Lin's voice replied. "Here is coffee, Missus and Mister."

Cecy accepted a cup. "Linc, can you sit up?"

"No," he moaned.

"I brought spoon. I help."

"I feel . . . weak," he murmured. "Thanks. So thirsty."

Cecy listened to Linc sipping and swallowing the coffee. She brought her own cup to her lips. Her hands shook. Maybe today the fires would stop. Maybe today.

Linc asked in his weak voice, "What does it look like outside?"

"Big smoke over San Francisco. Color red over city, show through bad black-black smoke."

"Is something burning close by?" Cecy asked, sniffing the air.

"Tent burn! Look up!" Kai Lin exclaimed.

Reflexively, Cecy did look up.

"Sparks," Linc said with despair. "Water—quick."

"Isn't anywhere safe?" Cecy half rose, but Kai Lin pushed the child into Cecy's arms and ran out.

Soon, Cecy heard men's loud, hurried voices and footsteps outside the tent. The sound of water being splashed and a faint spray from overhead told her that the sparks were being put out. Fighting despair, she gripped Linc's free hand again. With new faith, she prayed, "Please can't the fires end, Lord?"

"The children," Linc murmured.

"They are in God's hands." Saying the words gave her comfort, joy, a new sensation. Cecy closed her eyes and prayed aloud for the thousandth time for Meg, Del, and Susan.

"You . . . praying?" He squeezed her hand weakly.

"Last night God was all Kai Lin and I had left. His love filled me." She waited for his reaction.

Cecy felt Linc's smile. How could that be?

"I love you, Cecy. Thank you, Lord." Linc's voice, though dreadfully weak, sounded confident. "Children . . . God . . . send someone."

Cecy bowed her head until it touched Linc's hand. How dear he was to her. He wouldn't die. The children would be found. She had faith. Softly she sang the words from an old hymn, "God has led us safe this far. And he will lead us home."

※ ※ ※ ※ ※

The second day passed like a month. The baby, now fed, quieted—even gurgled when Cecy tenderly rocked him in her arms. But Linc's fever rose again. The nurse brought aspirin but to no avail. Using a small basin and cloth, Cecy bathed and bathed Linc's burning face. Kai Lin continued to douse the tent against the shower of sparks blown over the Presidio from the raging fires.

Explosions punctuated the long hours. Rumors that Nob Hill had been demolished saddened Cecy. Were her servants safe? The remembered image of her mother, Nana, Susan, Meg, Del, and Linc all together in the lush conservatory made her heart ache. *I don't care if I never see again, Lord. I can live with blindness, but I can't live without my family. Bring them safely out of the cauldron of suffering.*

The odor of burning flesh came on the wind. She realized parts of the city had become pyres for the dead. Names of friends came to her mind. Fleur, Clarence, Little Ann—even Victor and Clarissa. Were they safe?

Every once in a while, someone, a woman would wail out in shock and grief. All other voices would fall silent. The wailing would drop into moaning, the other voices would start up again loudly, discreetly shielding someone's grief. Often came shouts of welcome, of reunion. Loved ones found. How were Nana and Mother? Where were the children?

Cecy recited the Twenty-third Psalm silently and clung to Linc's good hand. He lay still, too weak to talk, almost too weak to swallow broth.

✱ ✱ ✱ ✱ ✱

April 20, 1906

"Papa, Papa." *Meg's voice.*

"Meg! Come here!" Feeling a shock of joy, Cecy sat up from where she had slumped in sleep on the cold ground. She held out her arms. Her prayers had been answered!

"Meg, Thank God," Linc's frail voice spoke in the darkness. "Del? But where is…Susan?"

"Oh, Papa." Meg began crying and must have bumped the cot. It moved. Linc moaned.

Cecy held her hands over the cot to protect Linc. "Meg, dear, your father's shoulder is hurt," Cecy cautioned, then held out her arms reaching for the child. "Don't touch his sling."

Del mumbled, "Grandma died."

Cecy's heart hurt. "Oh, no."

"How did it happen?" Linc's feeble voice showed strain.

"We got out of the house," Meg whimpered. "Then we started walking and then Aunt Susan had to sit down. She couldn't breathe. We tried to get someone to help—"

"But no one would listen to us," Del added grimly.

"Then she had to lie down and she couldn't get up." Meg began to sob.

Cecy's searching hands connected with Del's arm. She pulled him close to her. She couldn't take it in. Susan gone. She hugged Del and whispered her love for him.

"They made us leave her." Del's stark words reverberated with raw pain. "They said she was dead. Kang died too."

Cecy stroked Del's moist cheeks and kissed him. "You're safe now."

Meg went on tearfully, "They took us away. They said we had to go to Oakland. We ran away. But they found us again—"

"Who?" Linc asked.

"The army," a man's voice replied.

Linc looked to the entrance of the tent. He hadn't noticed the soldier who'd wounded him stood there.

"I found them, sir. They were at Golden Gate Park."

"Thank you."

"The fire is dying and it looks like rain."

Cecy asked, "Have you found out about my mother?"

"Ma'am, from all the information I've been able to glean, your mother's sanitarium wasn't affected much. She should be okay too."

"Thank you!" A lump of cold dread in her middle dissolved. *Mother, Nana were safe!* Cecy wept for joy.

Though it trembled weakly, Linc held out his only good hand.

The soldier doffed his hat and left without a word. His debt paid in full.

Linc tried to believe what the children said about Aunt Susan, but he couldn't really take it in. In his memory, the faces of his mother Jessie and Susan captured for one moment in time. They stood side by side on the back porch of the Chicago house before The Fire. They were laughing. *Oh, Mother, she's with you now. Susan, dear Susan.*

Linc let his eyes close. "Lord, we commend our beloved Susan to your care. She has fought the good fight. She is with you now and those who went before her. Bless us. Make us strong again. Heal our pain."

"Papa?" Meg bent her head and lay her cheek beside his.

"It will be all right." The children were dirty, torn, and singed. "You're both here."

Sniffling, Meg pointed to Kai Lin. "Who's she?"

"She is Kai Lin, our new friend," Cecy replied, dabbing at her eyes.

Linc glanced at the sad, young Chinese woman who sat on a drab army blanket holding the smiling baby in her slender arms.

"Is that her baby?" Del asked.

"No, we found the baby." Cecy stroked Del's curly hair. "The poor child is an orphan. Meg, let me touch you, dear. I need to hold you."

Linc closed his eyes remembering seeing the mother lying dead, so near her helpless infant. The baby left all alone as the deadly fire had drawn nearer and nearer. Tears slid down the sides of his face. *Thank you, God. Over all the noises, Cecy had heard the baby's cry.*

After Meg kissed and hugged Cecy, Meg drew near to the baby. "Can we keep her?"

"It boy baby." Kai Lin smiled wanly. "Good baby."

Cecy spoke up, "We've named him Shadrach because he came through the fire. If we don't find his family, we'll adopt him."

"I'm an orphan now too." Del looked close to tears.

"As long as we live, you have family," Cecy said, reaching out, drawing him close again.

The words were exactly what Linc would have said.

Sitting on the bare ground, still wearing her driving hat and coat, Cecy smiled. Her beautiful face was smudged with dirt and smoke, her driving coat torn and her auburn hair bedraggled. So weak he still couldn't lift his head, he saw clearly Cecy had changed. Her lovely brown sugar eyes had no sight, but she looked at peace, at home even in the cramped, primitive tent.

Drawing a shaky breath, he didn't want to know what he looked like. He felt like a flattened flour sack. But they were all alive. They'd made it through the crucible.

"We won't be afraid anymore," he stated. Speaking took so much energy, but healing words needed to be said. "The six of us are family now. If you agree, Kai Lin?"

"God take care of us all." The pretty Chinese woman nodded though tears ran freely down her face. "We come through fire together. We family."

Linc touched Cecy's hand lightly. "You know God's love is true now. I've put the guilt behind me and I love you. Do you love me, too?"

"Oh, yes." She kneeled, then ran her hands over him till she found his face. She kissed him. "If only you and God stand beside me, I can face anything."

He kissed her in return. Del and Meg knelt on either side of Cecy. Thinking of her mother and Nana, Cecy felt confident they were safe too. She whispered the words that had brought healing. Now they spoke truth, "Surely goodness and mercy will follow me all the days of my life. And I will dwell in the house of the Lord forever. Amen."